A Time of Trial

Carol Buchanan

Carol Buchanan Books

Kalispell, Montana

Carol Buchanan

Publisher's Note: This is a work of historical fiction. With the exception of Charles S. Bagg, John X. Beidler, Governor Sidney Edgerton, and Chief Justice Hezekiah L. Hosmer, names and characters are a product of the author's imagination. The towns of Virginia City and Bannack are real, and exist today. Virginia City is the county seat of Madison County, and Bannack is now Bannack State Park. Otherwise, any resemblance to actual people, living or dead, or to businesses, companies, events, institutions, or locales is completely coincidental.

Ordering Information:
For all sales inquiries, email Carol A. Buchanan at her website: https://carol-buchanan.com

A Time of Trial / Carol Buchanan. -- 1st ed.
ISBN 978-0-9864203-6-8

Dedication

For Richard Alan "Sir Richard" Buchanan
(1946 – 2023)
All My Love and Gratitude for 47 Years

Thank You To...

Sue Greskowiak of Artistic Barbering, Kalispell, Montana, friend and beta reader, for her willingness to read and give honest opinions on the early drafts of this book.

Pastor Al Jensen. Director of Pastoral Services at Immanuel Living, Kalispell, Montana, for taking the time to read the "final" draft, ask questions, and give honest opinions from his perspective.

Heidi M. Thomas, who edited the book. I'm grateful for her eagle-eyed approach, even to noting the difference between the length of Em and En dashes! And for her honest feedback and spotting things I was too close to the manuscript to see. All errors are mine, and mine alone.

Historical Note

The Montana Post was established August 27, 1864, in Virginia City, Montana Territory, and was published until 1869. The "clippings" at the head of each scene are taken just as they were printed, in the style of the writer, usually Thomas J. Dimsdale, Editor. Dimsdale edited the newspaper from September 17, 1864, until August 30, 1866, when he became too ill with tuberculosis (then known as "consumption") to work. He died September 22, 1866, at age 35.

1 ~~~

The Montana Post: 1/7/1865, p. 2:

Fatal Accident.

> About half a mile above Virginia, in
> Fairweather district, on a claim – we did not
> learn the number of it – two men were killed
> on January 2d, 1865. The two men, James
> Dick, a Scotchman, and C. W. McBride, from
> Illinois, were at work on the day named, in a
> drift. The rest of the workmen had been to
> see the prize fight, and got home to supper.
> The others not coming to their evening meal,
> were looked after, and the drift they had
> been at work in found caved in. One of them
> was heard to groan when the accident was
> first discovered. Assistance was procured
> and both exhumed – dead. It appears that
> the drift they were working in was twelve
> feet wide and badly timbered.

He could get killed.

The notion had rode him all day, and here he still was, though he cussed himself for an idiot. Fifteen feet into the mountainside, starting a new drift, what miners called a tunnel in a gold mine. On a hunch. By himself. After Mam and Dan'l had told him not to go alone. If only the sounds of the mountain's insides didn't make him think of it as something alive, liable to take a fit and come down on him.

1

Carol Buchanan

Trickles of water splashed at his feet. The air smelled of wet rock. The mountain rumbled, shifted, sighed almost too soft to hear over the chunk of his pick or shovel biting into its gut. Beyond the lantern's circle of light, absolute darkness.

Like Jonah and the whale. Only the whale had et Jonah. He, Timothy McDowell, would not let a mountain eat him. No, sir.

God willing.

The point of his shovel rang on rock. Not pebbly dirt. This – striking at it again – sounded like solid stone.

He'd hit a boulder. Drat. He'd never be able to dig it out by himself.

Stooping, he took the lantern and lifted it up to shine on what he'd struck.

A chill raised the hairs on his arms and the back of his neck.

The most beautiful thing he'd ever seen. Pale rock threaded through with – almost he didn't dare even think it – Gold?

Bending down, he brushed at it with his bare hand. Lifted the lantern to light it from a different angle. A good-sized nugget, it looked to be. Maybe the size of Albert's fist. Scraped some more. Revised his idea. Both of Albert's fists, and then some.

He set down the lantern and scraped around the rock to find the edges. Raised the lantern again, two more times, maybe three. Maybe more. Wished the candle in the chimney would stop jiggling. Burn slower.

2

Wished he had more candles.

He raced the candle now, to find the edges of the rock before the flame guttered, fool that he was for not putting more candles in his pockets.

He couldn't find the edges.

He dared not dig farther into the wall, make a new, proper drift. He couldn't timber the drift by himself even though the three of them – Jake, Albert, and him –they'd cut enough logs to hold up the mountain. For a few more feet, anyway.

He stopped digging, shined the lantern all around where he'd exposed the rock. Golden gleams showed through stone, pale and gauzy like Mam's best silk shift that Dan'l had brought her from New York.

Almost he couldn't believe his eyes. He'd found a boulder made of quartz, that beautiful, nearly transparent stone shot through with gold. Like the nugget in his pocket. Only bigger. Way, way bigger. He'd never seen nothing —

The candle sputtered.

He tied the shovel and pick to his belt, grabbed the lantern, and ran for the entrance. Before he reached it, the candle guttered and went out. In absolute dark he finished the last few feet by the feel of wet ground underfoot, the splash of his boots in shallow pools, and the current of fresh-smelling air on his face.

Worse'n the belly of the whale.

Outside, he paused in the starlight on two days' snowfall, to breathe. He didn't see moonlight, but he could see his way well enough.

3

He'd paid the hostler up front for the horse's keep, so there was no one to stop him from saddling the gelding, tying his tools on behind the high cantle, and setting off downstream to Virginia City. A fierce wind swirled around him and the horse, at times obliterating the trail along Alder Creek. This time of year, even on a clear day, the sun might light the mountaintop, but between the snowstorm and the time of this day, the road lay night dark.

He rubbed the animal's neck, under the mane. He'd have to trust him to find the way home.

With every hoof-fall he asked himself what he'd found – Rock? Boulder? Lode? Every time he came up with one answer.

No knowing until it was all uncovered.

He'd ask Dan'l what to do when he got there for his tutoring. He'd leave the horse at the Elephant Corral and get to Dan'l's office quick as he could. He was later'n he'd planned.

Looking up into the sky, he judged by the fading stars in the lightening sky that it must be close to time Dan'l would go to his office. Dan'l hated tardiness.

2 ~~~

The Montana Post: 1/7/1865, p. 4:

Carrier's Address to the Patrons of the MONTANA POST.

[The carrier of the Post...]

Is come to wish you happiness,
And Fortune's tenderest carress,[sic.]
for all the twelvemonth born to-day,
with showers of gold-dust 'long your way.
.... The Vigilantes, staunch and true,
Have done a useful thing or two,
By making this, for vice and crime,
A rather insalubrious clime;
For outlaws, if they didn't slope,
Were apt to take a dose of rope.
Now, Justice holds her even scales,
And law with calmest reign prevails,
While Order walks her peaceful way --
Welcome! Thrice welcome, be their sway!

Dan Stark hoped he would never again have to hang a man.

Standing close to the potbelly stove in his law office, waiting for the fire he'd built to warm the stove's cold heart, he felt his scalp itch. He touched the bandage covering the crown of his head. Flinched.

"Although," he muttered to himself, "in the case of Tobias Fitch, I could make an exception."

Fitch's attempt to brain him had not succeeded, but the place where his blow had landed – what? ten days ago? – was still tender, and a pulse throbbed at his temples most of the time, changing now and then into a stampede of hooves thudding in his head and pounding in his ears.

The wall clock between the back door to his office and the stove pipe chimed the half hour. Nine-thirty. Timothy was late. Thirty minutes late. Drat the boy. Why could he never be on time?

At last feeling his hands warming, he turned toward the door and draped the skirts of his greatcoat over his forearms, the better to warm his backside.

Yes, he could make an exception of Fitch, depending on the outcome of Fitch's trial for attempting to murder him. If it ever came to be.

At the hearing a week ago, Chief Justice Hezekiah Hosmer had postponed that trial until after February 9, exactly one month from today. By then, the First Legislative Assembly for Montana Territory, now meeting in Bannack should have passed a Criminal Law and Procedures Act. Without it, Fitch could not legally be tried and hanged.

If that body of squabbling, self-seeking lawmakers moved as fast as the sloth, they might meet the deadline. Then the law could hang Fitch. A legal execution would free him and the other Vigilantes of the necessity.

The Bar Association had appointed a committee to help the First Legislature write codes of criminal and civil law for Montana Territory. If they did not succeed, he might again, as he'd heard it was said of him, "pull his own rope."

Until a criminal code was written, passed, and signed by the Governor, the Vigilantes still handled criminal matters, particularly capital crimes – attempted murder and murder. "Will our job never end?" he asked the muttering stove.

The *Post* was right, though. The Vigilantes – we, he said to himself, made the trails safe between Virginia City and Bannack, south toward Salt Lake City and northward to Hell Gate. People could take their gold home to the States without fear of armed holdups, though caution was still advised. Time would tell, though, how many lived to make the trip with their gold, one way or both ways as he had done.

Not many brought gold to Virginia City, the heart of gold country. They came to get the gold and take it back home. But when he'd taken his gold back to New York to pay Father's debts, he had ventured into the Gold Room just off Wall Street.

There he'd struck it rich. Then he'd brought his treasure home. Home was Martha, and their growing family.

Now the gold, in coins, was distributed among three dilapidated wooden crates labeled "Law Books." They were haphazardly stacked among other crates that held up his desktop, and the shelves in a bookcase against the wall between his office and Number Four. The bottom shelf rested on bricks at each corner and

7

two in the middle; the top two shelves lay across crates, one at each end and one in the middle.

The bookcase held a veritable library, at least by Virginia City standards – Sir Walter Scott's *Heart of Midlothian, Ivanhoe,* and *Kenilworth;* an 1863 volume of *The Atlantic Monthly.*

Of course, he had a law book. *A Practical Treatise upon the Criminal Law and Practice of the State of New York,* in two volumes, each nearly 800 pages. He had shipped that tome from the City when he knew he was coming back, in a crate identical to those in which he had shipped his treasure. If anyone had stolen the box, thinking they would get their hands on some gold, they would have been sadly disappointed. The joke was on him, though. The boxes of treasure came safely to Virginia City on various stagecoaches, but so did the *Practical Treatise.*

"Why," Dan grumbled aloud, "do law writers have to be so blasted long-winded?"

The storm whined an answer around the back wall of the building. The mercury in his outside thermometer had frozen. That meant it was at least forty degrees below zero. Not even the thick stone walls of Content's Corner, the fire-proof building where Dan occupied Number Five on the second floor, could hold out a wind so relentless, so cold. Ice covered the water in his clean bucket.

Downstairs, men moved heavy items across the floor. Display bins, Dan supposed. This was a brutal day for moving, especially groceries. He went to the door to look out the window. Rockfeller and Dennee, wholesale grocers, were moving across Jackson Street to this building. No one was yet moving into their vacated premises across the way.

The storm had turned the false fronts of buildings into vague rectangles and wiped out their business names. Winter had stolen the income from real estate.

Head bent to use his hat brim to shield his eyes from the north wind, a man topped the stairs and hurried past Dan's door.

Dan swung round to escape the drafts seeping around the door.

The floor moved. The outside wall soared.

He grabbed at something to steady himself, grasped the edge of his desktop, a warped door, not nailed to the crates. It slid with him, tipped his papers, pens, inkstand, slate, and chalk onto the floor.

Stumbling, he groped for the back of a chair near the stove and caught himself, to wait out the spasm.

Steady again, he stooped carefully and snatched up the inkstand now dribbling ink onto the floorboards, stoppered it. Straightened the desktop. Set to putting everything in order. Understood, this must be how a sailor felt, standing in a ship's wheelhouse during a snowstorm at sea.

He could thank Tobias Fitch for that.

Men's voices came clear through the single-board wall dividing his office from Number Four.

"Burns, you've almost let the fire go out again."

"Unless you want to help me write these statutes, you can keep it going yourself."

"Statutes?" The other voice rose in pitch. "What's taking so long? You're just copying Missouri laws."

"I am not. I'm making revisions for our particular situation."

Dan ground his teeth. In less than a month the Legislature would close, and Burns still copied from the Missouri lawbook?

"Lord help us," he muttered to himself, then: "Where is Timothy? Where can that boy be?"

3 ~~~

The Montana Post: 12/31/1864, p. 2.

New Quartz Lode Law.

> We present our readers with a copy of the
> new quartz lode law, as passed by our
> Legislature. It will remedy many of the
> present evils complained of by miners. The
> miner's claim is made real property by the
> act of recording. Jumping will be prevented,
> and also an undue extension of claims from
> their discovery. We shall revert to the
> subject in our next issue, and meanwhile, we
> are happy to realize a beginning of the end
> proposed — viz: justice to miners.

Footsteps clomped up the stairs.

The silhouette of a broad-shouldered man appeared in the window. He pounded once on Dan's door and lifted the latch. The wind blew the door inward out of his hands, and he leaped to catch it before it banged against the wall and broke a windowpane.

"Colder'n a witch's heart out there." Timothy McDowell brandished Saturday's *Montana Post* as he joined Dan at the stove. "What's this mean?" He jabbed a forefinger at a headline, "The New Mining Law."

"Good morning, Tim." Dan spoke deliberately, to slow his stepson down. At the same time the boy puzzled him. Timothy was lit up, incandescent with suppressed excitement, a fuse about to ignite an explosive. What had happened?

"Oh. Yeah. Good morning." Tim rattled the newspaper. "Well? What's this mean?"

"You tell me. What does what mean?"

"It's something about the new quartz law. Read it to me." Melting snow ran off his wide-brimmed hat onto the paper. Tim thrust it at Dan, who batted it away. The sheet dropped to the floor.

"Read it yourself. You know how." Dan bent to rescue the paper from a puddle of melting snow. Straightening, he congratulated himself that he had not toppled over.

He smoothed the paper and hung it to dry over the back of a chair by the stove.

Timothy peeled off his gloves, stuffed them into a pocket, and held his hands out to the warmth. "I'd take too long. I have to spell out big words. An-im-ad-ver-sion. Why can't you just tell me?" He hung his greatcoat on the hall tree, adjusted its folds to hang straight.

Dan had gone with him to buy the coat, to help get the best price and style. It was the boy's first winter coat, bought with his own money, earned working his late father's placer claim. His father had never bought him a winter coat.

"You won't learn if I do. Read it."

Tim's face folded into a frown. The change from boy to man had come late and uneven. He'd grown in four months from five feet, three inches to almost looking level at Dan, who stood six feet tall in his socks.

"I ain't never going to learn how to read all them words." Tim stared at the drying paper and pulled Dan's other armchair up to the stove.

Dan winced at the squawk of chair legs across the plank floor.

"Yes, you can. You will. But not if I tell you everything. You have to. Or you won't be fit to manage the Nugget when you're twenty-one. A little more than four years."

The boy's eyes widened at the threat. "You'd do that? Keep me from managing it?"

"Yes, if you can't read, you'll be incompetent. I won't have you endangering your mother's and sister's futures because you can't read a document."

Timothy tramped around the floor, four long steps from the back wall to the shared wall, three from the stove to the door. He stopped beside Dan.

"What if I decide you're the one to run it?"

"I don't know if I can, legally."

"Why not?"

"A judge could rule that it's a conflict of interest."

"What's that when it's at home?"

"Because I married your mother, and we have the twins, I might have an interest contrary to yours and Dorothy's."

"You wouldn't, would you?" Tim bit a fingernail. "Um, cheat us?"

"No." Even as he replied, there came a vision of the two wrinkled red faces and four tiny doubled fists, and he knew he lied. What could ever be more important to him than the two squalling morsels of his and Martha's joining, tiny beings who had wrecked his sleep for the past nine days? He was responsible for bringing them into existence, two human beings, two men in chrysalis. Just as Timothy, Dotty, and the orphan girl, Eileen, all half-grown, were his responsibility. Five young people to see right.

The weight of it all settled on him, and a headache came like a wave from the ocean, a constant wash-and-thump.

He stood as close to the stove as he could without scorching his waistcoat. Taking a deep breath, he set himself to explain. "You, your mother, and sister inherited the mining claim from your father."

Tim made a face; he already knew that.

"Steady on. This is important for you to understand. Because you're the oldest male heir, its management will be yours when you're twenty-one. The twins and I have no share in it. My only responsibilities are to make sure you're ready and give you the best legal advice I can once you're of age and become the manager. If there's anything to manage." So far, nearly a year after its discovery, the mine was a hole in the mountain, its mysteries hidden.

Tim made another circuit around the room, scraping his boots along the floorboards, occasionally stomping them as though to rid them of caked snow. "My feet are cold."

Silence reigned at the shared wall.

Tim stopped close enough for Dan to smell his breath. Lowered his voice. "I was up there, yesterday and early this morning." He looked his stepfather in the eye.

A chill ran up Dan's spine that had nothing to do with the temperature in the room, warming as the stove's black iron skin turned pale. Putting a forefinger to his lips, he pulled the two chairs close to each other – and to the stove. Of all the stupid risks…. He clamped his lips tight against the words he wanted to say. They would do no good, after the fact.

"Let's see what the paper says." Dan spoke to give himself time.

Sitting side by side, they bent their heads so close over the article they nearly touched.

"You went up there in this cold, in a blizzard?" The words squeezed between Dan's tight lips. "What are you trying to do, die young?"

Tim scratched at a hangnail, bit it off. "I get so blamed tired of waiting for the snow to melt. The weather was fine when I figured I'd give it a look-see."

"You took tools?" The redness mounting in Tim's neck told Dan he'd hit it right. "Pick? Shovel? Candles?"

"Yeah. All that. Lantern, too."

"How many times have your mother and I told you, don't dig alone?"

"About a million." Tim ducked his head, his shoulder-length hair falling forward, uncovering the curve of one flaming ear.

"At least. She'd be heartbroken if something happened to you."

"She's got the twins. I ain't so much to her now."

Dan seized Timothy's upper arm. Felt the strong muscle harden under his grip. "Never say that! You hear me? Never! You're her first." He released the boy. "If anything happened to you, she'd be lost."

"I didn't —" The red in Tim's neck drained away. "I never thought —"

"Right. You didn't think. You rode up there. All right. And you rode back down because the weather was foul and you couldn't find the entrance."

Laughter in Number Four resounded through the wall.

"I ain't told you the whole story." His hands, held out to the stove, trembled.

Ah. Now they were getting to it. The reason for Tim's excitement. "Shhh." Dan poked a thumb toward the bookcase. A coffee grinder stood on the top shelf, an opened bag of coffee beans on the bottom shelf. "Wait. We need something hot in our gullets. How about coffee?" He rose, went to the bookcase, lifted the nearly ten-pound bag onto the top shelf.

"Sure thing," Tim said. "You know me. I'll never say no to a cup of java."

Dan pointed to the word on the sack. "It's Sumatra coffee."

"Either one." Tim shrugged. "Coffee's coffee."

Dan didn't argue. It was an old joust between them, he didn't understand how some people could not tell Java coffee from Sumatra.

"Talk. What's happened?" While Dan poured raw beans into a frying pan and set it on the stove's cooktop, Tim muttered low, under the jovial sounds next door.

"You and Major Fitch left for Bannack afore Christmas to talk the Legislature into a thousand feet of ground for quartz claims, so we'd have room for tailings and machinery and such. All right. You done that. I got that much from that article. Well, while you-all were gone, me and Albert, we kept digging. Racing the snow, to get an adit dug far's we could." He looked sideways at Dan. "A portal's a mine entrance, and an adit's the tunnel in from the portal."

"Yeah, and a drift is a tunnel off a shaft or an adit, and a shaft is a hole in the ground deeper than a well, that connects drifts on different levels. I know." He stirred the beans, lying inert while his heart jumped. "How far in did you go?"

"'Bout fifteen feet."

Dan shook the pan across the cooktop. "How often did you go up there while I was gone?"

"Whenever I could. Yesterday, I figured I'd start a new drift off the adit." Tim dug into his trousers pocket, extracted a lump of gold quartz. A nugget, big as his thumb and nearly pure gold. He had named the mine for it. The Nugget.

17

"You what?" Dan managed not to shout. "Don't you know the danger you put yourself in?"

"Yeah, but. I wasn't going to dig through the whole mountain." Tim tossed the nugget. Caught it. Did not look at Dan.

A whisper of something unsaid brought Dan's head up. "How'd you know which way to go?"

"I d'know. I just felt like I should dig thisaway." He flapped a hand to one side. "Seemed one way was as good's another."

A few roasted beans jumped in the pan. "Thank God you're alive." Dan held up a finger to stop Timothy. "Where did you sleep?"

"In the livery with the horse. I wrapped up in the saddle blanket, and it was warm enough. Then I went back and dug some more until I guessed I'd be late meeting you." He tore off a hangnail with his teeth and winced. "Ran out of candles by then."

Dan kept his eyes on the roasting beans, his mind busy rejecting things he wanted to say, to convince Tim of what a fool he'd been to take such a risk. What could he say, how could he intervene when Martha's boy had been mostly on his own, without a father's good example – thanks in part to the War – for most of his life? Not that the elder McDowell provided any example except foul ones.

"No wonder you've got hay in your hair."

"Better'n hay on my horns." Tim's attempt at a joke died under Dan's glare.

Dan reminded him, "The beans are ready to grind."

Tim brushed his fingers through his hair, and a few broken bits of hay tumbled to his shoulders, onto the floor.

All was silent on the other side of the wall.

Tim dipped water from the clean pail into a pot and put it on the cooktop, as Dan rose to grind the beans. He signaled Tim to stand close to the grinder as he poured the beans into the funnel and turned the handle. A miniature grindstone growled its way through crushing the roasted beans.

"You could have been caught in a cave-in, like the two fellows in the *Post*."

"I didn't dig very far. Less'n a foot in, and no higher'n my head. I hit a rock." Tim inhaled, his chest expanding and stretching his sheepskin waistcoat, making gaps between the buttons. "That smells fine. I do love the smell of fresh ground beans."

Dan murmured, "So. You're digging in the Rocky Mountains, and you hit a rock."

"What? Oh. Right." His smile broke open like sunshine. "Yeah. A rock. An almighty big rock. A boulder, maybe. I tried to find the edge of it and couldn't."

"And then?"

The last of the grounds dropped into the grinder's drawer. Dan stopped turning the handle.

Boiling water sputtered across the cooktop. Tim wrapped his hand in a rag and snatched the pan partly off the heat. Dan poured the grounds into the water, his mind racing, speculating on what the boy might have

19

found. He stirred the grounds in the water, did not see it turn dark brown.

Tim whispered, "I shined the lantern on it, see what it was."

Dan held a hand up to stop Timothy from saying more until he estimated the coffee had finished brewing. He filled two thick ceramic mugs, set the pan aside, gave Tim a mug. Took the other for himself.

When the boy had poured canned milk into his coffee, they sat. Although separated only by the width of two chair arms, Tim lowered his voice until it sounded muffled in Dan's good left ear. "What did you say?"

"The rock had a shine. Not water-shine. Gold."

"All of it?"

"Much as I could see." Swigged some hot coffee. "Ouch." Rubbed his breastbone. Breathed deep.

"How much was that, do you think?"

Tim set the mug on the arm of his chair, held his hands about a foot apart. "It was big. Maybe this wide." Held one hand perhaps three feet above the floor. "About this high." Took hold of his coffee mug. "Hard to tell. I didn't dare dig more out, on account it was just me." A sidelong peek at Dan. He coughed. "I uncovered just that bit. It was –" coughed again "– mostly all gold."

Dan's scalp crawled. When he'd found that nugget resting now in Tim's pocket, he'd been afraid the ground was salted. That fear now dissolved like the sugar lump in his coffee. The nugget was a piece of something larger, maybe a piece of this boulder or more like it, forces of nature in their eons of work grinding off pieces and squeezing them to the surface. The nugget had assayed at 99.3 percent pure. But now – a gold rock? Boulder? Or something bigger? A lode?

He could not grasp the possibilities. They were too grand. Too immense.

He got up, carried his coffee to the window, where he sipped, swallowed, hardly noticed the hot liquid burning down to his stomach. His mind sparked. Questions, possibilities, flashed like pistol shots. He almost expected Tim would hear them. Or Burns and Pemberton, next door.

Tim came to stand with him.

"You think you may have found a lode." Speaking the word made his scalp tingle; the headache pounded faster.

"'Pears so." Tim took a sip of coffee. "Maybe."

"The question is, now what?"

"Dig it out. See what we got."

"Yes. That's first." Dan paused to shape his ideas. When he had them in order, he said, "The gold is there. Only question is, how much."

"Yes." Tim wrapped both hands around the mug.

"Who else knows about it?"

"Nobody. I come straight here after I stabled the horse and put my tools away at Jake's place. He wasn't home."

"Probably at the bank." Dan mused as though to himself. "The correction in the *Post* today gives discoverers two claims each instead of just one. You're

21

entitled to another claim because you were there first. Discovering the claim."

"Preemption. I figured that much out. But wait."

"Yes?"

"We didn't discover the claim. Pap did. He's the discoverer, and he's" – a hitch in his voice – "dead."

Dan's ideas moved fast. He walked to the stove, poured himself more coffee, carried it with him. Glanced at the clock. Tim had been here for less than an hour. Forty minutes to change their lives. Maybe.

"If –" Tim began to say. Stopped.

"Yes? What is it?" He stood by Timothy at the stove.

"We discovered the claim after Pap marked it wrong. That makes us – you, me, and Jake – the discoverers, don't it? So we're all eligible for two claims each, right?"

Dan's hand, raising the coffee cup to his lips, stopped in mid-air. "Yes. Of course. Probably. But the real problem is the difference between discovering a placer claim and a quartz claim. We're between two legal systems. The Fairweather Mining District laws rule placer claims, and placers are surface mining."

"Not underground?"

"Right. Not underground mining."

Timothy made a small raspberry sound.

"All right, yes, yes, I know you know that. But hear me out. You have to be clear about this. We registered the Nugget claim under Fairweather law last year when there was no other government here. But now this is a Territory, and the first legislature has made this new Territorial quartz law that governs underground mining. Quartz claims. And since there's an adit with a drift off it, and you found – what you found – the Nugget is now a quartz claim. We'll have to re-register it."

"What do you mean, re-register it? We already registered it when we found it."

Dan paced from his desk to the bookcase and back. Only three strides either way, but movement helped him think. "All right. Listen close. We registered it as a placer claim, because the gold lies in the topsoil and in the bedrock where the creek water washed away the topsoil. Now that you've gone so far underground, it's a quartz claim. We have to re-register it as such."

"But we still inherit it, right?"

"Yes. Doubtless. Your father would have had the rights of the discoverer, but as he died without a will, we'll have to be extra careful to make sure the new judge, Chief Justice Hosmer, will uphold the next of kin's right to inherit. That's you, your mother, and Dorothy. You jointly inherited all rights pertaining to the Nugget. The miners court judge already ruled that you three are its legal owners. That means, as owners, you are each entitled to two claims, one by discovery and one by preemption, according to the new quartz mining law."

He stopped to drink more coffee, see if Timothy would raise the next problem.

While Tim chewed on the idea, Dan worried that he might not have understood the point, that the right of preemption justified seizing the Nugget claim and claims adjacent to it. Current squatters on adjacent claims could challenge the family's right to take those claims by preemption, but they should not prevail in court unless they had registered their claim with the recorder.

The boy shook his head. "Major Fitch, he'll fight it hard, and he don't fight fair. He already tried to murder you once."

"I'm not forgetting him. How could I?" Dan gestured toward the bandage on his head. "I'm expecting a battle." The headache beat a message in his ears in time with the pounding of his heart: 'Bring it on. Bring it on.'

Tim's voice quavered, the boy wanting to cry fighting the man who kept a stiff upper lip. "He let Pap die because of that claim. Not that he knowed it was anything but a hole in the mountain, but he paid Pap to look for gold. Pap had that contract with his mark on it, and maybe it was to make Pap think he'd own a gold mine. Pap didn't know what he'd found. Major Fitch, he might not of knowed Pap was dying, but he saw Pap walking, and his blood dripping on the snow, and he didn't do nothing." He stopped, swallowed, and tears shone in his eyes. "He'll say he grubstaked Pap, so the Nugget's his."

"I'll handle Fitch, Timothy. That contract has Sam's name – and his mark – and another name on it. Not Tobias Fitch. Besides, the other name is a figment." To Timothy he could sound sure of himself, but inwardly he was not certain of the case at all. He would have to formulate this legal argument to give Judge Hosmer no choice but to agree. Because they could not admit Fitch to this discovery, not under any circumstances, and he had been Sam's partner. Like Tim said, Fitch had grubstaked Sam – paid him to do the prospecting – and the contracts on each claim Sam found gave him fifty percent of whatever the claim yielded. Mostly, nothing.

"A fig –what?"

"Figment. A chimera. A figment of the imagination. Like a child's imaginary playmate. He doesn't exist. Fitch insists he does, and lives in Atlanta. Even if that's true, the Fairweather laws forbid them. That name exists only on paper to get around the two claims rule."

"That true? How can you be so sure?"

"The miners meeting of the Fairweather Mining District passed a law against absentee owners last summer. The *Montana Post* printed them in October."

"That won't matter to the Major. What's his is his, and that's an end to it."

"Listen to me." Dan faced his stepson square-on. Timothy was at an awkward stage. He was of a size to be treated like a man, but the strong man's body had outstripped his boy's mind. Had he been younger, or smaller, Dan could have held both of his shoulders and looked into his eyes, treated him like the child he often was. "He won't succeed. I'll fight him, and I'll win. The law is on our side."

"What law? We don't have law yet. The Legislature ain't finished writing all its laws." He jerked a thumb toward Number Four. Whispered, "On account of the committee ain't done."

"The committee is working on the Criminal Code. We have the Quartz Law for Montana Territory." Dan tapped the newspaper. "Before Montana became a Territory and Justice Hosmer came to establish the Territorial court, the miners court was the only court we had."

"I know that. A miners court hung George Ives." Too late, Tim bit his lower lip and mumbled, "Sorry."

Dan, who had prosecuted Ives in that trial, nodded, silently accepting the boy's apology. "It's all right. The Fairweather laws were our only laws, but they ruled placer mining, and their intent was to give everyone a fair chance at getting rich. Justice Hosmer hasn't overturned any of Judge Duncan's decisions."

Slurping his coffee, Tim raised an eyebrow. "There was the Vigilante tribunal. I was never so scared in my life."

"We only took care of capital crimes. Murder, armed robbery, attempted murder. Because we had only one punishment."

"Yeah."

"The Tribunal found you innocent. I got well." Except for a troublesome partial deafness in his right ear. The boy hadn't meant to kill him when he'd lashed out. He just hadn't stopped to think before he flew off the handle, as the saying went. That was Tim's biggest problem. He was good-hearted, but too quick to strike, too prone to snap judgments. Like Sam before him.

"You gonna tell me what you're thinking?"

The blasted headache again. He couldn't think as clearly as he had before Fitch hit him. He leaned toward Tim. "The rock you found makes the Nugget a quartz claim. It may have begun as a placer claim, but you finding the rock changes everything. Like I said, we'll refile it as a quartz claim under the new law, and gain an additional hundred feet of ground, and a thousand feet for workings."

He waited while Tim considered it, watched his face change from a puzzled frown to the excitement he'd brought with him.

Tim's laughter burst out, a boisterous deep sound that poured over Dan, who laid a finger to his lips just in time for the boy to turn a shout into a whisper, a stage whisper to be sure, but the men in Number Four would not hear it clearly.

"You believe me." He punched Dan softly on the shoulder. "You believe me."

"Yes, of course. Did you think I wouldn't?"

"I didn't know. It's so farfetched. Folks like me don't discover gold like this."

"Why not? Bill Fairweather hoped to pan a little tobacco money, and he found more gold than California."

Dan set the cup with the dregs of his coffee on the desk. "Come on." He lifted Timothy's coat and his own off the hall tree.

"Where?"

"To see Jacob. We need a banker."

27

Carol Buchanan

4 ~~~

The Montana Post: 1/7/1865, p. 2. Col 1.

The Quartz Lode Law.

We find that an error has crept into our Quartz Lode Law as published in our last issue. The first section reads thus:

"That any person or persons that may hereafter discover any Quartz Lead, Lode, or Ledge, shall be entitled to one claim thereon by right of discovery, and one claim each by preemption."

The official copy arrived after the first that came to hand had been printed.

"Why'd we bother with coats?" Tim shouted through the scarf over his mouth and nose. "Just takes longer to freeze."

Head down, Dan concentrated on navigating Jackson Street among wind-scoured frozen piles of horse droppings and garbage.

John Ming's building, directly across from Content's Corner, housed more than his bookstore. Left of the doorway, the jeweler who rented the first stall bellowed, "Shut the door!" when swirling, wind-driven snow followed them in.

"Sorry." Dan nodded to him as Tim hauled the door closed.

The jeweler plucked the loupe out of his eye, returned Dan's nod, and wiped his dripping nose on his coat sleeve. He mumbled something Dan did not catch. Replacing the loupe, he bent to his work, engraving an intricate design on the cover of a gold watch. Minute flecks of gold flew off the smooth surface and dropped onto a piece of Mrs. Sanders's Brussels carpet, where they disappeared into the dense pile. Eventually, he would burn it and pan the ashes for the gold.

Across from the jeweler's stand, a grocer's stall occupied the middle of the room. The grocer roamed a four-sided space bounded by mostly empty bins, their slanted bottoms bare of anything but dust. A few shriveled potatoes sprouted in one, onions in another. He would have little to offer until supply trains could cross the passes from Salt Lake City. Or from Walla Walla, in Washington Territory.

Come July, local gardeners would have produce to sell.

Tim murmured, "That grocer looks worried."

"Ming charges rent per month by the square foot." Dan lowered his voice, tossed his comment over his shoulder, away from the grocer. "But he won't throw the man out. Come summer they'll both make a fortune."

"I'd give two ounces of dust for a heap of spinach. We're close to eating meat straight."

"Don't worry. You'll keep your teeth. Your mother has an endless supply of sage tea."

Tim crossed his eyes. "That's what I'm afraid of."

Their laughter carried them through the turn toward the rear of the building and along two empty booths that backed onto the outside wall. Harold Abbott, president of the Virginia City Bar Association, played cards with a newcomer to Virginia City. The young man, not much older than Timothy, had a discouraged look to him. His face had a gray cast and his spine bowed. Probably hungry. None of his business, though, not with the young fellow on friendly, card-playing terms with Abbott.

"Gotcha!" Abbott, a hugely fat man in a country of lean men honed down by their troubles, their obsession with getting the gold, or drinking themselves to death, slapped his cards down face up on the box that served as a table.

"Good show." For politeness' sake Dan stopped to pass the time of day. Timothy walked on to where Jacob Himmelfarb stood under a sign – "Bank" – suspended from a rear crossbeam.

Abbott grinned up at Dan. "Winning sure feels good." He slid the cards over to the new man. "Glad you happened by. I have a new client." He smiled at his opponent, who crossed out a number on a piece of paper and wrote a new sum under it. "Tobias Fitch."

Fitch. "Is that so?" Dan removed his hat, so both men could see the bandage, blood-stained and dried to a shade somewhere between red-brown and black. He managed a smile; it was either that or snarl. "I wish you joy of him."

"Who will represent you?"

"I haven't decided."

At that the new man looked up. His face was blank, but his eyes gleamed. "Do you play cribbage?"

"No, sorry to say. Poker's my game." Dan extended his hand. "I don't believe we've met. My name is Daniel Stark."

A damp, limp hand rested briefly in his own. "Vaughn Ryder."

Dan resisted the temptation to wipe his hand down his coat.

Abbott leaned back. The chair creaked under him. "You know the saying, Stark. 'A man who represents himself has a fool for a client.'"

"Sayings aren't always true." He'd won the hearing before Judge Hosmer that jailed Fitch. His trial for the murder of Timothy's father was due to begin at the next session of the District Court, in less than a month.

A loud voice came to him from under the "Bank" sign. Jacob shook his finger at Timothy, angrier than Dan had ever seen him, scolding the boy in a flood of Yiddish, German, and occasional English for all of Ming's to hear. The fringes of his prayer shawl thrashed about below the hem of his waistcoat.

"Excuse me, gentlemen. Welcome to Virginia City, Mr. Ryder."

"Thank you." Ryder's mouth turned down as though he smelled something off.

Jacob stopped lecturing Timothy when Dan reached the white picket fence surrounding the bank's area, the far back corner of the room. Tim's face was pale, even below its winter pallor, and his eyes were blank, stunned. His hands dangled at his sides.

Jacob included Dan, opening the gate, in his glare. "Do you know what this – ungrateful – this – what he has done?"

Dan stepped into the bank's space. Thinking a small delay might cool Jacob a bit, he took an extra few seconds to fiddle with the latch as he closed the gate behind him.

"He has come close to killing himself, that much I know."

Tim stared steadfastly at the plank floor. His face was set in the stubborn lines of a much younger boy. "I was careful. I didn't take chances. I'm here, ain't I?"

Jacob ignored him. "Two days he disappears. Two days." Shook his finger at Tim. "Saturday and Sunday, and now – now!" He stomped his foot. "Only now do I see alive he is, and tells a fairy tale."

Dan waited until Jacob had wound down to a stony silence. "Apologize to Jacob, Timothy."

"Jake, I'm sorry. I didn't mean to be gone so long. And I didn't think —"

"Ja. You did not think. You do not think. You can go off for almost two days, and I will not worry? Dan will not worry? Your mother will not worry?"

Jacob was saying what Dan had not, though he knew it needed saying. If he had scolded Tim this way, he would have caused a rift in the family that would take time to heal, and knowing Tim's mulish nature, he couldn't blame Jacob.

At first, when Dan and Jacob came to Alder Gulch, they had shared a tiny cabin, known as bachelor's quarters. When Tim's father threw him out into a snowstorm during a drunken rage, Dan had brought him into their cabin, where he shared their bed, three to a bed being not uncommon in the overcrowded gold camp that was Virginia City. Then, when Dan and Martha, Tim's mother, came together after Sam McDowell disappeared, Dan had bought the cabin they currently lived in. Something like eight-hundred, eight hundred fifty square feet in two rooms and a lean-to, that Dotty, Timothy's little sister, shared with Eileen, the help, sleeping on camp beds among boxes and stored foodstuffs.

Tim continued to live with Jacob. Dan had been grateful every day for Jacob's generosity toward the boy.

But now Jacob was angry.

Jacob, who had always regarded them with affection and friendship, owed Dan much, including his life. Plainly, they had come to a barrier thrown up by Tim's thoughtlessness. Dan knew he would be hard pressed to convince Jacob to listen to any proposition based on the possibilities of the boy's find.

He had to try. Dan said, "Jacob, you have every —"

Tim broke in, talking across him. "I'm sorry. I just had a feeling, and I figured I'd be back before dark.

Only I found something." When Jacob glared at him with hard dark eyes, Tim gulped, lowered his voice. "I found a gold rock. A big one."

"So? You forget me? You go somewhere, and I don't know, and you don't come back? This storm comes, but you don't? Injured I think you may be. Or worse."

"It was gold."

"Ja? This is why you do not come back?" Jacob stamped a foot, and the floorboard bounced. "For a rock you leave me to worry? Why you ruin my Sabbath, when I must study God's word?"

"I found something —"

"Pah! You might have been buried with this rock. There are more rocks everywhere here. What is a rock to make you forget your duty to your friends?"

Tim's frustration rang out. "Didn't you hear me? It was gold."

Dan winced. His stepson had revealed the find to the world.

Jacob crossed his arms over his chest, and glared at Tim. "So? Is no surprise. Every week, in the *Montana Post*, we read of great gold strikes. You know of Christenot, he finds the Oro Cache almost on the summit of the mountain, and you think you find another quartz mine, maybe you find the mother lode, ja? You value gold more than your friends?"

Tim tried again. "But, Jake, it's big. I couldn't find the edge of it."

Jacob brushed his hand to one side as if brushing off dust. "So. You make this excuse? You risk being killed in a cave-in and your friends—" a sharp glance at Dan, standing mute "—and your family do not know where you are, if you live or die?"

"Jake, I'm sorry. I didn't think. I'm so sorry."

Jacob turned to Dan. "This I cannot do any more. I cannot have him in my house, make my Sabbath – how you say, not respect?"

"Disrespect."

"Ja. Disrespect my Sabbath. And me. You must take him home where he belongs. This I am sorry, Daniel. You have ever been a friend. When I had no English and no money, you taught me how to help with survey and brought me here, showed me the way of making much money. But I cannot have this – how you say – look out for him."

"Responsibility?"

"Ja. Responsibility. It is too much."

"All right, Jacob. I'll take Tim home with me." Dan kept his voice low, conciliatory. There was nothing he could say now. Whatever could be done to repair the damage Tim had caused would have to wait for the opportunity. It would have to be something Tim could do for Jacob. Merely saying he was sorry had clearly been useless. Being sorry didn't make up for the pain he had caused. It was a start, though. And he would keep watch for an opportunity for Tim to mend this break.

Perhaps. He hoped so.

In the meantime, with Jacob so angry at Tim, and so unbelieving that the rock could be gold, how would they fund the excavation? No one gave money to anything without believing in it. Like religion. Or, with a mine, believing in a return on the investment.

And Jacob did not believe Tim had found anything but granite.

5 ~~~

The Montana Post: 1/7/1865, p. 3. Col 1.

Local and Other Items.

> The hydrants in town are all up now, and a supply of good water is to be had, without getting this element mixed with all imaginable substances, from an ox's tail to pieces of old shoes or clothing. We hope the proprietors and builders will get a charter, and substantial assistance in subscriptions from all those who use water from the hydrant.

Dan rescued the banked fire in his office stove by shaking the blanket of ash down into the ash pan, while Tim picked two quarter rounds – each a quarter of a log cut to stove length – from the woodbox. Using the poker, Dan stirred the coals into a fresh blaze, then stood aside for Tim to thrust the new wood into the firebox. He hung up the poker as Tim shut the fire door.

Huddled as close to the stove as possible, they waited for the fire to build enough to warm them and reheat the pan of coffee.

"I don't understand Jake." Tim turned his back to the stove. "He's always been kind and friendly to me. Let me stay at his place after you and Mam got together. but now he don't want me there no more?"

Dan looked past him toward the wall behind the bookcase. "Keep your voice down."

Tim's voice rose, as though he had not heard Dan. "Well? Can you figure it?"

Dan made a damping gesture and answered Tim in a near whisper. "Yes, I can. He feels you've disrespected him."

"I never —"

"Listen to me." Dan took a breath to calm himself. He wished he could put both Jacob and Tim in a room to battle their differences out, like Hugh O'Neill and Con Orem, but what would be the point of that? They both felt they were in the right. And each was right, at least in part. Like the saying went, 'Two wrongs didn't make a right,' but what about 'two rights don't make a wrong?' "You did. He's changed. Haven't you seen the signs? You've been living with him."

Tim went quiet, nibbled at his thumbnail, spat the shreds onto the floor. "Yeah. I guess so. He's more religious. Leastways, that's how he acts. He always wore that fringed shawl under his waistcoat, but now he spends more time reading a book he sent away for. You were with Fitch in Bannack when it came. I looked at it once. Couldn't make head or tail out of it. It's all in a funny alphabet, and he reads it back to front." Spat out more nail fragments. "Right to left."

Ever restless, Tim pivoted as though he turned on a vertical spit. Glancing toward the shared wall, he said in a low voice with a quaver in it, "He must've knowed I'd come back. He didn't have to spend his Sabbath worrying instead of reading that big book and praying, like he does with the Morris brothers and some other Jews in town. I didn't make him do that."

"Not everything people do on your account is because you make them do it. People who care about you will worry if you're late getting home."

"I don't see why. I can take care of myself."

"Oh, can you?" Dan took his overcoat off and hung it on the hall tree. "Can you withstand a snowslide? Can you stop a river flowing? Hold up a mountain?"

"Well, no. No one can do them things."

"All right. You were working alone in the Nugget. What was that like?"

Tim scuffed his toe at a spot on the floor. "I kept hearing noises. Groans. Now and then something like a sigh. Water dripping. It was eerie. Like I was hacking away at something alive."

Dan waited to be sure Tim had finished. "It gave you the willies, did it? It would me."

"Yeah. Especially at the end. When the candle almost went out. That's when I saw it. The gold. I held up the lantern, to see how much candle I had, and it – it shined on something that gave the shine back. Gold." He looked toward Dan then, but not as if he saw him, but gazed at something beyond that only he could see.

Dan took off his hat to scratch around the bandage, glanced toward the door. Nothing but wind-driven snow appeared in the panes. Only that. But even as the idea took shape, he knew he lied to himself.

He'd glimpsed something, seen with what they called the 'mind's eye.' As though he'd been with Tim, looking over his shoulder as the lantern swung around, and something gleamed out of the dark.

He shivered.

All unaware, Tim poured coffee into mugs. "I hope this swill is hot enough."

Truly the boy thought he'd seen something far bigger than what he'd uncovered – the rock that had no edge. No edge.

He swallowed coffee. It scalded his esophagus all the way down into his stomach. He bent over, coughing. "Water," he gasped.

Tim poured him a dipper of clean water.

Still preoccupied with his conjectures, Dan drank it. "That's good." Cold, sweet water, such as he had not tasted in months. The new hydrants. Worth whatever the builders wanted to charge.

He put the dipper back on its hook. Tim gave him his mug of coffee. Dan took a careful sip, and his ideas straightened themselves out.

Men climbed Baldy Mountain, following the trail blazed by Alder Creek, and the higher they went the more likely they were to find gold, but not in the stream, because the placers were playing out. Men had just about dug all the gold the creek had hidden in its bed, in its shoulders. In the mountain. Gold quartz. The beautiful, pale, sometimes nearly translucent rock shot through with strings, threads, of gold. In the very fabric of the mountain, part of its heft, its tissue.

Tim might have seen the edge of a lode? Did he have dreams of a wall of gold reaching all the way to daylight, perhaps to the summit, something over 9,000 feet?

Probably not. He had, though, seen something, sensed the presence of something larger than the boulder, the – his thoughts stumbling a bit in his eagerness to find a word, maybe limitless? No, that promised too much. Edgeless would have to do. For now. The edgeless boulder.

With a sense of relief, Dan retreated from the difficulty of finding the best word for his idea, to a language he understood. Facts. Numbers. The rock or boulder or something larger – whatever it was, it needed excavation. To find out what they had, it had to be dug out.

Not by Timothy. At least not alone. He must never again go alone into the mountain.

Wrapping his hand in a rag, Dan took hold of the pan's handle. He watched the dark liquid flow out of the pan into their cups and did not look at Tim.

"Promise me two things."

"What?" Wariness vibrated in Tim's voice, as though he expected something dire, something his father might have said or done.

"Never again go into the mountain without telling me where you're going. That's one." Dan handed Tim his coffee cup.

"Okay. What's number two?"

"Never again go alone. Tell me when you plan to go up there, and who you're going up there with." Dan felt his way with an idea forming in his mind.

Timothy raised his head, shook it, reminding Dan of a mule refusing the bit.

He waited. The next step, if there was to be a next step, depended on Tim making this promise, a promise being sacred to him. If he promises, Dan told himself, we'll see about the next step.

Excavating the boulder.

They had to know what it was, if it was worth going on or not.

He waited, while his own breath quickened along with the pulse beating under the bandage. If the rock held as much gold as Timothy reckoned, if it turned out to be the edge of a lode, then and only then – maybe – a very big maybe balanced on the point of an if – then there would be a gold mine to develop. Hope blossomed in his mind, a night-blooming Cereus, beautiful but doubtful and fleeting, on a plant full of thorns.

He reined himself in. Time enough for fancies after the rock was known.

Blast this headache.

"I promise."

At first Dan did not think he had heard right. "You do?"

Tim met Dan's skepticism with a steady gaze. "Like I said, I promise. I won't go up to the mine without I tell you first, you and Mam, and I won't try digging without taking someone along."

"All right. Shake on it." Dan held out his hand, prepared himself for Tim's usual bone-crushing grip.

But Tim grasped his hand without making the simple handshake into a contest of strength.

"Good. Now then —" Dan started to say, but a sudden notion caught him, and his mind grappled with an idea, carried him into the woods, where he groped for a clear path forward. Should he break his habit of secrecy and trust Timothy? Reveal what some of the crates held? Could this impulsive boy keep a secret that big?

First of all, should he do what the idea demanded?

Fund the excavation himself?

The rock had to be excavated before they could attract investors, even friendly ones like Jacob — if Jacob were still friendly, if Tim's thoughtlessness had not ruined the friendship.

What alternative was there?

Timothy's voice broke into his thinking. "With all your woolgathering, have you thought about eating something? I'm about starved."

"What? Oh, yes. Come to think of it, I'm feeling a little hollow myself."

"I ain't hankering after going out, but I can't think of nothing else to do."

Dan heard the wind whistle around the corner of the building. "We don't need to go out. I have sourdough bread and a hunk of cheese here."

"Fine with me, as long as there's coffee to wash it down."

"If there's water in the clean water bucket, we can make more."

"There ain't." With a big sigh to show how abused he was, Tim put on his new coat. "At least I won't freeze my backside."

While the boy was out, Dan set about cutting the bread and cheese, but his mind was not on the task. He made a mental list of what they would need to excavate the boulder.

First of all, men.

Strong men willing to earn a few ounces of dust underground, in the middle of winter. Rough, dangerous work, but warmer than outside. How much to pay them? He didn't know. Six or seven dollars a day? Chief clerks made three dollars a day, as did top cowhands. But miners had to be paid enough not to be tempted to high-grade the ore. The term stopped him. Before he came to the Montana gold fields, he'd never heard it: High-grade. A fancy way of saying 'steal.'

He would make a simple rule: Steal, and you're fired.

Even as he imagined himself saying that, he knew monitoring the men was impossible. Or was it? He would have to figure that out, find economical ways to prevent high-grade theft. Perhaps a changing room?

Ensuring secrecy would be impossible. Everyone in Ming's had heard the argument between Tim and Jacob. Besides, there were other clues to sudden fortunes. When men suddenly had money, or disappeared for set times every day, people noticed, and rampant speculation started. Whenever a man disappeared, talk of the Plummer gang started again, even though the Vigilantes – Dan among them – had taken care of that problem a year ago.

Besides, the *Montana Post* published stories every week of new discoveries, new fortunes in the making. Country rock or lode, the entire Gulch would know which had been found, just like everyone knew now which mines paid and which were a bust, and how each sample assayed. The *Montana Post* printed it.

The knife thumped down on the desktop. Ah. He stopped, held the knife point up. He knew just the man to help Tim, but would Tim agree? After all, he was a young McDowell, and before he left one of the Confederate armies, his father, Sam, had been an artilleryman, aiming his cannon into masses of charging bluecoats, blasting living men into bloody clouds of red mist.

Tim returned in the midst of Dan's thinking. If he noticed Dan's preoccupation throughout the coffee making, while they ate the bread and cheese, he kept his silence. Or if he said anything, Dan did not hear.

Not until they sat warmed from the inside out, over coffee, comfortable before the stove, did Dan say what was on his mind.

"How are you at keeping secrets? Can you play your cards close to your vest?"

"Sure, I guess so." Timothy set his tin cup on the arm of his chair. "I ain't much of a gambler."

Dan took a long drink of coffee. His swirling ideas tossed up one word: Risk.

"What're you —" Tim began.

On the precipice of bringing the boy into his greatest secret, that one word blocked him. Dan shook his head and held up his hand for silence. Should he risk Timothy's knowing? His feet carried him to the bookcase, back to his desk, to the bookcase, so deep in thought he hardly knew he moved.

He stood at the edge of great risk. He should back away. He owed Martha and the twins – the entire family, including Eileen – safety. To make this region safe he had joined the Vigilantes. To keep them safe, to keep this boy, his sister, the waif – Eileen – safe, he wouldn't, what?

Jump. No, he would not. Not again.

He remembered:

Poised on the lip of a quarry in upper Manhattan Island, he and his friend Peter, both twelve years old, stripped, Dan's skin raised goosebumps on this warm July day, goosebumps of sheer terror. Behind them, other boys chanted, "Jump! Jump!"

Dan's heart pounded now at the recollection, as if he'd returned to that time on the brink looking so far down into the unknown. He'd asked the air, 'How deep is the water? How far below? Are there water snakes?'

'Jump! Jump! Jump'

They'd jumped.

The air whistled past his ears. He'd hit the water feet first, plunged down and down until there was a roaring in his ears, and his lungs demanded air. Kicking hard, he'd reached for the bright sky, visible as light fragments in splintered water above him. Blood rumbled in his temples when he broke the surface, and as if from far away he heard himself and Peter laughing in the sunshine, shaking water from their hair, pulling sweet, sweet air into his lungs.

The drumming in his temples now was a thunder of countless hooves – a buffalo stampede.

It could take hundreds of dollars to uncover the boulder. Thousands to develop the mine if the boulder turned out to be a quartz lode. He had thousands. His own fortune, from trading in the Gold Room. He was rich enough.

He'd been rich before. Before Father gambled everything away ....

He knew the onslaught of poverty. He'd watched the bailiffs, their lips curled in scorn, carry out the family's personal possessions – Mother's jewels and furs, their books, the sterling silver, the Spode. Portraits of Mother, Father. The children's toys. Everything, almost down to the clothes they'd stood up in. He'd known it all: the contempt society heaped on speculators who lost, the humiliation waiting for gamblers who came up short, the shame the family endured because Father had embezzled his law firm's funds – clients' money – and then shot himself.

The coward's despair.

Carol Buchanan

Would risking so much be fair to Martha and the family? His newborn sons?

Yet if he did not, what then? This opportunity would gallop into the mists of might-have-been. Could he let the buffalo run without taking a shot?

A hot current ran through him, as in the Gold Room when he'd called out his last order: Sell!

At the quarry, in the Gold Room, so now.

He jumped.

6 ~~~

Montana Post: 1/7/1865, p. 3.

MONETARY.
Reported by Allen and Millard Bankers.

Virginia City, Dec. 17, 1864.

Exchange on N. Y,, selling for Treasury Notes
at 3 per cent, prem.
Exchange on N. Y,, selling for coin at 5 per
cent, prem.
Treasury Notes, buying at 50 cts., for dust.
     "   "   selling at 60 cts., for dust.
Gold Dust, buying at $39.09 per ounce in T.
N.
Gold Dust, buying at $14.09 to $15.00 for
coin.
Coin buying at 10 per cent. premium in dust.

"Dan'l! You all right?" Timothy stood in front of him. "I asked you twice —"

"Shhhh! Yes. I'm fine." He gestured to their chairs. Somehow, he'd expected this room to have grown larger, but then, he'd transported himself back to the Gold Room, into the trading pit. "Sit down and listen."

Dan spoke in a near whisper. Tim leaned close to hear him. "You must keep this to yourself."

"I will. But Dan'l, what's the matter?"

"We don't need Jacob to fund the excavation. I will fund it myself."

"Wha –?" Tim's shout broke off as Dan clamped a hand in his arm. The mug of hot coffee rocked, spilled on Tim's hand. "Ow!"

After a fast wiping up, they settled again.

Dan raised his voice above normal conversation, "Sorry. Are you all right?"

"Yeah, I'll be okay." He searched Dan's face as though looking for a way to read his mind. Whispered: "You said you'd fund the digging?"

"That's right. We have to know what the rock is before we go any further."

"You have the money?"

"Yes."

"Where? How?"

For an answer Dan stared past Tim at the bookcase.

He twisted around, looked, shrugged. "There ain't nothing there, just–" His eyes widened. He whispered, "Them crates."

Six strong wooden boxes, battered and stained from their shipment more than two thousand miles across the continent on the tops and in the boots of stagecoaches.

"Yes. A couple of them have a little gold coin in them."

When he answered, Tim sounded as awestruck as though in church, his voice so soft Dan had to turn his better ear toward him. "Twenty-five pounds of gold in each one?" The limits to the amount of treasure allowed in each box on a stagecoach, a limit set by the Overland Stage Company.

"No. I wasn't that lucky as a gold trader." He smiled, hoped his lie would stand against the boy's awestruck excitement. "If I'd won that much, I'd have sent for you, your mother and the girls to come to New York." He took a sip of coffee, watched Tim to see how well his lie went down. "But there's enough scattered among them to pay men to excavate the boulder."

At once, he looked for a way to backtrack. Could he trust Timothy? Would the boy guard this knowledge, keep it to himself?

"Your mother doesn't even know about this."

"Rocks will talk before me," Tim muttered. Made a gesture of turning a lock across his lips.

"Good. Keep it that way." The wall clock struck twice. "Almost mid-afternoon." Time was wasting. For the sake of the family's future, decisions had to be made, and Tim had to learn how to make them.

Starting now.

"There are questions to be decided."

"Questions?"

"For one thing, how much say will your mother have in decisions affecting the mine?"

"Huh?"

"Think about it. When you come of age, you'll be the primary decision-maker. In law, you're the principal heir. You're the firstborn. And you're male. But what about your mother? Martha has a head on her shoulders.

"Even though she never went to school, she's not too proud to ask your sister to teach her what she learns from Professor Dimsdale. She traded dried apple pies to Mrs. Hudson for reading lessons. She can read her Bible, and that's not easy, since it's written in seventeenth-century English. She seldom has to ask for help with hard words."

"Mam is smart," Tim agreed, smiling.

"Yes, she is. She keeps increasingly accurate household accounts. I don't very often have to correct them. That's no easy task, you know. The arithmetic involves figuring the value of one or two ounces of gold dust – or a fraction of an ounce – against the shifting rate of eighteen to twenty dollars per ounce, depending on where the dust was panned and its purity. Or the varying exchange rate between dust and Treasury notes."

"Oh, you mean, 'Mr. Lincoln's paper'?" Tim sneered. "That stuff's worthless. All the government has to do is print more. It's just paper."

"Not really. It's tied to how much gold the government has. Treasury notes – greenbacks – are redeemable in gold after ten years, don't forget."

"Yeah, but it's nothing like the real thing. Have you got enough to dig out the rock? Really?"

"That remains to be seen."

"What do you mean?"

"How big is it? How big do you think it might be?"

Tim's mouth opened, as though he meant to protest that no one knew how big the rock was because he couldn't find the edge of it, when another consideration appeared to strike him. Open-mouthed, his eyes moved back and forth at speed, as he began to realize what Dan meant.

"I'm thinkin' we might have a lode. The boulder, like I said, didn't have no edges."

"All right. We don't know for sure. But if we do —" Dan broke off. His ideas flooded his mind too fast to give them words, until one idea clarified, and he could stop on that.

Martha was female.

Tim was male.

Dorothy was female.

Last month Chief Justice Hosmer had ruled in favor of the Idaho statutes. But the Idaho Quartz Law no longer applied, because the Legislature had repealed it in the final section of its own new quartz law, printed in Saturday's *Montana Post*.

The new law said nothing about women. Or men. It mentioned "persons," without regard to sex or race.

Sex or race.

Sex or race, he repeated to himself. Neither mattered to the law on quartz claims, just as neither mattered to the Homestead Law, which gave 160 acres of public domain land to "heads of households." Section nine of the new mining law made it clear, but even so, in either Montana or Idaho claims law, or in the 1862 Homestead Law, claim holders of either land or mining claims were persons.

Persons.

"Albert has been helping you some with the digging, hasn't he?" So deep was Tim in his own speculations that he did not hear Dan until he asked again.

"Yeah. He don't gossip, neither." Then, as if reading Dan's mind, the boy's eyes met his, and widened in sudden understanding.

"D'you think – ?"

"Think what?"

"Albert's done as much work as me and a lot more'n Jake. Maybe on account he's bigger and stronger'n me, and a lot bigger'n Jake. He's come out to help more often than Jake, too." He drank some coffee. "We oughta pay him if'n we ask for his help now."

"Yes, but that's not all."

"I'm listenin'."

Reaching back to his desk, Dan retrieved two issues of the *Montana Post* – one for December 31, 1864, and the latest paper still folded to the article with the correction. Laid them both in Timothy's lap. "Read them again. Section Nine in December and the new Section One."

Tim bent his head, braced his elbow on the arm of the chair, traced the words of each article in the law with a forefinger, whispering as he read. When he finished, he gaped at Dan. "Both of 'em says 'persons.' They don't say nothing about black. Or Colored. Albert's a person. Bein' Colored don't matter to —"

Dan waited. How far would Timothy distance himself from his father? Slavery had existed throughout humanity's time on earth, although people increasingly, he hoped, regarded it as evil.

"That's not all. Read the rest of it."

Tim swigged some coffee. "You mean about bein' entitled to one claim by discovery and one claim by preemption?" He wiped his hand on his trousers. "Albert wasn't there when we found the Nugget."

Dan recalled Chief Justice Taney on the U. S. Supreme Court. "True, but what do you think the article means besides?"

Silence spread between them. Voices rose in Number Four. Heavy horses clopped down Jackson Street, their hooves planted with certainty on the uneven surface.

Pitch exploded in the stove, a gunshot pop.

Tim jerked, struck his elbow against the edge of the chair back. "Ow!"

Rubbing the joint, he muttered between gritted teeth, "I think it means that you, me, and Jake – all three of us together – can own one claim along a lode because we found it, and we can each claim a second one because we was there first."

Dan swallowed his last bite of cheese. "Yes. Good. And preemption means..."

"We can jump any other claim on the lode that we want."

"Not exactly. We can seize a claim, if – and only if we could prove in court it's ours by rights, that we were there first. Or that it was improperly registered. That is what the law means." He smiled at Tim. "Still, you'd make a pretty good lawyer."

"No, sir. Not that. Not me. I ain't cut out for law. Too nigglin'. I like things that say what they mean."

"I don't blame you." Dan swallowed the last dregs of his coffee. His tongue hunted out the grounds around his teeth. "I didn't want to be a lawyer, either."

"You? Then how?" Tim waved his hand around at the office. "This? And you the Vigilante prosecutor?"

"I wanted to be a surveyor. I like math; it comes easy for me. I like being outdoors, too." Dan glanced at his transit standing on its three legs in the corner between his desk and the two outside walls. Looked out the window. Smiled. "Though not today."

"What happened? Why'd you become a lawyer if'n you didn't want to?"

"My grandfather won, eventually. He always won. Except in our last battle. He tried to force me to stay in New York." Smiling, Dan spread his hands. "I came home to your mother, and you and Dotty."

"Oh." Tim rolled the empty cup between his hands. "But you stayed on long enough to make more money?"

"Yes." For a moment the stone walls disappeared, transformed in his mind into the Gold Room, with its trading pit and blackboards hung high on the walls, young boys scurrying up and down ladders in clouds of chalk dust to write the day's trades as they occurred. Recalling the thrill of the trade, he felt his blood run faster.

He came to himself when Timothy left his chair to pace the room. "Yes! We – Mam and me, and maybe Dotty, too, could file on another claim each" – ignored Dan's hands waving him to quiet – "on account we're Pap's heirs 'n' you, Jake, and Albert – y'all could file on two claims each, so we'd have nine claims, ain't that right?"

Dan stood in his stepson's way to make the boy see him nod his agreement, remind him to keep silent, but Tim did not see him. He rushed on. "We'd – the group of us – we'd own pretty much the whole damn mountain, or at least this side of it. Right?"

When Dan, lost in a new view of the boy suddenly grown into a savvy heir to a potential gold mine, did not speak up fast enough, Tim stopped in his tracks and faced him.

"Well? I'm right, ain't I? Ain't I?"

"Yes. But don't shout." He jerked his head toward Number Four. "You're right," he muttered. "Fairweather laws have that, and so does the new Quartz Law. We could file on claims, and then form a co-partnership and operate all our claims together as one mine."

"Oh." Tim sat down, watched his big, rough-callused hands roll the empty cup between them.

Dan waited, while hooves beat in his ears, and his breath stifled in his chest. What would Sam McDowell's son say about this radical idea? Scandalous — white men going into business with a Colored as an equal partner. It was a stab in the eye of the memory of the late and widely unmourned Chief Justice Taney, Confederate and slave-owner, who had ruled that Dred Scott, and any other Colored man, had no rights a white man was obliged to respect. In effect, the Supreme Court had ruled that Coloreds were non-persons.

But not in Montana Territory. Not in the 1862 Homestead Act. It gave heads of households 160 acres of land to farm, without specifying their race or sex.

Dan realized he was shivering. He opened the door to the firebox and laid two more quarter rounds on the fire. When he straightened, he found Timothy staring at him.

"Have you made up your mind?"

"Guess so."

"And —?"

Timothy's response came so slowly that Dan thought he had decided against it.

The boy took a deep breath. "Bring him in on it. Albert, I mean."

"Are you sure? This isn't done, you know, blacks working with whites in equal partnerships."

"I know that. And I ain't sure it'll work. What's a slave – someone used to be a slave – know about business? Less than I do."

"How do we all know about anything? We learn it." Dan remembered the long hours studying gold trading in his brother-in-law's back garden, his apprenticeship with Peter, God rest his soul.

Tim sat, took his coffee mug in both hands, but instead of drinking from it, sat still, his head bowed over it.

Dan waited, almost afraid to breathe. He had to get this right.

Tim looked his stepfather in the eye, his voice trembling with emotion. "Slavery's about the worst thing anyone can do to someone. Maybe bringing Albert into a co-partnership with us will help. Besides —" His indrawn breath stretched his flannel shirt tight across his chest. "Pap wouldn't like it. It goes against everything he believed. Everything he taught me and Dotty about Colored folks."

Looking down, he traced a circle on his knee with the tip of his index finger, around and around.

Dan watched Tim's face as his notions chased across it.

"We got to do this." The boy's direct, blue-eyed stare brought Sam to mind. "It wouldn't be fair to leave Albert out. If it wasn't for him helping dig the adit farther into the mountain, I wouldn't have tried starting a side drift. I wouldn't've found the boulder. So, yes. Let's bring Albert in."

"Good." Dan wanted to shout something between Hallelujah and Huzzah. It wasn't every man who could decide on the moral thing and bury his own prejudices.

But Tim was not finished. "He swung his pick harder 'n longer 'n I ever imagined any man could. Even Pap. And Pap was a good worker when he'd put his mind to it." Tim looked away from Dan, his lower lip in his teeth to stop its trembling.

Dan let him be, counted sixteen audible jerks from the wall clock's second hand.

"Pap wouldn't of liked that, me workin' side by side with Albert. And I wouldn't of liked that idea much myself 'fore me and Albert dug so much of the adit. Jake, he wasn't having any of it by then, around Christmas time, you know. He said it was their holy time and he oughtn't to do no work. But Albert, he said he'd stay with me. So we kept on. Then Miz Hudson told him to help more at the Eatery, said she and his wife needed him there, so he had to stop. He made me promise not to go on my own."

He broke off, but Dan kept his silence, though he raged internally at the boy's stupidity – going into the mountain alone.

After awhile Tim continued. "You know the rest. While you were gone to Bannack with Fitch, I went back from time to time, and started picking away at the side drift, until I had to stop yesterday on account I hit the boulder."

Still, Dan remained silent.

Tim squirmed in his chair as if the hard wood had grown thorns. "Bein' with Albert, though, it was like workin' alongside with any hard-goin' man. We'd dig into the adit, and then go up the mountain and saw some timber and bring the logs down and use 'em to prop up the mountain." He peeked at Dan from the curtain of his hair, falling across the side of his face.

"After two, three days working with Albert, I wasn't noticing he's a different color 'n me. Pap, he could never forget folks' colors, but Mam always told me it was like God wanted a bouquet, like flowers, so He'd made us all different colors." He smiled and raked his fingers through his hair to brush it back from his face. "I guess Mam knew what she was about, her being a quarter Eastern Cherokee. That makes me an eighth. Dotty, too, only you'd never know it, us takin after Pap like we do."

Outside, the mid-afternoon light faded. Dan itched to get going, but Timothy hadn't talked himself out yet.

Abruptly standing, the boy stretched his arms up, his waistcoat lifted, and his shirt came out of his trousers, revealing the grayed suit of long underwear underneath. Grasping his shirttail, he said, "One day it was pretty warm where we was diggin'. And we took our shirts off and hung our undershirts around our waists. And he was diggin', his back to me, and I saw his scars. His back had been ripped up something awful. All healed over, of course. But I near puked my guts out. Don't know how I held it in." He unbuttoned his trousers and tucked in his shirt, watched his fingers button up again.

"Albert's a good man, I don't care who says different on account of his color." He frowned. "Pap's dead and gone and we – me and Dotty and Mam – we're free."

7 ~~~

The Montana Post: 1/14/1865, p. 2. Col 1.

Sherman's Christmas Gift to President Lincoln

The noblest and most welcome Christmas gift ever presented by one man to the representative of a nation, is the city of Savannah, which Sherman has given to President Lincoln, as a voucher for the success of his enterprise. Never since the war was first proclaimed, till now, did the Union cause appear so prosperous as it does today; and never did the dark clouds foreboding the storm carrying ruin in its track so darkly lower over the Confederacy. The desperate game will soon be played out, and remorse alone will be the portion of the guilty leaders who have seduced their ignorant followers to the commission of the hellish crime of rebellion. One by one the armies of the South are being conquered and destroyed...., Soon will the earthquake shout of victory announce the triumph of the cause of liberty and justice .... The tide of victory sets surely and strongly onward and soon will the fervent prayers of thousands be answered, and peace with all its blessings again dwell in the land.

From inside the Eatery, a heavy bar scraped against its brackets. A dark face glared out at them through a narrow opening, from a height that made Dan look upward. Recognizing Dan, Albert smiled. "Miz Hudson," he called over his shoulder, "it be Mistah Stark and young Mistah Timothy."

A woman's voice called back, "Wait a moment, Albert. I'll be along directly."

Timothy pursed his lips and made a rude noise. "How long's she aim to keep us out here in this wind?"

"Sorry, Mistah Timothy. They's cleanin' up from dinner."

Dan clapped his hands together, and wished he dared to remove his fur-lined gloves and blow on them. "It's all right, Mr. Rose. We've come to see you, anyway."

"Yessuh. Here she come." Albert stepped away from the door, and a woman's face and a bit of her black-clad form took his place. She stood only three or four inches above Dan's elbow, but short as she was, Mrs. Lydia Hudson made a formidable blockade. "Daniel Stark. Have thee come about thy injury?" She had neither smile nor welcome for him.

"No, ma'am. Not unless you'd like to check it. We've come to talk business with Albert."

"Vigilante business?"

"Of course not. Financial business." How long would she think about letting them in? He stamped his feet. The dratted woman disliked him, considered him a man of violence because of his involvement in the Vigilantes, but keeping Timothy waiting also —

"Very well. I suppose thee may as well come in."

Albert Rose had reseated himself at the small table by the door where customers paid for their meals. He weighed their gold dust in a balance scale, like nearly all businesses did in Virginia City. A stack of tin wafers stood next to the scale, which occupied another foot-square piece of Brussels carpet. A notebook lay beside the carpet, and a stub of pencil in the gutter of the closed book marked his place.

The restaurant's one room held two long tables with a long bench on either side. Mrs. Hudson and Tabitha Rose, Albert's wife, served meals to customers and retrieved dirty dishes from aisles along each wall. The right-hand aisle was wider, to accommodate Mrs. Hudson's stout form, while Tabitha, tall and lean, used the narrower left-hand aisle.

"Come down by the stove where it's warm." Mrs. Hudson turned her back on Dan to walk down the right-hand aisle. "Thee can talk there."

"Yes'm."

"I can finish the accounts later." Albert laid the two-by-four bar in its brackets.

A dog that resembled a half-grown bear crawled out from under Albert's worktable, shook himself, and offered his massive head to Dan, who obliged by removing his gloves and digging his fingers into the dense winter fur around the upright ears.

"Hello, General."

The dog responded with a yawn of deep satisfaction, displaying a mouthful of sharp, white teeth. At the Eatery, most people willingly paid the quarter-ounce of dust, or $4.50 for whatever meal was on offer that day, but if anyone ventured to argue about it with Albert, the dog's deep rumbling growl persuaded him to change his mind.

Part way down the aisle, Mrs. Hudson paused. "Tabby and I have to go on with our tasks."

The women prepared the meals in plain view of customers, especially those sitting at the back table. Mrs. Hudson chatted with them as she worked, giving more than one lonely miner, Dan had been told, a feeling of sitting in his mother's – or his wife's – kitchen. Tabitha Rose, working near the left-hand wall, never talked to customers, and answered Lydia Hudson's requests with a single nod, followed by quick compliance.

Dan had heard some people wonder if she could talk. Or if Mrs. Hudson was such a hard slave-owner that Tabitha Rose was afraid to offer less than obedience.

From Martha, who knew Mrs. Hudson very well, and knew Tabitha some, too, Dan had learned that this Quaker woman was no friend to slavery. In fact, she had helped the Roses get away from slave-catchers in Missouri. He had his own theory about Tabitha's silence: she plain hated white people. Maybe she believed they were beneath her notice.

For that, he couldn't blame her.

It was regrettable, he decided, but what could they expect, after she had been held in slavery? Why Albert did not harbor the same all-encompassing hatred, he didn't know. Or maybe he kept it better hidden.

The two women were washing up from the only meal the Eatery served. Tabitha Rose washed the dirty dishes in one tub and rinsed them in the second, then stood them in a box fitted with slats to hold them upright. Holes drilled in the bottom let excess water drip onto the hard-packed dirt floor. Mrs. Hudson dried them and put them away in cupboards made of wooden boxes stacked against the back wall.

Seeing her husband behind Dan and Timothy, Mrs. Rose straightened from the washtubs, her hands dripping, and cocked her head at him.

"Good afternoon, Mrs. Rose." Dan touched the brim of his hat but did not take it off. Putting it on again could be a bit of an ordeal. Around Virginia City, in most towns, it was just not done for a white man to offer a Colored woman this polite gesture, not in these times.

Dan did so almost always – when he could without disturbing his wound – and let people fume how they would.

He and Timothy sat together on the bench facing the kitchen. From a cupboard against the wall, Albert took a sack labeled "Java Coffee." Waiting for the coffee, Dan tried to make conversation with the women. Intent on getting on with their work, Mrs. Hudson offered him replies so scant as to stop just short of rudeness, while

Tabitha Rose ignored him entirely. When Albert set full mugs of fresh, steaming coffee in front of them, Dan was relieved to stop the effort of making conversation.

Tasting the brew, he smiled. "Very good."

Albert settled on the end of the bench near his wife. General wriggled under the table until he laid his head on Dan's feet.

"This business." Mrs. Hudson picked up a plate to dry it. "What is it?"

Dan pulled the newest *Montana Post* from an inside pocket and held it out to Albert. "It's about Timothy's discovery." Pointing to the headline, "The Quartz Lode Law." Ignoring Mrs. Hudson, he directed his conversation to Albert. "Have you read this?"

"No, I ain't had the time." Albert folded his hands in front of him, made no move to take the paper.

His defenses would not be easy to breach, Dan saw. A lifetime of betrayal by whites shone in his narrowed eyes. How could he, with whip scars on his back, ever trust a white man? Dan recalibrated his approach. Beyond polite greetings in the Eatery or on the street and greeting him as 'Mr. Rose' – as though he were a white man – he'd had little interaction with Albert. Most of what he knew about him came from Timothy. Or Martha, who repeated some of what Mrs. Hudson had told her.

Easy does it, he warned himself.

"It's what we've come about." Dan stayed still, holding the newspaper out for Albert, who continued to ignore it.

Drafts, seeping through cracks in the mud chinking the walls, ruffled the paper.

Albert glanced at Tabitha, who had stopped scrubbing dishes and held her hands quiet below the water. She gave no signal that Dan could see, but Albert reached for the sheet.

Dan laid it in his grasp.

"Read it to me." Tabitha wiped her hands on her apron and sat down on the bench by her husband, her back to Dan and Timothy.

"They made a mistake last week, Mistah Dimsdale did." Albert pronounced "Mister" so the T stood out and the R had rounded corners.

"That ain't no never-mind." Tabitha lacked patience with unnecessary details.

Dan managed not to smile. They were so like any married couple.

Albert read, "'Any person or persons that may here – hereafter discover any Quartz Lead, Lode, or Ledge shall be — '"

Dan interrupted. "That's the point. It's the first four words. 'Any person or persons.'"

After a slight hitch in his voice, Albert read the rest as though he had not heard Dan. "'... shall be entitled to one claim thereon by right of discovery and one claim each by pre-emption.'" He held out the folded paper as though inviting Dan to take it back.

Dan ignored the newspaper. Albert laid it on the table between them.

"The Supreme Court done said we ain't persons."

The paper fluttered. Because of air moving in the room? Or did Albert's strong feelings rattle it, even though it lay untouched between them?

Timothy's voice startled Dan. "The Emancipation Proclamation said blacks is persons." He closed his eyes and recited, "'All persons held as slaves within any State or des – uh, designated part of a State, the people where – whereof shall then be in rebellion against the United States, shall be then," ended in a rush, "thenceforward, and forever free.'"

Not only had the boy remembered the Emancipation Proclamation, he'd quoted it from memory. Yet as far as Dan knew, he had not read it before this morning. Maybe he was smarter than he'd let on.

"It's been in effect since January first of 'sixty-three."

"Two years," Tim said. "And then some."

Albert's eyes narrowed, and a crease appeared between his brows. He picked up the paper. Read it again, in a whisper to Tabitha.

A sound escaped her. "Hmph."

Impossible to know what the sound meant. Perhaps, Coloreds did not trust President Lincoln's Emancipation Proclamation, either, because it came from a white man.

His head throbbed, but he would not own up to it. He sensed an undercurrent circulating among them: himself and Timothy first, and then Albert, Tabitha. And Mrs. Hudson.

They were all separated not just by the wide table, but by the deep divide of their races and their backgrounds.

Would it be possible for them to see each other as persons? Man to man? The silence stretched thin and tenuous as smoke.

"Persons." Albert laid the newspaper down closer to Dan.

"Yes. Persons." Dan ignored the headache, the drumbeat pulsing in his ears. "Not white, black, or purple." A glance at Tabitha and Mrs. Hudson. "Or male or female."

Mrs. Hudson replaced the plate in the rack and sat down by Tabitha. She quoted a letter from St. Paul: "'There is neither Jew nor Greek, nor bond nor free, nor male nor female, for you are all one in Christ Jesus.'" She lifted her head and looked at him with a challenge in her eyes: Deny this if you can.

"That's about what the Homestead Act says. And the Emancipation Proclamation. 'Persons.' 'Head of household.' That's all." Dan waited then, struck by the power of words. Four common words that carried revolutionary change. 'You are all one.' St. Paul had written it first eighteen-hundred years before, 'neither bond nor free,' but here it was again, in these four words that turned the country upside down and shook out its deepest sin – slavery.

Tabitha had been watching her husband, her eyes intent on him. Now, hearing Dan, she twisted around to look at him. Mrs. Hudson kept her fixed stare into

Dan's eyes, as though she could strip away features, skin and bone, and read the mind of the real man beneath. He met her gaze directly, as he would a man's.

"Albert, Jacob, and Timothy – they dug the adit." The two women frowned, puzzled. "An adit is the tunnel into the mountain from the outside." Looks of comprehension satisfied him.

He focused his attention on Albert. "You, Timothy, and Jacob, Tim tells me, dug a portal – the mine entrance – and an adit fifteen feet into the mountain. That fifteen feet and the timbering, he says, took nearly all the time I was meeting the legislature in Bannack." He watched their faces, especially the women's. If he read them right, they would have a powerful influence over Albert. Just as Martha had on him, although he would never own up to it. "On Friday last, Tim went up by himself and started a side drift. He'll tell you what happened."

Tim, caught with his coffee cup at his lips, swallowed too fast and coughed hard. Dan pounded his back. Recovering, the boy pulled a grimy rag from his coat pocket, dabbed at his eyes, and blew his nose. Replaced the rag. Took a breath.

"Yesterday, I started a new drift off the adit. I didn't get far, on account I couldn't do the timbering by myself."

"How far did you get?" Dan prompted him.

"Maybe about half a foot or so. I dug some over my head, too." A sidelong peek at Dan. "Just a little. Then I stopped that and shoveled just to here." He laid a finger on his shoulder. "I didn't want the whole mountain coming down on me."

Picturing it, the boy driving his shovel or pick into the mountain over his head, rocks and dirt raining down on him, Dan wanted to yell at him, or shake him, or anything to make him think how close he'd been to killing himself. Instead, he tempered his language in deference to Mrs. Hudson's hatred of profanity. "I should hope not. You shouldn't have been there at all, by yourself."

"Yeah. Well." He picked at a scab on a knuckle. "I won't no more." In a rush, he continued, "I got stopped by a boulder. It was too big to dig out by myself, so I had to leave it and go home."

Mrs. Hudson opened her mouth, began to say something, but Tim overrode her. "I was running out of candle, too. But afore I left, I shined it on what stopped me. It was quartz, some crystal, but mostly gold." The Roses and Mrs. Hudson stared at him. "I didn't dare try to dig farther into the drift." He flicked a sidelong glance at Dan.

"And so? Just what does all this mean?" Mrs. Hudson sounded like she considered Dan was wasting their time.

"It means that we may have something."

"Or nothing," Mrs. Hudson's lips clamped shut, but her eyes lighted.

"Yes. But to know for certain, we have to excavate that boulder. And that could be a matter of digging out a big rock." He took a deep breath, as though he dove off a cliff. "Or Tim may have found the edge of a lode."

Tabitha Rose gasped. "You think this could turn into a quartz mine?" For the first time in more than a year's acquaintance she addressed Dan directly, not through her husband.

"Yes, Mrs. Rose. If the snow weren't so deep, we could climb the mountain and see if there's a crevice or an exposed wall on the surface above the portal. For now, we'll work from Tim's rock upward and inward."

"If that's where we're led." Tim bit a fingernail. "We have to dig where the boulder is. Where it leads us."

For a moment no one said anything. Albert and the women sat still.

Dan breathed carefully, so as not to upset the moment.

He'd give them time to think about this before he came to the point of this visit, but so far it seemed as if it might turn out better than he'd hoped. He sidled toward the main point.

"Albert, you've been helping Timothy without pay, out of the kindness of your heart. If you'll help him and me excavate that boulder, I'll pay you eight dollars a day."

In the moment's silence among them, Dan heard only the soft bubble of water heating on the stove.

"Eight dollars a day?" Albert's eyes shone in the candlelight, as if he wanted to believe Dan, to believe that he could earn such a high wage, when even skilled craftsmen and top cowhands earned three dollars a day and found – their room and board.

"Yes, or —" He stopped on a sudden guess. Perhaps Albert had never in his life worked for pay. Had Mrs. Hudson paid him? Or had he worked for room and board, or did the three of them share what the Eatery brought in, after expenses? He did not know.

Whatever their arrangement was, Dan realized he had no idea what a radical anti-slavery employer might pay former slaves. Perhaps he and his wife had both worked out of gratitude, or – or – not knowing they could earn good money?

"Thee are busy here, Albert." Mrs. Hudson's voice scraped through tight lips.

As though he had not heard her, Dan offered, "Or, you could exchange work for a share in the mine."

"A share in the mine?" Albert's voice cracked, ended in a squeak.

"Yes. How much of a share we can work out later, but my offer is firm."

Mrs. Hudson put in, "And that offer is, what again?"

Speaking as if to Albert, Dan explained, but wanting to be certain Mrs. Hudson understood, what he had in mind. "You put in as much of a day with Timothy as you can, what with your responsibilities here, and I'll pay you eight dollars a day." Another notion struck him. He added, "In dust. Not Treasury notes." He was offering to pay Albert in gold, not in federal paper money, discounted as much as sixty percent.

Albert was silent while his wife and Mrs. Hudson sat as though frozen in amber.

Through the drum beating in his temples, Dan heard Timothy breathe.

At last, Albert said, "Miz Hudson, you been better to me 'n Tabby than I ever figured a white could be. You and Doctor made to come with us when we heard the slave-catchers was gettin close. You just packed up and made ready to come with us your own selves, not knowing where we'd all end up. And when Doctor slipped on the cellar steps and broke his neck, you had me roll him up in a rug and put him in the wagon, and bring him along until we could find a decent place to bury him proper."

He added with a quick look in Dan's direction, "Which we done. And said the Good Book's words over him."

Talking to Mrs. Hudson again: "The good Lord guided us to take this and that fork in the road, and we ended up on the Oregon trail, all the time you masquerading as our slave owner to keep us safe. And the Lord brought us here with the gold-seekers. Here we're safe, thanks to Mistah Stark and the other Vigilantes. Ain't nobody here gonna tell Tabby and me we're going back to slavery. Ain't nobody'll lynch us for having ideas above ourselves. They might think to, and they might wish us nothing good, but it won't be the rope. Not here and not now. Nosuh."

He paused to breathe, and perhaps to let Mrs. Hudson speak, but she sat silent, her fingers toying with the black jets on the front yoke of her dress.

"Ma'am, you been talking about selling this place. You're tired, and Tabby's tired of always cooking and washing up. I'm tired of always sitting in a chair, saying Yessuh and Nosuh. So maybe it's time to change ourselves. Mistah Stark coming here today with this offer, it seems to me like a God-send. Truly it does."

Again, Albert waited, but Mrs. Hudson's mouth made a crease above her chin.

Beside Dan, Timothy stirred as if he were about to speak, but Dan coughed, and he subsided. Albert, Dan realized, was not through.

"Begging your pardon, Miz Hudson, I want something to grow on. Become somebody. I hear white folks talk over they dinners, about what big folks they gone be when they get home with all the gold they've collected. I want to take care of Tabby and our young'uns like good white folks take care of their families. There's more to me than just muscle and a strong back. I feel the Lord calling me to something better." As though suddenly realizing how he had not meant to open his heart to these white people, he ducked his head down like a man afraid to look them in the eye. Or perhaps he feared Dan would take the offer back and laugh at him for having aspirations to better his life and Tabby's. Them being only blacks.

Dan pulled his feet out from under General's warm bulk. "Timothy and I should leave you to discuss things among yourselves." He swung around on the bench, and Tim stood with him.

"Timothy has decided to move home," he told them, "so we'll collect his things from Jacob's place and take them to my house. I'll be in my office tomorrow, Albert, if you have your answer ready."

Albert wanted this job. He had made that plain to all of them, Mrs. Hudson especially. What happened between them now was for Albert to determine without his interference. For a former slave, it was bound to be an unfamiliar situation, but something he would have to navigate on his own. Remembering Grandfather's relentless insistence that he become a lawyer, Dan promised himself he would not interfere.

"Let me know what you decide."

But it was Mrs. Hudson who said, in a softer voice than she had ever used to him, "We will do that, Mister Stark. Thee may be sure of it."

8 ~~~

The Montana Post: 1/7/1865, p. 3

Local and Other Items

> Union Church Festival — Preparations on a large scale are being made for the Church Festival on Friday the 13th inst., in the new Union church, Idaho street. The amusement and comfort of the spectators is being amply provided for and large as is the building, we feel sure its capacity will be tried to the utmost. The cause, the company, the programme will ensure the success which all well wishers of society must desire.

When Dan and Timothy came out of the Eatery, storm clouds had broken up and sailed onwards, leaving the sun's ferocious brilliance to shine on Virginia City.

"Now what?" Dan shaded his eyes against the sun's glare to see his stepson. "If we collect your things now, while Jacob is still at the bank, we could spare ourselves another confrontation with him."

"Might's well." Tim pivoted to the corner. "Get it done and over with."

As they trudged through drifted snow down the Jackson Street hill between Wallace Street and Daylight Creek at the bottom, shredded clouds sailed eastward past the hill on the north side of the creek, where five road agents lay in their graves. Remembering their hanging in the unfinished drug store building, Dan kept his eyes on the icy stepping stones as he followed Timothy across the creek. Relieved to be on the other side, he refused to think about the way back, when they would be loaded with all of what Tim called his 'plunder.'

Returning, he carried Tim's shovel and pick, while the boy brought his meager wardrobe in a gunnysack tied to his belt. The smaller tools, and the lantern he hauled in his hands and skipped from stone to stone as if he played hopscotch.

"Watch out," Dan called. His own balance threatened to fail him, and he stabbed the shovel into the stream to save himself from falling as he jumped to the next stone and from there onto the south bank, where Tim stood.

"Yeah, old man?" Tim teased him. "You had something to say?"

"I'll show you who's an old man." Brushing past his stepson, Dan set a fast pace up the slope.

At the corner of Jackson and Wallace, where the Eatery's blank log wall sheltered them, Tim bent over to catch his breath. Sunset hurled bright lances between dark blue blocks of shadow cast from the buildings on Wallace's south side. Low in the southern sky, the sun would soon disappear behind the Tobacco Root mountains, and another long winter night would set in.

Tim kicked snow on the boardwalk. "I never seen such a country for snow. We had snow in the Blue Ridge Mountains, but it beats all here." He jumped down into the street. Snow blew in a cloud up over his head and floated down onto him. With his belongings, he emerged laughing. "Look at me. I'm a snowman."

Dan stepped off the boardwalk into the street and sank into snow halfway up his thighs.

Sleigh bells jingled in the clear still air. As they stopped to listen for its direction, a sleigh behind two fast-trotting horses rounded the corner off the Jackson Street hill above Wallace and slid sideways toward them. Jumping onto the boardwalk, they teetered on the edge and grabbed at each other to avoid falling off, nearly dropping Tim's things.

"Outa the way, tinhorns!" the driver yelled. His passengers' merry laughter swept back to Dan and Timothy in blown snow.

Snow coated his face as Tim stared after the sleigh. "If they'd knowed who they nearly run over, they wouldn't be so carefree."

Dan leaned the pick and shovel against the Eatery wall to brush at the snow on Tim's face. The beat in his head centered over his eye in time with his pulse.

"Let's hike on home instead of the office. It'll be dinner time soon. The ladies probably need wood chopped, and the path cleared to the necessary." He set off across Wallace, striding through snow that parted like water.

Carol Buchanan

Tim hurried after him. "Is there room for me? Maybe it'd be better if'n I stayed someplace else."

"Of course you're coming home!" Dan plowed through a hip-deep drift. "I can't promise a comfortable night, though. The twins sleep in the bed with your mother, and I've rolled a bedroll on the floor behind the stove in the reading corner. It's not a feather bed. And the twins are on a mighty crying spree."

"Ha! What y'all need is a few decent nights' rest."

Forging ahead of Timothy to break trail for him, Dan called over his shoulder, "We'll catch up on sleep when they're out on their own."

In an effort to make the boardwalk passable, most business owners had shoveled snow into the street, where it camouflaged piles of offal Dan didn't want to think about. Snowbanks five feet high lined the path to Dan's house, which he'd made wide enough for two people to walk side-by-side. The path was clear except for some drifting. As they climbed the three steps to his front door, to stand shivering on the porch, the sun sank, almost rock-like, behind the mountains. The first stars glittered in the darkening sky. Leaning the tools in a shadowed corner, Dan pounded on the door loud enough to wake a hibernating bear, but he felt like they would turn into pillars of ice before he heard the rasp of the bar being lifted and set aside. His stepdaughter peeked out at them.

"Oooh, Dan'l!" Dorothy McDowell stood aside to let him in through the least possible opening.

When her brother followed Dan, Dorothy squealed, "Timmy!" She threw herself onto him, never mind how the cold had stiffened his snow-crusted coat, how much he carried in his arms.

Nudging the youngsters aside, Dan closed the door and dropped the bar into its braces.

At once chaos enveloped him. The stench of used diapers and unemptied chamber pots in closed-in rooms rolled over him like the miasma, along with the screaming of very young babies.

When he turned, Martha stood in the big room near their bedroom, holding a struggling baby in the crook of each arm. Deep purple circles underscored her brown eyes in their nests of red lines, and her dark hair hung in loose tangles around her shoulders. Stains of liquids Dan did not try to identify spotted her wrinkled blue nursing dress.

"My love." He dropped his greatcoat on one of a row of hooks driven between the logs of the wall, pulled off his winter boots, and went to her. The floor covering of tightly woven cattails squeaked and crackled under his stocking feet.

He gathered the three of them into his arms. His heart beat fast in his temples.

Her tears soaked into his waistcoat.

From the bustle around them, he knew that Dotty had showed Tim where to stash his outfit, and he and Eileen hurried about the evening chores. Pots and pans clanged, and Tim's heavy tread passed by them twice. By the smell, Dan realized he carried chamber pots out.

Keeping her in his embrace, he guided Martha, holding the twins, into the bedroom. Heavy curtains pulled across the window darkened it and kept the drafts out. The stink was well nigh unbearable, but they could not risk the twins in winter's cold drafts.

Two baskets stood on the unmade, rumpled bed. He helped Martha to sit on the bed, took dark-haired baby Luke from her and laid him in a basket, then put blond little Danny in the other basket. Both babies continued to howl as he wrapped them snug in their own Hudson's Bay blankets. Sweeping Martha up in his arms, he laid her down and pulled the covers over her.

He bent to stroke her hair away from her face. "I'm going for help. I'll be back soon."

She attempted a smile.

He read, "Hurry home," on her lips under the babies' crying.

As he was about to close the door, Dotty hurried toward him with a small pot full of warm milk in one hand and two braids made of twisted cotton rags in the other. "This may help. I soak the cloths in warm canned milk and give it them to suck. It quiets them, for a while, anyway."

"Good. You're a great help for your mother." He patted her shoulder. Startled, he noticed that it rose to the second button on his waistcoat. She was growing up. Fast. "I'm going to get Lydia Hudson to help."

Standing on one foot, he pulled on the other boot. "Where's Tim?"

"Shoveling the path to the outhouse." Dotty blushed. "I mean the necessary." She had trouble remembering to use the polite word for the little building thirty feet behind the house. "Mrs. Hudson? Why do we need her?"

"This situation is beyond you and Eileen." Dan slipped his arms into his coat and shrugged it onto his shoulders. "And I'm useless. Have you been here all day?"

At her nod, he chided her. "You should be in school."

"But Mam needs me!"

"Your mother needs more help than any of us is competent to give. Lydia Hudson knows homeopathic medicine and herbal remedies. She learned all that from her husband, the doctor. She knows women's complaints and the problems of childbirth. She'll bring Tabitha Rose, too."

"I don't want to go to school, and sit and read Latin about the Helvetian migrations, or how to divide three-and-three-eighths by two-and-a-quarter. Not when I can help Mam. Or other women."

About to wrap his scarf about his neck, Dan looked at his stepdaughter's stubborn face. "You can watch and learn from Mrs. Hudson while she's here."

Putting on his hat, he forgot about the wound until he tugged it down tight. Reeling, he put his hand out to steady himself against the wall.

"Dan'l, are you healed enough to do this?"

"Yes. Don't worry. I'm fine."

As he stepped onto the porch, Tim climbed the steps in one leap and set down the empty chamber pots. "The path is clear, for now, but the snow's so dry it'll blow back quicker'n scat." He leaned the shovel against the house. "Where're you going?"

"To get Lydia Hudson. Your mother needs her help."

"You think she'll come?"

"She'll come if I have to drag her." Dan walked down the steps.

"Let me come with you. I can't do no good here. I'd just be in the way."

"No. After you get warmed up, go back to Jacob. Tell him I said you have to live there another night. We'll get you settled here when this crisis is over."

Pulling his scarf up over his nose, Dan half ran downhill through the drifting snow.

9 ~~~

The Montana Post: 1/7/1865, p. 2. Col 1.

GLORIOUS NEWS!
SAVAN'AH FALLEN
Complete Defeat of the Rebs in Tennessee!

We stop the press to give a slight synopsis of the dispatches, which arrived by last night's mail. It brought dates to the 28th ult., from which we learn that Savannah fell into our hands on the morning of the 21st.

....

Owing to the lateness of the hour, and want of space we are unable to give further particulars.

A gloved fist wouldn't open a door on a night as dark and cold as this. The sound was too muffled. Dan banged the side of his bare fist on the Eatery door. If it didn't open soon, he'd kick it in. He drew his foot back.

A thunderous bark warned him.

Dan kicked the door. If a fist didn't bring Albert, the toe of his boot would.

A heavy tread, calls to hold on, and Albert opened the door a scant crack, just enough to squint at whoever made such a racket. Behind him, General growled. If he hadn't known General since the dog was a small puppy, he'd have fled to the nearest saloon rather than cause any more commotion.

Mrs. Hudson called out, "Who is that, wreaking mayhem on my door?"

Holding the snarling dog back, Albert called out, "It's Mistah Stark." Then, "Hush up, Gen'ral. Stop your noise. Down!" He stood aside to let Dan in. General wagged his tail, his growl traded for a tooth-filled grin.

"Daniel Stark?" Mrs. Hudson peered around Albert's arm. "What brings thee back so soon? We're not —"

"It's Martha. Please come, Mrs. Hudson. My house is chaos. The babies won't stop crying, and Martha is distraught. I can't get through to her. She doesn't seem to know me."

"When did this start?"

Albert held the door open wider, and Dan stepped into the restaurant. Mrs. Hudson had turned off the wall lanterns, so he saw the woman only by the candle Albert held.

"Last night, but things were better when I left for the office this morning." Forgetting his sore head, Dan swept off his hat. "Ahhh!"

Mrs. Hudson pivoted for the back of the room, where two lanterns lighted the stove. "Bring him along, Albert. Tabby, do thee please round up my medicaments for post-childbirth ailments. Mister Stark, sit thee here on this bench and let me look at thy head." She pointed to the bench closest to the stove.

"No. Please. I don't need tending. It's my dear wife. Don't waste time on me."

Albert's voice rumbled among the hooves beating on Dan's temples. "Best you do as she says. She'll be with Miz Stark smart-like if she does what she's a mind to."

Mrs. Hudson parted his hair to look closer at the wound. As she bent to get a better view of it, Dan smelled mixed odors – something mild that he couldn't identify, along with the pungent smell of sage, the usual barrier against scurvy in winter.

General sat, leaned against his leg. He wound his fingers in the dog's fur and gripped hard to keep silent as she peeled off the two-week-old bandage she had put on when he returned with Tobias Fitch. "Thee should have come to me to have this changed days ago. It's dirty. Thy head needs a good wash, too."

"I talked to the new doctor, what's his name? He sold me a bottle of elixir for it."

Mrs. Hudson left off her examination to wash her hands in the pan of soapy dish water. "Doctors. Pooh. Most of them can saw a man's limb off in less than two minutes, but they don't know a thing about medicine. The best they can do for wounds is to pour whiskey in them."

Shaking the water from her hands, she said, "Albert, thee knows what to do. Wash his head and don't let him out until it's dry. Thee can leave off a bandage until he's fit to go out." She paused, cocked her head to one side, considered Dan as she might if he were a small boy with no good judgment. "Though I truly do not know when that will be."

Plucking her shawl from its hook, she wrapped it around her neck and head, and stopped to think. "Dr. Glick, now, he's knowledgeable about wounds and illness."

"He's not in town." Dan's voice rose with an urge to yell at her to move, stop wasting time. "Please. Go. See to Martha and the babies. Dotty and Eileen can't cope with this – this hysteria." He bent forward, his face in his hands. "Nor can I."

Tabitha Rose emerged from a curtained area at the back. She hauled a wheeled portmanteau behind her. "The necessities be ready, Miz Hudson."

The portmanteau was a large suitcase, nearly a standing trunk on wheels, that opened in front. While Dan ground his teeth to keep himself silent, Mrs. Hudson checked the contents of each drawer before drawing the two sides together. "Good, then. You remembered the paregoric."

Dan picked up his hat to put it on his head, but Albert's heavy hand pressed down on his shoulder.

"Nosuh. You'n me, we'd just be in the way. We wouldn't be no help at all. You bide here and talk to me. I've got questions for you. Miz Hudson and Tabby, they be takin good care of your family."

The Quaker woman pulled on a heavy wool mitten. "He's right, Mr. Stark. This is women's business. Thee would just be in the way. Stay here until we return."

"But that portmanteau. I'll carry it for you. The snow is too deep —"

"Thee think we're so frail?" Mrs. Hudson made a contemptuous sound, as she tucked the ends of her scarf around her neck. "We've carried that thing part way over the continent. A little snow won't bother us."

The women pulled on knitted hats, drew their scarves over their mouths and noses, drew on their thick woolen mittens. With Mrs. Hudson holding the handle on top, Tabitha picked up the portmanteau by one of its rear axles.

Albert held the door open for them and closed it when he saw they were across Wallace.

"I'm thinkin we clean your head before supper, Mistah Stark. If'n it's fine by you." Not waiting for Dan's answer, he went behind the curtain to the cupboard his wife had brought the portmanteau from and came back a square bottle of an unsavory-looking brown liquid and a blue, white-speckled basin piled with rags. He set the basin in front of Dan and arranged the other things ready to hand.

"Soon be time to melt some more snow," he said as he shook the bottle. "Hold your head over the basin, if you please, suh."

Dan set his forearms to either side of the basin, let his head droop toward it. Whatever Albert was about to do, it would not be pleasant. He tightened his jaw, muttered, "Just get it over with."

93

"Thank you kindly, suh. I'm sorry about this. Your head needs a good cleanin. Dried blood and dirt and such, you see."

Dan smelled a suspicious, sharp odor just before his head caught fire in spasms of white pain. For the next while, he had no idea except to stay still and lock any sound behind his teeth. He would not cry out in front of a man whose back bore welted scars of the lash.

After an eternity, Albert said, "We done now, suh."

Dan cracked his eyelids enough to see reddish, dark water in the basin.

"That was the worst part." Albert spoke softly, almost in a murmur. "I got to rinse and comb it now, suh."

"Do what you must." Vowing silence, he tightened his jaws and stiffened his neck.

Twice Albert emptied the basin into the slop pail to be thrown out. After the second time, he picked up the comb when he set the basin down.

"This will hurt," Albert warned him.

As though what had gone before was a sweet lozenge? Dan stared at the stove. This time, there being less danger of water getting into his eyes, he would keep them open. Before he thought the ordeal would end, Albert spoke.

"We's done, Mistah Stark."

Dan sat straight, rolled his shoulders to loosen the muscles. "Thank you. That needed doing."

"You were mighty quiet. Most folks would've been yellin' and cussin' somethin' fierce." Albert gathered up the wet cloths, glanced sideways at Dan. "Leastways, I'm thinkin' white folks would." He dropped the rags on the floor behind the washstand.

"I don't know about most folks, white or black. Or Indians, although I understand they can be very stoical." He smiled, though sharp new pains lanced across his scalp and his eyes teared. The treatment had been almost worse than the original blow, and as bad as Mrs. Hudson's first care. "I was calling down the fires of hell on Fitch, though."

"Sometimes that's enough." Albert scrubbed his hands in the wash tub. "I think if somethin smells bad, it ain't good for you. My hands stink like that brown stuff, but Miz Hudson, she swears by it." He rubbed his hands together, dipped them in the clean water bucket, which Dan suspected was not so clean now.

"How much do I owe you for your trouble tonight?" Dan's fingers burrowed into his trousers pocket for his poke.

Albert's raised hand stopped him. "No, suh. I won't take money for what I learned treatin' other slaves. I have a heap of questions I'd be obliged if you'd answer for me, as you're able."

"Of course. Until your wife and Mrs. Hudson return."

"I'm thinkin they won't be back tonight. You'd best stay here."

He went behind the curtain again and emerged carrying a pile of quilts and pillows that he spread out on the tables, making two beds. He built up the fire in the stove and motioned for Dan to move to the end of the bench, closer to the heat. "I'll warm up some moose stew, and we can set here until your hair dries. That way, you won't take cold in the night."

"Moose stew?"

With a woof, General walked partway up the aisle.

Someone pounded on the door.

A man's voice hollered, "Let me in! Please."

Dan and Albert stared at each other. This time of night, with the cold so deep – who could this be?

10 ~~~

The Montana Post: 1/7/ 1865, p. 2, Col. 1:

Local and Other Items.

The weather, after a week of spring-like sunshine and balmy breezes, changed suddenly on Wednesday evening [1/4/1865], and a snow storm of no mean magnitude visited this place, and reminded us that winter was not quite over yet.

"Gen'ral! Back! Back, damn it."

Dan twisted around to see who would be at the Eatery door so late on such a cold night.

Albert raised the bar, leaned it against the wall. As he pulled the door open, a man nearly fell into him. "Mistah Stark! It be Mistah Timothy!"

Dan jumped up, and almost dropped. He sat down hard. The candles in their wall sconces swam, and his feet felt disconnected with the rest of his body. When the candles steadied, he swung around, put his feet over the bench, and stood, bracing himself while the room settled.

Then, moving faster than he knew, he reached for his stepson as Albert handed the boy to him. Dan threw one of Timothy's arms across his own shoulders and helped him down the aisle. General whined close behind them.

Albert slammed the door shut, dropped the bar in its brackets, and hurried after them.

"You're half frozen!" Dan removed Tim's coat. Stopped. "You're wet."

Tim's trousers, boots, and socks were soaked. The ice stiffening them was beginning to melt.

"I sl – sl – slipped. F – fell."

Against his chattering teeth, Dan understood he had slipped from a stepping stone and fallen into Daylight Creek.

Then Albert was there, handing him a pile of heavy wool blankets. As Dan wrapped the shivering youngster in blankets and knelt to pull off his boots, Albert poured water into the same basin he had used for cleaning Dan's head. The water came from the same bucket he had used to rinse the liniment from his hands. Setting it on the stove's cooktop to warm up, he helped Dan strip off the rest of the boy's wet clothes.

When Albert tested the water on the stove, he told Dan, "It ain't hardly warm. We put his feet in it, they don't thaw out too fast. Maybe, Lord willing, he don't get frostbit."

In the almost-warm water, Tim's feet soon came awake, judging from the tears rolling down his face. His jaw muscles bulged as he stifled the sounds fighting to escape.

Understanding his pain, Dan offered his hand. "Hang on."

Tim clung to the hand as a drowning man grabs a floating branch. His grip squeezed Dan's knuckles together, but Dan braced himself against the pain, willed himself to silence. If the boy could endure the agony of awakening numb feet, he would not complain.

He watched Albert, who stayed at the stove, stirred the stew, tasted it to check the flavor or judge how hot it was. He slid the pot off the burner, onto the wide area over the oven. There he kept it hot, stirring it between other tasks, as he assembled supper for the three of them.

After what seemed hours to Dan, Timothy breathed deep and loosened his grip. Dan dropped his hand to his lap to hide it while he stretched the fingers and doubled his fist to work the stiffness out.

Tim reached down to test the water. "It's cold."

Dan bent to retrieve the basin. Albert took it from him, and gave Dan an old, dirty towel to wrap Tim's feet in, saying at the same time, "Y'all ready for some dinner?"

"You bet."

Tim swung his bare feet under the table. "What the—?" He twisted to look. "You gotta see this."

The men bent to look.

General lay under Timothy's feet; the boy's toes burrowed into the dog's fur.

"He moved there so's my feet could get warm in his fur." For a moment he could not speak. "This dog is kinder to me than —" Fighting for control of his emotions, Timothy could say nothing more.

"What do you mean?" Dan felt heat in his face. Had Jacob not let Tim stay with him? Was that why the boy had fallen in the creek as he climbed the hill to the

Eatery, looking for him? A memory overtook Dan: Rawley, whose feet were so far gone from gangrene – the result of frostbite – that he had crawled into Bannack.

God save Tim from that fate.

And God save the boy from the life of a cripple – not at the age of sixteen. Dear God, no.

If Jacob had caused this, God Himself could not save him.

"Now we best be gettin' somethin' hot into our bellies." Albert set mugs of hot coffee in front of Dan and Tim. "'Pears to me like you need it special, Mistah Tim. Warmin' the inner man is good for gettin' cold and fallin' into a creek."

"Why – yeah. I'm – I am hungry." Tim groped in a pocket to find a rag. He wiped his face and blew his nose.

"You sound surprised, like growing boys shouldn't need to eat."

"No, it's just – I forgot about eating." He took a breath and let it out. "Smells good, Albert. What is it?"

"Moose stew."

They waited for Timothy's reaction. After a second, it came. "Moose stew?"

Dan and Albert shared a smile. "He sounds like me," Dan said.

"I don't care if it's skunk stew. This boy's that hungry."

Thinking of nothing to say, Dan squeezed Tim's shoulder.

"Comin up." Albert turned away, busied himself loading stew into tin bowls.

The stew smelled so good, Dan forgot about the moose. He asked Timothy, "Why couldn't you stay at Jacob's house?"

"I tried. When I got there, I could see Jake was home. There was light in the window, and I could hear Jake and other men singing. I knocked on the door, but nobody answered. Not even when I pounded fit to wake the dead. They just kept on singing. So I give up and come to find you. That's when I fell in the creek."

"Tomorrow." Dan laid his fist on the table and emphasized each word with a soft bump, a caricature of what he wanted to do – hammer it into splinters. "Tomorrow, I will learn why Jacob did not answer his door."

"I can't believe he wouldn't let me in." Timothy picked at a splinter on the tabletop.

As Albert set three bowls with spoons on the table, Dan said, "I promise I will sort this out. First, though, we take you home. You will rest your feet until we're certain there is no frostbite." Seeing Tim's lips part on the beginning of a protest, he hardened his tone. "Yes. You will sit with your feet up until we know they're healthy. Mrs. Hudson can see to the state of their health while she visits your mother." He took up a spoonful of stew and ate without tasting it. "Then, after you're settled at home, I'll find Jacob and learn why you couldn't stay one night with him."

Albert sat next to Dan, with a bit of extra space between them. Now he spoke up. "I don' think I'd like to be in Mistah Him'farb's shoes when you commence your learnin'."

"That depends on his explanation." Silence followed Dan's comment. He spooned up another mouthful of stew. Turning to Albert, he managed a smile. "This is surprisingly good, Albert. I had an idea moose meat would be tough and gamy."

"Thank you, Mistah Stark." Albert finished his own mouthful. "My Tabby's a dab hand with cookin. Mr. Gohn said it must've been a younger bull that maybe challenged an older one and lost. That's the best explanation. It's usually the old 'uns get left behind. Someone shot it not far out of town and brought it to Mr. Gohn for butcherin'. Took his pay in the choice cuts and left the rest to Mr. Gohn. He sold it to Miz Hudson and the hotels. So you get moose stew for dinner. We had it midday."

"Along with half the town," Dan said.

"Them what had the dust." Albert nodded his agreement.

They lapsed into silence.

Dan listened to the question circling his mind: Why could Timothy not stay at Jacob's house one more night? Somewhere, amid the wind's whine around the building, the faint, sporadic tinkle of a saloon piano long out of tune, and the creak of wood on wood in the roof, the thunder of stampeding hooves in Dan's head eased to the four-beat step of one walking horse.

His notions cleared. He would discover what lay behind Jacob's refusal to open his door to Timothy. There had to be an explanation, perhaps something simple. Even just off the boat, Jacob had been grateful to Dan for showing him how to make money in this immense country where he didn't speak the language. And now he was set to make a fortune in Montana gold. Even though his attitude to Timothy had been almost hostile of late, there had to be a reason why he would not let him sleep there one more night.

To himself, Dan vowed, 'I will know why.'

11 ~~~

The Montana Post: 1/7/1865, p. 4:

Local and Other items
Debating Society — We have received a communication from Mr. H. N. Elliott, of Biven's Gulch, informing us of the organization of a debating society in that place, on Dec. 20th, James Duckworth, Chairman, H. N. Elliott, Secretary. The society resolved "That Love of Woman has more influence on the mind of man than the love of gold." If it were made to read "ought to have," we would venture our last linen envelope on the argument. It was not the love of woman that built Virginia City, peopled Montana, started the rebellion, created commerce, or generally ruled the world; Solomon, Mark Antony, & Co., to the contrary notwithstanding. We wish our friends success.

Albert got up from the table and took their bowls and spoons to the washstand, where he set them in the tub with the remaining dishes from the midday meal.

Dan swung around and opened the oven door. He crouched down to comb his fingers through his hair – gingerly near the healing wound – to help it dry faster.

"How are your feet. Tim?"

"They're hurting some, but not like before. They're getting warm, too." He leaned around to reach under the table to pat the dog. "Good job, Gen'ral. Good dog."

A soft woof answered him.

Hearing papers rattle, Dan took his seat again.

Albert sat across the table from the two whites. "We see pretty soon if they missed bein' frostbit." He held some papers. "After our talk, Mistah Stark, I wrote down some questions. Mine, Tabby's, and Miz Hudson's."

Dan waited until he realized something held Albert back from asking. "And?" Still no response.

After a few seconds, he guessed at the reason. In Albert's slave past, he hadn't been allowed to ask anything until the master gave him permission. Did he speak freely to Mrs. Hudson? "You don't need anyone's permission to ask a question, Albert. What are they?"

"Yassuh."

In that one word, Dan heard the echo of slave talk. And still Albert hesitated, shuffling his papers as if looking for something.

Dan waited.

Timothy stirred, restless about waiting as only a half-grown boy could be. Or maybe his back protested at sitting so long on a backless bench with his feet up. Whatever the reason —

Albert cleared his throat a time or two. "I've told Tabby – and Miz Hudson – I'd be a fool not to put in with you on this mine. When would black folks, uh, like me ever have a chance like this? When I was a field hand, I had nothin to look forward to but work harder, and the lash when the overseer thought I was shirkin'. When I was taken to the house, t'others thought I'd have it easy, bein' a house niggah. But it was just the same 'cept we ate some better. All there was, was work and —" a quick slide of his eyes toward Tim – "other duties, and the lash, just like allus. That don't hardly make mornin's worth gettin' up for. Except for the books in Massa's library. I snuck 'em whenever I could get away with it." He paused to sip his coffee. "And sometimes when I couldn't. But now. Lord, I never expected nothin' like this. It's like the earth turned over under my feet and we's sittin where China used to be."

Albert's face contorted as he fought to control his emotions.

To give him what privacy he could, Dan turned his shoulder to him as he asked Timothy, "Are you still certain about the single mine idea?"

"'Course I am. It's only fair."

Facing Albert square again, Dan saw the puzzlement on the Colored man's face, but he knew what he wanted to say. And if he kept working at drying his hair, maybe it would help Albert ask his questions.

"You've helped Timothy and Jacob in the mine. You know what it's like going underground. Tim and I don't think you ought to do that without some assurance of a reward at the end." His fingers caught on a tangle, and he paused to unsnarl it. Somehow, he did not think the questions Albert asked would be his only ones, but he would try to answer his unasked questions as they went.

"Like I said, if you help us excavate the boulder, I'll pay you eight dollars a day. But Tim and I have talked this over, and if the excavation turns out well, if the rock is the edge of a lode, I'll help you file on an adjacent claim as soon as we can see how it goes." He considered the claim process a moment, then added, "Or before, if necessary."

He took a deep breath. "It works like this. According to the new Territorial quartz law, Timothy can file on one adjacent claim by right of preemption, because he was one of the original discoverers, and I'll file on another claim that follows the lode – if there is one. From that, we intend to run all the claims as one mine. That's what we're offering you. There's no guarantee it'll work out like that, but in the meantime, you'll have a salary for helping us find out what's there."

"You'd help me own part of a gold mine?"

"Yes."

Albert stood, hands thrust deep into his trouser pockets, and walked to the front door. He stood, head bowed, as if he prayed. Or contemplated his record book. He didn't see it if so.

General crawled out from under the table and stood in the aisle, looking from Dan and Tim toward Albert and back again. He stretched his spine, front and back, then sat down and wrapped his feathery tail around his paws. Cocking his head toward Albert, the dog whined softly. To Dan it sounded like a question.

Coming back, Albert's heavy footsteps vibrated through the dirt floor, like the earliest warning rumbles of an earthquake. When he took his seat, he fondled the dog's ears as he spoke, his voice unsteady. "I'll take you up on that offer, Mistah Stark. I don't need nobody's say-so. Eight dollars a day is, shoot, it's a whole lot better'n the three dollars most men make hereabouts. Clerks and such. White men. And the chance to be a partner, a mine owner? I know it's only a chance, dependin' on the rock, but it's more'n I've ever had anywheres else."

"I'm glad, Mister Rose. Very glad." Dan combed his hair back from his face with his fingers so Albert could see it well enough to judge his sincerity, rose to his feet, and held out his hand.

He nudged Timothy, who raised his own hand for Albert without getting up.

Albert hesitated, wiped his hand down his trouser leg, and met Dan as though uncertain what would happen. His hand lay in Dan's grip, until he closed his fingers gingerly, as though afraid of breaking something.

Timothy reached across the table and laid his hand on thers. Albert hesitated, then clasped Tim's hand, too.

"It's a deal, then." Dan's unsteady voice betrayed the awe he felt in this moment. A Colored former slave and two whites shaking hands on a partnership in a gold mine. Unheard of. There was a sea change coming over the nation, and it wouldn't be easy, or finished when all the slaves were free. And it wouldn't be just a matter of weeks. Or even years. But as Timothy had said, tonight they were making a start.

Breaking out, Albert's wide, generous smile lighted Dan's mind.

12 ~~~

The Montana Post: 1/7/1865, p. 4:

Advertisement:
CLAYTON & HALE / WHOLESALE & RETAIL / DRUG EMPORIUM,

Virginia city, Montana Territory, Corner of Wallace and Clay sts., Opposite Creighton's Stone Block.

We take pleasure in informing the citizens of Montana Territory, that we have opened and offer for sale one of the largest and best selected stock of Drugs every brought west of the Missouri River, embracing all kinds of [long list of items, including] DRUGS, MEDICINES, CHEMICALS, ... TURPENTINE, COAL OIL, ALCOHOL, BRUSHES, GLASSWARE, KEROSENE LAMPS, WINDOW GLASS, TOBACCO, CIGARS, PAPER AND BLANK BOOKS, PERFUMERY, PATENT MEDICINES, PURE MEDICINAL WINES AND LIQUORS, FANCY GOODS AND NOTIONS.

... Particular attention will be given to Physicians' orders and Prescriptions, and nothing will be dispensed from this establishment by (but) what is STRICTLY PURE.

Carol Buchanan

The prices of all goods shall be as low as they can be bought in the country.

Call and examine before buying elsewhere.

Dan and Timothy forged their way uphill through knee-deep snow so bright in the sunshine it hurt to see, but they stayed on the sunny side of Jackson Street for the sheer pleasure of seeing their own shadows against the side of Content's Corner as they passed. When they reached Dan's house, he sensed a change before they turned onto the path, and hurried his steps until he jogged up onto the porch.

Timothy, with his sharper hearing, knew it first. "Music. Mam is playing her dulcimer!"

For a few seconds, defying the cold, they stood on the porch to listen; music floated in the crystal air, rippled around them, while snowflakes danced and sparkled in the sunlight. Dan let the moment warm his soul, until Canary whined inside the house.

"Let's get you inside." Slapping snow off his trouser legs, he rapped on the door.

The music stopped, and a woman's alto voice ordered Martha to stay in her chair. The hairs rose on the backs of his hands at that insolent at tone of voice used to his wife. Then he heard the wood-on-metal sound that told him Mrs. Hudson lifted the bar. A key scraped in the lock. Mrs. Hudson looked out at him, no welcome in her face. As if grudgingly, she moved aside to let him shepherd Timothy across the mudsill.

Canary, the yellow coon dog Martha's family had brought from Appalachia, whimpered and wriggled a joyous greeting, then scratched at the door. Dan let the dog out, while Tim sank gratefully onto the bench to take off his boots.

"Dan'l!" Martha laid the dulcimer in its case and came to him, arms outstretched.

He unbuttoned his greatcoat and opened it wide to bring her into his warmth. Her arms circled his middle for the first time in a month. He bent his head to avoid seeing Mrs. Hudson watching, and inhaled Martha's clean scent, tinged with a milky smell that he associated now with babies.

At last, he let her step slightly apart from him, he murmured, "I've missed you."

Her brown eyes glowed amid the ravages her ordeal had made of her face. Though she smiled up at him, he understood that it would take time before she was fully herself. He reached for her again and held her until she pushed against him. He set her loose, and she brushed at his hair. "You have a clean head. Your hair is all gold."

"Thanks to Albert Rose." Dan's face warmed at the pleasure of Martha's approval, until he noticed Mrs. Hudson. The woman stood a gimlet-eyed watch that seemed to consider Dan and Timothy as intruders into her female realm. Hastily, he added, "Mrs. Hudson has taught him well."

The woman did not smile.

"And Timmy!" Martha reached for her son.

113

He stepped onto the mat and winced, stood still in place, afraid to take another step. Dan moved his footstool behind Tim. "Sit here." As Tim sank onto it with a sigh of relief, he handed him his own moccasins – winter's indoor shoes, made of muskrat hide turned so the fur comforted his feet. "Put these on."

Martha's happiness faded to worry. "What's wrong?"

"We're afraid he might have frostbitten his feet."

"How?" Martha started forward, but Mrs. Hudson squeezed around Dan to crouch in front of the boy.

"I'll tend to him." It was a command for Martha to stay out of her way.

Settling into her chair, Martha gave no sign she resented being ordered about in her own house, except that her mouth tucked in at the corners.

The Quaker woman crouched down in front of Tim, stripped off his socks and held a foot, peered between the toes, raised it to examine the sole, squeezed here and there, asking, "Does this hurt?"

Tim shook his head. His teeth held his lower lip until she finished, apparently satisfied, and set that foot down. "Thee may put on the slipper."

Dan stood behind Martha in her chair, one hand on her shoulder, the other a fist in his trousers pocket – parents waiting for the doctor's opinion of their boy's condition. Is this what fatherhood feels like? Dan asked himself. This fearful hope – almost prayer-like – for a good outcome. Only when Martha whispered, "That hurts," did he realize how tight was his grip.

"Sorry," he dropped his hand. But he followed Mrs. Hudson's every gesture until she sat back on her heels and stood in one smooth motion.

"How did this happen?"

When Timothy did not answer, Dan explained about his ordeal. Midway through the account of it, he heard a whimpering at the door and interrupted himself to let the dog in. Canary circled wide around Mrs. Hudson, slipped behind Dan's reading chair, and edged behind the wall at the back of the stove. A canine sigh and a shuffle of clothes told them he had flopped onto his bed – a pile of rags near the men's bedrolls.

So, the dog agrees. He hid his internal amusement to finish the story of Tim's ordeal.

"I see." She patted Tim's head as if he were a small boy – or a likable dog. "Thy feet were numb after thee fell in the creek?"

"Yes'm. It was like walking on blocks of ice, but ice don't hurt."

Mrs. Hudson stood still, one arm bent under her bosom, the hand cupping her other elbow, her chin in her hand.

They waited.

"He fell in the creek about fourteen hours ago? And you and Albert thawed his feet within minutes? Ah, yes. I don't believe he'll sustain any permanent damage if he's careful." She poked his shoulder. "Young man, pay attention. Thee must not go out in the cold for two days."

"Two days?" The boy's face flamed.

Dan knew he was thinking of necessary tasks that had to take him outside.

"Two days. Do thee want to lose thy feet?"

Even though he could not see her face, turned away from him to Timothy, Dan knew she had trained her spotlight glare on the boy. He would disobey her at his peril.

"No, ma'am."

He sounded positively meek. Defending Timothy, he assured Mrs. Hudson, "We'll make sure he stays off his feet and doesn't go out in the cold for two days." Dan stared at the boy, who seemed about to fight him on that, until his shoulders slumped. "What should we watch for?"

"Blisters anywhere on his feet or ankles."

They talked just above a whisper. Dan understood the habit of quiet for the babies' sakes was so much part of them now, but even so, from inside the bedroom, a baby squalled.

Martha launched herself out of her chair, moving so fast that Dan had barely enough time to sidestep a collision. She flung up her hands as she swung toward the doorway. "We can't be done with this stage soon enough to suit me." She disappeared inside the bedroom.

Dan hid his feelings of dislike for Mrs. Hudson. "You've worked a miracle."

"The Lord did. We've just been His servants."

"That's right."

Dan had not noticed Tabitha Rose, standing by the cookstove. She wrung out a rag into a bucket on the floor behind the table where he could not see it. Her sleeves were rolled to her elbows, and smudges of black dotted her apron. She had been cleaning the oven.

"That's all we be," she said. "The Lord's servants."

"The Lord's servants, maybe, but not mine." Dan reached into his trousers pocket. "I want to pay you both for your help. I did not expect so much." He moved his hand around in a wide circle to indicate everything he could not say – the calm, the cleaner house, Timothy's examination, Martha's rest. The dulcimer, lying in its open case. He was indebted to these women in ways he did not yet understand.

"Where is Dorothy? Eileen?"

"They're both sleeping." Mrs. Hudson hesitated. "That child – Eileen – has surprised me. Both girls have been good helpers all night. But Eileen – in spite of where she was reared – in that – house, and then killing – she is an innocent soul."

Dan knew she referred to Jacky Stevens's death. "She acted in self-defense."

"I know."

They faced each other in an awkward silence before Mrs. Hudson said, "Sit thee down. I would see thy head."

Dan straightened, stood to his full height, something over six feet. Albert had tended his head. There was no need for Mrs. Hudson's inspection.

"Please." The word came out hoarse, as if long unused. "Thee are much too tall for me to see."

Perched on Martha's footstool, he resolved to make no sound as he anticipated the pain when she removed the cap-like bandage Albert had fashioned to protect the wound. But he felt little pain as she meticulously separated his hair from the wound and pried the bandage little by little away from the area. Finished with her inspection, she laid his hair back in its proper combing, and replaced the bandage with great care as though putting a cap on a baby's head.

Finished with him, she stepped back.

"Thy wound is clean and healing well. It's a blessing thee are young. It will heal quickly if thee protects it. I have a salve for it." As he stood up, she added, "I would shave the crown of thy head, but I might damage the wound. Keep thy hair clean and wear a hat to protect it. Thee will not need the bandage in another few days. A week at most."

"Yes, ma'am." He reached for his poke, but remembered he had no scale here. "Reckon up a bill for me. I'll bring the dust to the Eatery later today."

Mrs. Hudson wiped the back of her hand across her forehead, and for the first time Dan saw, besides the dark exhaustion of the night's work in the shadows around her eyes, a deeper weariness in the lines around her mouth, and a downward set of her lips, all of which reflected how her life had tried her.

"About Eileen," she began, stopped, then went on. "She should not be here. Thee are a man of violence, and a constant reminder that evil is repaid with evil. Thee does not deserve the great love thy family has for thee. Especially thy wife. Thy sons should learn the way of peace, but they cannot from a father who resorts to violence an—"

Towering over this small, stout woman who dared to lecture him, Dan held himself back from shouting at her, and lowered his voice to a murmur.

"Why do you think I became a Vigilante? To make this place safe for the family I did not yet have. And for others. If there had been a way without hanging the criminals infesting our roads, I would gladly have chosen it. But there was not. You know very well we had no law, nor law enforcement, nor even a jail. I asked you once before, 'When others were at the mercy of murderers and armed robbers, should I stay out of the fight and keep my own soul safe while innocents died?' I'm telling you again. I will protect those in my charge, even if I burn in hell."

Glaring at her, he turned away. "If you'll excuse me, I'll see to my wife and babies." At the bedroom door, he paused with his hand on the latch. "Thank you for your care for my family. And for me."

Inside, the heavy curtains were parted an inch or two to let in sunlight. Luke cooed happily in his basket, his voice rising and falling in pitch. Was he already learning the sound of his own voice? At just two weeks? White-haired Danny burped contentedly at his mother's shoulder, his eyes fixed on the light streaming through the crack between the curtains.

"You look so handsome." Martha patted Danny's back.

"You're beautiful," Dan told her, but he was preoccupied. What had Mrs. Hudson done to work this miracle in the entire household? The babies' fretfulness, Martha's hysteria and her bone weariness, Dotty's frenzied worry – he had seen all this for himself. Overnight, all had disappeared in this transformation.

Luke gurgled as he punched and kicked with fists and feet; the blanket stripes bulged black, green, indigo.

Martha must have seen where he was looking. "He takes after me. Black hair, but he's got blue eyes. We'll have to wait 'n' see what color his eyes turn out t' be. Lots of babies' eyes are blue when they're born."

Was she slurring her words a little?

By the sounds from the big room, Dan guessed that Mrs. Hudson and Tabitha Rose were gathering their things and giving someone last-minute instructions.

Martha said something he didn't catch, the words blurred. Then he had an idea how the miracle had been worked. "I must speak with Mrs. Hudson."

He had to know if his sudden insight was correct, if he had guessed how she had worked this change in his household.

Clad in house shoes and her night robe, Eileen held a small notebook in one hand and wrote with pencil on its pages. She glanced at him from half-closed eyes, through smudges of exhaustion. Some of her hair had escaped its nighttime braid.

"Mr. Stark!" Mrs. Hudson halted with one arm in the sleeve of her buffalo coat and the other groped for the second sleeve.

Without thinking, he helped her on with the coat. Made from a buffalo-calf hide, it was too big and almost too heavy for such a small woman.

"What did you do to work a miracle in my home?"

Stopped as she fastened a frog on her coat, she looked up at him, and he caught a hint of defensiveness in her eyes. "Paregoric."

"Ah." That accounted for Martha's deliberate movements, her slurred speech. "I thought so. How much did they have?"

"Just a teaspoon in a quart of boiled water. The babies had a stomach upset, and it soothed them. Thy wife needed badly to sleep, and so did the girls. They all had a good rest, though they'll be ready tonight to sleep when it's bedtime."

"It has opium in it, does it not?"

"Yes, a very small amount. Perhaps one quarter of the undiluted mixture is opium, and I mixed it with twice-boiled water and gave both girls the least possible amount to calm them and give them rest. Mrs. Stark I gave only slightly more."

He wanted to shout, but for the sake of not frightening the others, he kept his voice down to a low, soft rumble. "You are aware, are you not, of the dangers opium carries? How soldiers coming from the battlefield hospitals cannot break its hold?"

"I am very well aware. If the case is not severe, I do not use it." She wrapped her wool scarf around her head and face, leaving only her eyes visible. "Thee need not fear my handling the poppy's gift. I err on the side of too little rather than too much."

He held the door open for her and Tabitha, then lifted the portmanteau over the mudsill and down the steps. "We'll see how they go."

As he climbed the steps to them, Mrs. Hudson said, "Thee are a good protector of thy family, Mr. Stark. I only wish thee had no violence in your makeup."

"I have only the violence necessary to protect those who can't fight for themselves, Mrs. Hudson. Good evening."

Shutting the door behind the two women, he laid the bar in place and leaned against it to savor the calm of his house. He was home again.

Eileen had a question about vegetables for dinner. Agreeing that they were scarcer than hens' teeth, he said, "Do the best you can." She kept her face turned away from him when he talked to her. He took her chin and turned her face up so he could look directly at her, past the dark smudges under her eyes, the hollows in her cheeks. "Try to get some rest, child."

For answer, she squirmed out of his grasp. "I'm well, Mr. Stark. I like keeping busy."

Yes. Dan realized she kept busy so she didn't have to remember killing Jacky Stevens. It didn't make any difference that she had shot him in self-defense when he came at her with a knife. Poor child. Grown men sometimes couldn't reconcile themselves after a killing, by gun or – by rope, no matter how necessary it might have been.

In his mind, as if the gallows stood in this room, he saw the frozen corpse swinging on its rope – the frozen corpse whose legs ended in stumps of bone and blackened skin where feet should have been.

Rawley.

Returning to the bedroom, seeing that Martha slept again, he lifted a baby – Danny, as it happened – out of his basket and sat down with him. Raising an ankle to the opposite knee, he laid the sleeping infant in the crook of his lap, keeping one hand under him. Just in case.

As he watched his little boy breathe, a shudder ran through his body. These six people, the babies, and Timothy, Dotty, Eileen, and Martha – especially Martha – they were his to keep safe. He had told Mrs. Hudson that he would protect them even at the cost of his soul.

So he would.

13 ~~~

The Montana Post: 1/14/1865, p. 2.

Latest by Telegraph

The Richmond Whig of the 20th says, the situation in Tennessee is melancholy enough. It was a black day for the army of Tennessee when Johnston lost its command. Hood was soon flanked between and compelled to abandon Atlanta. He stepped out of the way, hat in hand, and asked Sherman to walk through Georgia. He himself moved up into Tennessee, where he has now again got himself beaten, and this time, we fear, badly enough.

"By Jays, this can't be true!" In a corner of the cell he shared with five, maybe seven other men – depending on why and for how long they got stuck in this rotten pigsty of a jail – Major Tobias Fitch flapped the most recent *Montana Post* in his attorney's face. "This can't be true. No sirree. Not one bit true. It's a pack of lies dreamed up by that devil incarnate Dan Stark and that pal of his, that that – that –" words failed him "– pencil-pusher Tom Dimsdale! They want to undermine our war effort." He took a great breath, nearly choking on the thick, stinking air. "The Confederacy is not losing the war. I tell you, we will win, and all Yankee mudsills will rot in hell." He slapped the paper. "'Latest by Telegraph'? Hell! It's lies, I tell you. All lies!"

Forgetting, he hit the stump of his left arm on the wall to emphasize his words. "Ow!" He screamed and clutched raw end of the stump against his stomach. Sweat broke out on his face and glistened in the candlelight from the overhead lamp.

"Are you all right?" Harold Abbott mumbled through the perfumed handkerchief he held to his nose.

"No," Fitch snarled. "No, I'm not all right. Whaddaya think? This." Held up the stump. "Stark did this to me. Tried to burn me, too." He lowered his voice. "I'll get him, though. I'll burn him. Just get me out of here."

"Yeah," said another prisoner. "Get him out of here so we don't have to listen to him no more."

A second man growled, "Way I heard that story, Fitch tried to brain Stark and fell in the campfire and set hisself on fire, but Stark rolled him in the snow. Saved his useless life. Carried him to the Overland station at Point of Rocks, brought him here on the stage, and found him a doctor."

"Will you all shut the hell up?" A man lay on one of the two bunks with his face to the wall. "It's my turn with this flea-bag, and I need to my beauty sleep."

Abbott leaned closer to his client. "I'll talk to Justice Hosmer about getting you out on a writ of habeas corpus. You know what that is?"

"Sure. It means have the body, and I show up before this mudsill judge and tell him to let me out because there's no reason to keep me in here."

"That won't do." Abbott began, but Fitch cut him off.

126

"Then what do you say? I want out of here so I can even things with —"

"Never say that. Never, do you understand? You have to be released in order to – What do you have on the outside other than revenge on Stark?"

Fitch was quiet as the sweat rolled down his forehead and into his beard. He swiped at it with his good arm. "I've got a child to look after. A little boy. He's seven months old. Maybe eight. I've got him over at a wet nurse's place in Nevada City."

"What's his name?"

"Name? He's got no name. I haven't named him since he killed my wife. He's a half-breed, anyway. Berry Woman was a full-blood Injin. I forget her tribe, if I ever knew it. I bought her from some passing Injins."

"Well." Abbot, thinking, drew out the word. "Here's what I'll do. I'll draw up the writ on the grounds that you have an infant son to check on, to make sure he's doing well. You'll get your hearing on February 6, probably —"

"That's a month off! I don't want to wait so long."

"That's when the next session of the District Court begins. Today's the twelfth of January. It's only a little over three weeks."

"Can't we do this sooner? What about the Justice Court? Or Probate Court?"

"No, they're not authorized to issue Writs of Habeas Corpus. Only the District Court or the Supreme Court can do it."

Fitch glared at his useless ninny of an attorney. Abbott had done him no good at the December 31 hearing that landed him in here, thanks to Stark and that mudsill judge. Mudsills, yeah, both of them. Yankees. Interfering with a man's property rights, telling him he couldn't own slaves. Next thing you knew, they'd say you couldn't own a horse. Or a jackass. The lawyer looked down at the floor, probably scared to look him in the eye. No matter. He didn't have long to wait before Abbott's usefulness, even as little as it was, would be over. Never trust a man who won't look you in the eye, he reminded himself.

"All right. I'll see what I can do."

"Do better than that. Get it done." Fitch eyed the second occupied bunk, where a man lay on his back. "I need to rest, if I can."

Abbott buttoned his coat. "Oh, I nearly forgot." He leaned toward Fitch and dropped his voice to a soft mutter. "Stark's stepson, Tim McDowell, went to the Nugget claim and did some more digging on his own."

"Yeah?" Fitch's head, bowed over the arm held to his chest, snapped up. "That's my claim by rights, you know. I grubstaked his worthless pappy to find it."

"Is that a fact?"

"You bet it is."

"Ah. The McDowell boy says he found a gold boulder."

"He did what?" Fitch shouted.

The sleeping man woke up. "Wha —? Who —?"

"Aw, go back to sleep, Ed," another prisoner said. "It's only Fitch sounding off again. You'd think he's God, the way he thinks he owns the world."

Ed turned onto his stomach and fell to snoring again.

Abbott said, as though he hadn't been interrupted, "Found a gold boulder. A rock made of solid gold, or part of one. They have to dig it out before they can determine the extent of the find, but I'm betting it's the tip of a lode."

Fitch seized Abbott's arm, muttered under his breath. "The Mother Lode. The Mother Lode. That breed, that stupid get of an imbecile father, he's found the Mother Lode. Just my godforsaken luck." Something in Abbott's eyes warned him to shut up, but his thoughts raced on. He'd been chasing the Mother Lode ever since he'd come west, and that breed might have found it? He'd vowed to find it himself ever since he'd come back home on that recruiting trip for General Price and found the bluecoats had burned his plantation and run off his slaves. Even the freed ones.

"What are you talking about?"

"Shut up!" Fitch lowered his voice to a breathy whisper. "That damn boy has found the Mother Lode, and he doesn't know it. But I know it. I've known for a couple of years. With all the gold lying in the streams around here, the Mother Lode has to be here, in Alder Gulch, someplace. We find the apex, its highest point — Ow!" Forgetting the wooden cap was gone, he clapped his hand to the stump. "Damn!" When the pain subsided, he ordered Abbott, "I need another cap. See to it, won't you?" These caps, well padded, made a useful club. But never mind that. He'd soon be rich. He'd be the richest man in the whole damned country, Atlantic to Pacific, and the mudsills had better mind their manners, because he'd show them what's what. He'd show them. He threw back his head and laughed, a high-pitched giggle that turned Abbott's face pale.

"I'll get to work on that writ." The lawyer edged around Fitch, toward the door. "I'd better be going so I can get that done." He shouted, "Hey! Deputy! I'm done here. Let me out."

Fitch was not finished. "Yeah, you get me out of here." He jabbed at Abbott's chest with his forefinger. "Then we sue Stark for ownership of the Nugget. Win that suit, and you'll be rich. I'll sign a contract that makes you a part owner of the richest gold claim in Montana Territory." He looked into his lawyer's eyes, noted the hunger there, the worn elbows and shiny seat of his overcoat, the hole in one of the fingers on his gloves, his shivering in this cramped and overcrowded cell, choked with the body heat of several hungry, filthy men. Yeah, he told himself. He'd hooked his fish and reeled him in.

14 ~~~

The Montana Post: 1/14/1865, p. 2.

"Change of Time"

"The following law has been passed by the Legislative Assembly of Montana, relative to the time of Holding the District Court in this county:

"An Act designating the time for holding a Term of the District Court in Madison County.

"Be it enacted by the Legislative Assembly of the Territory of Montana:

Section 1. That the first term of the District Court for the County of Madison, for the present year, shall commence on the second Monday* in March next, instead of the first Monday in February, as designated by the Governor's proclamation, and at such other times as may hereafter be prescribed by law.

Sec. 2. — All writs and other processes heretofore returnable to the February term, shall be returnable to the term of court to commence on the second Monday in March.

Sec. 3. — This act shall be in force from and after its passage.

Approved, January 10, 1865, Sidney Edgerton, Governor.

Late in the afternoon on Saturday, when the light had dropped into dusk, Dan crossed the street to Con Orem's Champion Saloon. Pushing open the door, he closed it before anyone could yell at him, and paused to scan the room. Men stood at the bar against the right-hand wall, where a large mirror nearly the length of the bar showed them the opposite wall, festooned with sporting prints. A mahogany statue of half-naked women flanked either end of the mirror and held up the draperies covering their loins with one hand, while the other rested half-open between their breasts. Their tantalizing half-smiles seemed meant for the winners in the prints they looked to be watching, the boxers Tom Sayers and John Morrissey.

That left-hand wall, visible in the mirror, boasted an artist's rendition of a horse race between the great Eclipse and other horses trailing far behind the blaze-faced English Thoroughbred. The race seemed to run toward a portrait of a bare-chested Con Orem who faced off, fists up and cocked, against a similarly posed likeness of Hugh O'Neill on the wall beside the mirror.

Would there be a rematch between the two men? Dan doubted it. The "Great Fight," as the *Post* called it, had gone 185 rounds, and the two combatants had inflicted so much damage on each other, they both recuperated at home.

Below the picture of the horse race, Deputy Sheriff John X Beidler sat alone at a table for six.

X, as his friends called him, had positioned himself like a man whose hard work ferreting out criminals had earned him enemies, and he didn't know who they might be. He faced the door, his back to the bare-knuckle fighters.

His over-under shotgun leaned against the wall within quick reach.

X gestured toward one of the vacant chairs. Dan cocked an eyebrow in a silent question. The unsmiling deputy, who was not much taller than his favorite weapon, nodded.

Dan ordered two beers. As the bartender reached for clean glasses, Dan met the saloon owner's eyes in the mirror. Though painted, they were so lifelike it startled him. It was as if Orem guarded his establishment with a close eye, although Dan knew he still recuperated at home.

"How's Con doing?" Dan asked the bartender.

"Passable, passable." The man talked in gusts without looking away from the rising foam. "He still hurts. Some here and there. Leastways, he ain't puking blood no more. Most days, he's walking. Around his house, y' know." He spat tobacco juice at a target below the bar that he didn't look at. The gob whanged against brass.

The bartender adjusted the flow of the beer. "He'll be back maybe in a week. Less, if he has his way."

"I take it O'Neill hasn't been himself, either." Dan handed over his poke for the bartender to weigh out ten cents' worth of dust. He tasted his beer without watching which wafer the bartender put on the scale pan for his drink.

Finished weighing out the dust, the bartender handed Dan his poke. "Hugh's doing pretty good, too, from what I hear. You know, I call that a miracle. They didn't kill each other. Not that they'd mean to. But fights can sometimes – you know. After the beatin' them two give each other? Shoot, that fight went – what was it? Near two-hundred rounds?"

"Near that, until the crowd begged the referee to stop it."

The bartender was in the mood for more conversation. He leaned both elbows on the bar. "What'd he do that for? They was both standing up."

"Maybe so they would both live to fight another day." Dan stashed his poke away and lifted his glass. Taking another sip, he smacked his lips, the approved sign of a good drink. "Still serving the best."

"Wouldn't have it any other way." The bartender said over his shoulder as he went to answer another customer. "Brewed here, in Virginia, y'know."

At Beidler's table, Dan set the glasses down, draped his coat over the back of an empty chair, sat down, and clinked glasses with X. "Heard from Howie yet?" Sheriff Neil Howie had gone to Boise in southern Idaho with an extradition order for a criminal.

"No, and I don't expect to for awhile. It's a long, hard road to Boise City in winter. Them Idaho officials ain't pleased with losing Montana Territory, either. It cut theirs down to less than a third what it was."

Dan chuckled. "It left that skinny little strip all the way to the Canadian border, too. What is it? Ninety miles wide?"

"About that, I think." Beidler's dark eyes shared Dan's amusement.

"I expect it will take him awhile to convince the Idaho Attorney General to honor the extradition order."

"I think you've got that right."

"Meantime you're acting sheriff?"

"Yup. What's on your mind?"

"Tobias Fitch."

"Ah." X took a long swallow of his beer and set the glass down.

Dan waited while he sucked the foam out of his heavy soup-strainer mustache. "That son of perdition. His lawyer saw him today."

"You don't say." Dan pretended interest in his beer. Somehow, he had lost his thirst.

"Fitch has him filing for a writ of habeas corpus. If Hosmer goes for it, you'd better watch out. I think he's addled. I heard him tell Abbott that the Nugget claim is his because he grubstaked Sam McDowell."

"He's had that burr under his saddle since Sam died and he escaped being hanged for his murder."

"Yeah, but now he's convinced – absolutely, positively, mind you – that your mine is the site of the Mother Lode."

Speechless, Dan stared at X. "The Mother Lode is a myth. How can anyone seriously believe in it?"

"I wouldn't say it's a myth. Gold in its molten state, maybe sometime in the six days it took the Almighty to create the world, could've flowed downhill from somewhere. So much of it ended up here when the earth cooled off that maybe the source of it is hereabouts someplace."

Dan smiled. "You've been reading too much Darwin."

"Nah. Just keeping me eyes and ears open. Liquids flow downhill. Water does, anyway. So must gold, when it's melted."

Both men sat in silence. Dan pictured streams of gold sliding down among the rocks. That was logical, if the rocks were hot enough. But the idea of having one source for it all – that was plain crazy. No one knew how gold originated. It melted, sure, at nearly 2,000 degrees, but the idea of having a single source somewhere – No. How could that be when gold was found here and in Last Chance Gulch, a couple hundred miles away? In California? And in Africa?

But — another consideration stopped him. X was right. In its molten state, liquid gold moved. What if it pooled in places? Dan raised the beer glass to his lips and swallowed without tasting it. If so, the boulder

Timothy had found might – his heart beat faster – be something.

"Dear God. Fitch truly thinks the Nugget holds the Mother Lode?"

"Yeah. But like I say, he's not sound in the head. It's been getting worse ever since Nick was murdered. He loved that boy like a son."

"I know. It about broke him up when Palmer brought Nick's body in."

"Yup. I recollect how eager he was to get up that night ride."

"If he gets out —" Dan's memory showed him Fitch's shadow wavering in the firelight, against the wall of a cave in Beaverhead Rock. The clubbed left arm rose over his head. And descended. "If —" He paused a moment to collect himself. "Judge Hosmer can't release him. He's awaiting trial for attempted murder. My murder."

"Which he says is backwards. You tried to kill him first and he fought you off in self-defense." X spat tobacco juice in the general direction of a spittoon. Missed. It splattered on the floor. "That grayback is more trouble than all the other prisoners together. He bellyaches about everything – the food, the water, the buckets, the bunk, his cellmates, the noise – you name it. He even whines about the length of time he has to wait for a trial. He wants that trial over with so bad it's like a disease. He's convinced it'll prove you're a liar and a thief. He thinks your mine belongs to him, and what's worse – well, you know." X drained his glass, wiped the back of his hand across his mouth. He did not have to explain the slang term, grayback, or be cautious about using it with Dan. Unionist friends and fellow abolitionists, like X and Dan, felt free to use the slang term for the insects that infested unwashed clothes and hair. Lice. If Confederates could call Unionists 'mudsills,' the threshold that people scraped their shoes on before they entered a house, he felt no twinge of guilt for calling slave-owners and their supporters 'graybacks.' The term was, after all, accurate. They were an infestation on the body politic.

Rather than wait for the Deputy Sheriff to hint that talking made a man thirsty, Dan went to the bar for two more beers. "You might as well put them on my tab."

"Can do." A hole in the bartender's smile showed where he'd lost a front tooth.

Returning, Dan waited for X to take a first pull at his beer.

"Do you think there's a chance Judge Hosmer will release Fitch?"

"I d'know." X looked at Dan from under his eyebrows and tugged at one end of his mustache. "You're worried." It was a statement, not a question.

They leaned toward each other to talk below the room's noise.

"Yeah, I'm worried, but I'm considering all possibilities. That's the only way I can block him." He paused to get his ideas in order. "His child, a boy about seven or eight months old, is with a wet nurse. If I were

Abbott, I'd make a strong case for letting him out on compassionate grounds to check on the boy."

"You think Abbott will try that?"

"Yes. If Abbott doesn't see it himself, Fitch will persuade him."

"It wouldn't be the first time the client was smarter'n the lawyer." X almost whispered, so that Dan leaned closer to hear him and got a whiff of his sour breath. "If that happens, we'll be on the lookout. He won't get away with nothin. We'll deal with him."

With his half-empty glass Dan made wet, interlocking circles on the table that mimicked his swirling memories of men coming to the ends of their ropes.

X broke the silence. "Face it, Stark. We have a lawful court and a judge who says, 'No more midnight hangings.' But we're still in about the same fix as before. All we've got in Madison County – all 3,600 square miles of it – is one overcrowded, nasty jail. As for official law enforcement – there's me. And Howie, when he's here."

"Besides that, God help us," Dan murmured, "we still have no code of criminal law. The Bar committee that's writing the criminal code won't be finished before the Legislature adjourns."

"How do you know that?" Beidler sat up so suddenly he knocked against the shotgun and snatched it quick to catch it.

Dan waited as he stood it up in its corner.

"I hear Burns and his partners talking through the wall between our offices."

X blew out his breath. The hairs of his mustache rose and fell. "What a fix this is. It might as well be 1863 again. It's still up to us to maintain law and order."

"I hoped we'd finished with all that." Dan drank the last of his beer and set the empty glass aside. "Though I could make an exception for Fitch." Startled at having said it aloud, he added, "Only if it passed the Executive Committee."

"Like Slade?"

"I didn't want that under any circumstances. Rawley was worse. Both times, we were cornered. What else could we have done?"

"Nothing else, less'n we wanted to give up and let people know we didn't mean business." X glanced up as a chill draft signaled an open door. He muttered behind his mustache, "Here comes Hal Abbott."

Sitting back on his chair, Dan raised his voice. "Do you mean to tell me that you have to pay for the prisoners' meals out of your own pocket?"

"Durn tootin'. Now you know why I'm in favor of that blasted income tax."

Abbott, wearing a triumphant grin and reeking of something sour and unpleasant, stopped by their table.

For form's sake, Beidler pulled out an empty chair. "Have a seat, Hal."

"I can't stay. I have work to do." His self-satisfied smile made the hairs bristle on the back of Dan's neck.

"You should know, Stark, I'll be filing a writ of habeas corpus to release Major Fitch."

The hoofbeats had quieted while Dan talked with Beidler, but now they stomped as though attacking something nasty. "Oh? On what grounds?"

"Incarceration without sufficient grounds." His smile toward Beidler was condescending. "That means without a good reason for holding him."

Dan took a deep breath, felt his waistcoat tighten across his chest. "And why would that be? Attempting to murder me isn't sufficient grounds to be held for trial?"

Abbott shifted from one foot to the other. "He didn't attempt to murder you."

"Is that so?" Dan removed his hat and set it on the table. Across the room, a man standing at the bar glanced his way, then hastily turned away, carried his beer to the pool tables in the back of the room. In the mirror, Dan caught a gleam of white – the new bandage – already showing the dark reddish signs of blood.

"Indeed so. We'll prove it, too. His Honor won't want to keep an innocent man incarcerated." Staring down his nose at Dan, Abbott delivered the challenge as though he bestowed a favor.

Dan shifted his chair around in hopes of avoiding Abbott's odd smell. He failed. "You realize you'll be arguing that reasoning before the same judge who ordered Fitch bound over for trial, don't you?"

"Yes, of course, but that should hardly matter to a fair-minded man." When Dan remained silent, Abbott went on, "And in any case, if he denies the petition, we can appeal it to the Territorial Supreme Court."

Dan stared at him.

Abbott's brow wrinkled as if he sought to understand why he didn't react as expected.

As Dan spoke, he didn't believe he had to explain it to another lawyer – even one as thick as Abbott. "You don't understand the court system? You call yourself a lawyer? If your case got that far, you'd be arguing in the Supreme Court before Chief Justice Hosmer and Associate Justice Williston."

Abbott's eyes darted from side to side. Clearly, the man was flummoxed. Attempting to recover, he sputtered, "Regardless, I have asked for a hearing on the writ in no less than a week, or at his earliest convenience."

A great boom of laughter escaped Dan. Men set down their glasses, stopped their conversations to watch him. When he recovered, he pulled a handkerchief from his trouser pocket and wiped his eyes, blew his nose. "For that, Fitch will have sit in jail until at least March 13." He stuffed the handkerchief back in his pocket.

"What do you mean?" Abbott blew his nose on his fingers and wiped the result on his pants leg. "Scheduling a hearing on a simple habeas corpus shouldn't take long."

"Don't you read the *Post*?"

"That Union rag? I wouldn't dirty my hands with it." Abbott's disdainful sniff caused X to shake his head.

When Abbott looked around to receive other men's silent approval, some openly grinned at him. Others turned away, their expressions contemptuous.

"Then you miss reading the laws of Montana Territory as the *Post* publishes them. You missed the 'Change of Time,' as the editor headlined the Act. The legislature moved the opening of the first session of the First District Court for 1865 to March 13. If I may quote it, 'All writs and other processes returnable to the February term, shall be returnable to the term of court to commence on the second Monday in March.' That is March 13."

"So?" Abbott thrust out his lower jaw.

"'Returnable' means your writ of habeas corpus cannot, by law, be heard before March 13."

The blood drained out of Abbott's face, leaving it pale and sallow. His mouth opened and closed.

"Where," Dan turned another laugh into a moderate bellow. "Where on earth did you get your legal training?"

Abbott swung around on his heel and stalked out, slamming the door behind him so hard it bounced open again.

The bartender hurried to close the door. "Lawyer, is he? Born and raised in a barn." He paused, then added, "Probably studied with the cows."

Laughing, his customers raised their glasses and cheered him.

Beidler muttered, "Abbott shouldn't be a problem to defeat. At anything."

Dan pictured the long column of sums the new man – Ryder? Ritter? – had added up. "He's not as stupid as he appears. He's a card shark."

"Not surprising." Beidler drained his beer. "None too choosy about how he wins, I've heard. Don't underestimate him."

"I won't turn my back. He and Fitch make a pair." Dan put his hat on. "You bet I'll be careful."

15 ~~~

The Montana Post: 1/14/1865, p. 4.

For Sale.

I have for sale two ranches on the Stinking
Water; also one good business house in
Virginia City, and one good residence; also
one Ranch on the Madison. Enquire of

Wm. Chumasero

Through Martha's voice in his right ear as she
instructed Eileen on how he liked his eggs, Dan
strained to hear Dotty's attempt to explain the income
tax to Timothy.

The two female voices mingled together. Martha
said, "Mr. Stark likes them over easy." At the same time,
Dotty spoke with all the authority of her thirteen
years: "Mr. Lincoln says everyone has to give ten
percent of what they have —"

The girl was wrong about the percentage. As he
opened his mouth to correct her, Eileen turned her
back on the sizzling eggs to face Martha. "Nobody
complained at the – the —"

Timothy sputtered, "That's just, uh, it's just a plain,
stupid. It's — "

Eileen got out "the other place —" avoiding the name of the saloon Dan had rescued her from "— 'bout how I cooked eggs."

Timothy finished, his voice louder to rise above Eileen's protest "... stealing a man's hard-earned money."

Eileen pivoted to glare at Tim. "What do you mean my cooking's stealing a man's hard-earned money?" Covering her face with both hands, she sobbed, "I ain't no thief. Mr. Stark, I ain't stealing your dust."

Into the sudden vacuum in the breakfast hubbub, Tim dropped his final comment: "I don't see why we gotta have an income tax nohow."

As Martha sat, mouth open, Dotty stood up and gathered the other girl in a hug. "Nobody accuses you of stealing anything." She patted Eileen's back. "Dan'l can eat his eggs however you make them. Over easy, sunny side up —"

"Even scrambled," Martha chimed in.

Dan protested, "Let's not go too far."

Eileen's tears stopped on a giggle. Dotty released her and sat down at her place facing her brother across the table.

"Nobody accuses you of stealing, Eileen," Dan assured the hired girl.

"But them eggs ..." Timothy pointed toward the stove.

"The eggs!" Eileen swung back to them. The whites had browned around the edges. Seizing a spatula, she scooped them up. "They're ruined. Mister Dan'l, you can't eat 'em like this." Spatula in hand, she edged behind Dotty's chair toward the slop pail by the washstand.

"Eileen, stop."

Teetering on one foot, the other beginning to rise into the next step, Eileen stared at the spatula. Its load of eggs slid toward their doom on the floor or in Dotty's hair.

"Watch out," Tim warned the girls.

Dotty glanced over her shoulder, snatched up her own plate, and thrust it under the spatula in time to save the eggs. And her curls.

Dan held his own plate for Tim to take. "Here, Tim, put them on my plate."

Eileen wailed, "Mr. Stark, you can't eat them! They ain't fitten!"

"I most certainly can." He waggled his fingers for Timothy to hand him the plate of overcooked eggs. Looking at them, he asked, "What about the toast?"

"Oooh, no!" Eileen let out a scream and swung toward the stove where a thick slice of scorched bread on the cooktop had started to smoke. She snatched up the blackened bread and tossed it in Dan's direction.

Dan caught it on his plate; his thumb stopped it from skidding onto his lap.

No one made a sound as he set the plate down and regarded his breakfast: brown egg whites, hard yellows, and blackened bread.

He took the plate, shook a little pepper over the eggs, and took a bite.

"Mmmm." As he pretended to savor the bite, he reckoned he owed his stomach an apology.

The three females watched him with identical nervous, round eyes as though he might fire Eileen. Or feed eggs and toast to the dog, the last word in insults.

Except he couldn't be cruel to Canary. The mental picture of the dog turning up his nose at his breakfast tickled his funny bone.

He chewed the first unpalatable mouthful and washed it down with coffee. "I might get to like this breakfast." A laugh built up. Despite his attempt to hold it back until he had finished the bite, it exploded in a guffaw that he nearly did not catch in his napkin. His eyes ran tears, and he recalled his mother's voice complaining about a lack of decorum.

After a shocked moment, everyone joined in, Eileen last of all.

When the laughter had faded into an occasional hiccup, Timothy demanded. "Now, can we talk about this here, uh, doggone income tax?"

"If we can have more coffee," Dan held up his mug. It, at least, was worth drinking. "Good coffee," he told a nervous Eileen, before turning his attention to Timothy. "What do you want to say about the income tax?"

"Why do we gotta have it?"

"Yes, Dan'l, why?" Dotty demanded. "People work hard to get their living, and the government takes ten percent of what they earn? All politicians do is sit and talk."

Surprised, Dan held up his coffee cup to give himself a moment to think while Eileen circled around the table to fill it. What was this, this challenge from Dotty? This flibbertigibbet – curious about the income tax? As long as he'd known the family, going on what? – two years? – she'd never had a notion beyond "pretties," her word for ribbons and such gewgaws to dress up a hat, or bits of glass to put in chains of apple seeds woven into a necklace of her own blonde hair.

Thinking how to answer her, he debated with himself: Should he tell her straight, as though she were a man? This new tax President Lincoln wanted was a business matter, and business was the domain of men. Not women, and certainly not of young girls.

What had changed her?

Was it witnessing her mother's long and difficult lying-in on the night the twins were born?

Or Eileen shooting Jacky Stevens in self-defense that same night?

Timothy, sitting next to him, swallowed his toast. "Dotty, what d'you care —"

"Don't call me that!" The girl flashed back at her brother. "Don't ever call me that, ever again! I'm not 'dotty.' I'm not! I'm not crazy!" Tears stood in her eyes.

Dan set his cup down. All right. She'd asked for an answer about the income tax, and he'd give it to her, just as if he spoke to a man of business.

Her face flaming, the girl stared at her cup as she stirred canned milk into her coffee and dabbed her handkerchief at her eyes.

"For one thing," Dan said, "the government isn't taking ten percent. It's taking seven-and-a-half percent."

"How do they know how much they'll get from everyone?" Timothy reached a long arm across Dan to the plate of sliced bread.

Dan held on to the plate, fixed him with a pointed stare. "Repeat after me, 'Please pass the toast.'"

"Oh." The boy's cheeks reddened. "Please pass the toast."

Dan handed him the plate. "They made a form."

Picking out a softer slice, Tim laughed. "Of course. It's the government. They'd have a form for breathing if they could."

"Probably." Dan smiled at Tim. "On it I listed everything I could deduct, and then I have to pay seven-and-a-half percent of the rest."

Timothy whistled. "That's a lot."

"Oh, not really. Not as much as they could take."

"Ten percent would be fair," Martha broke into the conversation. As her son gaped at her, she added, "It's the tithe."

Eileen, filling the coffee pot with water, set the dipper back in the clean water bucket. "Tithe?" She set the coffee pot on the cooktop and picked up the grinder.

"Don't forget to roast the beans first," Dan reminded her.

"I done roasted them already yesterday," Eileen didn't look at him as she dumped beans into the grinder and paused before she turned the handle. "What's a tithe?"

"It's the sum we're expected to give to a church if we belong to one. It's ten percent," Martha told her.

"Why on earth would President Lincoln come up with this, da–um —" a glance at his mother's frown made Tim grope for a different word to use – "er, stupid, idea?"

"The war has to be paid for." Dan took a sip of coffee. "We can't ask men to risk their lives for their country without a reward. Or do all the other work. They need some compensation."

"You like the tax? Why?" Dotty held her cup in front of her mouth, as though to hide behind it.

Martha gasped. Dotty looked at her. "What's wrong, Mama? Are you all right?"

"Yes, I'm fine. I just marvel at how you talk right up to Dan'l."

Timothy explained to Eileen, "Pap would never have a conversation with womenfolk. Or let them talk up to him."

"But Dan'l does," Martha said.

Dan ignored the exchange to push his plate of uneaten food away. "Getting back to the income tax, understanding the reason for something doesn't mean I like it. This tax, like Timothy says, is unfair. And it's unnecessarily intrusive. Is it any of the government's business to know everything I have?"

Dotty wouldn't quit on the subject. "But if you understand why it's needed, and you think soldiers have to be rewarded, why —?" She gestured with her fork, and a bit of syrupy pancake dropped into her cup and splashed coffee on her sleeve.

"Now look what you've done!" Martha scolded. "That shirtwaist will have to be washed, and Lord knows what the laundry bill is already this month–" waving her fingers toward the babies. "–what with them."

"My dear." Dan reached across Danny's basket to lay his hand on hers. "Don't worry about the laundry bill. I can pay it."

Timmy said, "That's right, Mam. He can —"

"Timothy." With that one word, Dan warned the boy, reminded him never to so much as hint that he was wealthier than anyone else knew.

Timothy closed his mouth. Eileen set the coffee pot down hard on the burner. Dotty's eyes rounded. But before anyone could take another breath, Dan set his fork on his plate like nothing had happened and spoke as if he had nothing more important on his mind than the laundry bill.

"I've been thinking we need a bigger house."

"What for?" Martha wrung her napkin in her lap. "We can't – the little'uns are too young to move and it's too cold and we're doing fine right here."

"My dear, the first thing you said to me after the birth was to build a bigger house."

"I did?" Martha looked around the table as if she hoped one of the youngsters recalled it.

"Yes. You did. Anyway, I didn't mean we'd move this afternoon, but Timothy will be living here now, and our little boys will soon be walking. This house was all right when it was you and Dorothy and me, but now we've added four more people, counting Eileen. Seven people in an eight-hundred square foot cabin is much too crowded."

"Lots of folks don't have this much," Martha retorted.

In the sudden quiet, Timothy's arm stopped as he reached for a piece of toast. Dotty's forefinger tangled in a lock of her hair. Eileen's back hunched over the coffee pot. Martha held four fingers against her lips as though to protect them.

Dan frowned. What were they afraid of?

Luke yawned and burped in his sleep.

Danny sneezed without awakening.

Even as he asked the question, Dan knew the answer. They feared the ghost of Sam McDowell. He kept his voice quiet, used a gentle tone as if he spoke to a nervous pony. "I know that, my dear."

What had he done to any of them that they feared he might turn into another Sam? Or what had he done to anyone... And then he knew.

He was a Vigilante. And more, a leader of the Vigilantes, one of those who had hanged members of the Plummer gang – more than twenty men – after secret trials hardly anyone ever saw.

They feared what they didn't know, and he could never tell them, bound as he was by the vow of secrecy he had taken when he'd helped to form the Vigilante organization, a vow as binding, as sacred as any vow sworn by a monk Rumors were plentiful, whispered among people who knew nothing of what went on in the tribunals, and would never know. They would —

Little Danny awoke with a cry, and the moment broke.

Timothy picked up a piece of toast and brought it to his mouth.

Martha scooped up the crying baby.

Dan put his hand into Luke's basket and murmured to him.

Martha drew her shawl around the baby to cover hrself and the child while she arranged her clothing to nurse him.

Luke, the sounder sleeper, did not awaken as his father held him in the crook of his arm and rocked him, studying the distinctive cast – even so early – of his baby son's features, so like someone he had never met. He could see nothing of either Martha or himself in this tiny son of his.

"I wish..."

Martha's voice roused Dan from watching Luke. "You wish what, my dear?"

"I wish we could do something for Tobias Fitch's baby son. He's at a nursemaid's place and she's not – well, what she should be." She swallowed and cleared her throat. "I feel sorry for the poor little tyke."

"Why should you? He's no concern of ours." He heard a stiffness in his voice and decided it was well-earned. Glancing around, he realized the others looked as surprised as he was.

"I've been thinking of Berry Woman, poor thing."

Martha's nasal Appalachian tones, pitched higher by her nervousness, grated on Dan's ears. She looked half-scared of him.

Dotty dropped her fork on her plate, and the clatter broke the pause.

"Why would you be thinking of her, just now?" Dan recalled the young Crow girl Fitch had bought from Indians who had stolen her from her tribe.

Martha answered him, looking very like her daughter with her chin up, though her voice steadied. "The poor girl, she was near enough to being a child herself, and she died bringing that baby to life."

Dan doubled his fist by his plate and emphasized each primary word with a soft thump on the table. He would put an end to any talk of Fitch's infant son. "I said, that baby is not our concern. Let Fitch take care of his own."

Now Dotty lifted her chin. "His father's in jail, and he's just a helpless baby."

His females were aligned against him in this, but he'd be damned if he'd give in and take responsibility for the get of a man who'd tried to kill him. Dan'l only looked at her again, and the girl stared into her coffee cup as though she expected to find a spider in it.

The entire table went quiet until Timothy broke the silence.

"I want to go back up to the mine."

Dan looked at him, and something about his silent expression made the boy add, "If'n it's all right with Mam and you, Dan'l."

Dan made himself smile in Martha's direction, though he wanted to say a flat no to that fool notion. "Wait another day until we see how your feet are healing. Then we'll let your mother decide." He didn't want Tim to go up there at all, but if he said no, the young fool might go anyway. Sometimes he thought caution – or good sense – had been left out of the boy's makeup.

Then he remembered jumping into the quarry. Maybe foolishness belonged to most half-grown boys.

"Just two things." Martha paused to adjust baby Danny under her shawl. When she was ready, she sat in silence, thinking, taking her own time about her answer as the family waited.

"Two things?" Her son prompted her.

"One is, you take someone with you. Someone good and strong, and for t'other, you come back by sundown the next day."

"But that don't give hardly any time to —"

"You heard your mother." Dan did not speak as sharply as he might have, but Tim's mouth turned down at the corners. He glanced at Dan out the corner of his eyes as though judging what he could say.

"If that's how it's got to be." He sighed as one much put-upon.

"Yes, that's how it has to be." Dan reached his knife toward the butter plate.

"All right, I'll wait until we see how my feet are tomorrow, and then I'll be back by sundown the second day after I start up there."

"Why not take Albert?" Dan scraped butter onto his cold, dry toast. "Or at least ask if he'll come with you. I'll pay him what we agreed on for two days." He pointed the knife at him. "Don't hurry the timbering."

"And don't be starting any more new drifts, either," Dotty warned her brother.

"We won't be needin' to. We've got us a big old hunk of gold —"

"Timothy." The sound of Dan's voice warning him to say no more stopped the boy, who put three fingers to his lips. "I'm sorry, Dan'l. I forgot."

"Forgot what?" Martha asked.

"How much Dan'l said he'd pay Albert?"

Martha looked toward Dan, who vowed to have a word with his stepson soon. Meanwhile, he did most certainly not trust either Eileen or Dotty to say nothing of the boulder Timothy claimed he'd found.

Dan studied how he might answer her. Some men – definitely Sam – would have shut her right down, because women had no business mixing in men's concerns. But he recollected how his mother and sister had complained that his father had told them nothing, kept them ignorant of his business affairs until after his death they had learned why he'd been so secretive. He had hidden his thefts and his drinking well from the entire family. Especially his own father.

So Dan told Martha – and the youngsters – the truth. "Eight dollars a day."

"So much?"

"As hard as he works, he'll earn it," Dan added, with a smile for his wife.

She patted the baby under the shawl and returned the smile. "He is worth his hire."

Eileen finished her breakfast and rose to fill the wash basin. "We're needing more clean water."

With that, the family was back to normal, although Dan resolved to begin work on plans for a much bigger house as soon as he could, no matter whether Martha wanted it or not. A house that would have an office for himself, so he could guard the family.

16 ~~~

The Montana Post: 1/14/1865, p. 2:

The Mineral Resources of Montana.

> Anticipating the inevitable result of the
> continued industry of multitudes, Nature has
> pointed to the hills that enclose it, and each
> day brings news of quartz lodes discovered
> around and about it on all sides. At the head
> of this vale of wonders, the General Butler,
> Oro Cache and Kearsarge, among scores of
> others, contain treasure that invites the
> labor of years. At Prickly Pear creek silver
> lodes in dozens are already discovered, with
> many a crevice of golden ore and the work is
> not yet 1-10 part completed.

Sunday morning, Dan negotiated the snow-mounded hazards of his walk down Jackson, his mind worrying over Tim's safety like Canary with a good stew bone.

If he'd been a praying man, he'd have sent up a plea to the Almighty to watch over Tim and Albert, that nothing bad would happen to either of them. As it was, he fervently hoped they stayed safe.

Meanwhile, he had a job to do. Jacob owed an explanation to both Timothy and himself – but beyond that, an apology to the boy for shutting him out in one of the coldest nights of the year, when Tim had almost frostbit his feet.

Why the hell had he refused to answer Tim's knocking?

Just thinking about it, he felt a familiar heat at his breastbone, that he'd felt only a few times in his life – once when the bailiffs seized his books, and one had sneered at his liking for novels, especially *Les Miserables*: "Too good to read English, are you?"

Again, when he'd viewed the partially nibbled face of Nicholas Tbalt. He could have strangled Nick's murderer with his bare hands then, if he'd known who it was.

Eventually hanging George Ives for that murder had been nothing but satisfactory, and what the man had deserved. And now, it came again as he pictured Jacob in his warm house while Timothy slipped off into icy rocks into the near-freezing water of Daylight Creek.

He put his foot on the bottom step up to his office and began to climb. He was so focused on keeping his temper with Jacob, that he had reached the third step from the top of the stairway before he saw a man standing by his door.

Jacob.

He shifted from foot to foot, marching in place, as if he'd waited awhile, as if he fought the cold.

Dan squinted to see him better. So, he's cold. Serves him right.

"Good morning."

"It is that." Unlocking the door, Dan left it open for Jacob to follow.

Inside, he set about reincarnating the fire in the stove as though Jacob were not there.

A crease appeared between Jacob's eyebrows when Dan finished building up the fire, but he said nothing. Perhaps he expected to be offered a seat, take off his coat, make himself at home, have some coffee or whisky – all Dan's normal invitations to him.

"What brings you to see me?" Dan stayed by the stove, aware of the other man's puzzled frown.

"My mind, I have changed. You need investors, I have an amount of gold I would invest. Is not great, but you I trust. Timothy is just a boy. He may not know gold, the mine's gold is maybe fool's gold, but if you trust him, I trust you, and I would invest."

Bent over to fit an unnecessary log into the pile of quarter rounds already beginning to blaze, Dan hid his expression, tamped down his outrage, that Jacob could sink so low as to refuse to open his door and then come with an offer of investment tantamount to a bribe.

Dan shut the fire door harder than neeeded, rose to his full height, more than half a foot taller than Jacob. At their first meeting on a Manhattan dock, Jacob – newly disembarked from Eastern Europe with hardly a word of English – had quailed before him. Since then, some five years past, Dan had never given Jacob reason to fear him.

Jacob took a step back, toward the door. "You are angry. With me. *Warum?*"

"Why? Because you would not open your door Friday night when Tim was looking for shelter. I told him to tell you to let him sleep at your house one more night because all was chaos at my place. But you shut him out."

For a space, Jacob gaped at him, as though unable to grasp why Dan should be offended.

"Well? What have you to say for yourself?"

"I have said. I must keep the Sabbath. Too long I have gone without obeying YahWeh. No more. It is the law from – as you say – the Almighty."

"You put Sabbath observance ahead of his safety? God commands us to love our neighbor. That is God's law."

"I did not know it was Timothy."

"But it was someone needing help. Whoever it —."

"I serve YahWeh. Not you. Not Timothy." Jacob thrust the poke into his pocket, drew on his gloves, and swung toward the door. There he stopped. "The things we did a year ago, the executions, I must pay for them, before YahWeh Himself. I must – must make all good with Him before I die. That is why, to keep every jot and pen stroke of His law respecting the Sabbath is most important. To be in harmony with YHWH is why I live now."

"In harmony with God justifies the loss of a boy's feet?"

Unspeaking, Jacob pulled the door open.

Dan sent him out. "That's right, Jacob. Go."

17 ~~~

Montana Post: 1/14/1865, p. 2.

From Prickly Pear
**During the recent cold weather, when those
less courageous were glad to content
themselves in doors, might be seen the
hardy prospectors apparently heedless of the
wintry storms, going to the neighboring hills
to delve deep into the earth in search of the
hidden treasure — gold.**

"About time you came back. When are you getting
me out of here?" Tobias Fitch growled at his lawyer
over his shoulder as he stood at the piss bucket in a
corner of his cell, his back to everyone. Finished, he
faced Hal Abbott while he buttoned his trousers.
"When do we see that mudsill judge? And don't tell me
it won't be until next month."

The misbegotten excuse for a lawyer was scared of
him, Fitch could tell by the way he licked his lips. Good.
And just look how close he stood to the door. Trying to
burrow through it, by the sound of scratching behind
him. Or maybe it was rats. Fitch couldn't rightly track
the noise because his hearing had got worse after all
the artillery fire. But no, it was the shyster. Probably
calculating how fast Deputy Beidler could unlock the
door. In case. Baring his teeth, Fitch grinned at him.
Yup. He was scared, all right. Bah! Some fixer he'd be.

Probably scared of jailhouse stink, afeared it might rub off.

Abbott cleared his throat. "Not before March thirteenth, sorry to say."

"What?" Fitch bellowed.

Judge Hosmer must've heard him through the walls – if that misbegotten Yankee excuse for a judge was in his office on such a cold day. No doubt he was sipping decent whisky in front of a good fire, telling lies with some other damn Yankees.

Such an angry dark haze came over Fitch's eyes, he almost didn't see Abbott holding out a folded newspaper – the cursed *Montana Post*, again, full of Yankee lies and drivel.

"This is why." When Fitch refused the paper, Abbott dropped his arm to his side, but stayed close to the door. "The legislature – over in Bannack, you know –"

Damn it, of course he knew. In here, it was talked about every day, cellmates wondering what would be illegal next — would he never get to the point?

"— passed an act moving the first session of the First District Court to the second Monday in March. That's the thirteenth."

"Let me see it."

Without moving farther into the cell, Abbott held the folded *Post* out toward Fitch, but another prisoner, pretending to be asleep on a bunk, sat up and grabbed it out of his hand, tearing a corner of the sheet. He swung his feet to the floor and stood up, loomed over Fitch, and held the sheet almost to the rafters.

"What'll you give me?" he demanded. "You're always saying how you'll be the richest man in the country, so you want this ass-wipe, you gotta pay."

A reddish haze covered Fitch's vision. He lunged for the man and knew nothing else until he sat on the other's bunk to look at the paper. The other prisoner lay groaning on the mud-crusted floor.

"Some legislature. I knew that bunch wasn't to be trusted," he muttered as he scanned the sheet. "Too many mudsills. I thought our boys had more sense." He found the headline, "Change of Time," and read it through, his eyes flicking from side to side as though reading a line at a time. Slapping the paper, and tearing it more, he demanded, "This is dated the fourteenth. Why am I just getting it?"

"I'm not late, Fitch." Abbott's voice was rough. He cleared his throat. "Climb down off your high horse, or you can find yourself another lawyer – if any would take your case." He kept his eyes from the man on the floor.

"Had it coming to him." Fitch scanned the rest of the paper, refolded it haphazardly, held it out to the shyster, who reached to the ends of his fingers and snatched the sheet back.

Through the greyish cloud that overlaid his vision, Fitch noted with glee how a pulse beat over one of Abbott's eyes, how fast he blinked. Whatever he'd done to the varmint on the floor had put the fear of God into him.

Carol Buchanan

Cradling his short left arm, Fitch cupped his right hand under the elbow, breathed deep. When the red fog had cleared, he promised himself he would get Abbott. For now, he needed a fixer, incompetent though he had proved to be. He couldn't help the rough edge in his voice, like a dog's audible waning growl. "So, what is today?"

"Monday, the sixteenth."

"I've got to get out of here. You've got to get me out. You hear? Get me out." In a softer tone that made Abbott edge toward the cell door, Fitch murmured, "Get me out of here – or else."

Abbott seemed about to salute the Major. "I'll think of something, but don't worry. You won't have to wait until March."

"I better not. That claim is mine, you hear? Help me, and you'll be rich, too."

In a pig's eye, he told himself, as that cursed Deputy X, a mudsill himself, unlocked the cell door behind Abbott, who scuttled out like a scared rabbit. He'd be damned if he'd share any of his lode with Abbott, the fool. "It's mine," he whispered to himself. "Mine. All mine."

18 ~~~

The Montana Post: 1/14/1865, p. 2.

The Mineral Resources of Montana

Here, where we write, in this enchanted city,
the great gulch traversed by Alder creek for
twenty-two miles, challenges research, never
yet fruitless. Though thousands of miners
have, in every conceivable method, delved
and dug from one end to the other, yet years
of labor will have passed ere it ceases to
yield the rich harvest that has made so many
of the poor of the land wealthy and
Independent. ....

Trudging upstream on snowshoes reminded Timothy how much he hated the blasted things, needing as he did to swing his feet wider than usual, watch that he didn't put the edge of one on the other. He'd done that before and wound up on his face in the snow. He'd feared he'd never dig his way out, trapped and suffocating as he'd been, held down, unable to move his feet in the snowshoes. How he'd wriggled out at last he still didn't know.

By the time they'd gone half a mile along Alder creek, he bitterly regretted his decision not to use horses. Besides his shovel, pick and lantern he packed an extra can of kerosene, and more candles.

The load was already heavy, and by the time they'd've gone another mile he knew he'd be plumb tuckered. His pack, like Albert's, towering above his head, held food, dry socks, and anything he'd considered needful to last them in case they stayed on.

He had no intention of going back the next day if they hadn't found the edge of the boulder.

He had to know what he'd found.

Albert hiked on hard and fast like he was some kind of machine, never once acting like he had to work at this snowshoeing, even on a trail that wound among boulders and stumps turned into snow-mounded barriers much bigger than their summer sizes.

Sometime during what Tim reckoned might be the second half mile, though, he got his wind. Albert must have done, too, because although the going didn't get any easier, they arrived at the mine entrance sooner – and for his part less blown – than he'd expected.

After all, horses might have been faster, but he still didn't know if he'd have done better to have used them. Like Dan'l talked about, what did he call it? The return? Except for how tired he was.

He was that glad to stop, he nearly fell on his knees to give thanks.

No time to rest, though.

In the week since he'd been here, snow had drifted enough to build a partial wall across the lower half of the portal. Over it, he and Albert had built a roof mounted on upright logs that held the weight of snow. Above it on the mountainside, maybe ten feet or so up, a big old dead fir tree lying angled across a boulder held back tons more snow. If nothing disturbed that tree, the portal would remain open.

Albert didn't hesitate. He shucked his snowshoes, pack, and tools and climbed up the slope to study how the tree laid. "It'll hold," he called down to Timothy. "It be hung up on a boulder bigger'n Massa's house."

Relieved at the reassurance, Tim lay both pairs of snowshoes on the snow and piled their tools and packs on them. Then he and Albert dug a path from the main trail. The dry, fluffy snow made for easy shoveling, and he warmed to the task. He made the path wider than necessary for a man on horseback, while Albert came behind him, widening it enough for two horses.

Sooner than Tim had thought possible, they stowed their gear and supplies inside the portal.

The portal itself was wide enough to drive a small wagon into or out of – looking ahead to when they would haul ore out to be crushed – if they found what Tim guessed they'd find. It widened out inside to a good-sized, timbered cave. Off to one side, sawn timbers of various lengths lay ready to shore up new or extended drifts. They dropped their packs and blankets near the back wall, close to where they'd built a small fire, then melted snow and boiled water for coffee. Eileen had sent sandwiches, and Mam had put in the last of the oatmeal cookies. With what Albert had brought from the Eatery, they could eat for a week. Or at least a couple of days. Warmed by the coffee and the fire, they watched snowflakes drift down outside, almost dancing, or so Tim felt, out of his great happiness at being here again, with Dan's permission, and with Albert to help. Before they went home again, they'd find what this mountain had hidden since the Almighty created the world.

On that, he finished his coffee and stood, Albert with him. They threw the last dregs of coffee onto the fire.

"We best set to it, then, right? If Mistah Stark wants you back by tomorrow night, we better hustle."

Tim knew a bright tingle that must have been pure happiness. "Yes, we'd better hustle. We have a lode to find."

They hoisted their tools – an axe, pick, and sledgehammer, and two single-jack, or one-man, hammers and a mattock – the snowfall had become a lacy curtain pulled over the outside world. Tim laughed at himself. *Getting fanciful are we?* Lacy curtains, indeed.

At the end of the adit where Tim had left off, the lantern cast broken shadows in weird shapes amid rough stones and boulders too large for one or two men to move.

Hunkering down when they reached the rock, Tim's breath came faster when he shone his lantern on it. He was almost afraid of what they would see. Had he imagined the gold? Or was this just a chunk of granite? The shine could be mica – pretty, but worthless.

Afraid to look where the light shined, he watched Albert's face, thinking he'd know the truth by Albert's expression. The fickle candlelight glanced off the boulder. Albert touched it with his fingertips, took out a pocketknife and scraped at the surface, turned to Tim with the scrapings in the palm of his hand.

Tim brought the lantern closer. Candlelight danced over the scrapings.

Gold.

He hadn't imagined anything. With people refusing to believe him, he'd begun to doubt himself, but he'd seen what he'd seen. This was no water shine. No rock crystal. No mica.

This was gold.

He moved the lantern around for the candle's light to stroke all the boulder they could see. From every facet of the rock, gold shimmered and glowed.

"I wish Dan'l could see this," Tim whispered.

"He ain't seen it?"

"No. He's just going on what I told him."

"He believes you, without he's seen this?"

Timothy shook his head, swiped at his hair – or maybe at a piece of grit – to get it out of his eyes. Dan'l believed him. Sight unseen, he'd believed.

"We best get to work, then." Albert's voice rumbled deeper than usual, deep as the mountain itself. "We's got to have somethin' real for him to see when he comes up here." By the lantern's shifting light, they studied the situation.

"Follow the rock." Embarrassed, Tim felt certain he'd stated the obvious.

Albert only nodded. "Dig out enough room on the side to work."

"Go up as high as the rock?"

"Higher, to dig it all out. We need room on top."

In the candle-lit darkness they regarded each other.

"It be needin more'n us."

"We're all we got for now," Tim said. "We just have to make do."

"Do what we can afore we have to go back." Albert took up a pick and pointed it at a spot over his head, a few inches to the side of the rock. "Good a place as any, you reckon?"

"What we know now." Tim, standing between Albert and the rock, moved away. "You first."

Albert swung the pick, yanked the handle upwards, and dirt and stones dropped down.

Beside him, Tim sank his pick into the wall, jerked it out. Nothing happened. He sank the pick in, to the left about a foot, and pulled it out. Following him, Albert went at the higher reach. Tim swung the pick again, and it sank into the mountain's belly. He lifted the handle's end, pushed up with all his strength, stopped to breathe, and pushed up on the handle. As an almighty creak started up, he jumped out of the way, pulled Albert with him.

Rock and dirt cascaded to the floor of the drift.

They laughed out loud to see the pile spread out into the adit, and the man-sized cavity opened up beside the boulder.

Tim picked up the lantern, and they stepped across the pile to see.

"Let's clean this up a bit," Albert said.

They set to work to remove the debris still clinging to the boulder as far as they had gone. Tim decided they had uncovered about three feet along the side, and perhaps eight feet upward, judging by how high Albert had lifted the pick above his head.

When that job was done, Tim whistled. "It ain't – there ain't no edge there."

They stared at each other, and Tim watched realization slowly came to Albert, faster than he could grasp it, himself. The rock – the boulder – wasn't either one of those. It was more. A wall. Maybe a lode.

"We've got to find the size of it."

"More diggin," Albert spat on his hands. "We ain't come to the edge of it yet."

They worked feverishly as long as the candle in the lantern chimney lasted. When it fluttered, it reminded Tim that he should change it before it left them in the dark. As he lifted the chimney, he spoke aloud. "First, let's get rid of this pile. Then we better see about timbering?"

"Yup. We best be doin that before we go any farther."

Lighting their way to the portal with the sputtering candle, Tim's plans skipped among jobs to do, and how to do them. Near the entrance, they sat at their fire. Albert poked at the coals until flames flickered among them before he added more wood.

Tim passed the tin of cookies over to Albert, who took one daintily between a thumb and forefinger.

173

"I never done this work afore," Tim said. "I got a lot to learn." He chewed a bite and swallowed it, washed it down with a cup of melted snow. "You ever done anything like this, Albert?"

"No, nothin like. But it don't seem to me like there's an art to it. Just common sense. Prop up the mountain so it don't come down on us. Be careful of blasting powder and such. Keep a lookout for yourself."

"The devil's in the details." Tim helped himself to another cooky. "What's the best way to prop up a mountain, I wonder."

Albert got to his feet. "I don't know." He reached a hand down to help Timothy up. "Them logs there? We best use 'em."

Tim closed the cooky tin. "Help yourself when you want another."

For the first time, he looked out the portal. "It's still snowing. About three inches more. Shoot. It keeps this up, we'll need the snowshoes. I'll go find them." He put on his knitted wool cap, snugged up his bootlaces, buttoned his coat, and pulled on his gloves. Outside, he found the snowshoes sooner than he'd expected. He turned around to take them into the mine when he heard a rumble deeper than he'd ever heard before, deeper than a bear's growl, like the mountain roared at him for something he'd done.

Snow engulfed him, tossed him head over heels, and he lost all track of up or down, light or dark. Then with an almost contemptuous flip it slung him partly out, curled up like a new baby, his head above the snow. He scrambled, almost swimming in the soft, light snow, floundered, slid until his feet found solid purchase, and he could stand up.

The snowslip had carried him twenty or thirty feet beyond the mine, as near as he could tell. He saw the slanted shape of the downed tree, still where it had been, leaning against the boulder.

He stood below the tree, which had been ten or so feet above the base of the portal.

There was no portal.

The mine entrance was gone.

Help. He needed help. He waded through the snow as far as he could toward the snow-buried portal. When the downed tree lay closer above him than it had been, he stopped.

"Albert!" he yelled as loud as he could. Waited.

Nothing.

"Albert!" He yelled the Colored man's name until he could not yell any more, could make hardly any sound at all. No one answered him.

Turning, he looked for the snowshoes, but they had vanished. He waded through waist-high snow, downward. Follow the creek downstream was all he could think of. Downstream was Virginia City. Down was home. Down was help.

Downstream was Dan'l. He had to find Dan'l.

Dan'l would know what to do.

19 ~~~

The Montana Post: 1/14/1864, p. 2.

The Mineral Resources of Montana

The national currency will provide the commercial medium which alone is needed to furnish the key for the unlocking of the dark caves which even "the vulture's eye hath not seen," and from which we may draw forth to the light of day those sinews of war and guarantees of peace which shall discharge all our national liabilities, heavy though they be, and give to our beloved country, favored so much by the fostering hand of Providence – a dowry for all her fair daughters and a competence to all her industrious sons.

Rolled into his blankets, Dan awoke to black darkness and could not get back to sleep. On the other side of the stone wall he had built for safety, the fire mumbled in the stove. It was colder behind than in front of the stove, but he took no chances with fire.

Wondering what had awakened him, he lay listening to night noises.

Canary snored at Dan's feet. The house creaked. The logs, shrinking in the deep dry cold, rubbed against each other as the ground settled under them. All was as usual.

What, then, had awakened him?

A baby whimpered, and Martha's voice came to him: "Sooo, little one, sooo, Mama's here." She hummed a few bars of a song, and the baby – which one? – quieted. Twisting in his bedroll, he got up. Padded to the bedroom door and put his ear against it. Both babies slept again, it seemed. He didn't dare open the door – it squeaked. The little ones occupied his side of the bed, to be close at hand for Martha when they awoke hungry or uncomfortable. When they were older and stronger, they would be moved to cribs, and he could take up his place beside her.

Chilly now, he shuffled back to his blankets. Outside, silence reigned. Even the Champion Saloon, directly across the street, was quiet: no raucous sporting songs, no fisticuffs from drunken men upholding the honor of their chosen pugilist.

He imagined the world lying encased in ice, motionless. Waiting for spring.

The girls, Dotty and Eileen, slept deep in their innocence.

He listened a few minutes before turning over and pummeling his pillow.

He heard nothing but the fire and the wind outside, the occasional gunshot sound of ice breaking in the creek. All was well.

A log snapped in the stove, and instantly he was wide awake once more. Would the little stove need more wood? After Martha's husband, Sam McDowell, disappeared, Dan had bought this cabin. He'd anticipated Martha and her two youngsters, Tim and

Dotty, coming to live with him. Dreaming of long winter evenings as a family, he'd laid a stone ledge and put an extra little stove on it in the front corner to keep them warm while they took turns reading to each other. He'd also built the stone wall behind the stove to prevent stray sparks from getting into the log walls. Once he'd finished it, he'd discovered that small space would make a private sleeping area.

He should be able to go back to sleep.

Thoughts of Timothy and Albert at the mine pecked at him. What would they find? What could they do in less than 48 hours? So short a time. Would they timber the new drift properly? Would they stay safe? Did they have enough food? Could they —?

Somewhere among his fretting he fell asleep.

Canary's sharp-edged barks yanked him into partial consciousness.

Before he came fully awake, he stood at the door, rifle in hand, willing to say a lead "Hello" to whoever disturbed them at this ungodly hour. He slid the bar through its brackets enough to lift the latch.

Timothy stood on the porch, teeth chattering, his body shaking with cold, arms wrapped around himself, hands under his upper arms. Snow crusted him from head to toe.

Dan laid the rifle back on its pegs and pulled the door wide open. Seizing Tim around the waist, heedless of the snow melting into his thick wool socks, he half carried the boy into the house, bumping the door closed behind them with his hip. So close to his near brush with frostbite, the boy had to be warmed, quickly. Safely.

Timothy slumped down on the end of the bench closest to the stove. Melting snow ran into the metal pan.

Only then did Dan realize the twins howled. He shut the door and replaced the bar. Shrill questions preceded the girls, in heavy, quilted winter robes and fur-lined slippers, coming out of their room. Martha peeked through the doorway. Seeing Tim shivering on the bench, she closed the door on the infants' commotion and snapped instructions that sent Dotty back into the girls' room for extra blankets while Eileen built up the fire in the kitchen stove to heat water.

"You're nearly frozen." Dan crouched down, tugged off Tim's boots and heavy socks, chafed his feet. Surprisingly, they looked pink, as though his mother's knitted socks had kept them from freezing. Cold, yes. But not frozen. Not frost-nipped. Still, Tim being so near to escaping frostbite, he could only hope the boy suffered no ill effects.

Dotty brought two blankets, draped them over the chairs next to the reading corner stove and went back for another. Martha held one as close to the stove as she dared. When Dan had the shivering boy out of his coat, Martha draped the warmed blanket around his shoulders. Together, they helped him into Dan's reading chair and put his feet on a footstool. Dotty brought another blanket, and soon warm blankets wrapped Tim, leaving only his eyes visible.

"Al – Al – Al." Tim brought his chattering teeth under control. "Albert ..."

Dan knew what he tried to say. "Albert's still back at the mine, right?"

"Y – Yes."

"Don't try to talk."

Desperation helped Tim find his voice. "We've got to go up! We've got to find him!" Tears leaked from his eyes and trickled down his cheeks. He struggled out of his wrapping and swiped a hand across his face.

"We will." Dan looked at the grandmother clock standing on the table between the reading chairs. "It's two o'clock in the morning. There's nothing we can do tonight. It'll be daylight about – seven-thirty. Then we'll get up a crew, go up, and find him." But he could not resist one more question. "Was it a cave-in?"

"No. Av – av– av'lanche." Timothy gasped for breath. "It's all my fault. We shouldn't a gone up there."

"The avalanche wasn't your fault. You're not God. You don't command the elements."

Eileen brought a cup of sage tea, hot and strong, and spiced with a concoction of healing herbs. At the smell, Timothy's face scrunched in distaste. The girl looked at Martha, an unasked question in her eyes.

"Drink it," Martha ordered her son. "It's Miz Hudson's recipe for chills." To Eileen and Dotty she said, "You girls go back to bed. We'll handle things from here."

"Let me stay, Mama," said Dotty. "I want to hear what happened."

Dan overrode whatever Martha would have said. "You already know. Whether the avalanche caught him, or – or something else, Albert is still up there. Now go back to bed, like your mother told you."

"Oh." As she turned away, Dotty's shoulders slumped.

Eileen lingered to murmur just at hearing level, "Timothy, I'm glad you're safe." Then, before either Dan or Martha could speak to her, she spun around after Dotty.

When the door closed behind them, Martha cocked her head to listen. "It's quiet. I best check on the little'uns." As she stood, she looked down at herself and blushed. "I didn't think – oh, my." Holding the skirts of her nightdress, she sprinted to the bedroom and shut the door.

Timothy looked a question at Dan over the rim of his cup.

"She's only wearing her nightdress."

Tim rolled his eyes. He tried to say something, but the words were an unrecognizable stutter.

A log snapped in the corner stove. From his heels, Dan rocked upward and went to stir the coals and put more wood on the fire. When he came back, he crouched beside Tim.

"What happened?" Dan's voice was soft enough not to disturb Martha or the twins. "You can tell me now, or wait until morning."

"Now." Tim held the mug out for Dan, who seized it, as his stepson tucked his hands under the blanket.

Stammering, pausing occasionally to collect himself, he told Dan about the avalanche. "I rode down in it, and I ain't never felt the like. I couldn't see nothing, and up or down was all lost to me. There wasn't any light, just me tumbling in the dark. Like I didn't weigh nothing. And the cold."

"How did you get out of it?"

"D – d – d'know. It tossed me out and set me down with my head in the open. Seemed like it took hours to get my bearings, and dig out, and then I went back to see about Albert." As he finished, his stuttering and shivering lessened, though his eyelids drooped.

Dan put the warm cup into his hands. "Finish this."

Tim stuck out his tongue and crossed his eyes. "I can't."

"Drink it."

Maybe the boy heard the Vigilante in Dan's stern response, but he took the cup, raised it to his lips and drank it off. Thrust the cup back at Dan.

"Now you turn in." Dan started to rise, his one desire to get Timothy down for a much-needed rest before he fell asleep sitting there.

Timothy shook his head. "I gotta tell you. When I got back there, I yelled and yelled, but Albert, he didn't answer. Leastways, I didn't hear him. I d'know if the portal roof caved in, or the avalanche blew it out, or maybe it's buried under snow. All the tools are inside the mine, and some of the houses around was smashed flat, or buried, so I come to get you." Tears shimmered in the candlelight. "Folks had their own problems, so I wasn't about to bother them about Albert." His chin dropped to his chest. "'Sides, I wasn't sure who up there would want to help dig out a Colored."

"They'd want to dig themselves out before helping you dig out a stranger, black man or not." Dan rocked upward. "We will." He seized Timothy's hand. "Come on. You need to get some rest. Tomorrow will be a tough day."

"What'll you do?"

"Get up a gang to help. If we're up early enough, we can have a bunch ready to start by first light. I'll talk to Beidler. He won't be able to come, himself, but he'll help find men." He did not mention Jacob.

The Jacob he had known for almost three years would not have hesitated to leave the bank to rescue Albert. That Jacob would have opened his door when a desperate man pounded on it, no matter what day it was.

The Montana Post: 1/14/1865, p. 4:

ELEPHANT CORRAL

Justus Cooke. J. A. Gray.   T. J. Newel.
Livery, Sale & Exchange

STABLE

Cover Street, Virginia city, M. T.

The Undersigned having removed their
Auction Stand to their corral on Cover Street,
would inform the public that they have a

FIRST CLASS STABLE

In every respect and solicit the patronage of
their friends and the public.

SUPERIOR SADDLE HORSES

can be obtained at all times.

Corrals for cattle in connection with the
Stables

Cooke, Gray, & Co.

Timothy slept the deep sleep of exhaustion when Dan slid his trousers on in the flickering light of the fire through the stove's firebox grate. The house was still as he checked on the fires in the stoves. He kissed Martha's cheek. By a gleam of reflected light in her eye, he knew she awakened. "I'll be back soon," he whispered. "I have to round up help to rescue Albert."

"Come back and eat something hot before you start up there," she murmured.

A baby whimpered. He sidled from the room before the infant could fully awaken.

~~~

Dan closed the front door as softly behind him as he knew how, but still it scraped along the floor. The hinges need replacing, a task he would get to in the spring. Listening for sounds from inside, he tugged his scarf up around his lower face. Not even the dog barked. The silence bothered him. When he knew he wanted to hear the sound of the bar being settled into its brackets, he understood. The house was essentially open, but Martha would not risk a baby's awakening, and he was letting Timothy sleep longer. He himself could find friends to come out to rescue a man, even on this piercing cold morning, and give the boy an hour's more rest.

He walked to the end of his path, where a bobbing light uphill caught his eye. He stopped before turning down Jackson Street. Someone carrying a lantern walked down the slope.

Dan waited until he recognized X Beidler. Shotgun in the crook of his arm, X loped toward him with his distinctive bowlegged gait.

"Good morning, X. You're out early."

Beidler stopped. "Might say the same about you, Stark. What're you doing, in this infernal cold before sunrise?"

He took Beidler's lantern and held it for them both as they walked on together. The light showed them a beaten pathway among the hazards of the street.

"Tim went up to the Nugget claim early yesterday with Albert Rose. He came in a few hours ago to tell us Rose is trapped up there. An avalanche came down and buried the mine entrance."

"Albert Rose? Him as works for Mrs. Hudson, the healing woman?"

"That's him." Dan didn't explain further, and Beidler did not ask. A man's business was his own until he decided to let someone else know about it. His silence wouldn't stop X or anyone else from speculating that something was going on upstream, but he would worry about claim jumpers when – or if – he had to. And then a Bible verse was in his mind: *Sufficient unto the day is the evil thereof.*

Beidler said, "You'll need as many men as will come to get him out. I've got something to tend to downstream, or I'd join you." He spat tobacco into the snow. "I've got some time yet. I'll round up some of our friends."

"Thank you, X. I'll make arrangements at the Elephant Corral. Have them meet me there in an hour. And tell them I'll pay four dollars a day and found."

"At them wages you'll have half the town sign up."

~~~

The gate of the Elephant Corral, two tree trunks so large he could not have put his arms around either of them, stood fifteen feet tall. Stripped of their bark, they had been polished to a golden sheen by the weather. Atop lay a crosspiece, perhaps another section of the same tree trunk, something like ten feet long, that overlapped the logs holding it at either end.

As a newcomer to Virginia City nearly a year and a half ago, Dan had helped raise this massive structure, and his hands still seemed to smart at the memory. As he put his hand on the section of fence that barred his way into the yard, he remembered also stories another Vigilante had told him of a hanging near Hell Gate the last winter, when the rancher's outraged wife had made her husband cut their gate down. It had made too good a gallows.

Dan lifted the loop of rope that held a swinging section of fence closed and walked in, pushing it ahead of himself. Inside, he closed it, replaced the loop, and walked across the yard toward the office in the barn reserved for fine saddle horses.

In a side corral, cattle lay in the snow munching their cud. One lurched to its feet, hindquarters and then forequarters, its horns longer than Dan had ever seen, and lowed at him. He walked on, perhaps a bit faster, more careless of his footing.

Above him, a beam thrusting out of the hayloft made a dark slash against the star-filled sky. Intended as a hoist for loads of hay, it had served another purpose nearly a year ago. Dan shuddered, chilled to the bone by more than air temperature.

The Vigilantes had hanged Slade from that beam.

The office door was locked.

He walked around to the barn door and slid it over enough to sidle through. Closing it behind them, he breathed to the bottom of his lungs. The barn smelled sweet to him, a mixture of good hay and horses. Moonlight followed the beam into the barn, and he gradually made out shapes among the shadows – a wagon hump-backed with a load of hay. As his eyes adjusted to the night-dark shadows, he heard the rustle of hay and small sounds horses' hooves made when the animals roused unafraid.

From the loft he heard footsteps, the rustling of disturbed hay. A forkful of hay slid down into the stall closest to him.

"Hello?" Dan called.

"What? Who's there?" A man called down to him. "State your business at this ungodly hour."

"More godly than ungodly. I've come to hire a sledge and horses to take men on a rescue mission." He added, "My name is Daniel Stark."

"A rescue mission?" The man in the loft came to the edge of its floor. In one hand he held a lantern, in the other a pitchfork. He twirled it around so the tines pointed downward. The lantern shone briefly on the man's face. "I'll be down directly."

Dan recognized Vaughn Ryder. Here? The Elephant's stableboy?

Ryder drove the pitchfork into a large mound of hay, and scrambled down the ladder as if it were a stairway, holding the lantern in one hand.

The bruised hay smelled sweet as springtime.

Dan held his peace, though he asked himself, why was Hal Abbott's assistant working as a stableboy? He pushed the question aside, to answer later. Now, he judged, was not the time. He would find out after Albert was safe.

Hanging the lantern on a stout nail in a post nearly the circumference of the logs defining the gate, Ryder stood in front of him in the wide aisle between two rows of stalls. From each stall, a horse's face stared out at them, ears pricked.

"You said a rescue mission?"

"That's right. There's a man buried under an avalanche about two miles upstream."

"You'll be wanting a team of Percherons and a sledge, then." Ryder brushed his gloved hands together, and Dan caught a faint whiff of leather. "I'll send someone for Mr. Cooke." Putting two fingers to his mouth, he whistled a high, shrill note. At the sound, the horses startled, and one kicked out at the door of its stall. "Calm down, there, boys. Easy now. Steady on."

To Dan's surprise, his deep, calm voice satisfied the animals, and soon Dan heard the horses crunching their hay.

Ryder peered at Dan. "It's Mr. Stark, is it not? We met briefly at Ming's a day or so ago." He extended his hand and Dan shook it. Remembering the limp, damp hand of their first meeting, he was glad Ryder kept his glove on.

A young boy, perhaps twelve years old, ran into the barn and stood at Ryder's side. "You need something?"

"If you will, run and find Mr. Cooke. We have an emergency here. This gentleman wants to hire a team of Percherons and a sledge to carry a load of men and tools up to a mine. There's a man's life at stake."

"Yes, sir!" As the young boy pivoted to run away, Ryder stopped him.

"Have you breakfasted yet?"

"I was just about to."

"Then when you come back, before you do anything else, be sure to eat."

"Sure thing." The boy called over his shoulder as he dashed out the door.

As they waited, Ryder asked, "Do you know the man who's trapped up there?"

"Yes." Dan picked among the facts of the situation to select the best ones, the most urgent, that would override any prejudice on Ryder's part against rescuing a Colored man. Then he recollected that Ryder had come from Gettysburg Lutheran Seminary, a school almost as noted for its abolitionist views as Oberlin College in Ohio.

"It's Albert Rose. He was helping my stepson, Timothy, excavate a boulder, underground. When Tim went out to get their snowshoes, the avalanche came down, swept Tim away and trapped Albert in the mine."

"Albert Rose? The black that guards the Eatery?"

"The very same."

"Well, then. Count me in. I don't know what Mrs. Hudson or – of course, Mrs. Rose – would do without him."

Talking close by the lantern's light, Dan watched Ryder. He was gaunt, his face pared of flesh, so that his skin covered sharp cheekbones. "Have you eaten?" Dan asked.

"Me? Oh, yes. Yes, I have."

"Do you have to let Mr. Abbott know you'll be gone for a day or two? We don't know how long it will take to dig Mr. Rose out." Dan felt his way along. To ask too many questions would be intrusive, and men were known to be shot because they pried too much into another man's business. Yet there was an odor about Ryder, the smell of hunger that Dan knew from the urchins hawking newspapers on New York streets. It was the smell of poverty. Ryder did not eat enough, and he moved as if he were not properly coordinated. Then, too, his plump form did not match his fleshless features. Dan suspected he wore all the clothes he owned, to keep warm.

How much help the young man could be, Dan did not know, but something was very wrong about him. Not his character, for he seemed an honest fellow, but something in his life in Virginia City did not – literally – smell right

"Very well, then. Come along with us, and I'll pay you the same as I will any other man who joins us. Four dollars a day."

"I – I don't know what to say. I would help rescue Albert Rose for nothing, but this —" The young man's eyes filled with tears, and Dan knew his suspicions were correct. Vaughn Ryder was close to starvation. But why? Why was a man going hungry when he had two jobs – with Abbott and in the Elephant Corral?

That answer, too, would have to wait until they returned from the Nugget. Meanwhile, he would roust out Timothy. By the fading darkness, he knew that sunrise was not far off. Excusing himself to Ryder, he stretched his legs to their longest stride and started for home.

~~~

Dan found his front door barred, while sounds of female voices and Timothy's deeper tones told him everyone was awake and up. He caught snatches: "You'll need this," "No, I won't, I got leather," "Girls, have you made enough?" A deep male voice answered: "Mam, there's enough food here to feed the whole dang Union army."

What he heard were the sounds of a family. His family. Joshing each other, like his siblings had done before – before Father's – For a moment, he stood poised at his own front door, his hand outstretched to seize the latch. He must protect them.

The dog barked. Before he could announce himself, Canary had known he was there.

Someone lifted the bar, and his stepson's man-sized frame blocked the opening.

"Are you going to let me in?" Dan's fist stayed in the air.

"Dan'l!" Timothy stepped aside for Dan to come into the chaos of preparations. Dotty and Eileen wrapped a pile of sandwiches, tied them with string, and Dotty placed them in a burlap sack while Eileen held it open. Tin cups for water and jugs of coffee went into another burlap bag that Dan wondered how either girl could lift.

Leaving them to their task, he eased himself through the bedroom door. Martha lay with a baby in the crook of each arm. Despite the noise outside the door, neither baby had awakened.

Martha murmured, "They're getting used to family sounds."

Dan bent over to lay a finger on a tiny, warm cheek. "You've made a miracle."

"Go with God," his wife breathed into his ear as he bent lower to kiss her.

"We'll come home safe and bring Albert with us."

"I'm prayin' for that."

As Dan stepped into the big room, Tim finished buttoning his heavy winter coat. Dan hefted one of the sacks and wondered anew which girl had been able to lift it onto the table. "We'll be home as soon as possible."

"But you don't know when." Dotty's eyes were full of fear. "We'll pray for you both, your safety, and a good outcome."

"Don't worry." Timothy yawned. "We'll all come home safe. Albert, too."

And then they were out the door, down the Jackson Street hill, the snow squeaking its mid-tones under their feet. Dan did not ask Timothy how he felt. It would be a pointless question. By the set of the boy's jaw, he knew Tim was determined to help rescue Albert. When he hesitated at Daylight Creek, Dan would have carried his sack, but Timothy held him off with an upraised hand, and stepped swiftly and lightly as a dancer on each stone. At the last one, he leaped onto the well-traveled road that led into the Elephant Corral.

As they walked toward the gate, the boy told him, "The trick is not to linger."

Dan agreed. "If you go quickly, you won't slip."

They exchanged a smile of mutual understanding. Dan did not hear Timothy's reply, and for a moment he stumbled, though the way was level, his mind reeled at a realization: He and Timothy were becoming friends, man to man, more than stepfather and stepson, although there was that. Timothy McDowell was growing up.

Carol Buchanan

Walking through the gate into the yard at the Elephant Corral, Timothy joked through the scarf wrapped around his lower face. "For a miracle, at least we're not starting out with wet feet."

"Let's hope the miracles keep coming." Dan closed the gate behind them and dropped the rope loop over the section of swinging fence.

As he turned from the gate, X Beidler joined him. "We got us a crew."

Dan and Timothy followed X into the barn. Six or eight men stood in the narrow aisle between two rows of stalls facing each other, where Cooke & Company kept their blooded horses. Dan could not see each of the men clearly, strung out as they were in and out of the light of one lantern hanging on a stout nail.

"Here they are." X paused to spit a brown stream into a stall. "All friends or friends of friends. I've told them you're promising four dollars a day, from now until y'all return."

Dan raised his voice to be sure every man heard him. "That's right. Four dollars a day, with a bonus if we find our man alive."

Someone near the back of the group hollered, "How big will the bonus be?"

"I don't know yet, but the sooner we find him the larger it'll be."

"Sounds good to me," a man called out.

Another voice sounded from among the men. "What if we don't find him alive?"

Dan clenched his fists. "We won't go in with that attitude. We'll bring him out alive. That's all." He beckoned Timothy to come forward. "Tim McDowell will explain the situation."

While he'd been talking, he'd heard the door to the barn office open and close at the end of the aisle between two rows of stalls. Slipping between the group and the stalls, he headed toward Justus Cooke, one of the partners of the Elephant Corral.

Cooke, a lean man with a short beard, stood a couple of inches shorter than Dan. Quickly, he understood what was needed, and they reached an agreement satisfactory to both.

Then Cooke surprised Dan.

"Ryder tells me you intend to rescue Albert Rose?"

"That's right. Also, he has volunteered to come with us."

"From the little I know of him, that's what I'd expect." He stooped to pick something off the floor and squint at it before putting it into his pocket. "It's a good undertaking you're on. You'll be wanting provisions for the horses, and someone to drive them. I'll drive up and bring everyone home myself. Don't get me wrong. I trust the fellow with my best team. He's good with horses. He likes them and they like him, but the ladies need special handling."

"There'll be something extra for you, if you're willing to do this." Dan expected Cooke to drive a bargain, but the stable owner named a price so low that Dan wondered what sort of businessman he was.

In the next thought he doubled it without telling Cooke. "We'd best be on our way, if we want a full day to work."

"I'll bring up the ladies," Cooke tossed over his shoulder as he walked away.

The men, loading provisions onto the sledge, were minutes from getting underway when Dan heard Timothy, who watched something by the main gate, mutter something to himself.

Jacob Himmelfarb walked into the yard. Over his shoulder he carried a sack bulging with odd shapes – some round, some sharp-cornered. Cans of food. As though unaware of Dan's hard face, he headed straight for him until he stood well within range to be heard.

How the hell did he hear of this? Dan asked the air.

Two men reached to help him with his load, but he shook his head to warn them off and spoke as if he and Dan were the only two people in the yard. "Deputy Sheriff Beidler, he tells me of this rescue for Albert Rose. These are provisions." He adjusted his stance, the better to carry the sack. "I give them to you if I come and help find him. You, I think, may need another man."

The men – all of them, it seemed – watched Dan's reaction. In a town that loved gossip, he had to assume that everyone knew he and Jacob, who had been great friends, were on the outs, as people said.

Dan had no welcoming smile. He reached out to take the larger sack from Jacob. "We can use all the help we can get. Thank you, Jacob."

"Ja. Is good." Jacob came closer to Dan and tilted his body to slide the sack from his shoulder.

Taking it, Dan wondered how Jacob had managed to carry it even the short distance from his house to the Corral. No matter. It was all the apology he would get – all the apology he needed.

Over Jacob's shoulder, he caught sight of Timothy's thunderous face. As soon as possible, he would have to talk to him, tell him they couldn't hold grudges when another man's life was at stake.

And sometime very soon, when Albert was safe, he would brace Jacob on why he had not opened his door for Tim on such a desperately cold night. The excuse of serving God rather than man was not good enough.

21 ~~~

The Montana Post: 1/14/1865, p. 1.

The Timber of Montana — the Lumber Interest About Virginia

This mill is located in Granite gulch, about three miles east of Junction City. It is driven by water power, having a twenty-foot overshot wheel, and a circular saw. Under the skillful management of its present though-going proprietors, it is doing a better business than any other mill in the country. During the past season they have been laboring under the disadvantage of having a saw which was entirely too small, to remedy which, Mr. Spencer has gone to "America" to procure one of the proper dimensions. The mill on Stinking Water is also said to be a good one, but the timber there is reported to be inferior. In addition to these, there are other mills within the limits of the Virginia trade – on Mill, Meadow, and Indian creeks.

By calling it a road, Alder Gulch people gave the track upstream from Virginia City more dignity than it deserved. Two ruts in the ground meandered around stumps of trees. Standing alongside Justus Cooke, Dan held on tight to the front rail of the sledge. He liked any skillful way of going about a task, but until now he had never seen such skill in a driver as the Elephant Corral owner showed. Cooke maneuvered the 'ladies,' his two massive Percheron mares, so that they glided along the nearly invisible trace without incident. About a mile and a half from town, they came to a place where the snow deepened until it rose to the horses' knees, then rounded a wide bend that curved around the shoulder of a mountain.

Dan stared across the expanse of white and could not speak. The track had disappeared.

Before him lay a sweep of tumbled snow from a downed fir tree part way up the mountain into the creek. The avalanche had obliterated everything in its path. Gone was the settlement that had been here. Besides the usual saloon, it had been only three or four cabins occupied mainly by prospectors, but one family had lived behind a store.

Standing on the roof of a buried cabin, men dug furiously by a toppled chimney. Below, a silent woman paced a beaten path. She clutched a bundle to her bosom under her cloak and watched the men's progress as she walked a few yards, turned, and went back.

A Percheron stamped a front hoof and shook her head. Bells jingled on the ends of the hames, the curved metal rod attached to the horse's collar. Her mate whinnied. The men on the cabin roof looked up and appeared to have a conference.

"Whoa, there, girls." Justus Cooke tightened the reins. "This is as far as we go."

"We're in the right place." Standing on Cooke's other side, Timothy pointed toward the downed fir on the mountainside, some twenty or so yards away from the bank of Alder Creek. "There's the portal."

"Where?" Dan could see only the wide expanse of snow draped over the tree.

The horses stamped their feet and switched their tails. Steam rose from their shaggy hides.

"I think we're needed here." Cooke watched the woman as he spoke.

"It's all right, Mr. Cooke," Tim said. "The portal is under that dead tree." Tim pointed to the fir. "That tree got hung up on a boulder in a windstorm awhile back. The portal's about ten feet down."

"You'd never know anything was there." Vaughn Ryder shaded his eyes.

"We'd better work fast." Dan jumped down from the sledge. "Bring the tools and supplies, and let's get as close as we can." He hauled a bundle of shovels off the sledge and slipped the knot. The tools fell out into the snow. "Help yourselves."

As the men grabbed up the implements, Cooke tossed down more sacks. "Don't forget the provisions, boys. You'll need 'em before you're done." He set a final two sacks down gently, with a clink of glass. "Here's the most important ones of all." Seeing their puzzled faces, he laughed. "Beer, gentlemen. Beer. You can't save a man's life drinking only melted snow and weak tea."

He turned the horses toward the creek. "I'll be helping these folks. You need anything, holler."

"We will." As Dan turned to the work, Cooke beckoned to him. From under his driver's seat, he brought out a well-cushioned burlap bag and gave it to Dan. Though fairly heavy for its size, it made no sound.

"Take care of this, Stark," Cooke muttered. "It's two bottles of good single malt whisky. Glenlivet. It'll make a good celebration. Or a restorative."

Dan took the bag. "Celebration. I won't think of anything else. Thank you."

Cooke grinned at him. "Us New Yorkers gotta stick together in this benighted country. Best of luck to you. Me 'n the girls will be ready when you're done." He poked a thumb toward the back of the sledge, where a pile of hay had cushioned some of the men on the ride up. Nodding toward the toiling men of the settlement, he added, "We can help these people some. It looks like me 'n the girls" – patting an equine shoulder – "could be useful around here till you find your man." The horse gave him a playful nudge that nearly knocked him over. "Hey! Mind your manners." But he scratched the animal's forehead under the pale forelock.

"We've brought a short ton of supplies." Dan gestured toward the loaded sledge. "There'll be some to share." He tilted his head toward the group of men waiting for direction. "I'll talk to the others."

Smiling at the play of the man and his great gentle beast, Dan seized a shovel and hoisted it onto his shoulder. Low clouds squatted on the mountain, and big fluffy snowflakes floated down. He kicked at some snow. It lifted off, drifted away as though part of the air.

He joined the men clustered around Timothy. "You're lucky you got out of this, Tim. There's no purchase in this stuff."

Shovel in one hand, and carrying a sack of provisions over a shoulder, Ryder made his way over to the group. Snow lifted away from his shins as though he walked through a lake.

"Where's the target?" Dan asked Tim.

Tim pointed toward the downed tree. "Up there, almost. The mine entrance is about ten feet below that tree." He walked away without another word, leaving Ryder to gaze after him.

"Did I offend him?"

"Not that I know of. We're all determined to reach Albert quickly, while he's still alive." Dan hefted the sack of whisky. "Thanks for coming."

"Don't thank me." Ryder's smile held no humor. "I'm ashamed to say I came for the money."

Dan gave him a sharp once-over. "You look like you could use it."

"Yes. I wish I'd have come with a better conscience. I'm an abolitionist, and they tell me you are, too."

Timothy called, "Dan'l, let's get to work."

"That's true." With a quick nod to Ryder, Dan caught up to the other men.

He thanked each one and shook his hand. His friends among them had hunted down killers, and hanged them, and now they had come together to save a life. Looking into their eyes, he read their shared, secret knowledge.

One friend sidled up to him. "So you're paying us extra for finding the fellow alive, are you?"

When Dan nodded, he murmured, "That'll be a nice change."

Dan smiled, appreciating the unspoken dark humor. Someone thumped his shoulder. Jacob's smile was a twinkle in his eyes. For a moment, they were on the old footing.

"We save Albert." Jacob poked his thumb at his chest. "I have feeling."

"Let's hope your foresight is accurate."

From the head of the line, Timothy called him. "Dan'l, come up here and plot the most direct route to the mine. You're the surveyor, after all."

Turning to do as the boy asked, for a moment Dan regretted he did not have his compass and chain. Then he reflected that he wouldn't need them. He could plot the straightest line to the downed tree just by sighting on it.

Striding about a yard or two forward from where they stood, he pointed. "Dig straight to here."

Men bent to their tasks, some to shoveling snow, while two relief men brought up the supplies.

Catching sight of Ryder looking forlorn, Dan bent to his own work, digging an advance line. The greenhorn would have to get used to being left out of secrets.

~~~

The group of friends worked to clear a path to the unseen portal. They dug it wide enough for the team and sledge as Cooke hallooed the men on the cabin roof. Their unspoken idea, Dan reckoned, was to be prepared to carry Albert out.

They tossed snow as fast as they could. Although Dan heard some cheering behind him, he did not look up to confirm that Cooke's arrival with the powerful team had been hailed as a rescue. He only hoped that both groups would save their people.

His own group worked as if time were fast running out. Six men worked at the same time, flinging the snow outward. With no one directing them, they rotated in and out of the line as a man tired, rested, recovered, and took up a shovel again.

The closer they worked to the portal, the deeper and heavier the snow became.

Relieved for the second time, Dan wondered at the depth and weight of snow that had seemed so airy when they started. He estimated the remaining distance to the downed tree at perhaps eleven feet. The closer they came, the deeper the snow, and the slower the progress. At times they seemed to make no progress at all, shoveling snow from a pit rather than from a path.

Only the tree, thrusting against the boulder, held back the immense weight of a mountain of snow. If they could reach Albert without disturbing that balance, it would be a gift from Nature. Or God. He hoped as fervently as he had ever hoped for anything in his life that the tree's dense limbs would hold long enough to get Albert out of danger. If it gave way from the weight of snow on it – he couldn't finish the thought.

He went to spell one of his friends who looked about done in.

The man spat tobacco juice, and the yellow-brown stream made Dan's empty stomach edgy. "We could dig through this snow all the way to China and never get there."

Another friend retorted, "The way you're spittin' we won't be able to lift it nohow."

"We stand here talking, and we'll never get there." Dan bent to the work, found his muscles knew the rhythm of scoop, lift, toss. And again.

He called a halt when he judged the men were well past the half-way mark to the portal. They cleared a circle in the snow, brought up firewood, laid a fire. As it flamed up, each man took what he wanted from the food sacks, passed items around for whoever wanted them.

Cooperation, Dan realized. We learned it on the trail. No one had to give orders. We looked for what needed doing and did it.

Ryder, though, stood aside, as though he didn't know what to do.

"Help yourself," Timothy told him.

Even when he saw one or two stowing food in their coat pockets, Dan said nothing. There was plenty to eat and drink. When Cooke came up the trail, the friends shared a goodly portion of the supplies with him, for the victims of the avalanche. A couple of friends assured him they would have enough to feed Albert after they found him. Or – no. He stopped the thought. He would not imagine the worst.

The men hunkered down around the fire and talked. No one mentioned the reason for their hard work in the snow with temperatures moderating upward toward zero.

"Hey, Jack," one man called to a friend crouched across from him, whose red beard covered most of his chest. "You ever think of cutting that growth?"

"Nah." Jack patted the beard. "Keeps m' front warm. 'Sides, I swore I'd let it grow until I got rich enough to go back to civilization."

"Ha!" laughed another. "'You'll have to tie it up so's you don't walk on it."

Ignoring him, Mike reached toward the fire for a small branch to light his pipe. As he brought it toward the pipe, a glowing ember broke off and fell in the beard. Mike yelped and sprang back, slapping his chest to kill the sparks, as others snatched up snow and rubbed it into the hairs.

"That's enough!" Mike's voice rose to a high shriek. "You're getting me wet."

"Better wet than burned," said a tall, spare man.

Someone kidded Mike: "Wait till Dimsdale hears about this! You'll be famous. The first man ever to singe his beard in an avalanche."

"Didn't know you could sing, Mike," Dan said. Now that the man was safe with no serious burns, they all found the whole incident funny.

Mike wrung dirty, melted snow out of his beard. "Hah! You'd yell, too, was it you."

Ryder, with a cup of something and a two rough-cut pieces of bread holding a slab of meat, watched as if he'd never seen the like.

Then again, Dan reflected, probably men like us didn't walk the halls of his divinity school. Little did the greenhorn know, though, he was earning their respect by keeping quiet and working hard.

Jacob crouched next to Timothy. "Is very hard you work, yes? Maybe rest?"

Tim stared into the depths of the tin mug holding his tea and spoke through his teeth. "I got him into this. I gotta get him out."

"Ach. We get him out. Alive. I feel it."

Another of Dan's friends joined them. "That we will. You can bank on it."

Other men chimed in, "Never fear. If he's there, we'll have him out soon."

"Oh, he's there, all right." Tim pitched the last of his tea into the fire, stood up, and grabbed a shovel. Marching to the end of the path, he scooped out a shovelful and flung it as hard and far as he could.

Jacob shook his head and stood beside Dan. "I worry. Perhaps it is he strains something."

Dan was silent, thinking of something to say. If Jacob had really worried about Tim, he had chosen an odd way of showing it. "He's pretty much on his own now." The comment held a slur at Jacob, but Dan didn't care if Jacob might understand. Time was, they'd have had plenty to talk about, but Dan could think of nothing more to say. Finishing his insipid, lukewarm tea, he tossed the damp leaves out and went back to work.

Sometime later, he leaned on his shovel to catch his breath. The clouds lifted and scattered. The sun shone out of a deep blue sky from behind Baldy Mountain, yet the mountain was beginning its retreat into night, gathering shadows to drape around it. Still, some rays of the sun glanced off snow-shrouded evergreens, whose branches folded in on themselves from the snow's weight.

"Trees look like they're praying." Tim said as he took up a position next to Dan and pushed a shovel deep into the snow.

Ryder's tenor voice answered him. "Them and us both."

Some time later, when Dan took off his hat to wipe his forehead, he caught Ryder staring at the bandage. Hastily, he reset the hat.

"How did that happen?" Ryder asked. "Or am I not supposed to ask?"

Head down, Dan went on shoveling. "Your client tried to brain me about a week before the New Year."

"My client?"

"Keep your voice down. Yes. Tobias Fitch." Dan drove his shovel into the snow and hefted out a foot-high block of packed powder.

Thankfully, Ryder asked no more questions.

From the front of the line, Timothy called out. "We're getting close." Added, "How close, Dan'l?"

Dan measured the distances horizontal and vertical, with a practiced eye. "We've got about five more feet horizontal till we're at the portal." If it's still there, he added to himself. "Then what did you say, ten feet depth from the downed tree?"

"Yes. Maybe less."

Behind them the work of digging out the nearby settlement went on. A man shouted, "He's alive!" A cheer followed, seeming loud enough to shake snow from the trees.

A bit later, a woman's shriek broke into sobbing.

One of the friends said, "Oh, no, she's lost her little girl."

"God help them and us both," murmured Ryder.

As Dan tired, the digging took on a grim rhythm: bend, force the shovel under the snow, lift it, throw it. Each time, the load fell a bit shorter than the one before. His back cringed with every bend, and his shoulders complained at each throw.

The light changed, giving way to encroaching sunset. The shadows on the mountain's shoulder crept lower.

Studying the distance to the downed tree, now almost directly overhead, Dan estimated they were very close to the portal. Now, he said to himself, is the dangerous part. His head throbbed, but he pushed the headache aside, as a nuisance like a lapdog that wouldn't stop yapping.

Some time later, as darkness gathered, they had dug down and in to arrive at the portal. Knowing the adit entered the mountain beneath the boulder under the pine, Dan called a halt. Waiting for everyone to assemble around him, he found himself near to praying: God willing, the snow wouldn't shift, and the boulder would stay up where it belonged. God willing, the tree would stay blocked by the boulder.

Jacob, who had worked apart from Timothy and Dan, now came to Dan. "These men, they talk. It is, they want to save the man inside the mountain, but they are having for a room no money, and to go back now – it is too far."

Dan looked up at the darkening sky. "Tell them, Timothy."

"We're almost there." Stepping up to stand beside Dan, Timothy pointed at the tree leaning above them. He tossed a snowball up, and snow dislodged from an overhanging branch sifted down the back of his neck. He shuffled around in a weary sort of dance that had the effect he was after – some of the men laughed.

"That'll learn ya," called out one of the friends.

"The mine portal is just under the tree. The job now is to dig the snow away from the entrance without disturbing it. We don't know if the avalanche shifted the boulder, or loosened the tree, or —" He spread his hands apart, helpless to offer anything certain.

Dan decided to leave it to the men, how to risk their lives. "How do you think we should proceed?"

They argued among themselves, gestured upwards toward the tree, this way and that. One man, in favor of going straight in, put his hands together as if about to dive into a pond and thrust them forward. Others shouted him down.

"We could go up," Tim suggested, "and dig around the tree and the boulder before we start into the mine. Make dead sure it's stable up there. But if we tunnel in under it, the whole thing could come down on us."

Dan yelled over the clamor or voices, some for Timothy's idea, a few for quitting altogether. "We have to decide now and open the mine before the light's gone."

Dan waited while the men weighed their options against the life of the man inside.

Ryder spoke up louder than Dan had known he could. "We came to save a man's life. I say we go on in. I didn't come all this way to quit now."

As two or three men echoed him, Tim came to attention, stood straight and alert. "Do you hear it?"

Jacob whistled a shrill note for silence.

The quiet of a winter dusk was all around them, deepened as they listened.

"It's someone singing," one said.

"I don't hear it," another objected.

Tim stomped his feet. "Just listen, dammit."

Snow slid off the downed tree's branches and landed in the path. A cloud of snow billowed around them.

The men stared at each other, an unspoken wild question in their eyes: What if it all came down?

Dan heard, faintly, a baritone voice singing:

"Ona my knees when the light passed by,

Thank God I's free at last.

Thought my soul would rise and fly,

Thank God I's free at last."

Tim shouted, "Albert!! We're coming to get you!"

22 ~~~

The Montana Post: 1/14/1865, p. 2.

The Mineral Resources of Montana
**... Numbers of rich claims are almost
untouched. Anticipating the inevitable result
of the continued industry of multitudes,
Nature has pointed to the hills that enclose
it, and each day brings news of quartz lodes
discovered around and about it on all side**

Ryder yelled, "He's alive! He's alive! Let's get him out." Drew breath, bellowed, "Now!"

The mountain echoed, "*Now! ...ow!...ow!*"

"Yeah! Get him out now!"

"While he's still alive."

"Let's go!" shouted a voice at the back of the group.

Like some sort of giant machine not yet invented, the crew powered through the ever-deeper snow. Pausing only to spell each other, for a hot drink, a moment by the bonfire, they followed Timothy, who alone knew the exact location of the portal. The closer they came, the narrower and more direct a pathway, the deeper the snow, and the higher the walls of snow on either side of the path, well above their heads, and it was harder to throw the snow so high above themselves. They formed a line to pass snow back to where the last two men could throw it behind and to the side without blocking the way out.

Darkness dropped on them like a theater curtain. Bright stars shone in the sky, and the moon cast enough light for them to see their way.

Someone built up and relighted the fire. Others melted snow for tea. Dan drank hot water on a break, then traded his speckled tin cup for a shovel and went back to work.

Timothy broke through to the portal roof. Logs laid side by side, corduroy-style, those in the back were anchored in the mountain. He stomped on it. Two stout upright logs supported the front. They had not buckled under the snow's weight.

They cleared the roof, dug down to the ground, to mouth of the adit, the tunnel into the mountain.

Tim punched his shovel at the snow blocking the entrance, and nearly fell forward before Ryder grabbed his coat and held him. He caught his balance. Shouted, "We're in!"

Dan produced a packet of candles. He stood his shovel against the adit wall and struck flint and steel into his tinder box to light a candle. Jacob stood behind him as he and Tim walked into the mine and shone the quivering light around the chamber.

Albert lay with his back to a wall of the adit, curled into himself, knees drawn up, hands between them.

"Albert," said Dan. "Get up. We've come to take you home."

Albert sat up, rubbed his eyes, squinted at the candle lights wobbling in men's lanterns. "I's ready, Lord."

"I'm not the Lord." Laughing, Dan knelt beside him. "Far from it. It's me. Dan Stark."

Albert jerked fully awake, stared at Dan. "Mistah Stark, be it you? Truly you?"

"Yes, Albert."

Dan and Timothy helped him to his feet. He blinked at them as though alien beings had dropped from the night sky. Unable to speak, Dan nodded and squeezed Albert's upper arm.

"Mistah Timothy? Be you Mistah Tim?"

"Yes, Albert. I'm Timothy." Tim's voice shivered.

Albert whispered, "I thought I's a goner. I just laid m'self down and waited for the Lord to pick me up. But y'all picked me up, not Him."

"Didn't you hear me shout that we were coming to get you?"

"It sounded like angels." Albert freed his hand from Timothy's grasp and brushed both hands over his face, stared at Timothy, Jacob, Dan, and the other men who crowded around. Last, he spoke to Dan. "Y'all white folks, and you come to get me."

Behind him, Dan heard murmurs from some of the men. The men had come to see for themselves the state Albert was in, to know if their efforts succeeded or not. Their feet shuffled over loose stones that rattled away amid puffs of dust, as they crowded around. For the first time they saw the point of all their labor for – it must be – thirteen or fourteen hours.

"All these white men?" whispered Albert.

A voice from the crew rose in disbelief. "He's Colored! We dug tons of snow for —"

"We saved a man's life! You hear that?" Other voices rose at once.

Ryder forced himself to the front of the group. "He's a man, and we saved his life! That's what matters. Not his skin. Not one bit."

Still holding Albert's arm, because he was not certain if Albert could keep himself upright, Dan half turned to face them. "Don't worry," he told the man who objected to Albert's skin color. He used the courtroom voice he kept for heaping scorn on opponents in lawsuits. "You'll get your pay, same as if he was white."

He reached into first one of his trousers pockets and then the other and brought out two pokes. The contents clinked together, the peculiar dull metallic sound of gold. "Jacob, you're a banker. Pay the gentlemen, please." Louder, the scorn gone, he said, "You've all done a miraculous thing today. You've moved tons of snow to save a man's life. That's something you can carry to your graves, and maybe for some of you –" looking at the faces of his friends "– just maybe, it makes up for some of what had to be done a year ago."

Jacob walked through the group, dropping a five-dollar bit of a twenty-dollar gold coin – a Double Eagle – into each hand. He'd had several Double Eagles cut into fourths some time back. Just in case.

Albert said, "I'd like to shake the hands of them as saved me."

Dan and Timothy stood aside for all who wanted to shake a Colored hand. Ryder was the first to grasp Albert's hand. Most of the others shook hands as well, but Dan marked the two took their pay from Jacob and sidled away.

Dan turned his back on them. They could walk to Virginia.

~~~

Albert munched on jerky and bread, washed down with beer. When Dan mentioned leaving for home, Albert shook his head. "No, sir. Not yet. I gots somethin' to show you."

Following Albert, who carried a candle, Dan, Jacob, and Timothy, with Ryder behind them, went farther into the mine, to where the new drift branched off from the adit. Rocks and stones, a few of them big enough to qualify as boulders, stood on the floor of the drift, but Albert walked around them and led them a few feet farther in.

"You were busy, Albert."

"Yes, sir." Among these white men, Albert dropped the slave talk and sharpened his R's. "I was busy. I had nothin else to do but dig. And sleep."

He raised the candle high. "Look here."

Timothy whistled a long, low note.

As though a warm cape settled around Dan's shoulders, a scrap of poetry came to mind, something about the 'mantle of satisfaction.' but even wracking his brains, he could not recall where he'd read it.

In the candlelight, the quartz wall glowed. Threads of gold laced through pale, translucent quartz, so dense as to be nearly a solid mass of gold embedded in the crystal.

Timothy wiped the back of his hand across his eyes. "I never seen nothing so beautiful."

Jacob hummed low in his throat, nodded from the waist.

Reaching somewhat upward, Dan grasped Albert's shoulder.

"You were the first man ever to see this, this – " His throat closed on the word he needed. He cleared his throat, tried again. "This wall." His eyes filmed over, and it was a little time before he could speak.

Ryder whispered, "What is it?"

"Gentlemen." Dan's throat closed. He coughed. Swallowed. Cleared his throat. "Gentlemen, we have a lode."

23 ~~~

The Montana Post: 1/14/1865, p. 3:

Hugh O'Neil's Benefit

The friends of this courageous and popular
professor of the "manly art" have
determined to give him a monster benefit, in
token of their appreciation of the gallant
efforts and unflinching courage displayed by
him in his late encounter with Con Orem.
Hugh O'Neil is very popular with a large
class of the inhabitants, and they are
determined to make up for him a sum
sufficient to leave him on the sunny side of
"square" instead of in debt. The donation
will be presented on the 22d inst., at
Nelson's Leviathan Hall. Hugh will handle the
gloves himself, assisted by all the "knights of
the knuckle.

Riding back to Virginia City on Justus Cooke's
sledge, Dan gazed at the dark sky. Stars shone so bright
and close he might almost pluck one from the heavens.

He felt as if he held a star in his hands, something
very few men even in this golden country had ever
done. Tim's rock was not granite, nor even a boulder.
It was a lode.

Standing beside Cooke, he gripped the front rail as
the mares plodded on with the careful certainty of
knowing the way home to shelter and their feed.

As I do, Dan thought. What news to share with Martha. How would she take it, her mind these days centering all on the babies, keeping them warm and fed and clean? Picturing the twins, those tiny morsels of his and Martha's joining, he shivered. If he guided this thing right, this mine development, none of the family would ever have to worry about their next meal or a warm bed. Or know the humiliation of strangers carting away their possessions.

Behind him, Albert, Timothy, Ryder, and Jacob sprawled on a pile of hay much smaller than they had brought. The rest of the men had gone ahead on a second sledge as soon as they were paid, before Albert had shown them the wall. They could be halfway home by now.

One of the sledge runners lifting over a buried stump threw the men off the hay pile. Ryder landed on the floor of the sledge, slid forward and sideways, arms flailing as he tried to grab the side rail. Holding onto it, Timothy seized a leg while Dan snatched a fistful of his coat collar. Together, holding onto the side and front rails, they set him on his feet and held him there while he regained himself.

Dan met Timothy's eyes across Ryder's back. Dan mouthed the words, "Too thin," and saw the boy nod. This man was far too light a weight for his height and the breadth of his shoulders.

Another lurch, and Dan fought for his footing, rued the blow on his head that made balancing on the sledge questionable at best.

He did not care.

He had seen the lode.

"You fellas are mighty quiet, for a bunch that's dug a man's life out of a mountain." Cooke ruffled the reins on the horses' backs. "You look like you've seen the Holy Grail."

When Dan kept his silence, Ryder answered, "We shifted a lot of snow in a very short time."

"You're good at shoveling loads from here to there."

Ryder laughed. "I do enough of it for you. Shoveling manure was good practice, but snow is cleaner."

"Colder, though," Timothy said.

"Lighter," put in Jacob.

The men batted the joke back and forth across Dan, but he registered the joshing as he would track the ball in a game of tennis, which had not interested him.

His first sight of the wall held him in a kind of rapture, with its golden shimmer and its surface like fragile gossamer in the lantern light. It was neither gossamer nor fragile, but quartz was stone as granite was stone, yet of a different order of rock. And now all five of them – himself, Tim, Jacob, Ryder, and Albert – had seen it. They all knew the Nugget would be a lode mine. And knowing that, especially Ryder knowing it without an incentive to keep it secret, all of Alder Gulch would know it by breakfast tomorrow.

Or today? Whatever, it was impossible to keep any news from spreading into the various settlements, camps and gulches. Not only would people talk, but the *Montana Post* would publish the results of any scrap of gossip, especially if it had anything to do with discovering another lode, and the world would know they had struck it rich before they had a sample assayed.

Rich. They would be rich. Very rich. How rich would depend on many unknowns —

Thought stopped, as though he had developed a catch in his breathing.

Fitch.

Ryder would tell Abbott. Abbott would tell Fitch.

Fitch would use any means necessary to get the Nugget. Any at all.

He will not succeed, Dan told himself. Tobias Fitch will not possess a flake of Nugget gold, no matter what I have to do to stop him.

Fitch would not own even a crumb of dirt from the mine, he vowed. Never.

He drew a cross-hatch on one palm with the other middle finger.

From higher up, a mountain lion screamed.

The horse on Dan's side of the sledge shied, stumbled. The sledge veered toward the creek.

Dan grabbed at the rail he'd let go. Missed. The ice-bound creek rose up toward his face.

Hands seized his coat, his arm, and pulled him onto the sledge as it righted itself.

"All right?" Cooke glanced over his shoulder.

He had come so close to breaking his neck. "Just fine, but your horses don't like big cats." Why did his voice sound so steady, when he felt like a dried leaf in the wind?

The stable-keeper laughed. "Who does?"

Timothy held onto him. "Blast it, Dan'l. You can't go swimming this time o' year. The water's too hard."

"Ja," came Jacob's voice. "It is, how you say, 'schade'?" When no one answered him, "Bad. Very bad. Swimming now bad idea."

Dan put his hand out, around Timothy, to grasp Jacob's arm as he stood behind them. Jacob's English was better than this, and only a big emotion could have made him forget it. "I'm all right. If I had found the water a little hard, I could only blame myself. I was woolgathering."

"What is this wool?"

Ryder spoke to Jacob in German, and they struck up a conversation. Dan caught the word Gettysburg and decided Ryder was explaining how he had learned the language. Growing up in Gettysburg? Attending seminary lectures in German? Dan made a mental note to ask him sometime.

Albert stood at Dan's left, against the rail. "Anyone test the water 'round here, it be me, suh." The deep South accent blended with the other voices, all soft as though they might disturb the night, and the warmth of all four – he had to count Ryder in this – standing close to prevent another incident, gave Dan a peace he had not known since the night at Beaverhead Rock, when Fitch had tried to kill him.

He would fight Tobias Fitch. He would win. He had won that night, and he would have help to win again. His being here, now, proved that. Fitch would not steal the Nugget.

Timothy rested his hand on Dan's shoulder.

Yes, he would win. The futures of too many people depended on him. He had to win for Timothy. For Dotty. For Martha. For the entire family.

His mind raced, calculating possibilities. Probabilities. Perhapses.

The horses walked on. Snow muffled the scratch and scrape of their shod hooves.

Cooke drew rein. "Listen."

Music. Someone played a fiddle. The hairs on Dan's arms lifted as he remembered: music in the night, and himself standing outside a brightly lighted house. Through the undraped windows, he'd watched men in cutaway coats squire beautifully dressed women through the intricate steps of a quadrille. "How much farther do you think?"

"Another half hour, God willing." He swung an arm toward the sound. "But be on the lookout. This part of the creek," – he pronounced it 'crick' – "it's been worked over more'n higher up."

The horses moved out at a brisker walk before Cooke gave the signal. He lowered his voice, speaking to Dan. "Thanks to y'all, we don't have to look out for road agents."

"This cold would discourage them in any case."

Cooke laughed. "Maybe so. But better a sure thing than a maybe." He spoke louder. "This was another good day's work."

"You did a good day's work, too," said Ryder.

"Thank you kindly, but I had the ladies to help me."

"You saved another couple of lives and dug out a shack or two." Ryder meant to give a man his due.

"But the poor woman who lost her little girl. I hated to see that."

"You tried to save her, and that counts," Ryder insisted.

One of the horses whinnied, and the discussion ended as Cooke called out, "Easy does it, girls, easy does it."

Dan was grateful no one had mentioned Slade, hanged by the Vigilantes nearly two years before – at the Elephant Corral. That had been their most terrible duty. Along with Rawley. Dan shuddered. Let there never be another like them. Although he'd make an exception for Fitch — gladly.

Cooke interrupted his dark thoughts. "As for you, Stark, you'll be thanking me plenty."

Albert sang, "Rock-a my soul in the bosom of Abraham." He hummed a bit and came back strong: "I once was lost, but now I'm found, and now my soul is Heaven bound. Oh, rock-a my soul."

Ryder called to him, "Albert, what have you got to praise the Lord for, anyway, being poor as a church mouse?"

Albert's laugh boomed out. "I thought I's a goner, and here I am, ridin' home with y'all. Ain't that enough?"

Tim answered him, "Seems like it to me. Maybe we all ought to sing it."

Maybe we should, Dan said to himself. So many things could have gone wrong, but they all rode home.

Cooke's horses nickered and quickened their pace almost to a trot.

The trail rose, turned a corner, became Idaho Street, and they drove past the Court House. At Jackson Street Cooke reined the team downhill past the Planter's House Hotel. On the opposite side of the street, the Champion Saloon was shut tight, but from another saloon tinny music from a piano permanently out of tune filtered into the night.

Dan's house, in the middle of the block, lay in darkness. Not a light shone from any crack between the drapes. He wondered how the family slept, and wished he could shout out the great news: We're all safe and alive. And soon very rich.

~~~

Crossing Wallace, the horses bunched their hindquarters, slowing the sledge as Cooke tromped his boot on the brake to help them.

"Lemme jump off here." Albert put both hands on the side rail as though to vault it. "I's home."

"No. You could get hurt," Cooke shouted. The sledge bumped off Wallace onto the steep slope. "Hang on!"

In three or four strides, it seemed to Dan, the horses brought the sledge sailing down lower Jackson toward Daylight Creek, the brake shrieking all the way, so that Dan wished he could free his hands to cover his ears. At the bottom of Jackson, where Cover Street shared the gully floor with Daylight Creek, the horses' weight broke through the ice, and they splashed through the water, trotted up the bank and into the stable yard.

"Whoa, there. Whoa, ladies."

The horses stopped.

Grasping the rail, Albert vaulted over, landed both feet on the ground. The other men followed however they could, eager to be someplace warm – their own cabin or in a friendly saloon. As a yawning roustabout set about helping Ryder unhitch the horses, Dan told Cooke, "I'll be along tomorrow to settle our bill."

"Come day after tomorrow," returned the stable-keeper. "I'll have it figured out by then."

Dan smiled to himself. Cooke might tack on a generous extra percentage, but he deserved it. He had never quibbled about Albert's color, he'd come along himself rather than sending an employee, and he'd used his best team to help both Dan's crew and the buried settlement. All in all, the man was worth his hire and then some.

Dan turned away from Cooke to head for the gate and found Jacob nearly beside him among the general hurry to be anywhere else, out of the cold. He had nothing to say to Jacob, but he needed his banker's assistance. "I'll have to convert coin into dust, Jacob. Tomorrow. For the bonuses."

"Feel light." Jacob made as if to step around Dan.

Dan knew the word was the German, "*Vielleicht,*" and meant, "Perhaps."

Dan's weary temper frayed. "I can go somewhere else. I want to pay him."

"Ah, but tomorrow. Is already the Sabbath. Come next day."

"Jacob, today is Thursday. Your Sabbath doesn't start until sundown tomorrow."

Stopping in his tracks, so that a man behind nearly bumped him, Jacob stared at Dan. "Is so?"

One of the men who had helped free Albert stopped. "Mr. Stark is correct. Today is Thursday." Brushing around them, as they stood in the middle of the gateway, he hurried out of the gate and tossed over his shoulder, "Your Sabbath doesn't start until sundown tomorrow."

"Ja. So. Tomorrow you come? Friday? We make exchange then."

"Good. I'll see you tomorrow afternoon, then."

"Before sundown, ja?" Jacob turned toward Cover Street and his house.

"Before sundown," Dan called after him. Jacob plodded through the gate without giving a sign that he had heard.

Shaking his head, Dan turned toward the creek, where Timothy waited, but on a sudden impulse, he swung back. Justus Cooke led one of the Percherons toward well-earned oats. Ryder lifted the collar from the other horse as a roustabout held her by a lariat around her neck.

As Cooke disappeared into the barn with the horse, Dan asked Ryder, "Do you have a place to sleep?"

"Mr. Cooke lets me sleep in the hayloft."

So that accounted for him wearing all his clothes at once. The hayloft door yawned wide above them. Dan imagined how cold the loft would be, even if Ryder burrowed into the dwindling hay pile with all his clothes and a couple of wool blankets. "I'll see about that. Wait here."

Catching up to Cooke, he spoke softly so that no one else would hear them. "I want to steal your helper. He worked hard today, and he could use a good meal and a decent night's sleep in a warm room."

"Fine by me. If he worked harder and more hours here, I'd pay him, and he'd find lodging somewheres else besides my hayloft." Cooke tilted his head to one side, as though listening to an echo of his voice. "I keep him on because he's good with horses. Has the makings of a real horseman." Another pause. "Horses like him, you know. You can always tell."

Dan thanked Cooke, and let Ryder know he was to come with him.

"As soon as I see Rosie bedded down," the younger man said.

"Be quick about it, then." Dan joined Timothy and Albert, who stamped their feet and swung their arms in a futile effort to get warm. "I'm bringing young

233

Ryder home with us, so he can get a decent meal and warm place to sleep. We'll take you home, Albert, and then we'll head on up to my place."

Albert said, "Best we all get something in our stomachs, Mistah Stark. I bet Miz Hudson won't abide you-all leavin' hungry." A jerk of his head toward Ryder, walking toward them. "Him neither."

24 ~~~

The Montana Post: 1/14/1864, p. 2.

Local and Other Items

Water Rate. We see that the proprietors of
water works have been making their rounds
among those using water from the hydrants.
No men deserve their pay better, and we
hope their enterprise will be rewarded by
the prompt liberality of the citizens

"Go away!" Mrs. Hudson's strident voice shrilled
from inside the Eatery moments after Dan pounded on
the door. When he hammered again, she hollered
again, "Go away, or we'll let the dog loose."

"She sounds scared," Timothy muttered.

Albert put his mouth close to the sliver of a crack in
the door where planks of green wood had pulled apart
as they dried. "Gen'ral!" he bellowed.

A long, quavering howl erupted inside, and a
powerful body thumped against the door.

"Down, General!" yelled the woman.

The dog howled and scratched at the door.

"Jiminy!" Timothy shouted. "He'll dig through that
door!"

"Gen'ral!" roared Albert. "Down!" All quieted inside
the Eatery. More calmly, Albert said, "Miz Hudson, it be
me. Albert. I's back and freezin' my nose off. I got

Mistah Dan'l and Mistah Timothy and – we be cold. Let us in. Please."

The shivering men heard the bar removed from its brackets, and the door opened just enough to let a man in, but on the principle that what can come in can also go out, General barged through the gap, knocked the door wide open. Barking, tail thrashing, the dog flung himself at Albert. Man and dog rolled off the boardwalk into the piled-up snow, that billowed up around Dan, Tim, and Ryder as they stood on the boardwalk.

"Get off a me, you misbegotten mutt!" Albert could hardly speak for laughing.

Dan jumped down, Tim close behind him. Together they pulled the dog off Albert. Timothy held the dog's collar in a tight, two-handed grip, while Dan helped the bigger man to his feet.

Mrs. Hudson and Tabitha clung to each other, offering advice and scolding the men and the dog at the same time in a storm of sound no one understood.

Once free, Albert stepped up on the boardwalk, Dan close behind him.

"What do I do with General?" Tim stayed in the street, struggled to hold on to the dog, more than a hundred pounds of squirming determination. "I can't hold —" Breaking free, General bounded onto the boardwalk.

Tim threw up his hands as if to say, I give up, I tried. Dan reached out and gave him a hand up onto the walkway.

"Come in, come in," Mrs. Hudson held the door open for them. "Tabby, do let's fix something hot for these men."

Tabitha stood as if frozen to the spot. Tears flowed down her face. "Oh, Albert, we was so afeared."

"Wasn't for Mistah Stark and Mistah Tim, and – and Mistah…" Giving up on Ryder's name, Albert spooned up another mouthful of piping hot bear meat stew, left from the nooning and reheated for them. "Anyway, wasn't for them, I'd be dyin' slow in that hole in the mountain."

"It wasn't just us. Others helped. And you didn't give up." Dan chewed mightily on a chunk of gristle, then abandoned the effort as being too hard on his jaw muscles.

Pretending a coughing fit, he leaned away from Timothy, ducked down below Mrs. Hudson's view, and spat the partly chewed gristle out under the table. It landed about an inch from the sleeping dog's nose. Hardly waking, General snapped it up and laid his head down again on his paws.

By her tense shoulders and the continual frowning glances she sent Ryder's way, Dan imagined Mrs. Hudson awaited an opportunity to pounce on his identity and turn it inside out until nothing remained but lint in his pockets.

"We should talk about the mine." Leaving the idea lie on the table, Dan sipped his coffee, black and strong, the way he liked it. "We're all weary tonight, but in brief, Albert discovered something while we were shoveling snow." Pointed his spoon. "Tell them, Albert."

"Mistah Timothy's boulder, ma'am." Albert spoke to Mrs. Hudson as if he and the women were the only people in the room. "It's not a nugget. Not a rock. Not a boulder, neither." He paused, and Dan wondered if he enjoyed the way his employer seemed fit to burst before he finished, "It's a wall."

His eyes misted, and he broke off to collect himself. "When that avalanche come down, there I was inside the portal, and first thing I knew, when Mistah Timothy went out to find our snowshoes, the snow had got him, and nobody'd know I was trapped there in the mine, like Jonah in the whale. I 'member thinkin I'd die there, but then I decided I wouldn't be a'dyin' yet, so I might's well do somethin' while I was at it. We had a small pile of timbers, leastways that's how it seemed to me, and all the tools and matches and candles was there, so I started diggin'." He spooned up more stew and chewed on the meat while he considered.

Tabitha nudged him. "You eatin' in front of white folks."

Dan smiled. "It's all right, Mrs. Rose. Let Albert tell the story in his own time. I haven't heard it all before, nor has Timothy."

"I don't have much of a story, only that I'd hack away at what was coverin' Mistah Tim's boulder until I had to stop, for one thing and another."

It would have been slow, tedious, hard work, Dan imagined. Every time Albert swung the pick up into the ceiling of the new drift, he would be afraid the whole mountain would come down on him, like those two men the *Post* reported on last week. And if that had happened, who would have found him? Who would have known where to look, considering that Albert believed the snowslide had killed Timothy?

Ryder put his spoon in his empty bowl and left it there.

Tabitha laid her hand on Albert's, resting on the table.

"You didn't think you'd be found till spring," Dan heard himself whisper.

Wordlessly, Albert nodded.

Meeting his eyes, Dan read the fear he had fought, along with battling the mountain. He had felt a slow death coming, by starvation or thirst, and the mine his tomb, because in his slave's experience white men did not rescue people of color. Did he chop at the mountain, thinking to go beyond the timbering in hopes a shift in the earth would kill him quick?

Albert had known uncertainty. The men the Vigilantes hanged had known certainty. They had felt death. The long, twisted knot in the rope chafed the skin of their necks.

Dan ground his teeth against the sudden burn in his throat.

Ryder whispered, "Dear God in heaven."

Mrs. Hudson shushed at him, and Albert seemed to awaken. He took up his story.

"I kept goin' until I had two, maybe three candles left, and I shined one of 'em around to see what I'd cleared." He swallowed, looked down at Tabitha's thin hand resting on his own, and interlaced his fingers with hers. "That's when I saw it. The wall. Miz Hudson, it's quartz crystal, only so full of gold threads it looks to be solid gold. Almost. Mistah Stark can tell you. It's real."

To clear his throat, Dan drank a sip of coffee. "Yes, Albert. You showed it to us. It is really a gold wall. It's a lode. You took an almighty chance, clearing it, though."

Struggling to speak, Albert said, "I decided, why not? What else was I goin to do in that cave? Wait to die? No, suh." He squeezed his wife's hand. Her fingertips dug into his skin. "When I saw that wall, I took the candle and went out to the portal and waited. I reckoned I'd get me some shuteye, so I built a small fire and – and ..." His voice stopped. He blew out a breath. Inhaled.

They waited while he gathered himself to finish. "I slept more'n I thought I would, and then I woke up and heard angels singin'. That's when I sang about bein' free at last, on account the angels come to get me, and I'd be free of earthly trials." He laid his free hand on Tabitha's and looked into his wife's eyes. "I purely was hatin' to leave you."

"Those weren't angels, Albert. Far from it. They were us." Timothy waved his spoon at Dan, Ryder, and himself. "We came to get you, but not to go to heaven. Bring you home."

"Yassuh, Mistah Tim. Only angels with wings never looked as good as you-all."

Silence reigned among them until the dog snored, then gulped, followed by a woof.

"Speaking of home —" Looking to escape, Dan started to say it was high time they left, but Mrs. Hudson interrupted him.

"Mister Stark, I've been thinking as we've sat here tonight. If thee still want investors, I'm willing to join in. Albert's experience has shown me I – I've been —"

She breathed deep, as though before – what? – leaping into a quarry?

In a rush she finished, "Albert's experience has shown me I've been wrong."

Surprised out of thought, Dan stared at her. Mrs. Hudson had never in his acquaintance with her admitted that she might be or could be or was wrong. Not about anything.

"I've been wrong about the mine, but mostly, I've been wrong about thee." Pointing her index finger at him, she insisted, "Mind, I don't hold with breaking even a single jot of one of the Commandments, and thee have run roughshod over all of them except numbers four, seven, and eight. Thee are not a liar. And thee have a well of kindness I've seen in thy rescue of Eileen, and in thy care for everyone in thy family,

241

including this young man." She swung the pointing finger at Timothy. Lowering her hand to her lap, she swallowed. After a moment, she went on. "I do not change my mind that breaking the Fifth Commandment, 'Thou shalt not murder,' is a sure route to perdition. Thee are prone to violence, and violence is anathema to the Lord, but" —" She took a moment, as though she could not herself believe what she was saying. "Thee do not lie."

Dan's mind moved as through sludge, searching for something to say. True to form, Mrs. Hudson could not speak of him without accusing him, and he did not know how to thank her for her testimony about his truthfulness or object – as so often – to her calling him a violent man.

He had helped to hang only those who had robbed or killed others.

Mrs. Hudson took a breath. "Besides, thee has rescued a valuable man." She nodded toward Albert. "Perhaps not in many people's eyes, but in the eyes of God, who made all men in his image. Albert thinks I rescued him and Tabitha from the slave catchers, but on our journey here they rescued me. If not for his skills with fixing the wagon and caring for the animals and keeping his quiet bearing, we would not have arrived here safely. For both Tabitha and me, thee has rendered a great service. 'Thank thee' is too small a thing to say, but it's the only thing I have that fits. Thank thee."

Dan had no words. He sat dumbfounded, his mind reeling as from a shock. He could not grasp that Mrs. Hudson had thanked him for saving Albert.

She had disliked him from the moment they met two years before, and even a few days ago she had let him know she harbored no good feelings toward him. Dan had never imagined he would hear her admit to being wrong about him.

At last, after a second, or an hour, he found his voice. "Thank you, Mrs. Hudson. Perhaps when Albert has recovered from his ordeal, we can talk about the future of the Nugget."

"Tomorrow be fine," said Albert.

"Yes. Tomorrow afternoon, when we've finished cleaning up." Mrs. Hudson went to stand near the stove. The light of a candle on a wall sconce nearest the stove revealed a different face on the woman. Without her habitual frown upon seeing him, her face revealed the pleasant young woman she had been when Dr. Hudson first proposed marriage.

"All right, then, tomorrow it is. At my office." He stopped, struck by a sudden realization of how much he had yet to do. How much he had to learn. How to apportion shares in the mine? How would men pay for their shares? Sweat equity or cash money? Dust or Federal greenback? How much to discount the greenback? Because it couldn't be at par with dust, let alone coin.

What to tell Martha, in her current, broken-down state? She worried too much as it was, about the babies, about Timothy, the girls. Him.

A nudge in his side.

"Wake up, Dan'l. It's time to get on home." By the sound of his voice, Tim held back a laugh.

"I'm awake. I've been thinking."

As he pulled his coat around his shoulders, a new question assailed him: What about Ryder?

An overwhelming weariness swamped him, so that he ached to curl up with General. Tomorrow. He would leave all this – the mine, paying the men, money – for tomorrow.

"I'll be on my way, too." Ryder rose to the half crouch necessary to leaving the table. "Thank you for the meal, Mr. Stark. Mrs. Hudson." His nod to her was almost a bow.

"Where to?" Timothy half-growled at Ryder, but looked at Dan, who tried to think how they would fit a stranger into their little cabin, already overcrowded as it was with five full-sized people and two infants.

Timothy said, "We've got three good cooks at home." After a short silence, he added hastily, "Not like you'd get here, but...."

Mrs. Hudson's lips tightened, and her frame stiffened, so that, recalling the tirades she had visited on him, Dan felt sorry for Tim.

But her frown dissolved into a merry giggle that surprised him. "So you do, young Mr. McDowell. So you do. You have excellent cooks at your house. Especially your mother."

To Ryder she explained. "Mrs. Stark – Mrs. McDowell as she was then – took reading lessons from me after her children – Timothy here, and his little sister Dorothy – bought her a Bible for Christmas two years ago. She insisted on paying me, so I asked her to bake her dried apple pies for me to sell here. When she had baked enough pies to settle what she felt was her debt – although in truth I had made far more from selling her pies by the piece, and I never wanted to charge her for anything – she taught me how to make them."

"The best apple pie in Alder Gulch," Dan said. He gathered himself to leave. "Ryder, you'll come home with Tim and me. We don't have much, but the stoves keep us all warm." Feeling Tim watch him, he added, "That is, if Tim has kept the wood boxes filled." He rose with Tim following close behind him, to take his greatcoat off its peg. "And yes, my wife is a very good cook."

Somewhat shaky, Albert rose with Dan and Timothy. "We can talk when you wish, Mistah Stark. For me, I be ready after a good sleep."

Ryder stood up slowly, like a much older man. Though he kept his face turned toward the tabletop, Dan noticed a sheen of unshed tears as he nearly tripped over the bench. Safely standing on his own two feet, the young man met Dan's eyes, his own shining through unshed tears.

That would have been all the thanks Dan needed, even if Ryder had not managed to rasp, "Thank you."

Tim laughed. "Wait'll you wake up to thank Dan'l. You ain't met the twins yet."

25 ~~~

Montana Post: 1/14/1865, p. 1.

PLANTER'S HOUSE

Corner of Idaho and Jackson Sts., Virginia City, Montana Territory

Wm. & John A. Shoot

(Formerly of the Planter's House, Hannibal Mo.)

Proprietors

The above named house, formerly conducted by Wm. Sloan, Esq., having been itlarged (sic) and re-fitted is now open with every facility for the accommodation of guests and Boarders. Comfortable rooms and beds are provided and the table is carefully furnished with the best the market and seasons afford.

"Who is that man?"

Martha's fierce whisper shivered to the bottom of Dan's stomach. Although it was midafternoon, he had not yet eaten. Sleep had come first, and getting warm.

"Who is he?"

They faced each other in their bedroom, crowded between the bureau and an outside wall, as far from the door as the room's sparse length allowed. For the sake of the sleeping twins, they whispered, but Martha's hissing anger bit as hard as if she shouted.

Not letting him answer her, she raised her voice to just below normal speaking volume. "You come home in the middle of the night with a strange man into a household of women and babies? Who is he?" Fists doubled on her hips, she waited for him to answer.

"I – I'm not sure."

By a tightening of her lips, a raised eyebrow, she let him know her opinion of that answer. She waited.

"He's an assistant to Harold Abbott, the president of the Virginia City Bar."

"So?" Into that one syllable she packed all her scorn for Hal Abbott, and for lawyers in general. This time, Dan understood, she would not exempt her own husband.

"He signed on to help rescue Albert Rose. He did his share of the hard work, and he didn't object to Albert's color."

"That's all you know of him?" Unspoken lay an accusation of failure in his most important task as a husband and father — protecting the family. Bringing a strange man into this cabin, among females and infants, did not protect them.

Dan mustered what he knew of Vaughn Ryder. "He has no place to stay. He's been sleeping in Justus Cooke's loft. He's too thin. I think he hasn't been eating enough." If he'd considered letting her know his surmises about Ryder would gain her sympathy, he was mistaken.

Martha crossed her arms under her bosom. "Wake him up. Before he stays another minute in this house, we have to know who he is. Even wasters and their children can go hungry in the winters here."

As she had probably intended, Dan recalled a gambler's six children. Clad only in thin cotton shifts and shirts, and desperately hungry, they had gone begging in December. And they had knocked at the best door. Pamelia Fergus and other kind-hearted wives and mothers – including Martha – had found warm clothing and food for all of them.

"All right. I'll wake him up."

"When he's up and about, come get me. I want to make sure for myself if he's safe to let in."

What that said about his judgment Dan did not want to hear. Martha was the gentlest of women until her children were at issue. As he shut the door behind him, he faced three young people – Dotty, no, Dorothy as she demanded to be called now, Timothy, and Eileen – clustered between the table and the washstand. They left off murmuring to each other and turned toward him. They might well have heard every word, even though the twins – thank the good Lord – had slept through Martha's storm. Attempting a smile, he summoned Timothy. Together they went to rouse Ryder.

Snow had drifted into the path to the necessary and seeped onto the shelf inside the little building.

Ryder said, "This cold is enough to make you constipate yourself not to come out here."

249

Laughing, Dan and Timothy buttoned their trousers. Outside, they tramped small circles around each other to keep warm. Timothy spoke softly. "Mam has a powerful way of making herself known when she wants to."

A rueful smile in his voice, Dan said, "She certainly does. Since the twins came, she's turned into a mother bear with cubs. But she has a point. We have to hear his story. Otherwise ..."

Ryder emerged then, and they returned to the house.

Inside, they set their snow-clogged boots in the tin tray to melt and warm up.

Turning from hanging up his greatcoat, Dan discovered that despite her stern talk, Martha and the girls had set the table for a celebration dinner.

It was short one place-setting.

Clever, he said to himself, as he nodded to her. She sat in her reading chair with a baby burping over her towel-covered shoulder. Before she had said a word, her expression warned Ryder what the stakes for him would be.

A sudden intake of breath from that young man told Dan he had got Martha's message. He stood as though frozen to the spot.

The 'big room,' as the family called the cramped space, was lighted by beeswax candles. Martha was telling the newcomer that this was a family of substance, who could afford to burn good wax candles in the middle of a long Montana winter.

The chaos of blankets and clothes was stowed away, Dan assumed, behind the safety wall in back of the reading corner stove, leaving the room tidy. She intended to make a good impression of the family for this stranger.

Ryder's gaze left Martha to sweep leftward around the room.

Behind her the door to their bedroom was firmly closed.

The oval table in front of the cookstove seated ten people if they crowded together. The edge of a door frame just visible behind the stove led to another lean-to, that functioned as a storeroom and the girls' lean-to room. Facing both the stove and the table, the washstand stood on the outside wall.

Next to it was a large window. It was now blocked by a heavy damask and wool drape that guarded against all but the worst of winter's drafts, and in front of itstood the blue sofa. And on it, as close to the cookstove as possible, sat Eileen, the "help." Dorothy sat beside her, holding the other twin, little Danny, who sucked on a milk-soaked piece of cloth.

Timothy went to stand behind Eileen and rested his hand on the back of the couch behind her shoulder.

The effect – the people, the warm, lighted, tidy room – closed Dan's throat. He could not say why tears threatened.

This is the only important thing in life, he said to himself. My family. This tiny, smelly log cabin that Mother would scorn to set foot in – this was home. It's not the house, he realized, it's Martha and Timothy and the girls.

They had extended themselves to celebrate his and Timothy's safe return.

And to meet Vaughn Ryder, who might or might not be invited to join the celebration.

Seeing how Ryder looked the room over, Dan concluded he would know it in the dark. The only thing Ryder had missed was the gun rack on the wall beside the door. Even as the idea finished, the young man turned his head to speak to Dan and noticed the guns.

His eyes rounded, and his jaw dropped. It was a small arsenal. Dan's Spencer repeating rifle lay across the top row of pegs, above seven handguns that hung in their holsters from pegs.

Dan left him to his surprise while he took his place in his reading chair. From there, he could see everyone at once. One straight wooden chair, which faced the front door, stayed vacant at the table. Dan gestured Ryder to the chair. "Have a seat," he invited him, with an inquiring look at Timothy.

Tim shook his head, shifted his feet to a wider stance and stayed close to Eileen. Ryder moved like a good child to the chair Dan indicated. Catching Martha's eye, he read her unspoken message: This was a family occasion. Not just his own.

"Vaughn Ryder," Dan said, "meet my family."

~~~

Baby Luke, in Martha's lap, cooed and waved his pudgy little arms about, kicked his feet. Dan sent up a word of thanks that he had not covered the shoulder of Martha's nursing dress with green vomit in this time of crisis. Martha played with him as though they were alone, as though Dan's judgment were not in doubt.

Introductions had been made, names pronounced, smiles exchanged.

No one relaxed.

Canary ambled out from behind the reading stove wall, shook himself. He barked once at Ryder, went to his water dish to drink.

Dotty giggled. "He's saying good morning."

Dan doubted the newcomer heard her. Or the dog gulping his water.

Ryder fastened his gaze on Martha and waited.

Clearly, she had caught the stranger at a great disadvantage. Also clearly, he was not stupid. Even without an explanation he understood that he must sing for his supper, and his song would be at her desire and directed to her as his primary audience.

"Who are you, young man?" she demanded. "And I don't mean just your name."

Dan kept Ryder in his sights. Now that Martha had begun this inquisition, he would do nothing to stop it until she had the knowledge she needed. Kindness, he well knew, was not always repaid in kind. He had helped to hang a man given hospitality who had murdered his host, stolen his gold and his horse, and cut off his fingers for the rings he wore, then tried to hide his crime by burning down the man's cabin around him.

Ryder bent his head, watched the toes of his boots.

"Dan'l — " Timothy began.

Dan quelled him with a small sideways movement of his head.

For an eternal minute, the stove fire and the wind sang their mismatched duet in the stove pipe.

Ryder lifted his head and sat up straight.

Ah, Dan understood. He has come to a decision.

"You want to know my story, Mrs. Stark. I understand. I'm a stranger, and you don't want to inflict the wrong sort of man on your vulnerable children." He waved his hand around to include babies, Dorothy, Eileen, and even Timothy.

They waited again, while he appeared to assemble his ideas, perhaps to put them in some order, or to decide what to tell. What to leave out.

"Until two years ago," the young stranger said, "I was a theological student at Gettysburg Seminary – Lutheran. I was a third-year student when the war came to Gettysburg. July first, 1863. It went on for three days before the Confederate forces retreated. I'll never forget those three days." His clasped hands writhed together in his lap, and by force of will, it seemed to Dan, he made them be quiet.

"Or the days that followed," he added.

Another pause. He swallowed, and his Adam's apple jumped in his throat.

"Union and Confederate lines formed just below Seminary Ridge, where Schmucker Hall – that's our main hall – where it stands." He did not look at any of them but stared at a mid-point toward the rush-covered floor.

"The Union lines formed up facing the Confederates in front of our building. A Union general – Buford, I think his name was – climbed up into the cupola, and his aides didn't seem worried. Just as we finished breakfast, though, someone fired a shot, and then more shots. And men screamed. The Confederates kept firing and kept firing, and our men – Unionists – they fought back, hard, and wounded men came into the Hall, and we turned the Hall into a hospital."

He stopped. Gasped for air. Continued.

"It stayed a hospital even after the battle was over. I don't remember which general was there, they came and went, first Union officers, and then Confederate, and soldiers, mostly white men and some Colored, but who was in charge – Union or Confederate – it all changed as the battle lines shifted, so I never knew from one hour to the next until at the last the Confederates retreated and the Union army was left in charge.

"Some white men objected to being treated along with blacks, but we were abolitionists, and didn't care about their objections. Besides, all the blood ran red. Union or Confederate, white or brown or Colored, the blood all ran red, and got mixed up on the floor so no one could tell the difference in races.

"In the afternoon of the third day, the Confederates began to retreat, but always there were the wounded, and the screaming, and the blood. So much blood, all running red."

Elbows on his knees, he lowered his head and pressed the heels of his hands into his eyes.

Dan waited with his family. Eileen reached upward, and Timothy took her hand. Dotty – Dorothy – stared wide-eyed at Ryder.

And Martha? To Dan's surprise, she dabbed at her cheeks with the edge of the blanket on her shoulder.

"I was made a doctor's assistant, and I gave men –" Took his hands away from his eyes, swallowed hard, folded his hands together, the nails digging into the backs. Dan bet his wide-open eyes saw nothing in this peaceful, well-lighted room except the war's horrors in his own mind.

He went on, "I gave men chloroform or ether, whatever the doctors had, and during surgery they still moved about, not from pain I was told, but from the anesthetic, so I had to help hold them down. After surgery there was a bit of laudanum for their pain, and I gave them that, and took away the limbs the doctors amputated, and the bullets they dug out of men's guts, and flesh cut away from the living bodies. It seemed like it would never stop."

Another strangling breath. "But a few days later, we had treated the last soldiers, and they either walked out or were carried out and transferred to military hospitals." He paused so long Dan wondered if he had finished his story. "Or the burial details came for them."

Timothy rose and dipped a cup of water from the clean water pail, and gave it to Ryder, but he did not drink. He held it as if he didn't know what to do.

Dan could think of nothing to say. Young as he was, perhaps twenty, Ryder had seen more death and endured as much as, or more than, Dan and his friends. With this one difference: Ryder had not caused anyone's death. He had not had the terrible duty of hanging men, even if they were convicted murderers.

Ryder bent over, and Timothy jumped up to rescue the cup. Elbows on his knees, he buried his face in his hands. His shoulders shook.

Across his back, Timothy caught Dan's eye. His face was ashen, his eyes wide pools of horror. The war had swept over his family's farm west of Asheville, up in the hills of western North Carolina, and Martha had told how her boy had stayed Confederate marauders off from an upstairs window, using a scattergun he could barely lift. Whether they were surprised by his child's voice and the big gun's muzzle poking out the window, she hadn't known, but they left the farm alone and rode away, laughing.

After a bit, Dan said, "So then you left Gettysburg?"

Ryder sat up, wiped his hands across his face, darted a glance toward Dan. "No, not then. Some men in the town, like my uncle – civilians – fought in the Union lines. The town is solidly Union, and Doctor Schmucker, the Seminary president, is an abolitionist. At first, I had no thought of leaving. Then I – I helped clean up the fields after the battle."

He drew a deep, shuddering breath.

"It was horrible. So many corpses, men and horses cried and screamed. The poor horses. We put them out of their misery. The field of Pickett's charge was the worst. Lee ordered them into the face of Union cannon, and on the battlefield there were great patches of soggy ground, like a swamp of blood, where men had been blown to a red mist because they obeyed their commanders.

"Someone said, 'Blood's the best fertilizer we can get. Should be fine crops next year.'"

He was silent for a bit. Dan wished he could spare him this battle with his demons.

"That's when I knew I had to leave. The blood soaked into the ground, acres and acres of ground, and all that man and possibly others could think of —" He swallowed the words; his Adam's apple leaped.

"Where was God during that horrible three days of slaughter? Where has God been this hideous four years? We pray 'forgive us our sins as we forgive those who sin against us.' But how can anyone be forgiven for ordering Pickett's charge? Or –firing the cannon that blasted living men? When Lee faces his Maker, what will be the result?"

He rubbed his face, mumbled, "Where is God now? I just can't find Him."

"Is that why you came West?" Dan almost whispered. "To look for God?"

"No. I came West to get away from Him." Ryder did not meet anyone's gaze.

Dan looked past the bent figure at Timothy's anguished face. Though he seemed to watch Ryder, his unfocused eyes looked inward at a private horror of his own. "Timothy, what is it?"

Ryder turned toward Tim.

The boy did not see either of them right away but watched the shadows in his own mind for a time before he looked at the stranger. "My Pap was a Confederate artilleryman, on the crews that handled the cannons. He could've been at Gettysburg. I don't know. He never said, but he come home that summer, after Independence Day, sold the farm, and we moved West."

Dan asked, "How did you end up here?"

"We crossed South Pass, then turned off at Soda Springs and trailed north to Bannack. Pap, you know, he talked about the war. Bragged about how many Union soldiers he'd probably killed with the big guns. Never said the names of the battles." Tim shut his eyes, as if he watched moving shadows load the monster gun, then its recoil as it fired and flung the ten-pound ball into the charging enemy soldiers.

At last, Ryder asked Dan, "Were you a soldier?"

"No. My father gambled. After he" – a hitch in his throat – "killed himself, my grandfather paid three hundred dollars to buy a substitute to fight in my place and sent me out here to get enough gold to pay his debts."

"Did you? Pay the debts."

For a moment, Dan thought he would not answer. It was none of Ryder's business whether he had paid the debts or not. Then he considered how these two young men had talked about their worst nightmares.

"Yes. I did."

"And you're a Vigilante."

"Yes."

After a minute or two, Dan realized that neither of them was about to say more. Both young men – it seemed wrong, now, to call either of them 'boys' – had said all they intended. As he had.

Martha asked her voice soft, "You denied God and came out here? Are you just another greedy gold-seeker?"

Ryder's jaw tightened; the muscles in his thin face bunched. "I have not denied the Lord."

"Ah. You don't believe in God, you said. What is that but denying Him?"

"Yes – er – No!"

Dan saw what Martha was getting at. She had to be sure that this young fellow, confused as war had made him, was not about to turn thief. So many, losing their Sunday School faith, threw out all they knew that came from it.

He spoke more sternly than he felt. "We're waiting."

"Dan'l —"

Another warning look silenced Timothy.

This had begun as Martha's demand to know this young man, but now it was Dan's inquisition, and he would have the truth of who Ryder was and why he was in Alder Gulch, no matter how the younger man resisted him. He let silence press on him, do what outright torture would not. He wanted to know if Ryder had been taken in by whatever means Abbott had ensnared him.

The fire muttered in the reading stove, and a drop or two hissed on the cookstove as they waited for Ryder to give in. When the wind sang off key in the stove pipe, Ryder lifted his head and sat up straight.

"I have not denied the Lord. I just can't find Him any more." Then, blushing, he said, "I beg your pardon, but I seem to need to go out again."

Tim leaped out of his chair. "I'm in need, too."

When the door shut behind them and the latch dropped, Dan sighed. "I believe him, I think." But believing Ryder gave rise to a whole new set of questions. What were they to do about him now? How could he – and the family – rescue this wounded young man?

Martha set little Luke in his basket, rose, and took Danny from his sister. Sitting down again, she laid him against her shoulder, covered them both with a small blanket while she freed a breast to nurse him. "I do, too."

"So do I." Dotty tossed her hair in a way she'd started recently, to emphasize a statement.

Eileen sat silent a moment before she went to the stove. "We all have to eat."

Dotty gave Dan baby Luke, who now slept, and rose to help her.

Holding his son, Dan crouched by Martha's chair and murmured, "What do we do about Ryder? I don't see how we can just ignore him now."

"You can find a way for him to be useful, can't you?"

"Are you sure you want me to? Do you believe him enough to take the chance he's honest?"

"I think so. You and Timmy can watch him close. As for finding him a way to be useful, is that so hard? He's got book-learning, like you. You must know some way he can earn his living."

"Are you sure you want me to take him on? You've been dead set against him, on account of Abbott. I've had misgivings, too."

Martha looked a bit shamefaced. "I know. But now I've heard his story, and I've watched him, and listened to what he doesn't say."

"What he doesn't say?"

"Yeah. His story rings true. I don't hear any dis-chords." When Dan said nothing, puzzling over what she meant by discords, she shook her head. "You ain't followin' me. Hand me the dulcimer."

Dan laid the instrument across her lap.

Without the usual tuning that began her playing, she held the nursing baby Danny securely with one hand and strummed the fingers of her other hand once across the strings.

He winced at the sound, not unlike two tomcats fighting.

"That's a diss-chord," Martha said.

Dan laid the instrument in its case. "Now I know." He would not tell Martha that the dulcimer sounded little better to him when she tuned it.

"All right. I'll find something genuinely useful for him to do. But what about his sleeping arrangements? Do you want him back in the Elephant's loft?"

Martha smiled. "No, I think he's seen enough of the elephant, don't you?"

Dan chuckled. Seeing the elephant was the common phrase for adventuring out into the unknown. "Well, then, where do we put him?"

Danny let out a wail. Martha shifted the baby, her hands busy under the blanket until he was quietly nursing again. "The babies are big enough, and we're both quiet sleepers, so you can move back into the bedroom. He and Timmy can bed down behind the stove," Martha suggested. "With you both about, he'll be all right." She meant more than her words implied, and Dan knew it. She hoped that having one grown male, even young ones like Ryder and Timothy, would protect them if Dan was out and about.

Under the clatter of crockery and metal cookware, the rising delicious aromas of good cooking, and a snick–snick of knife strokes as Eileen peeled potatoes, Dan knew a sense of satisfaction. He and Martha had come to an agreement. He would find some way for Ryder to be useful, and Martha would let him stay.

"All right. I'll find something he can do." As if he had only now thought of it, he said, "He's well educated. He can help tutor Tim. Be a clerk for me."

Martha beamed, the brightest smile she had shown him since his return from Bannack. "That's a wonderful idea." Rising, she held Danny without disturbing his contented nursing, and turned to her husband as he rose to meet her with Luke in the crook of his arm. As she turned her face up, he leaned down to kiss her.

When they parted, both a little breathless, Dan said, "You do realize we need a bigger house."

26 ~~~

The Montana Post: 1/14/1865, p. 2:

The Mineral Resources of Montana.

> In the vicinity of Bannack, runs the far-
> famed Dakotah lode, which is indeed a mine
> of gold. In is it [sic] to be found the
> wonderful cavern, the subject of so much
> speculation, as yet, but little examined. Here
> are two quartz mills, one with ten and the
> other with twelve stamps – one belonging to
> a New York company, and the other, we
> believe to Col. Hunkins.

The random path Dan detected among the snow-heaped mounds along Jackson street took much of his concentration, but he grappled with one question layered in doubt as he led Timothy and Ryder down the slope. Now that Martha had agreed to offer Ryder a home, how should he test him? What did the young man know, and what was he capable of learning? Theological schooling was a poor background for life in a mining camp. Out of thousands who had flocked to Alder Gulch for the gold, two that Dan knew of were preachers, and their total attendance numbered fewer than a hundred people. The itinerant Catholic priest who came down from Hell Gate and Sun River drew more, but —

Carol Buchanan

Ryder interrupted Dan's train of thought at the foot of the stairs to his office. "I'd better see Mr. Abbott and pay my cribbage bill." The scarf protecting his nose and mouth moved, in a smile or a grimace Dan could not tell. "He'll want to know where I've been."

"Good. Come up to my office when you've finished."

Inside, they kept their coats on while Tim shook down the ashes that covered yesterday's coals, and Dan brought out the coffee grinder and bag of coffee beans. Tim built a new fire on the exposed, glowing coals. As the fire ignited and grew, he blew on his hands and marched in place between the stove, gradually fading to gray from black and his stepfather, who ground the beans.

"One way or another, we'll find out what makes Ryder tick." Tim spoke low, under the growl of the mechanical mortar and pestle. "What do you think Abbott will do when he hears he helped rescue Albert?"

"He won't be pleased." Dan paused the grinding. "Besides Ryder staying the night at our house. That'll add insult to injury for sure."

"I'd like to be a fly on the wall when that happens." Timothy broke the ice on the clean water bucket and poured the remaining water into the saucepan. Picking the broken pieces of ice out of the bucket, he dropped them in, too.

Dan glanced into the pan. "Better fill up the buckets, or we won't have enough coffee to go around, and this will be strong enough to walk on."

"I like it strong." Tim stopped unbuttoning his coat at the second button. "What do you mean 'enough to go around'?"

"Ryder." The handle of the grinder came loose in Dan's hand as the last of the grounds dropped into the drawer below the mechanism. "I think he'll be back soon."

"I hope you're right." Tim settled his hat, fastened his coat, and picked up the two buckets. At the door he hesitated. "My curiosity bump itches bad. I like him. He's seen more rough stuff than most men ever do, even Indian fighters." He picked up the buckets, but stood still, as though he saw something he hadn't noticed before.

"Don't forget your gloves."

"Oh." Setting the buckets down again, Tim pulled the gloves on. "Y'know, all that hasn't made him an SOB, like Fitch and them." He snatched up the buckets and ducked out fast.

Before the door slammed, Dan thought he heard, "And Pap."

~~~

So as not to waste any of his meager paper supply, Dan took up slate and chalk. He stayed on his feet, to guard the coffee from boiling over, but his mind was not on coffee. He sketched out questions to test Ryder's clerical abilities: How clearly did he write, both as to penmanship and for reading? How were his math skills? Could he figure tangents, and help with

267

surveying? Could he outline an idea? Not a legal idea, surely, but —

The door slammed.

Nearly dropping the slate, he wheeled around.

X Beidler stood by the closed door, his mustache unable to hide his wide grin. "You deep in the legal weeds there?"

"X, damn your hide, you know better than to sneak up on a man like that." Dan set slate and chalk on his desk and shook X's hand without bothering to wipe off the chalk dust. "Have a seat. Can I offer you something?"

"Nope, sorry. Thank you anyhow. I'd like to set and chew the fat, but I'm here on official business."

"Official?"

"Yep. I'll give it to you straight up. His Honor has decided to hold an informal discussion – them's his words – of a writ of habeas corpus that poor excuse of a lawyer handed him a couple days ago."

"You mean Abbott?"

"Yep. How that fraud ever convinced anyone he's a lawyer, let alone got to be president of the Virginia City Bar Association – you got any ideas?"

"He's a grayback, and Alder Gulch is populated mostly by graybacks. Including the lawyers."

"You got that right." X looked around for a spittoon. Failing to find one, he stepped outside to spit his chaw over the balcony railing. Inside again, he stood with his backside nearly touching the stove. "I think Hosmer's trying to walk a fine line. He has to show the

Confederates that he's impartial. So he bends over backwards to accommodate Fitch."

"That's probably true. Legally, he can't hold a hearing until the First District is in session, but he can get the interested parties together for a discussion of the issues. So to speak." To himself, Dan was thinking that His Honor put the family in real danger if he let him out of jail, unless he assigned a guard over him. A guard of friends.

X drew out his pocketknife to carve a generous chaw off a corner of the plug. "Want some?" He held out plug and chaw to Dan.

Suppressing a shudder, Dan refused. "Has he decided on a date for this so-called discussion?"

Footsteps clomped up the stairs and stopped outside Dan's door. Glad to escape the sight of X's open mouth as he began to work the chaw, he went to hold the door open for Timothy, carrying two buckets of icy water.

"The paper was right. The hydrant works, but I hope you've got the money to pay for it." The boy stomped into the room and set the buckets between the stove and the shared wall. As if noticing the deputy for the first time, he greeted him, "Howdy, Deputy. Things too warm in the jail?"

X buckled the belt around his coat. "Not likely. I brought some news for your stepdaddy. You can tell him about it, Stark." With that, he took himself off.

At the door, Dan shouted after him, "When is this discussion?"

From near the bottom of the stairs, X's voice floated up: "Monday next."

Timothy warmed himself as close to the stove as he could get without scorching his coat. "You didn't need to slam the door. What was that about?"

Dan told him how Hosmer was politicking by agreeing to hold a "discussion" on the merits of the writ of habeas corpus Abbott had prepared to release Fitch.

"Damn!" shouted the boy. "How can he do that?"

Dan made a damping motion with his hands. "Keep your voice down."

"I don't care. It ain't right. Him being a Union man and all. That ain't right, sidestepping the law that way." Tim's mouth set in a stubborn line.

Dan explained, as calmly as if he didn't completely agree with the boy, as if the Confederate sympathizers in Number Four were not listening closely, if not avidly. "He's calling it a meeting to discuss some issues relevant to the Nugget. it's not binding. It holds no water, because it will be held between sessions as defined by the law the legislature passed." He lowered his voice. "All it will do is calm some of the tempers around here that think a Union administration of the Territory is a dictatorship."

"I don't get it. I don't get it A-tall."

Dan studied how he could convince Tim that Judge Hosmer was trying to placate both sides in this situation. Deep in thought, he picked up the pan of hot coffee, swung it in slow circles as he thought how to make Hosmer's situation clear.

Footsteps thudded up the stairs. The door opened and closed so quietly that Dan knew trouble had come in before he saw it.

Ryder's voice startled him. "Abbott fired me."

Forgetting that he held the pan, Dan swung about. Coffee splashed out of the pan, onto his fingers. "Ow!" He set the pan on the cooktop. Shaking his hand, he faced the younger man.

"What did you say?"

"Abbott fired me." Ryder leaned against the door, stared at his boots. "I paid my cribbage bill and explained I'd earned the dust shoveling snow, rescuing Albert, and he fired me. On the spot." He shivered so hard, Dan wondered why he did not hear bones rattle.

"Come here by the stove. Get warm, then you can tell us about it."

Tim dragged the third chair up to the stove. "Here. Sit down."

Ignoring his scalded fingers, Dan took up the pan again to pour hot coffee for all of them. His mind leaped to an idea: If Ryder answered two questions right, he had solved two problems and answered the main issue.

They clustered around the stove, the arms of their hard wooden chairs touching. Full mugs of black coffee warmed their hands and gullets. Dan blew on his coffee as if the only thing on his mind was the hot, strong brew. As if he did not covertly study Ryder out the corner of his eye.

What could he do besides lose at cribbage and muck out stalls? Dan had to know.

This was not a country that paid men to sit and think. Even Andrew Torbet, the Baptist lay preacher with a congregation upwards of sixty people, worked as Judge Hosmer's court clerk to get by.

He began by steering the talk in the direction he wanted. "I'm guessing Abbott made no bones about his reasons."

"Ha!" Ryder snorted. "No. he wasn't subtle."

"What did he say?"

"He said if I wanted to be a 'damned strangling abolitionist' – his words, not mine – I could go to hell."

"And you said —?" Dan felt his own inner heat rising.

"I lost my temper," Ryder mumbled toward the floor. "I, er, I told him I'd rather go there for all eternity than spend a second in heaven with slave-holders."

Picturing this thin young fellow, who had seemed almost effeminate in his manner at first, confronting the tough Confederate – and not backing down – Dan laughed out loud.

Almost he did not hear Ryder: "I should have said unrepentant slave-holders."

Dan laughed harder. Timothy joined him.

As he wiped his eyes, Dan's idea took a clearer shape. Ryder had defied Abbott and — Dan's biceps tightened as though he had the grayback in range for a good punch. The bastard had cheated Ryder out of his meager earnings and allowed him to go half-starved, and sleep cold in the Elephant's loft.

Ryder was a destitute, starving, well-educated, former divinity student. Who had courage. Also, he was an abolitionist.

Martha liked Ryder.

Dan had promised her he would find something for him. He could not promise Martha and not come through. Life wouldn't be worth living. She had seen what Dan had only now discovered.

Ryder would be worth the trouble. Whatever that was.

Feeling Timothy watching him, he took a deep breath. "What are we to do with you?"

Ignoring Tim's gasp, Dan waited.

Ryder, staring at the coffee in his mug, looked up. "What do you mean?"

"How can you earn your keep? My wife and I are willing to let you stay in our house, as long as you mind your manners around the girls, but how can you pay for the food you eat? We are not a charity." Ignored Timothy's protesting noises.

"I'm not asking for handouts. I want to work and earn my way."

"But what can you do?" Dan shot Timothy a warning look to sit tight and leave this grilling to him.

In the silence, the fire mumbled its discontent.

In Number Four, Pemberton and Burns argued about a point of law having to do with property rights.

Neither of them mentioned the Emancipation Proclamation.

Pemberton hailed from Missouri. "Slavery will soon be illegal."

Burns, the Illinois man, retorted, "If not, it should be."

Pemberton's voice came again. "You're copying a Missouri statute. Missouri is a free state, even if many people are slave-owners."

"What do you know of the law?" Dan raised his voice to be heard over the argument.

"Very little, I'm afraid." Ryder looked at his boots. The sole had cracked across the ball of one, and wet, crumbling newsprint showed through it. Dan read '...*na Post.*' "It always seemed so dry to me. I'm a great disappointment to my father."

"Is he a lawyer?"

"No, he's a stonecutter. He cut stone for public buildings and Lutheran churches in Pennsylvania." He stared into his coffee cup as though to read his future in the grounds. "I thought he'd be pleased when I entered the seminary."

"You went far in your education." Dan did not wait for a reply; the answer was obvious. "How's your penmanship?"

"Good. I won prizes in school. I write a clear hand." He added, "I sharpen the nibs myself."

"What were your favorite subjects?"

"History. Literature. Math." When Dan raised an eyebrow, Ryder nodded. "Yes, I know. It's an odd combination, but there it is."

"Have you been a teacher at all?"

"Yes. I taught school for three years after I turned fourteen, to save money for tuition at seminary. My father thought education beyond knowing how to read the Bible was useless, so I had to pay for it myself."

Below the level of the quiet answer, Dan heard the echo of a long past, sharp disagreement. Something like Grandfather and me, he imagined.

"And you were in your first or second year at the seminary when the war came?"

"No, sir. I was a third-year."

All this time Timothy had sat silent, but Dan did not doubt he followed the questioning like Canary after a raccoon. "Do you have any questions, Tim?"

"Sure do." When Ryder met his gaze, Timothy asked point blank, "D'you think you could pound any book-learnin' into my thick skull?"

Surprised, Dan sat back to watch their interaction.

Ryder thought about his response. "You're not stupid, Tim. You just don't want to waste time. If I can convince you there's a reason for learning Latin, you'd learn it fast enough."

"Latin? Whatever for?"

"Maybe there is no reason for you to learn it, except for being considered an educated man, but it's the foundation for several modern languages. And scientific terms. You want a good reason for taking trouble, that's all I meant."

"Scientific terms? Like geology?" As Tim scratched at an ear, his hand hid his face from Ryder at the same time.

But not from Dan, who caught a brief upward curve to the corner of his mouth. Something about geology had aroused Timothy's mind.

It was a spark Dan wished had come from himself.

"Oh, yes. I'm no geologist but knowing Latin would be of great use to understand the names of geological formations and rocks." He turned toward Dan, produced an apologetic shrug. "Science is not my strong suit."

"You're honest, at any rate."

Ryder did not see Tim's vigorous nod to Dan. As though he'd spoken, the boy was telling him Ryder would make a good teacher. Almost, Dan heard him say, 'Keep him, Dan'l. Keep him, do.'

His idea could work. Dan tamped down his own excitement. Hiring Ryder would give him a clerk and a tutor for Timothy. "It looks like we should give you a trial, then. What would you think of two jobs? Tim won't sit still for an entire day. That's why I can't send him to Tom Dimsdale's school."

"Ha!" Tim protested. "Me? I ain't about to sit in no classroom with a bunch of babies learning to spell c-a-t and d-o-g."

"You see?" Dan spoke to Ryder as though Tim had proved his point. "I need a clerk, to help with the documentation involved in setting set up a mining corporation. You seem quick to learn, and you and Tim get along pretty well. So here's the job."

As though he had not noticed how Ryder held his breath, Dan paused to take a swallow or two of coffee. The young fellow had changed somehow. He held the same pose he'd had before, but there was a shift in the set of his head. A looking askance.

Why?

Dan mind sorted through what he had said. Hit on 'mining corporation.' Abbott represented Fitch. "Help tutor Timothy, and clerk for me. You'll be learning Montana Territorial law as it's being written for the first time. In return, I'll pay you four dollars a day in dust. What do you say?"

Ryder swallowed twice before he managed, "Four dollars a day? In gold dust? Clerks only earn three dollars."

"True, but you'll be a tutor as well as a clerk." He paused for a moment. "Out of that you'll have to pay your board and lodging someplace, if you'd rather not roll your blankets behind the stove at home."

"Don't forget the babies." Tim's voice held a teasing note. "Dan says we'll get a decent night's sleep in about twenty years."

Ryder's guard, Dan saw, was up. "What would you charge for board and room?"

Clearly, he expected the sort of treatment Abbott had handed him.

Carol Buchanan

And whether he meant to or not, he had Dan walking a tightrope now. Generosity did not mean foolishness, but he could not let Ryder think he was another Abbott. "How about a quarter ounce of dust? The hotels charge fourteen dollars per week. We'll keep it simple. A quarter ounce is four dollars and fifty cents in Fairweather Mining District. How does that sound?" This time of year, as snow twenty feet deep blocked the mountain passes, the hotels stood mostly empty.

Tim's smile told Dan he had struck the proper amount.

Yet something bothered Ryder. Even Timothy noticed it. One eyebrow cocked, he looked from Dan to the new man and back to Dan. A man in Ryder's destitute condition should not have to think so long about this offer.

"What would I be obligated to?"

On the face of it, he asked a reasonable question, except for the word 'obligated.' That struck the wrong note. To give himself a moment to think, Dan got up, wrapped his hand in a rag, and seized the pan handle. Obligated. A lawyerly sort of word. Did divinity students use it? Outside of lawyers' conversations and contracts he had seldom heard it.

Except Grandfather. Who loved explaining why his small grandson was obligated to him for the switch across his bare buttocks.

His heart beat faster. He needed a deep breath of fresh, clean air. Only, the air outside would freeze the lungs.

Instead, he filled the younger men's mugs and topped off his own. Set the pan aside and reseated himself. When he had taken a swallow, he held the cup in both hands.

"To answer your question, you would be obligated to do your best to educate Timothy to the point he can take his position as the managing owner of the Nugget quartz mine. We don't have a lot of time to accomplish this, either. He turns seventeen in a few weeks, and comes into his inheritance four years later, along with his mother and sister."

Ryder turned a surprised stare on Tim. "You inherit the mine? I thought —"

"You thought what?" Dan leaned forward, the better to fix Ryder in his own spotlight.

"Er, I heard you owned the mine." He had forgotten the 'sir.'

"Whoever told you that was mistaken." Or a damn liar. "I am the McDowell family's legal guardian. I have no ownership in any claims staked by their late father, Sam McDowell." Finished, he caught a bewildered look on Ryder's face.

Tim set one ankle on the opposite knee and jabbed his forefinger at the muscles of his calf to emphasize his own points.

"You see, Mam and Dotty and me, we inherit the Nugget because Pap discovered the original claim, but they being females, they can't manage it." He poked, winced, darted a glance at Dan. "So until I can stuff enough learnin' in my brain, Dan'l is the manager? Operator?" A sidelong peek at Dan to see if he'd stated the case right.

Reaching back, Dan thumped his coffee mug down on his desk. "Tim, to effectively manage a business as big as this mine could be, you will need at least a degree in mining engineering, and a knowledge of business. Accounting, for one thing."

"But where'd I get all that?"

"The two best engineering schools are West Point Military Academy and Rensselaer Polytechnic Institute. I doubt you want to become an Army engineer, so RPI would be your best choice. And to get in, you'd have to pass examinations in mathematics, geology, and whatever other subjects the college thinks are necessary. Like English."

He turned to Ryder, watched both young men for a long minute. Both looked as if they were in shock. Good. Let them stay that way. They had to understand the stakes facing them now that they had seen the lode.

"How's your math?" he asked Ryder.

"I know geometry, algebra, trigonometry, and calculus."

"You do? Why did you learn anything beyond plane geometry?"

The young man's face bloomed a bright pink, as though he confessed to loving the wrong sort of girl. "I don't know. Not for any practical reason. Just, well, I like math. Some fellows read poetry, I learned trig and calculus."

"Hmm. You could be useful after all." Dan went on, "If we had a spare room with a bed in it, I'd ask the same as the Wisconsin House. Fourteen dollars a week. As it is, there's only floor space behind the reading corner stove to sleep on, but my wife and the girls are all good cooks, so the meals are decent."

"Don't forget the twins." Tim's wide smile threatened to split his face.

"Oh, yes, we mustn't forget them. They serenade us with a little night music." At the back of his mind, he puzzled over where he could send both of them on an errand while he looked out the Eagles or Double Eagles he could have turned into dust.

Even though it meant seeking out Jacob.

And then he had an idea.

"Timothy, we shouldn't take a chance on your new tutor freezing to death between here and home. Take him to the Pioneer Clothing Store, or Dance and Stuart, and see that he buys a warm coat and boots, and whatever else to get himself through the rest of the winter. Tell them to put it all on my tab."

Tim jumped up, set his coffee cup on Dan's desk, and hauled a surprised Ryder to his feet. "Let's go while he's feeling generous."

Coats and hats on and buttoned, they stopped at the door. Ryder, in front, held onto the door latch. "Mr. Stark, I can't thank you enough for –"

Dan waved his thanks aside. "Get along with you. You're letting the heat out."

When their steps had clattered down the stairs, Burns and Pemberton were arguing about what the end of slavery would mean for criminal law.

Dan hollered through the wall, "For one thing, ending slavery will mean that Coloreds will be legal to testify in courts of law. Against anyone, including white men, for any criminal act."

That stopped them, as he had known it would. Maybe they pictured Albert testifying as a witness against a white man? Roger Taney, the erstwhile Chief Justice of the U. S. Supreme Court, would spin in his grave.

Dan chuckled to himself. The world was indeed changing.

He took out a number of coins, mostly ten-dollar Eagles, enough to pay all household expenses for some time to come, as well as the bonuses for Albert's rescue, Cooke's bill, and Ryder's salary for two months. After banking the fire, he put on his greatcoat and hat. At the door, he paused and patted the pockets holding the coins. He had many uses for his money, beginning now. He would take great care in how he spent it, but he knew exactly what he would spend it for.

He had seen the lode.

27 ~~~

Montana Post: 1/14/1865, p. 3:

Monetary. Reported by Allen and Millard,
Bankers.

Virginia City, Jan. 14, 1865

> Exchange on N. Y., selling for T. N. at 3 per
> cent. prem.
> Exchange on N. Y., selling for coin at 5 per
> cent. prem.
> Treasury Notes, buying at 50 cts., for dust.
> Treasury Notes, buying at 50 cts., for dust.
> Dust, buying at $30.69 per ounce in T. N.
> Gold Dust, buying at $14.00 to $15.00 for
> coin.
> Coin buying at 10 per cent. premium in dust.

When Dan put his foot over the mudsill into Ming's, the jeweler snarled, "Shut the damn door." He did not bother to raise his head to see who let in the frigid air, but hunched over his work, etching a rose into the back of a gold watch case. Dan realized it was the same watch he'd been working on the last time he'd stopped in.

Now, he waited in front of the high stand until the man took the loupe out of his eye to glare at him.

"Well?"

"Why don't you rent a space away from the door?"

"Too expensive." He blew his nose on his fingers, wiped his hand down his coat. "Got any more stupid questions?"

"Just one. Do you ever wonder why you don't get more business? If you did, you could afford to rent a warmer space." Touching the brim of his hat, Dan walked away. The jeweler had the reputation of being one of the most unpleasant characters in Alder Gulch. Whether or not he learned now that treating potential customers with friendliness brought more business was none of Dan's concern. He had done his best.

In the middle of the room, the grocer looked even more discouraged. Seeing Dan, he drummed up a smile and wished him a good afternoon. Dan returned the greeting and stayed to hear a little friendly gossip before he moved on.

Passing Abbott's enclosure, his hand away from the man doubled into a fist, and he braced himself for a verbal attack, but Abbott bent to tie his boot and remained concentrated on the task until Dan passed by. That suited him just fine.

Approaching Jacob, he stretched his fingers to loosen them, but stayed on his guard. What exchange rate would Jacob charge him? For weeks in the *Montana Post*, the Allen and Millard bank had quoted fourteen to fifteen dollars per ounce, if buying gold dust with coin. Would Jacob sell his dust at that rate? Or would he charge eighteen dollars per ounce, the rate used by everyone to buy over the counter in the saloons and stores and restaurants?

Whatever price he quoted would foretell the future of their friendship – if he apologized to Tim for keeping his door closed.

Jacob did not greet Dan as he opened the gate and closed it behind himself, and his tone was serious with no hint of the pleasure he had always shown. "Is good you come. We talk, ja?"

Dan had no smile for Jacob. "Not here. In my office. First, though, I have business." That in itself was a concession. For this exchange, Dan could have gone to Allen and Millard, but he wanted to test Jacob with this transaction. If he charged more than $15.00 per ounce, Dan would take his business to another bank. "I need dust."

"For pay the helpers of the rescue, ja?"

"To pay their bonuses, yes."

His back to Abbott's snooping, he took the pokes out his pockets. Coins clinked quietly. "I have Eagles. Can you change them to dust?"

"Ja, certain." Jacob gestured toward his desk and three chairs at a writing table placed so as to catch the best heat from the stove.

When they had sat so that no one could understand Dan's business with Jacob, Dan outlined the situation as he saw it, nine men digging and his promise, "to everybody," emphasizing the word to be sure Jacob knew the promise included him.

"Ja. We dig faster for more money and save Albert. I hear the talk."

Dan tried to smile. "Good. I hoped that would be the result. And we did find him alive. So each man should receive a dollar bonus."

"A day later, even, Albert not die. He will live." He lowered his voice almost to a whisper. "So, you need two ounces of dust? Two and a half?"

"Three. Some of them looked like they hadn't eaten in days. Ryder for one. You have it, don't you?"

"Ja, naturlich."

Yes, naturally. After knowing Jacob since he got off the boat, Dan wondered that he still clung to his native language. He had been eager to speak English at first, but now? Maybe clinging to the peculiar amalgam of Hebrew and German was part of his renewed obedience to the Almighty.

Jacob unlocked the safe.

Dan spoke quietly. "Can you divide it nine ways?"

Jacob set about changing the ten-dollar coins to dust. "Go look at books. I finish this, and we go to your office. Ja?"

"Yes, but I'll hover around you and keep Abbott from seeing what we're doing."

Back at his desk, Jacob did some calculations on a slate.

Dan sat on the straight chair beside the desk. Time was, Jaccob would have offered him a whiskey now, but the new Jacob, this very religious Jew, no longer kept whiskey for customers because it was not kosher.

What had happened to turn him into a – this – Dan was at a loss for words, even to himself. He wasn't sure what to call this sudden zeal applied to Jacob.

Zeal. Zealot.

It seemed Jacob had turned into a zealot.

"Your cost, it is fourteen dollars an ounce. Not fifteen, even though this is good, Alder Gulch dust, worth eighteen dollars an ounce everywhere except on the Exchange. But your coin buys more dust. Good Alder Gulch dust."

Jacob offered a rock bottom $14.00 per ounce, when gold dust traded for up to $15.00 on the Exchange? It must be that he wanted something more, something he wanted enough to offer a major consideration. Dan's trading instinct quivered, as though it had antennae. Buying an ounce of gold dust at $15.00, Jacob could make a healthy profit by selling at eighteen or twenty dollars an ounce, the usual rates, depending on the purity of the dust. And spending it on things priced at dust for eighteen dollars an ounce.

But by offering dust at $14.00, Jacob would pay him $43.00 in dust. The rescuers could then sell the dust locally for $18.00 per ounce, the current local valuation in Alder Gulch gold. Or they could use it to buy needed supplies. Jacob would lose $3.00 in profit, while he would make a clear profit of $4.00 per ounce.

Even before this new zealousness, Jacob had kept a close eye on profit.

Someone over at Ming's bookstore laughed.

Dan came back to business. First, he would have Jacob pay the rescuers. Then he'd have Jacob's dust in his possession assayed to determine its true value. The purer the dust, the more valuable it would be.

"Thank you, Jacob. That's very generous. But would Mr. Hershfield approve?"

"Is no more Mr. Hershfield. I own bank now. It is, I have bought it." As he spoke, he put a thin sliver of lead on one pan of a balance scale and divided the dust into separate piles of one dollar each. Then he wrapped the dust in small squares of oiled cloth and tied them with twine, ending in four square knots. Snipping the twine, he pushed the little packages toward Dan. "So. Is good, ja?"

"Very good, indeed." Dan pushed nine tiny packages toward Jacob. "May I ask you to pay the rescuers?" He stowed the remaining package in his inside waistcoat pocket.

"Ja. Tomorrow, yes?" Jacob glanced toward the window on the Jackson Street side of the building, where Ming's Books took advantage of whatever natural light the day afforded. "Sunset comes." From one of the bottom desk drawers, he removed a sizable poke.

Dan guessed it held considerable dust. His heartbeat quickened.

"Perhaps you still have Laphroaig?" Jacob stowed the poke in a roomy coat pocket.

Playing along, Dan pitched his voice loud enough for Abbott to hear. "You have time for a drink in my office, then?" In a murmur, he added, "Yes, I have Laphroaig." A rare single malt Scotch, the whisky was kosher. Dan had carried it three precious bottles back from Scotland on his second trip to Europe. And hidden them from Father.

Sitting with Jacob in his office, inhaling the rich peaty aroma, Dan decided what Jacob wanted must be of great importance. Although he raised the glass to his lips, he said nothing as the room slowly warmed a degree or so.

Someday, Dan promised himself, he would see to it that Jacob apologized to Timothy – and to himself as the boy's guardian — for shutting him out on a subzero night.

Neither man touched his lips to his glass. For all the pleasure Jacob showed in it, he might as well have sipped from a puddle formed by a suspicious mound melting in the street.

For himself, Dan wished him gone. He had work to do, to get ready for Hosmer's so-called meeting. He should be reviewing the three laws that governed his family's situation. He had won against Fitch in the Miners Court for Fairweather Mining District, but since then Alder Gulch had become part of Idaho and subject to Idaho's own Territorial mining statute. Granted, the Montana Territorial Legislature had repealed it in passing the Montana Mining Law.

But there was the problem of "prevailing custom."

How Judge Hosmer would rule in this legal quagmire was anybody's guess, but –

Timothy charged through the doorway and stopped at the sight of Jacob and Dan, apparently at ease by the stove. He left the door wide open.

"Close the door, Timothy."

28 ~~~

Montana Post: 1/14/1865, p. 2.

A Trip to Brandon City
(The town is only 3 months old ....)

One quartz mill, owned by Mr. Ceisler, and driven by water power has done very well during the fall, but is frozen up for the winter. Another, a 24-stamp mill is on the ground, ready to be erected in the spring. It is owned by Mr. Vanterburgh. The most notable lodes in the immediate vicinity of Brandon, are the Mountain Queen, which has yielded very well under the skillful management of Mr. Ceisler, since it was opened; the Eclipse, with a wide and well-defined dirt crevice; Lady Suffolk, Kelly, St. Louis and many more which have been discovered this winter, but too late to commence work on them. Few of the lodes mentioned are further than a mile from town. We predict that Brandon will become the centre of one of the richest mining districts in Montana.

Timothy shut the door with a soft snick of the latch, unlike his usual treatment of doors, and swept off his hat. Snow melting from it dripped on the floor.

Dan pointed to the third chair drawn up to the stove. "Did Ryder get everything he needed?"

"Seemed to. 'Cause he's warm again, he's convinced you walk on water." Tim unbuttoned the top two buttons of his coat and hauled the chair farther around the stove, away from Jacob, hung the hat from the end of the chair arm. Seated, he unwrapped his scarf and settled onto his chair with his coat on, his feet gathered under him.

Dan rose to fill a cup of coffee for him.

Jacob cocked his head to the side. "This Ryder. He works for Abbott, the lawyer?"

Tim snorted. "Hah! Lawyer? Him? Like I'm a preacher, maybe."

"Not anymore." Dan handed the cup to his stepson. "It seems Abbott took exception to an assistant who would rescue a Colored man. I've hired him as a clerk for me, and a tutor for Timothy."

"I have heard. They argue. Young Ryder, he is happy to rescue Albert, and Abbott would let him starve until spring." Jacob shook his head in disgust. "Everyone in Ming's everything hears. Abbott shouts, 'You put in with a damn Vigilante, be damned to you.'"

"Ah." Sitting again, Dan watched the flames leap behind the iron scrollwork in the firebox door.

Tim stared at his stepfather. "'Ah?' That all you can say? 'Ah'?"

"Something seemed off about Ryder this morning. That must have been it."

"Why should he mind that you're a Vigilante?" Tim made a spitting noise. "That's a load of bullshit."

Jacob shot him a swift, disapproving glare. He sat straight, a poker for a spine, telegraphing his displeasure.

Tim's face reddened as he stared at the floor, ignored the coffee.

Dan banged his fist once, hard and loud, on the arm of his chair, startling both Tim and Jacob out of their fuming.

"Enough! There's too much at stake for you two to carry on this way."

"You had no call to shut me out —" The boy's outburst collided with Jacob's shout, "The Sabbath must —"

"I said, 'Enough!'" Without knowing how, he came to his feet, one moment sitting and the next towering over the other two, who gaped at him, mouths open in their upturned faces. Dan had a crazy urge to laugh. Baby birds.

And then he did laugh. "If you two could see yourselves."

Their mouths snapped shut on a sound of teeth clacking together.

The legal wrangle next door erupted into a shouting match, escalating swiftly to sound like a dozen men, until one voice prevailed.

"The times are changing." Pemberton's voice came clear through the single-board partition. "Blacks will have the vote after the war, if they don't already."

"Yeah," said another man, "next thing you know women will have it, too, they already do in some places —"

A third voice dominated the discussion. "And then the country's doomed for sure. We might's well move to Antartica while clipper tickets are cheap."

Under their loud talk, Dan spoke quietly. "Tim and I have a gold mine to develop and protect. The lode has changed everything for me and my family. Done right, it could take care of us – and our investors – for years to come. So I'd like to talk about the Nugget. You've seen the wall, Jacob. What do you think?"

The brim of Jacob's flat black hat slanted upward as he lifted the last of his drink to his mouth and drained it in one swallow.

Dan waited for his answer.

Jacob set the glass on the floor. "Ja. Is correct. The wall, what you call, it is a lode. I think, certain."

"Do you want to invest in its development?" From his chair, Dan picked up the empty glass and set it on his desk.

"Ja. Also correct." Rummaging in his coat, he retrieved the fat poke. He laid the poke on the arm of his chair. "I would invest all of this dust. Five hundred dollars."

Tim's eyes widened. "Five hundred dollars? Jake, that's all you have in the world."

"No. Not all. Is, maybe, enough to risk. For now."

"But —" Tim stopped, stared hard at Dan, an unreadable message in his eyes.

Sitting where Jacob could see his every gesture, his every expression, Dan had to let Timothy go on as he started. He could say nothing, telegraph no warning with a gesture or a look. Would the boy act from emotion, or would he take a businessman's attitude?

Tim rotated his coffee mug between his hands.

Then Dan knew he could not rescue this situation from the error Tim would make.

Tim cleared his throat. "You're ready to hand over a small fortune now that you've seen the wall, but you wouldn't believe me when I told you I saw it? Why not, Jake? Why couldn't you trust me? Do you think I'd lie to you? Or Dan'l? He believed me, Dan'l did. Why not you?"

As Jacob seemed to weigh his answer, weak sunlight shone through the windowpanes in rectangular patches across the floor.

Dan imagined that his friend poised on a knife-edge. The mine could set them all up for life, and their heirs, too, but this new Jacob might also think it represented a violation of God's law. Which law, Dan had no idea, but it was a risk. Especially for himself. The lode – if it was indeed a lode – might top out somewhere higher up on the mountain on someone else's claim, and lead to an expensive apex suit, a legal battle to determine who owned the entire mine, because whoever owned the highest point of a lode owned the entire lode. Those suits could drag on for years while the courts tried to rule on who owned the mine. And costs piled up until it did not matter who owned the mine.

Jacob cleared his throat.

Dan came back to the present. Would Jacob apologize to Timothy? Or try to justify the unjustifiable, that he had shut the boy out on a night of Arctic cold?

Jacob regarded his hat.

Tim fidgeted, opened his mouth as if to say something. Closed it.

As if that small motion caused the plodding hoofbeats in his head to stumble, a recollection warned Dan: Fitch claimed the Nugget was his.

He would confront Fitch in a few days. He might be arguing law with Hal Abbott, but he'd be shooting at Fitch. He would stamp out all embers of Fitch's burning idea that anyone owned even a pebble on the Nugget claim except the McDowell family and the mine's investors. He would put an end to this before Fitch had a chance to prove he owned the damned. Mythical. Mother Lode.

"You would know what Sabbath means for me, ja?"

Startled, at first Dan mistook Jacob's question for a challenge to himself, but the question was for Tim, who crossed his arms over his chest. "I s'pose so."

Jacob's pointing finger aimed at Tim as though to pin him to a board.

The boy shrugged. "I would, Jake. Yeah. I mean, I do know. It's on a Saturday, and it's your religion's day of worship."

"You Christians, you don't know what a Sabbath means. You maybe sit in a church for an hour, two hours, but later, like today, you meet and talk about how rich you could be." He looked around as though he had forgotten something, then stared unblinking at the boy. "For us, the Sabbath is a most holy day. It is first commandment of the Most High, the Almighty as you say. Yahweh. And the third." Closing his eyes, he chanted a few phrases that Dan recognized from the months he had roomed with Jacob, when he would awaken to find him in another world, bowing and shuffling his feet, the fringes of his prayer shawl swaying, as he chanted in an ancient language from a thousand years before Christ. Dan caught one word he recognized: *Elohim*. God.

Tim watched Jacob wide-eyed, his mouth slightly open.

Had Jake never sung for Timothy as he had when just the two of them shared a bachelor cabin?

The chant ended. When Jacob spoke, hie voice trembled.

Whatever he felt he needed to say, Dan realized, must be of immense importance to him, seeing how much effort it took for him to say it.

"The first commandment is this: 'Thou shalt have no other gods before Me.' And the third, 'Thou shalt not take the name of the Lord thy God in vain.' And the fourth is this: 'Remember the Sabbath day to keep it holy.'" He stopped to breathe. No one spoke.

"I must obey the Most High God. I must keep the Sabbath holy."

Something held them as though suspended in time. Whatever it was, Dan knew Tim felt it, too, for he spoke just above a whisper as if he did not want to break a spell. "I wasn't stopping you."

"Ja. You were. You did."

"How? I didn't mean to. Show me."

"The Sabbath is sundown Friday to sundown Saturday."

Dan glanced toward the door, where the windows revealed the meager winter light fading.

"You've never been much of a Sabbath-keeper, Jake. Until recently, I mean."

"Ja. However, is more I have to say. It is, I want a wife."

Timothy's wide-eyed stare mirrored Dan's own confused surprise. What did a wife have to do with keeping the Sabbath?

Before either of them could ask, Jacob spoke into his hat. "I must obey Yahweh – God – by keeping the Sabbath, studying Torah, and marrying a proper wife who can keep a kosher house. It is why I – I would not let anyone in that night. Why you cannot come back. I cannot obey Yahweh if I live with gentiles, because the house will not be kosher. And I cannot bring a proper wife into a defiled house." He spread his hands, leaving everything he told them in their laps and on their minds.

The wall clock made a sound like a metallic throat-clearing before it struck the hour – 3:00.

A log exploded in the stove, startling them all.

Dan could not grasp the logic of this new Jacob. All right, his single-minded desire to stand correct with God maybe stemmed from the hangings they'd participated in, even considering that a 17-man executive committee had weighed the evidence against every suspect. And every sentence of death had to be unanimous by the Vigilantes' own by-laws. Why couldn't he just leave the guilt behind? Why couldn't he acknowledge that they might have made mistakes, like every formal court in the United States?

He himself battled with nightmares. He would never forget the horror of hanging Rawley, the man who had lost most of both feet to gangrene. Last month his ghost had followed him from Bannack to Beaverhead Rock and from there all the way home.

Even though it had left him, he still expected to see it again. Sometime, it would ambush him.

With that idea still suspended in his mind, he brought himself back to business. "Can you participate in a gentile investment, then, Jacob? Or do you risk your soul with that, too?"

"No. " Jacob shook his head; his hair bounced on his shoulders. "I have seen the wall. It is a lode. So now you take that and use it for me?"

Dan hefted the poke in his hand as Jacob rose to his feet and shook out the folds of his coat. Standing with Jacob, he held the poke out to Timothy. "What do you think?"

Jacob's eyes widened.

Tim stood. He looked at Dan straight on, and Dan realized that the boy had grown in the last month. They were eye-level now.

"If Jake can't let a gentile into his house on a night that's thirty below zero, because he'd dirty it – I'd dirty it – I – how can we take his dust? Wouldn't a return, even a good profit, from us pollute his investment?"

Dan waited until Jacob had left with his poke before he wheeled on Timothy. "What were you thinking? In business you can not refuse an investor because he's done something to offend you."

Before Tim could open his mouth to argue, Dan blasted on. "In business you don't ask a man's politics, his religion, or the color of his beard. Everyone has opinions, beliefs that differ from everyone else's. You might as well demand investors only have green eyes."

Fists jammed into his trouser pockets, he took a turn about the room. What could he say to convince Timothy?

"But —" Tim began.

"No. Listen for once."

"No, you listen. I could of died. Or lost feet. If you and Albert didn't help me."

"Yes. But stop and think. Did it ever occur to you that offering to invest in the Nugget was Jacob's way of apologizing? He made a bad mistake, yes. Then again, he didn't deliberately shut you out because he wanted you to freeze to death. For one thing, he didn't know it was you knocking."

"So you're taking his part now?"

"No, never! He should have opened up, no matter who was on his porch. The cold this winter is deadly, and we should all be like Pamelia Fergus, and let the Canary children in, poor little mites. There is no excuse for what he did."

"You'd take his money anyway?"

"Yes. Because what he did was wrong, as I see it, but he didn't set out to hurt you." Dan waited while Timothy stood at the door and watched the weather outside, although he didn't reckon the boy saw much of anything.

From the adjacent office there was only silence. They had no doubt heard him, Jacob, and Timothy, and now avidly awaited the next act. Dan could almost feel them panting with anticipation.

"I guess I can see that." Tim spoke to the thickly frosted, darkening windowpanes. "We can't be choosy whose money we take as investments. Not if we want to develop the mine."

"That's right." Dan knew there were limits to taking investments, but Jacob did not have any sort of dishonesty they would have to watch out for. "If someone robs a bank and tries to invest the money with us, that would be different. We could never take it."

"I see. Jacob is honest. So what do we do about him wanting to invest?"

"Wait and see. That's all we can do now. Wait and see." Dan raised his mug to finish the remains of his coffee but found only bitter grounds.

29 ~~~

The Montana Post: 1/21/1865, p. 3.

Discovery and Settlement of Alder Creek:

The appearance of Alder creek at this time is
strikingly different from what it then was.
The deer and the antelope fed undisturbed.
The low bottom was covered with a dense
growth of alder; the higher banks sent for a
pleasant perfume from the blossoms of the
wild cherry which were then in bloom, and
the grass was rich and luxuriant where there
was no timber. But the hidden treasure —
the white man's god, had been discovered,
and he was there to worship at its shrine,
with all his frontier habits of destruction.

In the log building they called the Court House, Dan
watched the court clerk, Andrew Torbet, direct people
to their destinations. Some came on county business,
but others sought to enjoy the fun of watching the
informal meeting presided over by Judge Hosmer. A
tall, thin man who looked astonishingly like President
Lincoln, he made an amusing contrast with X Beidler,
stocky who stood

Deputy Beidler stood guard at the doorway to His
Honor's office, which functioned as a courtroom
during sessions of District Court One. His feet spread,
the ever-present shotgun cradled in the crook of his

elbow, he surveyed the room as though he expected to prevent a disaster.

X expected disaster anywhere, any time, often with good reason.

As often as disaster arrived, it had never yet found him unprepared.

His heavy soup-strainer mustache bristled at everyone, even his friends. No one dared enter the judge's office until X allowed it.

Not even his fellow Vigilantes. Like Dan.

X guarding the proceedings made Judge Hosmer's "informal conversation" as unlike a conversation as anything Dan could imagine. Yet it was not officially a hearing, for Andrew Torbet stayed at his county clerk's desk near the front door, just as if it were an ordinary day.

Dan knew better. Call it something else, keep Torbet at the door instead of taking notes, it would be a hearing. Judge Hosmer might say its purpose was to help him understand the issues of Gold Country, but it would carry the weight of the law.

His Honor was the Chief Justice of the Montana Territorial Supreme Court, no matter where he presided.

As an unrecorded conversation, it might escape accusations of violating the law, but Dan expected no one to be fooled. Yet it might give the Confederate majority in Virginia City what it wanted – proof that their desires were being considered. Being ruled from two thousand miles away by a Union government did not sit well with any grayback, as Union men called Confederate sympathizers. And having a Union administration rule over the new territory pleased them even less. Whether this so-called conversation eased their fears of a Union dictatorship, Dan doubted.

Just ask Tobias Fitch. Never a Union supporter, Fitch had become ever more radical in the cause of a man's right to own whatever property he chose. Dan's lips twisted. As if another human being should or could be considered property.

The jail door opened on a draft of air stinking from long unwashed waste buckets and filthy, chilled men.

He drew out a handkerchief and breathed through it. After a few breaths, the jail odor seemed to disappear, being absorbed into the general pungent atmosphere.

He was wondering if he could detect a man by means of his smell. Dogs could probably detect different human smells with their long noses, but —

"Ryder said he'd watch the office." Rubbing his hands in their fingerless gloves, Timothy came to stand beside him.

"Good. We'd need someone there. Just in case."

Tim did not ask in case of what? "You think he'd do any good? 'In case'?"

"Probably not. The office being occupied would be enough to discourage most burglars in town."

On purpose, they did not mention Fitch, nor Abbott. Dan held himself still, feigning ease, hands in his coat pockets where no one could see his fists, doubled to strike. He leaned against the wall, a tongue-and-groove plank barrier one board thick, between Hosmer's office and the short corridor to the jail, and watched beyond his stepson's shoulder as though new arrivals interested him.

From there he heard every word Abbott spoke inside Fitch's cell.

"I tell you, it's a done deal." Abbott's voice had the flinty ring of empty bravado. Whistling in a thunderstorm. "You're as good as free."

A mumble responded. For once Fitch kept his voice down. Dan could not make out the words.

"That mudsill judge won't dare to hold you from seeing your little boy, you a Vigilante in good standing. And a brother Mason of His Honor." Abbott's voice held a sneer as he said, 'brother Mason.' "Besides, you're an upstanding Confederate veteran who only defended your home against the Yankee invasion." A sour laugh from Abbott. "Yankee invasion. That's the line to take. Self-defense in the war and self-defense against the damned Yankee thief here."

"Invasion and theft." Fitch's voice came clear through the wall. He seemed to savor the two words as he repeated them. "You think that'll work against a mudsill judge and all the other mudsills here?"

"It'll work better'n some things. These –" Dan lost the curse "– are on their last legs. We'll win this thing yet."

'This thing.' Did Abbott mean the war or the Nugget?

As Dan considered that, X turned toward the open doorway and came to attention. His Honor gave him an order with "please" attached.

Yes, sir." The tall crown of X's wide-brimmed hat rose almost even with His Honor's shoulder. He stepped into the short hallway and spoke to Dan. "It's time. You and the boy can go in now. Front row, next to Torbet's table. Like before." He dipped his head in what might have been sort of a bow. "When you're settled, I'll bring in Abbott and Fitch, and then let in them as want to watch the fireworks." The ends of his mustache lifted, but not enough to uncover his mouth. He measured the waiting men leaning on the walls or sitting on the commissioners' empty desks. "Bunch of real winners, them. They don't care about Fitch trying to murder you. They figure he's gettin' shanghaied because he's a Reb. To them it's all politics, that's all. Even murder. Just politics."

As X stalked to the jail door, keys jangling in his hand, Timothy whispered, "X is right, you know. Dead on."

And then he seemed to hear what he'd said as if by a sort of delayed transmission. "I didn't mean —"

"It's all right." Dan ignored him. Nothing anyone else said mattered now.

From this point, it was all the coming battle, and it wouldn't be until it was over. Until Fitch was in Federal prison, in Detroit. Or hanged.

Judge Hosmer sat at his desk on a platform raised a few inches above the floor. As Dan and Timothy took their seats, he nodded affably and wished them both a "Good morning."

"Good morning, Your Honor." Dan restrained himself from remarking that His Honor held the morning's goodness in his own hands.

Behind the judge and to his right, at the corner of the platform, stood a hall tree that held his greatcoat and, today, his judicial robe. For this "conversation," as he'd termed the meeting, he wore the usual men's outfit in this country of deep subzero winters – a sheepskin waistcoat over a shirt. Below his shirt cuffs, his long winter underwear showed glimpses of a cuff, red faded to pink from many washings. Mrs. Hosmer, it appeared, believed in cleanliness.

Directly behind him hung a large United States flag, the blue Union section with its thirty-six stars dominating over his shoulder.

Dan heard low mutterings from the Confederate contingent sitting behind Abbott's empty chair.

On the wall to the judge's right, his clerk's table and chair stood between the first row of chairs, reserved for the prosecution in any case, and the wall separating this office from the jail. A month ago, the clerk had been a man named Dobson, a 300-lb. giant called 'Dobbin,' from his last name and his great size. Dobson had decided the Montana climate was unhealthy, so he'd started for warmer country as soon as the previous session had ended.

His replacement, Reverend Torbet, was his opposite in almost every way – thin, precise, and a teetotaler. Tall and lean, he also bore a surprising resemblance to Abraham Lincoln with his high cheekbones and the short, dark beard outlining his jaw from one sideburn to the other.

On the opposite side of the room, facing the doorway, Hal Abbott wore a self-satisfied smile that seemed intended to convince everyone he had already prevailed in this so-called "conversation." He slung one arm over the back of his chair, as he half-turned to chat with a man behind him. If he aimed for an appearance of nonchalance, he failed. Having turned his back to Dan, he could not sit still Every few seconds, he shifted his weight on the chair, or flexed his back, or scratched under his own waistcoat.

"He's nervous," Dan whispered to Timothy.

"Me, too. I wish they'd hurry up and get this over with."

"So do I, as long as he decides in our favor."

"What? You think —"

"Shhh!" Dan whispered. "Keep your voice down! I'm not sure what Judge Hosmer will do. You can never be sure of a judge until the trial is over."

"This ain't a trial."

"No matter what you call it, it is still an argument in front of a judge, and his decision will affect our lives." He let Tim ponder that for a moment, then changed the subject to ask in a normal tone, "How are you getting along with your new tutor?"

"Vaughn? He's all right. He makes schooling more fun than I thought it would be. He showed me how the baby learning, like the Latin, amo, amas, amat" – a quick glance at Dan to see if he laughed – "feeds into knowing how to pronounce the scientific names of rocks and even flowers. I liked that. I didn't know a dead language still had scientific life in it, like Vaughn said."

Before Dan could recover from his surprise, Judge Hosmer wiped the nib of his pen and laid it down, thrust the cork into the neck of the ink bottle.

X nodded at Torbet, who eased around his table and moved to stand between the judge's platform and the doorway as X left his post.

Dan tracked Beidler's movements by the sound of his steps. At the door to the jail, the deputy's key rasped in the padlock, and a chain rattled through metal brackets.

Dan's pulse drummed faster in his temples as he listened to the rumble and squeak of a key turning a cell lock.

He knew the routine.

X would bring Fitch out, on a light logging chain, and keep a close watch on him until Judge Hosmer rendered his decision: put him back in his cell or release him.

Timothy demanded in a whisper, "Why release him?"

So. He had let slip his deepest fear. He didn't want to explain, but he had no choice. Not with his stepson. His entire family had too much riding on today's decision.

He whispered, "Worst case. Hosmer could agree to reopen the case of the Nugget's ownership if Abbott can show good cause. Also, he might consider Fitch's guilt in our fight unprovable."

"What?" Timothy almost shouted.

Heads turned toward them.

"Keep your voice down!" Dan pretended to straighten his coat.

Timothy sniffed. A drop hung at the end of his nose

"Wipe your nose," Dan said. "Quick."

The boy snatched a cloth from an inside pocket. Behind the cloth's folds, he muttered, "How could he?"

"Points of law. Fitch's word against mine."

From the jail men's voices came muffled through the locked door, then the scrape of a key in a lock, and a louder man's baritone, curse words distinct with a twang on a flat "A" and a nasal "N" that tightened Dan's jaw.

Fitch.

Footsteps shuffled. When they came through the door from the jail, Fitch's face contorted at the sight of Dan.

"I'm innocent! It's an injustice! Unconstitutional! Illegal! I demand a speedy trial." He shouted as if he expected a posse of his fellow graybacks to charge in, swords all a-glitter and banners ruffling.

He reeked of the jailhouse, the stench of men who wore the clothes they were arrested in, weeks or months before, garments that might not have been washed since temperatures dropped toward winter.

X Beidler's shotgun at Fitch's back prodded him into His Honor's office, onto the straight chair next to the wall, beside his attorney, facing the door.

X closed the door and stood against it. He held the shotgun across his chest. In less than a blink, he could swing it around to focus its close-set stare on anyone.

Dan had seen it. He'd heard its thunderous roar, ducked shreds of a target blown to bits carried on a breeze.

"So," Dan muttered to Tim, "he fought to break the Constitution, but now he wants its protection."

The boy brought out a handkerchief and breathed through it. Dan caught a hint of sagebrush that helped to mask Fitch's smell, that nothing short of immersing him whole, clothes and all, in a vat of hot soapy water could erase.

Or drowning him in it.

His Honor gaveled once; the sound block hopped. When Fitch had fallen silent, Torbet called for order and took his place at his table.

"Good morning, gentlemen." Without his robe of office, and wearing a heavy waistcoat over a limp gray shirt, Chief Justice Hezekiah Hosmer looked like a pudgy, balding businessman, which he also was. His voice, even though cordial, carried the ring of an authority backed by the might of the Union.

And the promise of X's shotgun.

Whether awed by the judge's bearing or the weapon, Fitch's pals maintained a church-like quiet.

From across the room, behind Abbott and Fitch, two or three of Dan's friends nodded to him. He let a smile curve his lips. With his fellow Vigilantes present, there would be order in this "conversation."

Despite Abbott's restraining hand on his arm, Fitch shouted, "This hearing is a charade! It's unconstitutional! It's —"

His supporters raised their voices: "You got that right," "Yeah, Major!"

So much for hoping to placate the Confederates. Hosmer would know immediately that was a lost cause.

"Yeah! You tell 'em!" shouted another man, who wore the yellowish trousers from his old Confederate uniform. The color was called butternut, after the squash.

"Remove that man!" Judge Hosmer pointed the gavel toward Fitch's ally. A few men, who had been among Albert Rose's rescuers, were already moving to seize him and hustle him Into the corridor. In the hallway, they shut the door behind themselves.

His honor hammered the gavel on the sound block. When he had complete silence, he pointed it at Fitch. "Another outburst, and you will go straight back to your cell and remain there until the date I set for your hearing during the next term. Whether that is at the beginning or the end of term will depend on you. Do you understand, or should your attorney explain it to you?"

"I understand." Fitch ducked his head as if to bow, but Dan caught a rebellious gleam in his eyes.

Judge Hosmer shot a warning scowl toward Abbott, who whispered in his client's ear. He broke off to say, "We apologize to the Court, your Honor."

The chief justice set the gavel down. "Very well. Let us have decorum in this Court, even though this is not a trial, nor a hearing, but a conversation to become familiar with the facts and issues under consideration."

He threaded spectacle bows over each ear and read from a paper lying between his forearms. "Good morning, gentlemen."

Several men, including Dan and Timothy answered, "Good morning."

"If no one objects, I'll get directly to the purpose of this informal meeting."

Again he paused, pulled his spectacles down his nose and studied the waiting men. Like a preacher waits for his congregation to settle, Dan thought.

"We are here to consider a request by Mr. Harold Abbott, attorney of record for Mr. Tobias Fitch, on behalf of his client, to grant him a temporary release on humanitarian grounds, so that he can see to the welfare of his infant son, now in the care of Mrs. Beatrice Running Tongue, in Nevada City."

"Major Fitch." Less than an outright protest, more than a simple reminder, Fitch's military rank rose from a couple of the Confederate spectators, who thought the judge should address Fitch – and refer to him – by his military title.

Judge Hosmer glared around the room.

Silence reigned.

He went on. "Because we are between terms of the District Court, First District, of Montana Territory, as stated in the Act noted in the *Montana Post* of the fourteenth instant as 'A Change of Time,' I have decided to hold this informal meeting of interested parties so that I may understand the virtue of Mr. Fitch's request. I do so at the request, again, of Mr. Fitch, who maintains that waiting until the next term of this court, to begin March thirteenth, again as prescribed by the same law, would unnecessarily work a hardship on him."

Pausing, His Honor looked up, his usually affable face now a stern mask.

"Let me stress – again – we will keep to strict rules of decorum, as if we were in a formal court. Anyone who cannot abide by civilized rules of discourse will be ejected forthwith. Do I make myself clear?"

He fixed Abbott, then Fitch with a hard glare, before he turned it on Dan, who lifted his chin to meet Judge Hosmer's look with his own level stare, patented in New York City courtrooms. As then, he intended to telegraph his respect for the law, at the same time registering his total opposition to this entire charade. If Judge Hosmer wanted to placate the Confederates, they were not having it. Nor was he.

"Yes, Your honor." Dan removed his hat, setting his jaws against the pain.

Though dirty, the bandage on his crown would remind everyone, especially Judge Hosmer, why they were here at all.

Would you, the bandage asked His Honor, release an accused murderer?

Hosmer's eyes wavered. He glanced down at the paper on his desk.

Ah. Dan kept his face as expressionless as he could, suitable for a hearing; even if this was only a meeting,. Hosmer understood.

"Let us proceed." The judge's open palm and half a nod signaled Torbet.

The clerk moved to his desk, picked up a single piece of paper, and called out, "Mr. Abbott, you have requested His Honor to allow Mr. Tobias Fitch to leave the jail for an unspecified length of time to look into the care of his infant son and make alternate arrangements if necessary. Why should he grant your petition?"

Fitch jumped to his feet. "I'll tell you why —"

Deputy Beidler again stood in front of Fitch, his shotgun ready. "Sit down. No one called on you."

Beside Dan, Timothy gasped.

Dan half rose from his seat. He had not seen X move, only that in one blink he stood at the door and in the next he barricaded Fitch, pressed forward, crowded the Southerner, who half-fell onto his chair as men sprang up amid a racket of voices, wood scraping against wood.

Judge Hosmer banged his gavel on its sound block. The hard, sharp cracks echoed around the room, bounced off the walls like guns fired in battle.

Dan sat down, his hat on his lap.

Over all the shouting, the judge roared, "Mister Abbott, control your client."

As suddenly as it had erupted, the commotion ended.

Fitch cradled the stump of his left arm against his chest, rocked back and forth, moaned softly.

How it had happened, no one could say, least of all Dan, who had kept X in his line of sight.

The deputy backed to his post by the door. His eyes glittered.

"Like a feral cat," Dan muttered under his breath.

Abbott rose, straightened his waistcoat, laid one hand on his client's shoulder. "Your honor, my client apologizes for his outburst —"

Dan laughed inwardly. Fitch only regretted the show of potential force had not succeeded.

"— and respectfully begs the court's indulgence to allow him to visit the wet nurse who has charge of his only child, the offspring of his beloved and deceased wife, who died giving him this son. Let not her sacrifice be in vain. Give this bereaved father the opportunity to ensure that all is well with his only child. It is time this court showed mercy to my client."

A few men chorused, "Yes! Mercy! Show mercy."

At that, Abbott reseated himself with a self-satisfied air. He smiled at Dan as if to challenge him: Top this, if you can.

Dan ignored him, kept his face aligned with the amusement he wished he felt.

Judge Hosmer turned his glare toward Dan, and the corners of his mouth softened, almost relaxed into a smile. "Mr. Stark? Should you like to respond to Mr. Abbott?"

"Yes, your honor." He stood, nodded an apology to Torbet for turning his back to the clerk. Speaking to the judge, he also included the spectators, hostile though many of them were to his Union politics and his New York City accent. "In the first place, Mr. Fitch was incarcerated on a charge of attempted murder." He turned his head to glance at Torbet, knowing that he displayed the bandage to everyone.

"As a new father and a stepfather myself, I can appreciate his concern for his child." Thinking of the twins, those morsels of squalling life, Dan had to stop to regain control.

"Mr. Fitch," – he cleared his throat – "Mr. Fitch has only been jailed since December thirtieth, if memory serves." He took a breath, knowing full well he recalled that endless day as if he lived it over again. "The first session of this District Court, set by an Act of the Legislature, gave Mr. Fitch —" interrupting himself to calculate — "only seventy-four days, total, to wait for his day in court." Drawing out the arithmetic he knew would be tedious in the extreme, but he proceeded in hopes that sheer boredom would cool the simmering tensions. "Of that period, twenty-two days have elapsed, leaving just fifty-seven days more. Granted that in so new a country all requirements for his comfort could not be met, nonetheless, his basic needs have been catered to as well as for any man now held pending trial, largely at the personal expense of Deputy Sheriff Beidler. Certainly he has received better treatment than that afforded incarcerated men in the infamous prison in New York City. I refer, of course, to the Tombs. His arm has received the best medical attention available. I saw to that, myself. I brought him here from Beaverhead Rock to find the most qualified doctor, in the treatment of wounds." Everyone present knew he referred to Doctor Glick, the surgeon who had saved Henry Plummer's gun arm.

"Yeah," growled Fitch. "After you tried to brain me."

Dan bowed his head to display the bandage. "*I* tried to brain *you*?"

Fitch barked, "Yes! You attacked me, just as I reached for —"

Dan laughed.

Fitch yelled, "He tried to kill me, Your Honor, because he knows the gold mine he's got control of, that gold mine, the Nugget, it belongs to me! To me! To me!"

Timothy leaped up. "The hell it does! You're a liar!"

Dan's hand on his shoulder pressed him into his seat.

Shaking his short arm at Tim, as though it ended in a fist rather than a folded sleeve, Fitch yelled threats, obscenities and curses on Timothy's father, on Timothy, and on Dan.

"Stop there." X stood in Fitch's way, the shotgun looking toward his knee.

Fitch babbled. He slobbered down his filthy butternut coat with its gray patches where his Confederate army officer's insignia had once been sewn.

Major Tobias Fitch.

Dan sat down.

Anything more would gild the lily.

Timothy grasped his forearm, began to say something.

Dan turned his good ear to the boy.

Tim whispered, "You should've let him die in that cave."

"No. I wouldn't let a snake burn."

The gavel cracked down on the sound block in a rapid-fire beat like a gatling gun.

Dan asked himself, why had he not heard it sooner?

Hosmer's face glowed red and shone with sweat in the chilly room, and his lower lip had disappeared between his teeth.

When he had silence, the pudgy, affable man had turned into a figure of supreme and stern authority, like an artist's rendition of God in the Bible.

"Mr. Abbott, you and your client will please stand."

X positioned himself near the front corner of the platform. From there he could protect His Honor without blocking his view of the attorney and his client.

No boot scraped. No chair creaked. The onlookers seemed not to breathe.

X's thumb bent over one of the shotgun's hammers.

"Mr. Torbet?"

"Yes, Your Honor."

"Have you the court calendar at hand?"

A scuffle of paper, a flipping of pages.

"Yes, Your Honor."

"Mr. Abbott." His Honor did not wait for the customary polite response. "Your client has destroyed the decorum required of a court, even in an informal conversation such as this, by causing a complete disruption. In so doing, he has proven himself incapable of managing himself well enough to be at large even under your supervision.

"I therefor remand him to jail to await the first term of this court commencing on March thirteenth. Mr. Torbet will inform you of further action to be taken against your client – and possibly yourself – regarding his total disruption of a meeting designed solely for his benefit.

"Deputy Beidler, escort Mister Fitch back to his cell." A slight emphasis on 'Mister' reminded everyone that whatever Fitch's rank had been in Sterling Price's army, it was not recognized in a Union court. Confederate soldiers were mere armed insurrectionists against the duly constituted, legal government.

Judge Hosmer raised the gavel.

Abbott said, "Your Honor, if it please the court —"

"It does not, Mr. Abbott. One more syllable from you, and you will find yourself sanctioned. Do you understand?" He brought the gavel down in a last report, so loud that Dan looked to be sure X had not fired his shotgun.

Abbott moistened his lips. His voice squeaked. "Yes, your Honor. Perfectly."

X beckoned toward the back row. Two burly men navigated through the seated onlookers toward Abbott and Fitch.

As one laid his hand on Fitch's good arm to lift him to his feet, he hammered the air at Dan with his short arm. "It's mine, and you know it! That lode is mine! It's the Mother Lode. I own it."

The second helper laid a heavy hand on Fitch's shoulder. As he screamed, "I own the Mother Lode! I own the Mother Lode!"

The first man took his whole arm in a hammer lock as the second helper seized Fitch's short arm at the bicep. They propelled Fitch out.

Dan listened to the sounds of Fitch being jailed again: the jail door unlocked and relocked, Fitch's muffled screams through the walls as he was put back in his cell.

"I own the Mother Lode!"

30 ~~~

The Montana Post: 1/21/1865, p. 3.

Discovery and Settlement of Alder Creek:
... those of us who were here from the
beginning ... well remember the danger... on
account of the lawlessness of desperadoes.
... road agents and robbers walked
uncontrolled through the land. Then came
pleasing visions of the vigilantes — God
bless them. The capture and trial of Ives
followed. The noble and fearless men who
prosecuted him — may they also have their
reward. We owe them a debt of gratitude.
The public execution of the ring-leaders
shortly after inaugurated the reign of peace
and order.... We rest safely under the
protecting shield of the civil law, with a
consciousness that there is still a power
behind the throne.

War.

Elbows on his knees, Dan waited while the judge's
office emptied around him.

Timothy stirred, cleared his throat. "Um, Dan'l?"

As Torbet helped Judge Hosmer put on his
greatcoat, the judge said, "Mr. Stark, this meeting is
over." His tone was kindly.

Yes, perhaps. But the war had just begun

Wordlessly, he and Timothy walked up the slope to the corner of Jackson Street, where they turned downhill. Passing his house, he gave it a brief glance.

Tim stopped. Caught up after a few steps. "We ain't telling Mam what happened?"

Without answering, he continued on, climbed the stairs to the veranda on the second floor of Content's Corner, and brought out the key, but the lamplight inside told him he would not need it. He pocketed the key, turned the knob, and walked into his domain.

Vaughn Ryder started up from his seat by the stove, sending a few papers cascading to the floor. Dan stepped around them, closer to the stove.

War.

He heard his desktop sliding aside, the glug of a liquid into a glass. Timothy poured him a drink of Laphroaig. Ordinarily, he would have refused it, but after he won this war – this court battle, not that flaming monster in the States – he would take the family to the British Isles, to the distillery in Scotland, and buy more.

He could afford it then. He would afford it then, by God.

Unbuttoning his coat, removing his hat, he accepted the glass.

Timothy hung his coat and hat, and his own, on the hall tree.

Ryder whispered a question. Tim answered, "Shush. He's thinking."

Thinking? Is that what this was? This bemused state, in which his mind settled his ideas, sifted out the kernels of certainty from the mess of unknowns?

He knew for sure Fitch's attack was merely the latest, if the most blatant, in their war over the McDowell family property. After Sam McDowell disappeared, Fitch had laid siege to Martha for the control he would have over all the prospects her late, unmourned, husband had staked. When Martha refused his advances, and became Dan's common-law wife, Fitch had not given up. Then Dan had been forced to return to New York. In his absence, the Southerner had besieged her again, even as her figure thickened and her belly swelled with Dan's twins. Not knowing whether he would return or not, another woman might have accepted Fitch's proposal to save her reputation for honesty from annihilation.

Not Martha. Scorned by most respectable people, she'd held to her faith in his return. Then, Sam's corpse had been discovered, and Fitch's indifference to the other man's fate became known.

When Dan had returned and married Martha as soon as it could be arranged, he had believed the snake was defanged.

And then, Dan confessed to the flames leaping behind the stove-door grate, he'd made the worst mistake of his life. He'd allowed Fitch to persuade him to make a trip to Bannack to lobby the legislature for a thousand feet of ground in quartz claims. 'To give them working room.' Even Timothy had advised against traveling with Fitch.

In Bannack they had been successful. The law had been enacted with the thousand feet of ground. Governor Edgerton signed it.

On the way home, Fitch had tried to brain him.

His rant at the close of Judge Hosmer's meeting, had been a fresh salvo in their ongoing war. Fitch had become unhinged, and the only way to manage a madman, like a mad dog, was to put him down.

There was no doubt about that. The only question was how to do it and escape justice.

The law required a crime to precede punishment, but what if a potential danger became reality? How could he allow the family to be at risk? How could he stand aside, protecting his eternal soul while a madman endangered helpless babies and women?

It was simple.

He would not let the family be frightened, let alone threatened.

Or worse.

He sipped his whisky and felt its warmth all the way to the pit of his stomach.

"You been doing some mighty hard cogitatin', so how about you let us in on it?" Timothy thrust the cork well into the opening of the whisky bottle and put it back into the box. Slid the warped door-desktop over it. Hooked his posterior on the desktop, and perched there, arms folded across his chest.

Dan drained the whisky and set the glass on the arm of his chair. Rising, he studied Ryder for a few seconds before making up his mind. "I'm taking a chance, Vaughn, that you have no remaining loyalty toward Hal Abbott."

The young man sputtered, "What? No. None. Not a lick."

Timothy spoke as if the other young man were not present. "He stands to lose something if he does."

The tone of his voice, the hard gleam in his eyes, heralded a different Timothy.

Ryder's eyes and voice did not waver. "I couldn't live with myself if I had any more truck with him or his clients. I've paid my cribbage debt. I'm a free man." He swallowed. "Thanks to you, Mr. Stark."

"You'd better be damn sure, because we're at war now."

"War?" Timothy brushed his hand across his face as though to clear cobwebs.

"War?" Ryder echoed him.

Tim said, "You think it's that bad?"

"You heard Fitch." Dan riffled through copies of the *Montana Post* he kept on the middle shelf of the bookcase. "What do you think?" He pulled out two sheets. Explained to Ryder. "A law has to be pubic, readily accessible to anyone to read or have it read to him, in order for it to be legally binding. Once it's published, no one can claim ignorance of the law, because it's a citizen's responsibility to become acquainted with it."

As he spoke, Dan resumed his seat near the stove. He folded one sheet so it would lie on the arm of his chair and laid another sheet, a different issue of the *Post*, on it.

"That's why the laws are printed in the *Montana Post*?"

"As soon as Tom Dimsdale gets them, the typesetter puts them in the formes." He scanned the sheet, his index finger sliding down a long column of print.

Ryder looked over his shoulder. "I read that article on the discovery of Alder Gulch. If Dimsdale wrote it, he's a good writer. But what did he mean by a 'power behind the throne'?"

Dan's finger stopped. The print blurred, and he seemed to walk again up Wallace Street to the building now occupied by the Drug Emporium. They'd escorted five men to their deaths by hanging on that walk.

Feet shuffled to his left: Timothy shifted his position.

"I – I'm sorry —" Ryder stammered.

Regaining his equilibrium, Dan said, "No, it's all right." To give himself time, he shuffled the sheets into order. "For most of a year, men who tried to go home with their gold were waylaid, robbed, and often murdered. To deal with this situation, a group of men took permanent action against the culprits. These same men are now unofficial deputies, available to help Deputy Beidler when he needs assistance." It was a well rehearsed explanation, one he had mulled over but seldom used, and he hoped it was not too fluent.

But meeting Ryder's searching gaze, he decided it would serve. No more needed to be said. Unless the fellow asked more questions. Unless it became necessary to explain his own involvement in the Vigilantes, that he had helped to write the bylaws. That he'd been and still was the group's legal counsel. That he had pulled his own rope.

"I see." Ryder gestured toward the woodbox. "It's getting low, isn't it? I think I'll bring up an armload or two."

As he thrust his arms into his coat sleeves, Timothy stood away from Dan's desk. "You want help?"

Ryder smiled. "I can find my way downstairs and back. Thanks anyway."

Tim waited until Ryder had closed the door behind himself. "D'you think he heard what you didn't say?"

Dan mulled that over. "Yes. He's not stupid. He'll eventually figure it all out, but I think he'll remain our friend. Within his own lights, of course."

"Yeah, because between us and Fitch's sort, what else is there?"

"Bystanders." Dan shrugged off the topic of Ryder's loyalties. "He'll be cold when he comes in. What about coffee?"

Timothy laughed. "You mean I should make a fresh pot."

Dan bent his head to the law he was reading. "Thanks for offering."

Carol Buchanan

As skimmed the long column, he reflected, not all wars were shooting wars. The law attempted to take war off the battlefield and into the courtroom.

He would not be unarmed when he went to legal war with Fitch. Or any other.

31 ~~~

The Montana Post: 1/21/1865, p. 4.

Local and Other Items
All you fellows who have gulch claims in the Prickly Pear and Deer Lodge county, had better represent them soon. They will be jumpable on the first of February.

"You fool!" Fitch screamed at Hal Abbott, who stood outside the locked cell door. "Dan Stark stole that claim from me, and you haven't done a blasted thing to get it back. It's mine! Strike me dead, but I'm telling you, that mine belongs to me, and all the gold in it, and I own all the gold from it because it's the Mother Lode. That idiot boy has stumbled onto the Mother Lode, and he's too dumb to know it. But I know it! I own the Mother Lode."

"There's no such thing as the Mother Lode!" Abbott's tone rose to a scream.

For answer, Fitch's high-pitched hysterics went on in a Gatling gun spray of foul words and imaginative blasphemies.

The other prisoners agreed later among themselves they had not heard most of them even in the worst saloons where Hal Abbott picked up some of his best clients. 'Best' clients meaning men who could be counted on to get into trouble and pay him to get them out of it. Or out of the worst of the trouble they got themselves into. Those whose sense of self-preservation kept them out of the Vigilantes' kind ministrations.

Who now shushed each other and listened in a grave-like silence so as not to miss a syllable. This was the most fun they'd had since their last drunk and disorderly.

They listened now.

"Don't worry." Abbott adopted a reasonable tone when Fitch stopped to gasp for breath. "It's not May first yet. Nothing can take that claim from you for another three months. We have plenty of time to win it from the McDowell family."

"What do you mean, May first? I'm worried about February first."

Abbott pretended to be a model of sweet reason. It was bad enough dealing with a madman, but Fitch still had a semblance of intelligence. Or cunning. "That's for Deer Lodge County and the Prickly Pear country over by Last Chance Gulch. Here in Fairweather district, claims can't be jumped between October first and May first."

Fitch's eyes appeared in the porthole at a man's standing height. "That's right. I forgot." He went quiet. "So what do you plan to do about my claim?"

"Whatever you want me to do. I need clear instructions, though."

"Hah! That's because you don't know nothing about mining law. You sue the McDowell family, and especially Dan Stark, for everything they've got. Let 'em go naked into a blizzard, that'll show 'em. All of 'em. Their brats and servants and everyone. But you sue 'em for theft of that claim."

"On what grounds? The Fairweather Miners Court and the People's Court both ruled that they do own that claim."

What Fitch said then would have been unprintable in even the most rotten rags, the gleeful prisoners told each other later.

"You hear me?" Fitch wheezed, "You sue them for ownership and theft and your grounds, as you call them, will be this: I paid Sam McDowell to find that claim. We had a contract that made it mine in exchange for paying McDowell his expenses and something over for his family. That contract exists someplace, I tell you. It was properly recorded when Sam discovered the claim for me. It'll prove Dan Stark is a thief, and that whole family colluded with him to steal my claim."

Later, the other prisoners told each other they hadn't had so much fun even before they got put in jail. It kind of made a man sorry when his sentence was up.

32 ~~~

The Montana Post: 1/21/1865, p. 2.

Discovery and Settlement of Alder Creek
Those of us who were here from the beginning ... well remember the danger from the Bannacks, and the still greater danger that existed on account of lawlessness. Now we rest safely under the protecting shield of the civil law, with a conscious that there is still a power behind the throne.

Dan's office door slammed open on a gust of snow.

He and Timothy reached for the nearest available weapon – poker or rifle – before they recognized the short, stocky man who saved the door from breaking a window and closed it, shutting out the wind.

Sliding the end of the desktop aside just enough to form a corner, Deputy X Beidler stood his shotgun upright and unwound his muffler from his face as he stood by the stove and shook the encrusted snow onto the floor.

"You auditioning for the theatre, X?"

Chafing his hands in the stove's heat, Beidler cocked his head at Dan. "I come to warn you, else you won't see it coming." He glanced around to find a spittoon. "You inviting folks to use the floor these days?"

Unspeaking, Timothy brought a gallon can that had once held stewed pears and handed it to X.

"Thank you kindly." X shot a gob of tobacco juice into the can. The mess made a hollow plop that turned Ryder's face pale. Setting the can on the floor by his feet, X wiped his mouth with a handkerchief the indeterminate color of dirt.

"Fitch has talked his lawyer, Hal Abbott, into suing you and the McDowell family for ownership of the Nugget."

"I've been expecting this. You heard him. He thinks he owns it because Timothy's father signed a contract with him to prospect for likely claims, and he thinks he owns this claim, especially."

"Why 'especially'?" asked Ryder.

X and Dan spoke almost at once. "Because the terms of —" X stopped, gestured 'after you' toward Dan as though they met in a doorway.

Dan said, "You tell him, Timothy."

Tim glanced around at the others as if asking their permission. "Pap had an agreement With Major Fitch —"

"Major Fitch?" Dan's voice didn't rise much above a whisper.

Tim's face reddened. "Sorry. Old habits, they die hard."

"All right. Go on."

"Fitch and Pap agreed that he'd pay Pap five dollars for every claim they filed on, and fifty percent if the claim paid, but he'd only file on paying claims. So Pap, he hunted for good claims. He'd find some promising ground, stake it, then work it a bit to see if it really had promise. He couldn't file on any old piece of ground or he wouldn't get paid. This here Nugget claim is one of the last ones Pap located for Fitch."

"That's the mine we dug Albert Rose out of." Ryder unclasped a pocketknife and inspected his fingernails.

For a moment they heard only the wind rattling the stove pipe and the fire muttering in the stove. A voice in Number Four asked how to spell 'mandamus.'

Smiling to himself, Dan resisted the temptation to shout, 'Just the way it sounds.' Laughter sounded from the other occupants of that office.

Tim said, "Yeah, that's it."

"Ah." Ryder folded his knife and put it in his trousers pocket.

"War." Dan exchanged a look with X. "It could get ugly."

X glanced at the two young men. "We'll provide protection."

"If it comes to that, I'll be grateful."

"Do you think he has a snowball's chance in court?"

"No. Abbott is off his nut if he thinks he can persuade this judge to override Duncan's Miners Court ruling from last year." Dan put his hand down flat on the sheets of *Montana Post* lying on the arm of his chair. "Between the New Quartz Law the legislature passed in December and the new law on the public domain, the Nugget is safe."

"Safe?" Timothy sat up straight. "You mean we don't have nothing to worry about? Fitch is all bluff?"

"Not by a long shot. He — "

"The Major." X sneered. His mustache lifted at one end as his upper lip curled. "The Major is mad as a hatter. You can expect any all-fired, downright rotten humbug he can think of to steal the Nugget away from your family."

Tim's voice trembled. "He won't stop at humbug. He half-murdered my Pap, and he tried to murder Dan'l."

"Mur—" Ryder cut off the word.

X turned his scorn on the young man. "You too qualmish for this? You work for Fitch's lawyer, don't you?"

Before Ryder could answer, Dan held up a hand. "Not anymore."

"Oh?" X 's glare aimed at Ryder like the twin barrels of his shotgun. "You sure about that?"

"As sure — "

Ryder spoke in a near-whisper that sliced sharp as a stiletto. "I wasn't too 'qualmish,' as you say, during the Battle of Gettysburg to administer ether and hold men down so the surgeons could cut off arms and legs, or sew lower jaws back onto faces. I wasn't too qualmish to avoid clean-up duty on the battlefield days afterwards, shoveling parts of rotting corpses – human and horse – into mass graves." He stood up, thrust his shaking hands into his trouser pockets and went to stand at the door.

Timothy rose to stand beside him.

The two young men stayed there, a few inches apart, but as solid together as a palisade. When did that happen? Dan asked himself. To his knowledge, Timothy had never before had a friend near his own age. But now, seemingly, he did. He smiled, remembering the two cousins from the Bible. David and Jonathan. Friends. He raised an eyebrow at X.

The little man stared back at him, unrepentant, perhaps, or satisfied at Ryder's reaction. Certainly he had learned more about the fellow in less than a minute than many people – Dan included himself – would have learned in several hours. If ever. Ryder had said more than his words. He would never be one to align himself with a sympathizer to the cause of slavery – no matter how the Confederates disguised slaveholding as a property right.

He would never be one of Abbott's minions now that he knew him for what he was.

"I think we could drink more coffee." Getting up, Dan went about the business of making the brew.

In Number Four, Burns and Pemberton debated "reasonable doubt." Were they making progress on the criminal code at last?

He had dealt with that concept in law often enough to have his own arguments firmly in mind. He'd happily meet Abbott in court, or on a battlefield – but what was the difference? A courtroom or the Battle of Gettysburg – the weapons differed profoundly, but the spirit was the same. He would annihilate Abbott. War was war. In a sense. Except for flying balls and cannonades.

He set to grinding beans left from yesterday's roasting. The simple task freed his mind to a sudden realization: Like X had said, Fitch was mad enough to do anything to own the Nugget. Anything. Anything at all.

"You're grinding air," X told him. "Them beans is ground. Grinding nothing ain't gonna help 'em none."

"Yes." His mind still fixed on 'anything,' he poured the grounds into a saucepan, dipped up enough water to make two cups for each man, and set the pan on the cooktop.

At once his hands went colder than the water dipped out of buckets of melting ice, and his throat tightened so he nearly choked. He looked around to see that Timothy and Ryder, still at the door, murmured to each other. They had not noticed his instant of panic.

"Anything." Dan spoke to the grounds. "Anything."

"You heard me," X said.

"We may need a crew, X. Protection for Martha and all the young ones." Meaning Eileen and Dotty, as well as the babies.

The babies. His breath caught. His little boys, only twenty-four days old. As if a rubber sheet had been thrown over his head, he could not breathe. Bent over, he struggled for air, coughed and gagged. Drowning.

Someone pounded him on the back, and like a chunk of meat had dislodged itself from his throat, he could breathe again. He wiped his streaming face, blew his nose.

Timothy supported him to sit down. "We can do that. Vaughn and me." He looked over his shoulder at Ryder. "That is, if..."

"Of course I'll help. Whatever you think I can usefully do...." The young man let his offer trail off, while his anxious eyes silently begged Dan for something.

But what? Dan pocketed the handkerchief. Did Ryder own a gun? Dan had not noticed a pistol about his person, and neither of his coat pockets sagged.

"Can you use a gun?" X radiated skepticism, as though he'd already judged Ryder's fighting ability and knew he wouldn't like the answer.

"A – a –" Ryder stammered. His face blanched.

"Then I don't see what use you'd be." X spat, his scorn as real as the chaw he let fly toward the can. "A divinity student." The tobacco hit with a squishy sound inside the can. "I'd liefer have a woman defending your family."

"You forget Eileen." Timothy leaned toward X, his fists doubled. "She took care of Jackie Stevens."

X's breath rasped in his nose, and the wind whistled in the stovepipe as the coffee bubbled in the pan, an odd syncopation of different beats like a small chorus of drums warning from far off. "That's right. Some females have more'n their share of sand."

Dan, recovering from his moment of terror, poured coffee into four heavy, stained ceramic mugs. He set them on his desk and gestured toward them, a silent invitation.

The strong brew steadied him almost as well as a shot of whiskey. "Someone will have to be in the house at all times. Not just one guard, but different men trading off every couple of hours." An idea surprised him, and he almost rushed it into words before he gave himself time to think.

"Ha!" X barked a sound that passed for a laugh with him. "You know what folks will say? That you're keeping a bawdy house, all them men in and out."

Dan looked toward Timothy. The boy's face reddened, and he seemed about to explode.

"If we're to protect my family, I can't be bothered with what people will gossip about. The family's safety comes before their reputations."

He let the silence draw out before he spoke again.

"On my way out here, I noticed that Indian men looked very idle when they're in camp. White people look at an Indian camp and feel sorry for the women, doing all the work while the men lounge about. But, so I've been told, we're not seeing the camp right. The men aren't loafing. They're on guard. They're on watch. If they hoed the corn or dug camas roots, they wouldn't be watching for the enemy. Letting their guard down could cost them everything. Their horses. Their wives and children. Their honor. No one has mercy for them in defeat.

"So when we're guarding my family, I can't let the ladies press all of us into service to get water from a hydrant, or chop more firewood. If I did that, who would be looking out for them?"

X blew on the steam rising from his mug. He swirled the coffee around, almost sending it over the edge. "You think we need two men in the house at all times?"

"There'll be me, and Vaughn," Timothy reminded them.

"Yes. Count me in." The young man's lips twisted in a sort of a smile, or maybe a grimace. "I'm no stranger to gunfire, but I've never shot at a man." He thought for a moment. "I can pump water and chop firewood."

"Empty chamber pots?" X almost did not sneer. Everyone knew this necessary duty was beneath a man. Females did it.

"In my house, everyone, myself included, takes a turn at that." Dan would not have Eileen subjected to this noisome task exclusively.

Dan and X exchanged silent messages that needed no words for them to understand each other. The Vigilantes would guard the house, but discreetly, to avoid the appearance of debauchery.

X put the mug to his lips and took a healthy swallow. "Whew!" He doubled over. Recovering, red-faced with tears streaming down his cheeks, he mopped his face with his handkerchief, rubbed his belly and let loose a low whistle. "That scorched my innards all the way down. Like a small bomb landed in my stomach."

He breathed deep a few times as Dan waited. "I'll let our friends know about this, er, situation, that might develop. Meanwhile, I'll keep an extra watch on

Fitch and make sure he stays out of the weather, inside where he belongs." He pointed a stubby finger at Dan. "You just make sure Judge Hosmer keeps him in jail."

"I'll do my best," Dan promised.

For a time, once the door closed behind X, Dan and the younger men were silent.

"Guarding the family will take more men than just we three," Ryder said.

"Dan'l's got plenty of friends," Timothy assured him.

"Friends? Are there Quakers around here?"

Tim laughed. "Dan's friends ain't Quakers, not by half. They're peacekeepers, though." He nodded, as though satisfied with the idea and the word. "Yup. 'Peacekeepers' suits them just fine." After a few seconds, he added, "Or maybe 'peacemakers.'"

"Oh." Ryder looked at Dan, who stood without speaking, sipped his coffee.

"Oh." Ryder said again. "You're a –" Words failed him. He tried again. "You are –"

"One of them." Dan set his mug on the top shelf of the bookcase. "Yes. I'm a member of the Vigilance Committee. Like the Indian braves who keep watch over their towns." He glanced at Tim, who sat, his ankle on the opposite knee, his foot bobbing in time with a beat only he could hear.

Leaning against the bookcase, Dan left his hands free, a habit he had acquired since coming to Virginia City in the summer of '63. He wondered if Vaughn noticed the Spencer rifle leaning in the corner formed by the top shelf and the wall of Number Four, or that he stood within easy reach of it, if need be.

If need be.

That was always a possibility, now more than ever since the last road agent had swung from a gallows. Dan had thought he was done with all that, but more trees looked as though they might bear unwholesome fruit. He shuddered as though a spider had run down his back.

"I read about them, didn't I?" Ryder set his mug on the desk and took the chair next to Tim, turning it so he had a clear, straight view of Dan. "Mr. Dimsdale wrote about it in this week's issue, did he not?"

"So he did."

"If I remember right, he said something about 'resting safely under the protecting shield of the civil law, with a consciousness that there is still a power behind the throne.'"

"Correct again."

"And am I to believe that the Vigilance Committee is this 'power'?"

"Yes."

"And you are a member of the Committee?"

"That's right."

Timothy snorted. "Hah! Not just a member. Dan'l's the prosecutor."

"No," Dan corrected him. "I'm their legal counsel."

Ryder set aside his mug, the coffee only half drunk, and folded his hands on the arm of his chair. "You prosecuted George Ives in 'sixty-three."

"Not alone. There was also Charles Bagg. Most of the credit for Ives's conviction goes to him."

Ignoring Tim's muttered protest, Ryder took a deep breath. "Ives, so I've heard, was hanged?"

"Yes." The single syllable dropped between the young men – boys no longer, grown fast into men. In the knowledge of guilt and innocence, murder and its penalty, Ryder had no experience, though he had far more experience of war's horrors.

"Am I to believe that the hangings afterward also had court proceedings with evidence and witnesses?"

"More or less." Now Dan asked himself how he had been maneuvered into defending the Vigilantes' necessary actions when at the time he had seen no other choice Nor did he now. Yet mistakes had been made, though not for lack of zeal to get the correct sentences carried out.

In human action, perfection was impossible.

If it were, he would not still be plagued with nightmares that awakened him sweating, with a name on his lips.

Not the same name every time.

He wished to God it was one name. Just one. Or better yet, none.

The wall clock clanked, prepared to strike the hour. Standing away from the bookcase, he looked at it, then at the window, now darkening. "We'd better go on home. We have things to do before supper."

33 ~~~

The Montana Post, 1/21/1865, p. 1, Col. 6

The Law Relating to Ranches.

*Sec. 1. ...the right as the same may exist, under the local laws, to occupy, possess and enjoy any tract or portion thereof not to exceed 160 acres, in such form as may be prescribed by the laws of the U. S., shall be respected in law and in equity, in all the courts and tribunals of this Territory, as a chattel real, possessing the character of real estate.

*Sec. 8. The declaration of every occupant of any tract or portion of the public domain mentioned in section five of this act, shall not be construed to include any gold bearing, quartz lodes, silver lodes, or gold diggings, but *said lodes or diggings shall be excepted from the tract of said occupant, and shall be subject to be occupied, possessed and enjoyed, according to the local law or custom of the district in which the same may be situated, and if there be no local law or custom in said district, then by the customs prevailing in the nearest mining district thereto.*

In his reading chair, Dan held baby Luke in the crook of his arm. As the infant wriggled and squirmed in his blanket, his father watched Timothy do battle with the *Montana Post*. The boy perched on the footstool, knees apart, the single sheet spread from knee to knee, anchored by an elbow on each leg, as he tried to read the long vertical columns dangling between them. He traced his progress with an index finger down the shallow paper valley between his legs, mumbling as he went. Abruptly, he whacked the paper and sat up straight as it dropped onto the floor between his feet. Raising a foot to smash down on it, he glanced at his stepfather.

Dan cocked an eyebrow at him.

Tim set his foot down gently a scant inch from the paper. Gathering the sheet, he smoothed its wrinkles. Refolded it. Dropped it on the floor. Sat up with a challenging frown at Dan. "What the h –?" He checked himself and looked around to see if any of the females listened. Poked a thumb toward the paper. Muttered, "What the Sam Hill is all this?"

Vaughn Ryder, cross-legged on the floor, leaned forward to scratch Canary's ears. Dan noted the quickly hidden smile.

At the wash stand, Dotty and Eileen giggled together as they cleaned up after dinner. Martha, sitting on her usual chair at the table, crooned a wordless lullaby to baby Danny, nursing under the brightly striped blanket laid for modesty over her shoulder.

"Yes?" Dan's one word dug at Timothy like an elbow in his ribs.

"I mean, what is all this?" The boy flicked his fingers at the sheet.

"What part? What has you stumped?"

"All of it. I can't make head or tail out of all this gibberish."

"It's lawyer talk." Dan struggled to keep his face straight. "It's the way we write laws, so they cover any situation that arises in the future."

"Lawyer talk, is it? Ha!" The explosion of breath was not nearly a laugh. "No wonder nobody can understand what lawyers write. Or say."

Tim's outburst had drawn everyone's attention. Eileen stopped talking in mid-sentence to watch Dan. Dotty turned into a statue, the cast iron frying pan and drying towel both held in mid-air. Martha's crooning halted. Everyone but Ryder watched Dan, who had no doubt but that the young man noticed everything.

He wished Martha and the girls had paid no mind, but they had to know sometime what the family faced. Back home in New York, Grandfather believed in sheltering women, even to forbidding Grandmother and Mother from reading newspapers so their tender minds would not be stained with ugliness. Mother had told Dan not knowing was worse than knowing; it left too much to the imagination. He had promptly agreed to be her accomplice in purloining newspapers for her and his sisters. He had told Grandfather they were for him.

"The legislators didn't do such a good job making things clear this time." Tim scratched the bridge of his nose.

"You truly want to know what it means?"

"Yes, Dan'l." Dotty – Dorothy as she demanded they call her – set the pan on the stove top and draped the towel over the handle. Sat on one of the dining chairs.

Tim echoed his sister and spoke for them all. "If'n it has to do with the Nugget, we all want to know. What in blazes does it mean?"

Ryder, though, had a different idea. "Why do we need to know something lawyers have to figure out?"

Dan took a deep breath to quell a sudden surge of temper. "Because we're citizens of this country, and we have to understand at least something about the laws that govern us." He fixed the younger man with a gimlet stare. "All right?"

"Yes, sir." Ryder quit petting the dog and sat straight.

"This new law, printed in the *Post*. 'The Law Relating to Ranches.' It's good news for miners. It means that the right to file on and enjoy any piece of land not more than 160 acres – as granted by the 1862 Homestead Act – will be respected in Montana because it's a federal law." When Tim would have interrupted, Dan held up his hand to stop him. "It also says – and this is important, too, that claims to land, where they do not conflict with federal law, shall be respected in both law and equity. That means mining claims, too."

Timothy shook his head. "Now I am lost. What's the difference between them last two? Law and – what?"

Martha chimed in. "Yes, Dan'l, what is equity?"

By now, Dan held the rapt attention of everyone but Canary. The yellow hound put his hind leg over his shoulder, and Ryder nudged him into to a more seemly position.

Dan sighed. He had not intended to turn this into a lawyer's schoolroom, but neither Dotty – er, Dorothy, nor Eileen would be fobbed off with the condescending advice not to worry their pretty little heads. As for Martha – he had as well argue with the Almighty as convince her, once her mind was set on something. And both Ryder and Tim had to understand the laws.

"No one can say beforehand they'll win in a trial. But I have an idea for a strategy. It involves the court of equity."

"The what?" Timothy and Dorothy spoke together. Ryder stayed silent, as though he had no stake in the outcome of Dan's possible court battle.

"I'll take the baby." Dorothy came to him, arms outstretched.

Only partly aware of her, Dan handed the baby over as he stood.

He walked back and forth from the door to the oval table, the rushes crunching under his leather-slippered feet. What a small building it was, to house eight people, even if two of them could not yet sit upright. When he had won against Fitch for once and for all, he would build a house he would be proud to provide for his family. He came to stand behind his wife's reading chair, his back to the bedroom door, and laid his hand on her shoulder, his long fingers partly under the blanket, resting on the rise and fall of her breathing.

Timothy left off inspecting his fingernails and looked straight at Dan. "So what happens now?"

"You asked about law and equity. All right. In a court of law, a trial is generally heard by a judge and a jury. Two lawyers – one for the defense and one for the prosecution – present evidence for and against the person or issue on trial. There are a few variations on this, but in general most trials in law are structured this way."

He paused, wishing he had a glass of whiskey to help him along. "The verdict is up to the jury. The 'jury of our peers,' so-called. They are twelve men selected from a much larger group, and known as the petit jury, or small jury, as differentiated from the grand jury. They hear the evidence in a trial up to and including Circuit Court level. When both sides have presented their evidence, including witnesses, the judge instructs the jury on the law, and they go somewhere private to discuss the verdict. All twelve must agree, or it's what we call a 'hung' jury."

He did not add that Fitch had a better chance against a jury than the McDowell heirs would. Fitch had been a major in General Sterling Price's army, which Dan vaguely recalled as having grown out of the Missouri State Guard. That made him popular – or at least respected – among Virginia City's Secessionist majority.

In the most secretive part of Dan's mind, the chances of Fitch winning the claim might be good – if the case were tried in law.

"If ownership of the Nugget goes to trial, the jury will be the men Judge Hosmer chose to be the petit jury during the upcoming District One court session. I think most of them would be fair-minded, but these days we don't know how much politics will influence men."

"All right." Timothy stretched his arms above his head as high as he could reach. "What about the other thing? The equity business."

Now came the tricky part. Monetary value always complicated a matter. Dan flexed the fingers of his left hand, surprised to realize he'd been holding his fist so tightly that he had to restore circulation. He did not want to explain this, the dangerous part, for it involved the potential monetary value of the mine. If he faced up to it, this battle with Fitch could impoverish himself and the family for the rest of their lives.

While he talked. Martha had rearranged the blanket to bring Danny into the open. She held him over her shoulder with a towel under his chin.

The baby let out a resounding burp.

Everyone laughed, and when the laughter faded, Dan knew how he should approach this part of the discussion so as to keep out the fear he lived with. The 'what-if', as in what if Fitch won in court?

Ryder lounged against the back of the blue sofa, an arm stretched out behind Timothy, sitting between him and Eileen.

Dan took a deep breath to steady himself. "Abbott is suing for Fitch to take ownership of the Nugget. Fitch believes it holds the Mother Lode, the source of all the gold in Alder Gulch. For all I know, he believes it is the source of all the gold anywhere."

Caught in mid-yawn, Ryder closed his mouth, and watched Dan wide-eyed. "There's no such thing, is there? The Mother Lode?"

"No, there isn't." Dan stood, went to the cupboard under the and retrieved his bottle of whiskey. Though it wasn't as good as the special stash in his office, it would help him now. He poured a modest drink into the mug that had held coffee for dinner. "But you'd be surprised at how many people believe in it, search for it, are obsessed by it. Like Fitch."

He took a sip of the whiskey and wished he had not bothered with it. Compared to the Laphroaig, it was swill. "As yet, despite a promising assay, there is no monetary value attached to the Nugget, other than what we say we saw. Because the lode could play out the next time you try to excavate it, Timothy, we can make a very good case that it is currently worthless."

"Worthless?" Tim looked as if he wanted to spring up and defend his discovery. "The Nugget ain't worthless. It's –"

"It's what? How much ore have you taken out of it? None, right? What would you base a valuation on?"

"Um, er, I don't know."

"Right. It's too early. Therefore, Judge Hosmer should hear the case in equity, because we have no value in a hole in the side of a mountain. The only value is potential."

"But that potential?" Ryder left off drawing circles on his trousers leg. "Has it no value?"

"I shall argue it does not. We can't spend actual dust for potential food, although many have done so. They call it buying and selling 'futures.'"

"Then Fitch is mad!" Timothy had been scratching one ankle, which rested on the other knee. Now he dropped his foot too close to Canary's tail.

The dog let out a "Yipe," jumped up, and went to sit near Martha.

"The mine is worthless unless the wall Tim discovered does turn out to be a lode. Of course, the current wall, as we're calling it, will have some value, but not like a lode will have if an assay shows that its gold is worth at least $7,000 a ton of ore."

"What else could give it value right now?" Dorothy asked. "The purity of the ore?"

"No." Dan met his stepdaughter's question with respect. "That's promising, again, but it's not enough to put a monetary value on the mine. We had samples of the claim assayed last year when we found it. It registered 97.6 percent pure. But even I thought the ground was salted.

"Any trial based on the value of the mine at the present time, which is the only basis possible at this

355

point, means it can be or must be tried a court of equity. That means —"

"Before a judge, without a jury." Bouncing in her chair, her excitement almost touchable, Dorothy interrupted him.

"Don't interrupt Dan'l," Martha scolded. "Just listen!"

Red-faced, the girl mumbled, "Sorry, Dan'l."

"Thank you, Dorothy." Dan let a small quiet space settle among them. "You're quite right, though. I will petition Judge Hosmer to hear our case as a bench trial. That's a trial without a jury. He alone can or will decide if the previous court decisions – from the Fairweather Miners Court, the Idaho Mining Statute, and the People's Court – were correct, according to the new Montana Mining Law."

Lines folded between Dorothy's brows. The corners of Tim's mouth curved downward.

"But —" Dorothy began.

Ryder spoke up. "I don't understand this. Miners court? People's court? Idaho Statutes? I've never heard of a place where there were, what, three sorts of tribunals like you're talking about. And this act, passed by the Montana Territorial Legislature, it might not override them? That doesn't make sense."

Careful to avoid any appearance of condescension, Dan said, "Of course, you weren't here through all the changes. First, in 1862, we were part of Dakota Territory, and had no need of government. Then, in the summer of that year, gold was discovered in Bannack, over in Beaverhead County. People started to come in droves.

"Then, in late May 1863, Bill Fairweather and some friends discovered the gold in Alder Gulch, so the Fairweather Mining District was formed. The men got together and made rules to govern gold-seekers and make it fair for everyone. But also in May 1863, Idaho territory was separated from Dakotah. And in December '63 and January '64, the Idaho legislature wrote the Idaho laws. In May 1864, Montana Territory was formed, and our legislature is writing Montana law over in Bannack because that's where Governor Edgerton lives."

"I'm baffled." Ryder shook his head. "How can anybody keep all that straight? What law would govern your case?"

"The new Montana law." Timothy stood up and stretched. His fingertips curved over on a beam. "Just be glad Abbott ain't our legal counsel. We're dam – er, real lucky to have Dan'l as our lawyer."

34 ~~~

Montana Post: 1/21/1865, p. 3:

Local and Other Items

The Richest Quartz heard Of.
A piece of ore from the Oro Cache Lode in Summit district assayed at the Philadelphia mint $7,500 the ton, and an average piece of the same $3,500 to the ton.

He'd been reared a Christian, and he'd done the correct thing all his adult life. Church on Sundays, never mind how enticing the weather for hunting. He'd freed his slaves when he inherited them in '61. Most of them had stayed on to work for wages, because like Ol' Henry said, 'Where'd I go, Massa Tobias? This farm be all I know, so I ain't fit to start up somewheres else.'

True enough.

Then a year later, as a soldier for the Confederacy, he'd scrambled home from the debacle at Pea Ridge, and found his blacks all run off by the cursed Union army, and him left with nothing but a burned-out plantation. He'd gone from defeat to ruin, and he hadn't done anything wrong.

Didn't the Bible teach over and over, if a man did what was right, God would smile on him? Not true. The Book lied.

So he was done with religion, done with all that folderol he'd been taught all his life, because he'd toed the mark, and look where he'd ended up? This filthy rotten jail with a bunch of drunks and diseased debauchers.

He wouldn't stay in here, though. He would not wait for that cursed Yankee judge to say he was guilty of attempted murder, that he didn't own the Mother Lode. No, sir. He'd vowed to all the angels of hell, that he'd get revenge on the Union. If it took the rest of his life, he'd have his revenge. He'd even the scales, destroy this damn United States. This Union.

Tobias Fitch spat in the direction of the spittoon. He did not hear the new prisoner, in for public drunkenness, yell, "Hey! Spit that gob on your own boots."

Yessir. He'd destroy the cursed Union. Beginning with Dan Stark. Daniel Bradford Stark. A Yankee name if he'd ever heard one. Yes, sir. Destroy Dan Stark, and he'd have the Nugget for himself. With all the gold in the Mother Lode. He'd be so rich the Union with all its armies, all its tax money, couldn't defeat him.

But first he had to get rid of Stark.

When the mine was his, he'd show everybody. They thought the Oro Cache was a rich mine, did they? His mine, the Mother Lode, would be richer than all the gold in Montana territory, and he'd own it because he owned the Mother Lode, and it would never play out.

It was the Mother Lode. He would send this filthy, rotten country to the devil. He, Tobias Fitch. He'd do it if it took the rest of his life.

And he wouldn't have to do it alone, either. There'd be others, yessir. There'd be others wanting to destroy the Union as long as it existed, down the generations. The greedy ones, the stupid ones, the ones with grudges. He'd buy them, and make sure they stayed bought, make them think they were the good ones, the ones with brains, the ones that wanted to make the country better. They liked themselves so much.

He'd be so rich when he had control of the Nugget, that he could fund that destruction without end.

After he'd got rid of Stark.

After he'd finished what he'd started in that cave in Beaverhead Rock. Then he'd be free to —

"Hey, Fitch! You grayback, you got company. Your lawyer's here again."

The cell door clanked open just enough to let Hal Abbott sidle into the cell, and was quickly slammed shut behind him, the echo of iron against iron like ships colliding at sea.

Rearranging his features felt like molding clay, but he had as good a smile on his face as he could muster when he stood up from the cot he claimed as his own.

"Hal Abbott! You're a sight for sore eyes. Where've you been?"

Abbott held a handkerchief over his nose.

He didn't fool Tobias Fitch none, though. He didn't have a cold. Didn't want to sneeze. The handkerchief would be perfumed, something flowery, lilac or lavender, maybe even sage. Ha! He'd show Abbott a perfume, all right. Someday.

For now, though, he kept his semblance of a smile on his face.

Abbott handed him a copy of Saturday's *Montana Post*, Union rag that it was. "Here," the useless fop mumbled through the hanky.

"What?" Fitch scanned the page, but nothing struck him.

Abbott moved close enough that Fitch could scan the page, but it was difficult because Abbott's smell, of weeks without a bath, clothes unchanged from month to month – not unusual with clean water a scarce and expensive article, in a long winter of subzero temperatures – made his eyes water. "Here." The lawyer thumped a finger on an article titled, "The New Laws."

When he saw what Abbott meant, Fitch had to sit down. This was the legal basis he'd been hoping for. With this, he and Abbott could go into court and make hash out of anything Stark said about the mine. His mine. His Vengeance mine.

'Squatting was virtually abolished,' was it? "When we get my day in court, you go in and convince that mudsill judge that the McDowell family has been squatting on that claim."

"It won't be that easy. They've done the proper filing and registered the claim in the family's name with Dan Stark as their legal representative."

"I don't give a rat's ass how difficult you think it would be. You just get it done, or you can forget about the one-seventy-second share I promised you." He treated the shyster to a bestial grin, the one he'd used on wounded mudsill soldiers before he'd ended their lives with his bayonet.

Shouting for the guard to let him out, Abbott like to have broke the door down pounding on it.

That was the only bright spot for Fitch in the entire month he'd been locked up.

Sleeping, another prisoner rolled over. His cot tilted against the wall, trapping him between the unpeeled logs and the cot's board bed. Wriggling in the blanket and yelling, he drew laughter from his cellmates.

"Hey, Ed, you turning into a fly on the wall?"

"You look like a bug, Ed, pinned that way."

Ed hollered, "If I get out of this, you're all gonna get it."

Alone, Fitch did not comment. He glimpsed the reason for the cot's tilt. The dirt floor had gone soft next to the wall. Why would that be?

With everything frozen solid till hell boiled over, why –

"Shut the hell up, you guys, and get Ed out of that." Suiting action to the command, Fitch grabbed the cot's free side and pulled it over. Ed floundered out of his blanket, and Fitch pulled the cot farther into the room.

"Hey!" one of the prisoners protested. "You trying to —"

"Shut up! You'll have Beidler on us."

"Nah! He's off today," another prisoner scoffed.

Fitch squatted on his heels and began to dig with his bare hands. Even in the meager warmth of the cell, the dirt was soft enough out of the packed areas that it yielded. At the sight of the growing pile accumulating around a hole under the wall, the men leaped to help. In a few minutes, while two men stood guard at the door singing raucous drinking songs, they had enough of a hole down, a short tunnel under the wall, and up the other side into freedom.

Fitch went first. Filthy, crusted with dirt already stiffening from melting snow that promptly re-froze when exposed to the subfreezing air, he slipped into the darkness and ran behind the Court House, ducked between two whores' cribs – tiny cabins only big enough for the necessities of their trade – belonging to Fancy Annie's, and came out on Wallace, next to Fancy Annie's saloon and brothel. There he paused to catch his breath. The cold night air stung his throat.

From inside the saloon came laughter and the clink of glasses as men toasted each others' winnings and called for another round. For a moment, Fitch wished he were in the saloon, enjoying the warm and friendly company of other men who had small troubles. In the next thought, he shook himself, remembering that he had a mission, and now that he was free of that squalid jail, he could act on it.

He could begin by destroying Stark, then his family.

Because not even gold was more important to him..

35 ~~~

Montana Post: 1/21/1865, p. 3:

Atrocious Murder.

> A man by the name of Thomas Watson was murdered in his bed a short distance from Fort Owen, on New Year's night, and robbed of about $1,000. It appears that Mr. Watson came to winter near Fort Owen from the Kootenai mines. Three bullet holes were found on his corpse and everything valuable about his person taken off, even his rings. Suspicion was fastened at once upon a desperado, well known in that section of the country, and 25 or 30 well armed men are in pursuit of the murderer. May they succeed in overtaking him. We learn that Mr. Watson was formerly a resident of Lewiston.

If he hadn't been in dire need, Timothy would not have come out at all into this sub-freezing cold, but he'd felt a growing tension in his nether regions, and the chamber pot needed emptying, so he brought it along to accomplish both necessary tasks. As he trudged as fast as he could down the slippery path to the outhouse, he tried to make a joke for himself about emptying both at once, but it was way too cold for jokes.

He'd get done and go back to a good fire just as quick as —

A large mound in the snow lay just back of and beside the outhouse, and he waded through the snow to see what it could be, then stopped in his tracks. It was the form of a big fat man, who'd laid there not more'n a quarter hour, judging by the snow dusting his overcoat. Dead? Not breathing. No rise and fall of that up-sloping midsection.

His necessary errands forgotten, Tim dropped the chamber pot. Wheeling, he ran for the house. Yelled for Dan'l before he'd taken more'n three steps in the longest thirty-yard sprint he'd ever made.

Dan'l met him at the door, his coat half on already, though when Tim had left him, he'd been reading a back issue of the *Post* in his slippers. He'd said it was to understand how His Honor might decide to judge the Nugget case, but that was all done with now, Tim having at last recognized the bluish face he'd seen once he'd brushed the snow off.

Abbott. That shyster puppy of Fitch's.

And now Dan'l had his boots on, and Tim brought him his hat, and sooner'n he thought possible they stood together looking at the man in the snow.

Dan'l knelt down and brushed more falling snow from his face, took off one glove and pressed a finger to the side of his neck. "He's alive! Get Ryder. We have to take him to the Recovery."

No need to get Ryder. He was already just a step or two behind when Dan'l ordered them to help pick up the great body, and they – all three – would get him to the Recovery, there being no time to tell Mam where they were headed for. But as they rounded the corner of the house and kept going down the path to the street, Dotty come out on the porch.

Dan'l shouted, "Hal Abbott! Recovery!"

"I'll tell Mam!" she shouted back and stepped back inside the house.

Tim had no more breath for anything but carrying his share of the load. The man weighed nigh onto 250 pounds if an ounce, a great burden even for someone used to breaking boulders down into gravel. They carried Abbott up to Idaho Street, along past the Union Church away from the Court House, almost to Van Buren, the next street parallel to Jackson. The Recovery had moved there when its old room by the Champion Saloon got too small.

The Recovery was where men as hadn't anyone else to help them when they got hurt or sick went to recover from – mostly – gunshot wounds. Though accidents accounted for a good share of broken bones and sprains, and lastly a few sicknesses.

There being only one man on deck this night, they had to help him undress Abbott down to his long johns, wrap him in warm blankets, and settle him on one of the strongest beds, a cot with sturdy legs. Even with the duty man, him knowing how to handle dead weights, they were nigh onto half an hour about the business.

As they were about to head home, the caretaker was putting a hot rock wrapped in old flannel shirts at Abbott's feet, the shyster came to enough to mutter, "Fitch. Fitch killed me."

Dan'l laid a hand on his forehead. "You're not dead, Hal. And you won't be, for years to come. Just go to sleep now." To the caretaker he said, "I'll guarantee him."

"Thank you, Mr. Stark. Sometimes it's hard to keep this place open, but you can see the town needs it." Sure enough, Timothy saw that most of the beds were full.

As himself, Ryder, and Dan'l were wrapping their scarves around their faces before going home, then, light footsteps pattered up the steps to the front door, and Dotty barged in, all askew as to buttons lining up, boots on the wrong feet, and her hair all every which way. She flung herself at Dan'l, and he opened his arms wide to her, and before she'd quite caught her breath, she wept into his chest, "F — Fitch, he hit Mam, and he's got Luk-key."

Right then, Dan'l changed. He wasn't only their stepfather no more. He turned into one of the men like Timothy read about in the dime novels he wasn't supposed to read. His eyes changed to flint, and his whole being looked carved out of stone. He seemed to grow a few inches before their eyes. He was the Vigilante, and Timothy saw how this man he'd thought he knowed so well, how he'd – like they said – 'pulled his own rope.' Right then he believed it, though he never had before.

Dotty pulled herself together a little, though still weeping, and gasped out the words, stammering, "H–he said, 'The Nugget – or – or your son.' He's w–waiting for you at the wet n – nurse's house, in Nevada City, where he – he keeps his own baby, B–Berry Woman's baby."

"Your mother?" Dan'l gazed over their heads head at the rafters, at something nobody else could see, afore he let go of Dotty and turned her, careful-like she was made of spun glass, toward Ryder, but Tim took his sister, his little sister, that he had guarded all her life, put his arm around her. Told his stepfather, "I'll see to Dotty."

Dotty sank against her brother. "Mam, Mam's hurt, and I don't how to help her."

Already at the door, Dan gave orders in a deadly tone Tim had never heard from him before, giving orders to him and Ryder to take Dorothy home, and Ryder to stay with her, but Timothy wasn't having that. He interrupted Dan'l, on account Vaughn couldn't use a handgun, didn't have what it took to shoot Fitch when he snatched Luke and hit Mam. He wasn't tough enough. But he, Timothy MacDowell, he could've killed the —

"Dan'l, I'll guard Mam and Dotty. I can do the necessary."

And Dan'l, the door open, and his hand on the latch, understood at once. "Very well, you're on guard duty,

Timothy. But first I'll look in on – " his voice broke on a sob, that he had to get control of, but when he got control, he gave orders like an Army general. "Ryder, you find X, the deputy sheriff. Tell him I've gone home, and then to the wet nurse's place. It's a crib uphill from the Star Bakery, in Lower Town. On my way there, I'll send Mrs. Hudson to look in on Mar —" Right there, he had to stop again, and he put on his gloves like a man somewheres else.

Timothy dared to ask, "And you, Dan'l?"

"After I've seen Martha, I'll find Fitch. And when I do, Major Tobias Fitch will answer to the Spencer."

When Dan'l said Fitch's name that way, and mentioned the repeating rifle, Timothy wished he hadn't asked. It chilled him to his core, considering everything.

36 ~~~

The Montana Post: 1/28/1865, p. 2.

"How are Times Altered!"

How are times altered! Two large and commodious churches are now built, and crowded congregations listen with reverence and attention to the "words of eternal life." Two Sabbath schools are in successful operation – five day-schools are to be found within the limits of our sister towns .... Law now reigns supreme. Offenders are promptly arrested and their punishment by the authority of judge and jury is a matter whose certainty is unaffected by any circumstances save the want of legal proof of their guilt.

Why hadn't he left Timothy—or stayed himself – to guard the females and the twins, instead of carrying that useless whale of blubber that called himself a lawyer – damn Hal Abbott's soul – to the Recovery? Why hadn't he foreseen what would happen? Why hadn't he known as soon as he saw Abbott lying there, so close to his outhouse, that his own household was in danger?

Running, slipping through the snow falling on icy pathways, Dan heard a sob. He wondered where it came from, but something wet froze on his cheek, and he knew he wept. Tears of rage, they had to be. He never cried, had not cried since he'd refused to give Grandfather the satisfaction when he was small. What, five years old?

No matter that now, he had to think. He slipped. Recovering, he slid onto the path to his house, took the porch steps in two leaps, thought in time to avoid charging through the door. That would have been sure to give the females the terrors. From inside the house a dog growled, then barked, and Eileen's shaking voice came a-tremble through cracks in the door where the drying wood was pulling apart – a common occurrence here – why the hell was he thinking of cracked wooden doors now?

"Eileen, it's me. Dan Stark. It's safe to open the door. Miss Dorothy, Timothy, and Ryder are not far behind. You're safe now."

The dog barked, whined. Dan heard the scratch of dog claws as the animal tried to dig through the door to get to him. "Canary! Down!"

Silence on the other side of the door. "Go lie down."

A whine, and a woof.

"He's laying down, Mr. Stark. I'll open the door."

Inside, Dan could not help giving the girl a bear hug, quick to be sure, but something he'd never envisioned himself doing to an orphan girl in his protection. She clung to him a moment longer than would have been seemly under other circumstances –hugging her was unseemly under any circumstances but this one, she'd been scared half out of her wits and trembling as though to tear her sinews from her bones.

When they parted, he sat down to unlace his boots. "How is Mrs. Stark?"

Eileen stood off from him a ways, her face flushed and her hands twisting her apron into knots. "Not so good, sir. She fought something fierce when that horrible man grabbed little Lukey out of her arms. I thought, there's tiger blood in her. Maybe grizzly bear. Only reason he got the baby, she was afraid to injure him. Lukey, I mean."

"I'll see her now." Crossing the room, he had presence of mind to tell the girl, little slip of a thing as she was, "You're very brave, Eileen. I'm glad you're here to help her. Let me know if you need anything."

"Thank you, sir." Her thanks followed him into the bedroom. The only one in the house, it had seemed plenty when he bought the place, but it was bursting at the seams – why the hell was he thinking of that now? He must keep moving. With his hand on the doorknob, he wanted to scream at the thought of what might be happening to his infant son. He must find him – and fast!

But first, Martha. Always, Martha first.

He crossed the threshold into the familiar heavy fug, closed the door behind him, and waited for his eyes to adjust to the gloom. The only light came from the stove in the room's front corner, by Martha's nursing lounge. He had sent all the way to New York for it, but she seldom used it. She preferred to stay with the family for something so natural as feeding her child, even in front of the boys. Mother would have been appalled, though Martha always covered the baby and herself, for modesty's sake.

"Dan'l?" Her voice carried all the fear and sorrow possible, and some of his own, too, as well as what little Luke must be feeling, though too young to know why he was so terrified.

He sat on the edge of the bed, took her in his arms, and discovered he held her and Danny both. Danny, his namesake, the firstborn, the blond baby as fair as his twin was dark. He did not ask how she was, how she did. He knew. She ached where Fitch had hit her, and her heart ached, too, because Luke had been stolen out of her arms.

Yet he asked, anyhow. "What happened?" He needed to hear about the attack as much as he supposed she needed to tell it.

"I was feeding Luke when someone knocked. Y'all had gone to carry that one, him that's so heavy, to the Recovery, and I thought one of you was come back to look in on me. So I told Eileen to open the door, and next I knew she was layin' on the floor and that Major Fitch busted in. I could see by his eyes he wasn't right in his head. I tried to get to the pistol hangin' in its holster, but he moved too fast. Hit me here –" Her hand went to a place on her lower jaw"– and here "– a nod to the breast Danny was not working. Then he snatched Luke away when I fell, and ran. And now you come, and – and ...." She broke down, sobbing, and he held her, wishing he could heal her, turn the clock back, but he knew there was only one thing he could do to help either of them.

"I will bring Luke home safe and sound." He spoke with his chin almost resting on the top of her head, inhaled the herbal smell of her black hair, held her and their son until the baby squirmed, made a sound very like a protest.

He did not embellish the promise with more words but laid two of his three best loves against the pillows.

From out in the big room, he heard more voices. Timothy, Dotty – er, Dorothy, Timothy, Eileen, and yes – X. So Ryder had found him, and hearing two or three more men's voices, he knew some of the friends had already assembled.

"We'll be home as soon as we can."

"Yes, I know," Martha murmured. "God be with you."

He paused at the closed door to button his greatcoat against the cold he would soon face. Yet he knew the chill he felt already went deeper than winter's bite, to wrap his heart in a bitter numbness at the thought of little Luke in the power of that madman. He heard himself say, "I hope so."

37 ~~~

The Montana Post: 1/28/1865, p. 2.

Our Social Status
**Little more than a year has elapsed since
crimes against person and property were so
rife in our midst that imminent danger from
even stray shots confronted all who walked
our streets at nightfall, and sometimes even
in day time. ... In short, unrestrained
humanity in its wildest and rudest form,
displayed nothing of good but energy in the
search for gold which was almost universally
made the means for doing evil or of
procuring the facilities for riotous debauch.
The few wise and law-abiding people in this
neighborhood, were obliged to organize in
self-defense, and justifiable homicide was
the only means of terrifying criminals and
maintaining a partial security.**

When Dan closed the bedroom door behind him, he smelled the steamy scent of summer and knew Eileen was making tomato soup. From canned tomatoes, all right, but his mouth flooded. For a moment he could only swallow as though he had bitten into a fresh, ripe tomato.

X said, "Miss Eileen has promised us a bowl of soup when we bring your boy home safe and sound."

Dan could only nod. His heart and his mouth were too full for talk.

"You're in charge now. We're coming along to see right is done."

"Just so." Ryder wore his winter wraps, and stood as tall as he could in the new winter coat Dan's dust had bought him.

Beside him, Timothy wore his heaviest knitted jacket under the overcoat he struggled to button across his chest. It was harder work than it had been at the beginning of winter.

Timothy. Somehow, he had to earn the boy's agreement to stay home and guard the females. Never having fired a gun at another human being, Ryder would be useless. He would try to pacify an attacker, and by the time he realized it was impossible, the damage would be done.

Yet, if he ordered Tim to stay, he would rebel. Somehow he had to be made to volunteer.

Knowing no other way to say it than to put it in whatever words came to him, Dan crossed his mental fingers and plunged in. "Thank you all for your help. We will rescue my son Luke. There is no doubt. Or else ...." He broke off, leaving no doubt in anyone's mind what would happen if they found the unthinkable. Which, God knew, would not .... He took a shuddering breath. "Meantime, my wife and son Danny, and these young ladies — " glancing toward Dotty and Eileen, who stood still as rock behind the oval table "— must have protection while we're gone. Who will stay?"

The men looked at each other. Not one of the friends wanted to be lift behind with the women.

Dan watched Timothy, who looked around, saw no one volunteering. Met Dan's look directly at himself. Pointed a finger at his own chest. Shook his head, No.

Dan waited. While the seconds dripped by and God alone knew what was happening to Luke, he wanted to yell at Timothy: There is no one else.

A shift of Tim's eyes toward Ryder. Dan turned his head a fraction: Not him.

Timothy's shoulders slumped. He unbuttoned the first button on his coat. "I'll do it. I'll stay."

Dan smiled. "Good man."

Timothy stood straighter, his open coat hanging wide from his shoulders, He stood aside as the men left the house. As he passed his stepson, Dan squeezed his upper arm. "You should get a new coat when we bring Luke home."

Unspeaking, Dan led Ryder, X and the friends to the Eatery first. He pounded on the door, it being once again after closing, and the women would be cleaning up from the midday meal. It took only brief moments for him to tell about Fitch's attack and what he needed for Martha, before Mrs. Hudson and Tabitha Rose were ready to leave. To Dan's surprise, Albert insisted on helping to rescue Luke.

Looking at him, his face a mask of hard obsidian, Dan agreed. Not even a madman like Tobias Fitch would think of fighting Albert, who outweighed any man in the posse, and loomed over each of them, even the tallest, including Dan himself.

Albert sealed his inclusion in the posse when he clenched his fists and growled, "Anyone what threatens a little helpless baby don't deserve to get older."

"Amen to that," came from one of the friends, to accompanying nods and murmurs, "Yes, that's so," "You bet."

Albert banked the cooking fire and blew out the candles in their sconces on the wall. He closed the door with the dog outside. "Gen'ral, you lay down. On guard, now." As Dan led the men down Wallace Street, he explained, "Nobody gets by Gen'ral."

At the bottom of Wallace, the road curved to the right and became Main Street. It kept company with Alder Creek all the way to the mouth of Alder Gulch, some fifteen or so miles away. Along the creek, claims had been staked and mining districts mapped, so that the tents, wagon beds, and log cabins erected along the entire creek bed had no definable boundaries between them, and appeared to have merged into one settlement. People called it the "Fourteen-Mile City."

The men's boots pounded out a high-pitched litany of squeaks from the snow, that resounded in Dan's mind: *Find him safe, find him safe, findimsafe, findimsafe.* The words made their home in the thumping of his heart, a prayer he didn't know he said. They jogged around the curve of Main Street, downstream along Alder Creek, splashed through

Daylight Creek where it flowed into Alder Creek, then on to Lower Town. There they turned uphill away from the creek and the road, past the Star Bakery. At this hour, well after dinnertime, the bakery was dark. The baker had cleaned up the day's messes and would not start on tomorrow's meat pies, breads, and rolls for some hours yet.

At the wet nurse's crib, the men paused. The woman had been a whore who'd caught a man, but he'd abandoned her when he heard of richer diggings in Last Chance Gulch a few days before her baby was born. Her only occupation now was to nurse other people's children along with her own, a girl. No one wanted her in her primary occupation; there were far too many younger whores going hungry, now that so many men had left the gold fields for the winter.

When Dan stormed into her cabin with Albert, Ryder, X, and the posse of friends on his heels, the men filled the room. On the front wall, next to the door, an open fireplace, large enough for a man to walk into, was built into the front wall. A cot stood against one side wall, its foot close to the fireplace. On the opposite side wall, a narrow bare cupboard huddled into a corner.

The terrified woman shrank back, stumbled onto the cot. In her arms, she held a dark-haired, screaming baby wrapped in a thin, gray blanket. Another baby, a naked girl, lay howling on the floor in a box too small for her.

Ryder snatched the girl child out of the box, away from the danger of men's booted feet. Opening his coat, he closed it around the infant for warmth and edged himself and the baby between the cupboard and the rear wall, where they could be away from gunfire – if any place in this room would be safer.

Holding a third baby, a dark-haired infant who yelled a high-pitched note, Tobias Fitch stepped into the fireplace, where a dying fire smoldered. "I knew you'd come, Stark!" He held the baby by an arm over the coals. "Take a step closer, and your brat goes into the fire."

"Then so do you, Fitch." Dan brought the Spencer up. A shell already in its chamber, its single eye fastened onto the center of Fitch's forehead. Dan's finger slid onto the trigger.

The wet nurse sobbed.

Dan forgot to breathe. If Fitch opened his hand, baby Luke would die a horrible death.

If he shot Fitch, he would drop the baby.

Except for the crying babies, the room stilled.

"You kill me, it'll be murder." Fitch laughed, a shrill note of pure glee.

"Like hell," shouted X. "It's purely justifiable homicide. Ain't it, boys?"

Nods, murmurs of agreement: "You bet," "Fine by me," "We all saw it."

For an eternal moment, Fitch stood, arm outstretched, the baby held over the fire.

A bit of its dress fluttered close to the embers.

"You stupid pecker," shrieked the wet nurse. "You're gonna burn your own spawn."

The Spencer's roar deafened everyone as Fitch stumbled backward, empty-handed. Dan dropped the rifle, leaped, caught the baby as Fitch fell onto the cot, arms flailing for support he could not find. Dan's momentum flung him toward the side wall of fireplace. Protecting the infant, he landed on his shoulder against the side wall, bounced off, helpless, dropping onto the live coals, the child raised high, out of the fire.

Albert seized the baby from him, caught one of his arms. One of the friends grabbed the other arm, and together they dragged him out of the fireplace, where X and the others brushed him down in a shower of minute and glowing splinters. A man made comforting sounds over the infant, whose screams were fading.

"My son? Where's Luke?"

"I've got your'n," the wet nurse snarled at Dan. "That brat you saved was Fitch's."

Dan snatched his whimpering son away from her, soothed him in the low, soft, crooning sound he often made to the fretful baby. His fingers stroked the little body, which sent reassuring messages telling him the child was not hurt, appeared to relax under the fondling, gazed around blankly as if searching for the source of comfort and reassurance. But... "He needs changing." He looked at the wet nurse. "Where's a clean diaper?"

The woman sounded like she tried to laugh. "Ha! Whaddaya think this is? The Waldorf? Where'd I get the dust for laundry soap, or the wood to heat up the water?" She sniffed and brushed her sleeve across her running nose, flapped her fingers toward Fitch. "If he'd've paid me what he said, I might have something like you need. As it is...." She gestured toward the empty woodbox, the last embers of the dying fire, the congealing grease pale and thick in a pot on the stove. "I ain't got the wherewithal for nothin'."

Fitch crouched on his knees on the floor, his face in the crook of his left elbow, his right arm holding his stomach. He moaned softly to himself, in sounds that were not quite words, although Dan thought he heard, amid the groans, "... so low, sunk so low."

As the men of the posse stared at her, she glared at each of them in turn. "Who's gonna pay me what that one" – pointing a thumb at Fitch – "owes me for his brat's keep? Huh? That's what I'd like to know. I got me own to look after. I don't let other folks's suck for the fun of it." A leer began in her eyes, but looking at the grim men's faces around her, she lost the suggestion.

"Got a poke?" X was asking if she had the deerskin pouch commonly used for carrying gold dust.

Ryder shuffled his poke out of an inner pocket,

"Where'd I get somethin' like that? I ain't got enough to eat, and me and my own little one – " Her voice cracked. "We're starvin'."

Dan had not expected this sort of destitution. He knew – they all knew – of men like Henry Plummer. Prior to his marriage, he'd seduced a woman away from her husband and family in Nevada Territory, then abandoned her in Idaho, but they had never asked themselves what happened to the female left without a source of honest income or a character, as a testimony of her good reputation was known.

He reached into the inside pocket of his greatcoat and drew out his poke, plump with the dust from changing gold coins. Grateful as he was to be holding Luke – unhurt, though complaining of hunger – he was moved by this woman. This slattern.

And it struck him that if he had not returned from New York, a similar condition might have been in store for Martha. Dear Martha, dearest wife. Who had given him this child and his brother.

Following his example, one by one the posse men took out their pokes, pinched up some dust, and dropped the flakes on a piece of stained rag she found for them.

One man wrote out a note on a leaf from his pocket notebook. "Here." He thrust it at her. "Take this to the Pioneer Laundry. The people there will set you up with clean things whenever you need them. They'll bill me."

"You mean this? I can get clean things?" Her throat sounded raspy, and tears shone in her eyes.

"Not for you." The man waved a hand around, the gesture including the two infants, her own little girl and Fitch's boy. "For them."

"Hell, Jack," said X. "She'll only drink it up."

The woman hollered, "I ain't a drinker. I was a decent woman oncet, till some ..." Her voice broke, and, sobbing, she flipped her apron skirt over her head, and cried, "Thankee, thankee," her words muffled and distorted by the apron.

Jack answered X, "I'll watch her, and make sure she gets on a straight path. And stays there"

Then Ryder stepped forward, holding his poke, and set it beside the rag with the other men's contributions. "You can use this poke, Missus." He grew stern, spoke with an authority Dan had not thought him capable of. "But if you use it – even one flake – for drink, you will rue the day."

Looking at Ryder with new respect, Dan and his friends snugged hats onto their heads, wrapped scarves around their lower faces. When they had themselves as ready for the cold walk to the jail, before plunging into the diabolical cold, they dragged Fitch onto his feet, prodded him upright. He fumbled at the buttons on his overcoat until two of the men made a rough but swift job of getting him ready for the walk. They formed a phalanx with him in the middle and squeezed out the door.

He would not walk, but crumpled to the icy ground as they stepped outside.

One of the posse slapped his face. "Stand up, damn your hide, or we'll ride you up on a rail." There was a time Fitch would have shot back something, but he said nothing. He might not have heard the other man, although he stood on his own feet and kept up the pace as they marched away.

Holding the shotgun in one hand, X beat his free arm across his chest in an attempt at warmth. "We'll take him to the jail and I'll send someone to tell Judge Hosmer he's back where he belongs." He took a step or two away from Dan, then called to him, "Did you ever see the like?"

"No, never. He's probably playacting."

As Dan left with Luke well wrapped up and shielded in his coat, he thought there might be hope for the woman and her infant daughter. The kindness of strangers was a phrase he'd heard somewhere, and now he'd seen it. Begun by young Ryder, it had shamed the other men into following suit. As she'd said, she'd been a decent woman once. Now she had a second chance. He prayed she would keep to it.

For himself, he knew a great, aching gratitude. He wanted to shout his soaring joy to the Almighty: Luke was safe, unhurt, sheltered as best Dan could do for him in the bosom of his greatcoat.

He bent into the frigid wind and walked as fast as he judged safe toward home.

38 ~~~

Montana Post: 1/21/1865, p. 3:

Bannack Correspondence.
From our Special Correspondent.

Bannack Jan. 17th, 1865.

The Code progresses slowly, but it is the most cumbersome job of the session. It is folly to undertake to pass a code in a sixty day session, and the best way would be for the Assembly to select one from a State or Territory which would come near meeting our wants, and slide it through with the fewest changes possible.

(Signed) Franklin

Though cold bit to the marrow of his bones, Dan had not regretted the decision to walk to the wet nurse's hovel rather than taking horses. Time would have been wasted saddling up and assigning someone to look after the animals while the posse rescued Luke. Yet now, maneuvering among the pits and lumps of the street, keeping a secure hold on Luke nestled at his heart inside his belted coat, Dan thought he might have been shortsighted. True, the infant was well wrapped as warm as possible in his Hudson's Bay wool blanket, and cradled in the crook of his father's arm. Dan treasured the feel of his breathing, the small, constant movements of little arms and legs that proved he lived. But they could have ridden home faster, and Luke would have been warm in his mother's care sooner

Besides, Dan reflected, it would have been good to toss Fitch across the back of a horse and let him be carried back to jail, bouncing his stomach on the hard saddle seat with every hoof-fall. That ride would have given him a good beating.

As it was, two men, Albert holding one arm, half-dragged, half-carried him every step of the way. Several times he stumbled and would have fallen if Albert had not yanked him up on his feet again. Each time, X jabbed the muzzle of the shotgun into the small of his back, and snarled, "Get a move on, you rotten grayback."

When X gave up his place, another man took over. But Albert did not relinquish his hold to anyone.

Watching Fitch, with the Spencer slung across his back and Luke safe, Dan thought of a dead man, walking. He wondered if Albert relished the opportunity to treat Fitch as some white men would have treated – or did treat – himself. Except that Fitch would bear no open wounds as souvenirs of this walk.

He wanted to hurry. Fearful that their slow pace put Luke at risk from the cold, when they turned the corner onto Wallace Street, he quickened his steps onto the boardwalk and up the rise toward Jackson Street. He paused at the corner, before he turned up the Jackson Street hill and called to X. "I'll see you at the jail, after I take Luke home."

X prodded Fitch hard enough to send him stumbling forward, but Albert held him from falling. "If we get him there."

"Shoot me now." Fitch stopped, stood trembling with fear or perhaps cold. "I'm not fit to live." He watched the road at his feet.

"No." If not for keeping hold of Luke, Dan could have knocked Fitch down, and not known how to stop himself from murdering him. "You're not getting out of this so easy. You'll have plenty of time to contemplate your sins before Judge Hosmer sentences you to hang. And then you'll burn in the lake of fire for all eternity."

"I don't care what you do with me. Alive or dead, I'm in hell already," Fitch muttered to the icy track.

"See you later, X." Dan ground his teeth, as he turned on his heel and walked homeward as fast as he could. If he'd stayed two seconds more, he would have killed Fitch.

Ryder left the group and trotted after him. "Mr. Stark! Here comes Timothy!"

Sure enough, Timothy slipped and slid toward him, called his name: "Dan'l!"

"Timothy?" Hearing Tim, Dan quickened his pace, though carefully. "What are you doing here? Where is your mother? Is she all right?"

"Miz Hudson is looking after her. She sent me out to get you, and – and Lukey?"

"He's right here." Dan jiggled the baby, whose protesting whimper rewarded him.

"He's all right?"

Ryder answered him. "Near as we can tell. He needs proper attention, though, to make sure."

"He'll get that as soon as we get him home." As he hurried on, careful of where he put his feet, yet bring the baby home soonest, Dan knew a contentment he had not expected from this night. Luke rode safely in his arms, and the Spencer, slung over his shoulder, had not injured anyone.

"Miz Hudson's there, and Albert's wife." Timothy fell in beside Dan, who realized the boy's long strides nearly matched his own.

Ryder was telling Timothy the story of Luke's rescue. He left out his own contribution, which in Dan's opinion had been the biggest surprise. He had shown an unexpected moral courage when he set down his poke for the slattern and looked Dan in the eye as if to dare him to protest. Though he hated to see the young man throw away all his money on her, it warmed Dan to know someone in this gold-crazed world was capable of that great generosity.

"That's something, ain't it?" Timothy did not ask a question so much as make a comment. "I mean, Fitch. The way he is now. I never seen – er, saw him like that. What do you think happened? Is he truly sorry, d'you think?"

"I think he's honestly contrite." Ryder's voice broke through Dan's thoughts about the appropriate punishment for Fitch.

"Fitch?" Dan's foot slid sideways, and he was glad of Timothy's strength that steadied him. "Sorry? No. He's had the Mother Lode on his mind since I met him at your mother's dinner table. I wouldn't put it past him to fake this – whatever it is, contrition, or whatnot, just to get sympathy for his takeover of the Nugget. Fitch is smart, don't forget. Very smart. He went to school in England, to Oxford or Cambridge University – I don't remember which one, and came home just before the grayba – er, the Confederates fired on Fort Sumter." For the moment, he'd forgotten Timothy's own father had been a Confederate artilleryman.

"You can say graybacks, it's all right."

"What?" He'd been about to say, 'your own father was a Confederate artilleryman.'

Timothy held up a hand. "I've realized I don't hold with slavery no more. Yeah, I know even the Bible divides people into slave and free, so it's been going on since there's been people, but you know what? Albert's showed me it's wrong. He's done his share and more in the Nugget. I'm thinkin' he's been with the posse, too. Anyway, his color don't make him less'n me just because I'm white, like I used to think it did. So maybe Fitch has changed his mind. It happens." He kicked a clod of ice out of his path.

"Yes, I suppose it does. But you can't use yourself as an example. You never – I'll be bound – you never wanted to own the world, or thought the Mother Lode was your way to do that, or even that it exists. And most of all — you never intended to throw a baby into a fire, the way Fitch almost did."

Walking a bit behind them, Ryder put in, "If you hadn't stopped him, he'd have succeeded."

"What? He tried?" Timothy dropped behind Dan to hear Ryder tell what happened at the wet nurse's house.

"Yes, he did. He almost succeeded, too. When we got there, he held the baby over the fire. But Mr. Stark fired that rifle, and Fitch dropped the baby, and Mr. Stark threw the rifle to X, jumped, and caught the baby. I never thought anyone could move that fast. And it was Fitch's own, too. Why didn't he know that?"

"Fitch's boy? Not Lukey?" Timothy went silent for a few steps, as if he had to absorb this account. "How could a man not know his own child?"

Ryder could not explain it. "It beats me."

"Or how could any man throw a baby into a fire? That ain't human." Timothy fell silent for a step or two, then went on as if he thought out loud. "When Berry Woman died giving him birth, Fitch just parked him with that woman and tried to forget him. I don't think he ever looked in on the poor little tyke."

"I just don't under—" Ryder slipped on an ice-heaped mound of uncertain origin, but caught himself.

Dan heard his feet scrambling for purchase before Timothy steadied him. Weary of the discussion, as he turned the corner into his own cabin he hurried toward the welcome beacon the ladies had put out for them.

"Look, Tim, your mother's put a light out for us."

A lantern stood on the railing beside the steps up to the porch, a welcoming beacon guiding them home.

Timothy galloped up the path, leaped up the porch steps, and pounded on the front door.

Dan, cradling Luke, followed, placed each foot one at a time on a step and tested his weight on it before he trusted it to hold him and his precious, squirming bundle.

Ryder followed them so that when the door opened to them almost at once, he stood behind Dan. Timothy shouted loud enough to be heard all the way to Bannack, or at least to Idaho Street, "We've brought Luke home, and oh, Mam, Ryder says he never thought a man could move as fast as Dan'l did!"

As Martha fed Luke while Danny slept warm and snug in his own basket, Dan sat behind her at the head of the bed. She leaned against him while the child nursed. He wished he could pick them all up and hold them close to his heart. A fire burned in the stove, flames leaped in seemingly crackling joy, but nothing compared to his happiness at this moment. He had saved his family. The bruise on Martha's breast where Fitch had struck her would fade soon, she had told him, and there was no pain.

Now, she wanted to know the details. "Are you telling me, Dan'l Stark, that Tobias Fitch was going to throw his own baby into the fire?" Shuddering, she pressed into him harder, as if she could join her man inside his waistcoat.

"He thought he had Luke." The memory flashed through his mind and his stomach lurched. He gulped, swallowed against the acid taste of bile in his throat.

"Oh, dear Lord." For a minute she was quiet, thinking (he had no doubt) about the enormous wrong Fitch had almost done.

"Don't worry, my love. He will never have another opportunity to harm any of us."

"Is that a promise?"

"It's more than a promise." Bending his head, he kissed the back of her neck. "You have my solemn oath."

"I believe you." She nestled against his chest.

39 ~~~

Montana Post: 2/18/1865, p. 3:

The New Code.

— At a meeting of the county commissioners,
held on Tuesday, it was resolved that a
person duly authorized, be sent to Bannack
to obtain a verbatim copy of the laws
enacted by the Legislative Assembly. There
are now in custody, several prisoners whose
trial cannot be had, legally, without
consulting these statutes, several
modifications of the jury law and other
important provisions being therein
contained.

Dan's right heel drummed almost soundlessly on
the floor in Judge Hezekiah Hosmer's office. Twice he
had stopped it, only to have it start again when he
forgot about it. This time, he made no move to quell the
irritating motion. Maybe it would stop on its own.

He forced himself to focus on what His Honor was
saying, though he was already familiar with the
situation. After more than two weeks since the fight at
the wet nurse's hovel, Tobias Fitch could not be made
to stand trial.

Judge Hosmer rested his arm on the desk and bent
his left elbow, raised his hand. Counting on his
upraised fingers, he folded each down as one by one he

summed up the points already brought out in their discussion.

"One thing, Major Fitch's mental state has not improved. Isn't that correct, Deputy Beidler?"

"That's right, Your Honor. He sits on his bunk and stares at the floor. He mumbles something about deserving whatever punishment he gets. If anyone asks him to repeat what he said, he says, 'It doesn't matter what I said.'"

His honor bent down his middle finger. "Do you have to force feed him?"

The deputy replied, "No, sir." Corrected himself, "Uh, Your Honor. He eats and drinks like he has all his wits about him."

Before folding his ring finger, the judge considered something. "Can he participate in his own defense?"

The deputy seemed to inhale down to his boots. "He could, I think, but he won't. He refuses to see Mr. Pemberton, here, even though I've told him eleven times that you appointed him as defense lawyer now that Hal Abbott is – um, laid up."

In truth, Abbott lay in a coma, and people were asking if he'd ever wake up. A few had whispered something about putting him out of his misery and saving the county's money for worthwhile things. No one who'd said that had the nerve to suggest it to Chief Justice Hosmer. Or to the County Commissioners. Certainly the caretaker in the Recovery had said nothing about it. He was being paid for each twelve-hour shift after moving into the place to maintain a twenty-four hour watch over the patient.

"Mr. Pemberton, I ask you, is your client able to participate in his own defense?"

"I agree with the deputy, Your Honor. He could do so, but he will not. All he says is he's not fit to live, so what happens to him is of no account." William Young Pemberton, who occupied Number Four in Content's Corner, turned in his chair to ask Dan, "Mr. Stark, what do you think of this situation?"

His foot stopped its incessant tapping. "I suggest you ask him, Your Honor. Fitch understands what people say to him, and he's capable of responding."

Pemberton objected. "If we bring him out to ask him for a plea, guilty or not guilty, we're breaking the law. We can't convene a trial with witnesses, because we don't have a Criminal Code, although the Committee has worked hard to develop one." He sighed. "And even if we did copy a state's code, like Burns is doing with the Missouri Code, the Code Committee will have to codify our laws passed by the legislature along with the laws the legislature itself passed. We can't even use the Idaho Statutes as a fall back, because the legislature repealed them as its last Act."

"I'm aware of that." Judge Hosmer's face tightened.

Dan snorted. When His Honor glanced his way, he changed it to a cough, then brought out his handkerchief and pretended to wipe his nose. Hosmer had upheld the Idaho Statutes until the legislature adjourned *sine die*, but the Code Committee had not finished writing the Montana Territorial Criminal Code. It still lay in piles of paper in the office of Burns, Pemberton, and —

"Yes, yes." The judge laid his hands on either side of the pile of four or five papers before him. A thumb riffled one of the corners as he considered his options.

Dan had been thinking hard. What options were open to a judge, hampered as Chief Justice Hosmer was by the date for the District One Session set by the legislature? Perhaps because he had been thinking of it, explaining it to the family, it came to mind now.

"Why not hold a bench trial?"

"A bench trial?" Pemberton's eyes opened wide, but Judge Hosmer's eyes narrowed as he thought about it.

To Dan's left, behind the wall His Honor shared with the jail, came a roar of laughter.

"What do they have to be so hilarious about?" His Honor asked X Beidler.

X shrugged. "I'll ask them when I get back there."

"A bench trial?" Pemberton hung onto the subject.

Dan stifled a rising smile. The defense attorney was known around the mining camps as a bulldog, which explained some of his clients, the sort who needed a persistent attorney to get them out of some kinds of trouble.

The judge leaned forward on his elbows. "What advantages would a bench trial have for either side?"

Dan thought fast. He was not prepared to argue this before the Chief Justice, X (the chief law enforcement officer, even if the role was temporary until Sheriff

Howie returned), and the defense attorney. The idea
had just come to him.

"It seems the right solution, Your Honor. The
defendant will not defend himself or give any
assistance to his defense. He has committed two
crimes worthy of the death penalty – his attempted
murder of myself, and his attempted murder of his
own infant son. But I am the only witness to his
attempt to bludgeon me to death, and while he might
admit his guilt now, he probably would not defend
himself." He broke off to ask Pemberton, "Do you think
he would defend himself if I accused him in court
again?"

"Probably not. He only says his own life is
worthless."

"Ah, then." Dan inspected a scab on his left index
finger. He did not recall when he had scratched it, but
the small scrape had probably happened during the
scuffle when he saved Fitch's baby.

"Besides me," Dan continued, "there are plenty of
witnesses to his near-murder of his infant son."

Deputy Beidler nodded his head. "That's for sure. It
ain't something any of us will ever forget." He worked
a piece of dirt out from under a fingernail.

Pemberton opened his mouth to speak.

Not seeing it, Beidler spoke so quietly Dan had to
listen close to get what he said. "Wasn't for you, that
baby would've burnt. You and that long gun of yours.
'Bout took the roof off the woman's house, it did. And
you jumping to grab that baby afore he landed in the

coals. Lord. I ain't never seen nothin' like it, and I hope I never do again."

This time, Pemberton waited out the silence. "I suggest we bring in Major Fitch and ask him if a bench trial would be all right with him."

"Wouldn't he just say it doesn't matter?" asked the deputy.

"I'll be here to protect him against any sort of coercion." By the position of his legs and his hands on the arms of his chair, Pemberton signaled his eagerness to bring in the defendant.

"I'll get him," said X. "Your Honor can see for yourself what we've got."

When Deputy Beidler brought Fitch in, Dan was shocked at the change in him during the past couple of weeks. The formerly proud Confederate officer looked at his feet, as he shuffled through the doorway like a man fifty years older. His hair and beard had grown streaks of white and hung in greasy clumps around his head and neck.

He stood where Beidler had left him, near the front corner of the raised platform where Judge Hosmer sat behind his desk.

The judge moved his chair from behind the desk, near the edge of the platform, where he would not loom over the prisoner, who continued to stare at the floor.

Dan doubted Fitch saw it. He appeared completely sunk in misery. By now, Dan had expected Fitch to have regained some of his old fire, but in the grayback he only saw ashes of a flame gone out.

Pemberton coughed, cleared his throat. "Major Fitch, do you know where you are?"

Fitch did not look up. "Yes. Judge Hosmer's office."

"Good. Do you know why we've brought you here?"

"Probably a trial?"

"To ask you what sort of trial you would prefer."

Silence. Judge Hosmer raised his voice. "Do you understand the question?"

"Yes. You want to know if I want some sort of a trial."

His defense attorney went on, "What sort of trial would you like?"

"Short, simple, quick."

"What do you mean?"

A deep sigh. "What I said. I tried to kill Dan Stark last December in the cave in Beaverhead Rock because I wanted the Nugget gold mine, and I almost dropped a baby in the fire a couple weeks ago so that Stark would sign the mine over to me because it contains the Mother Lode." Another long, drawn-out sigh.

While the other three men listened to the flat, expressionless monotone in which he made his confession, Fitch continued, "I've told you. I can't live with myself. Give me a short, simple, quick trial and then hang me. Or, Stark." He did not look at Dan. "You and the others know what to do. Skip the trial, or the Tribunal. Just hang me. I don't want to live any more. I don't deserve to live. I'm too evil to live. Anybody that would burn a baby —" a wrenching sob "— isn't fit to breathe God's air. Alive or dead, it doesn't matter. I'm in hell now."

Dan objected in the same tone, using the same words as if he participated in a genuine trial, although this was nothing like a trial. "By his own admission, he's guilty of two attempted murders. Your honor, I would like to suggest that you sentence him to two life sentences in the federal prison in Detroit."

"Your honor!" Pemberton half rose from his chair. "I protest! This is by no stretch of the imagination any sort of trial. It is not even a bench trial. We're merely discussing a possibility that my client may have been guilty of certain alleged —"

"'Alleged'?" Dan bellowed. The shock of seeing an infant he had assumed was Luke – seeing any infant, he realized after he knew the baby was Fitch's own child, nearly consigned to a fire, even a fire dying in its embers, and seeing Fitch in the act of dropping the infant — He could not bear to relive that experience in his mind, and Pemberton, decent man though he was, claimed that horrifying event was 'alleged'? What about the testimony just given by the shell of the very man, standing a couple of feet from him, who would have —

Dan leaped to his feet and rushed out into the snow, but he did not have time to turn the corner of the building before the nausea struck him. It hit him in the stomach, pummeled him as though he faced Hugh O'Neil or Con Orem in the ring, so that he retched again and again until he would have collapsed, but Tmothy's strong hands helped him into Judge Hosmer's office, and brought him water and a towel that showed only a few signs of recent use. He drank some of the water, rejoiced as it chilled the rage burning in his gut, and used some of it with the towel to wipe away the worst of the signs that he'd been so upset.

When he had more or less control of himself, he sat quietly waiting for His Honor to decide something. Anything. So long as he ended this infernal waiting.

"Mr. Fitch, I find myself in agreement with those who would have you incarcerated in the federal prison in Detroit for the rest of your natural days. Your crimes, by your own voluntary admission, have been beyond the pale of civilization, and the great religion we hold by. Therefore, no later than February twenty-fifth instant, you will be placed on a stagecoach bound for Salt Lake City in the company of a trustworthy guard, who will ensure that you arrive there safely. In Salt Lake you will be placed on the Overland Stage that connects eventually to Detroit. The guard, who will accompany you on your entire journey, will then return with documentary proof that you have been incarcerated in that prison."

Leaning forward, he pointed the gavel toward Fitch. "Do I make myself clear?"

Fitch stood without being told, straightened himself to his full height. "Yes, your Honor." As Judge Hosmer was about to dismiss him, he added, "Although I wish you'd hang me."

"No," said the judge. "I'm consigning your fate to the Almighty. Let Him manage your lifespan." He looked at Deputy Beidler. "Deputy, could you find a trustworthy man to escort Mr. Fitch to his destination?"

"May I volunteer, Your Honor?" An audible gasp from Pemberton answered Dan.

Beside him Timothy whispered, "Mam won't like it." Timothy swiped at a lock of hair that had fallen over his eye.

In the light of the lantern on Judge Hosmer's desk, Dan saw the shadow of beard stubble on the boy's cheeks. Medium brown, a couple of shades darker than his hair.

In a quiet murmur, Dan explained it to his stepson. "I know she won't like it. It's something I have to do. For all our sakes, I must see for myself that he's inside those stone walls where he can never get out." He coughed to clear the lump in his throat. "I promised your mother I'd keep the family safe, and seeing that – that grayback into the federal prison keeps that promise. To her and to you. All of you.

"Your Honor, when I see those gates close with Tobias Fitch inside, then I'll know my family is truly safe."

When he had finished telling Martha of his projected journey as Fitch's guard, he knew by the tenseness in her body that she was not happy. He couldn't blame her. After all, he had twice left on protracted journeys – to New York more than a year ago, and to Bannack in December. Nearly, he not returned from either one. "What troubles you, my dear?" Perhaps he should not have told her about Fitch trying to drop his own son onto the coals. Perhaps Grandfather was correct that women's brains were too tender for stories of that sort. He should not have given her more cause to worry, even if he'd never meant —

She broke into his speculations. "We should take Fitch's baby."

"What?" He had not meant to shout, but neither twin awakened.

"The poor little fellow. I never thought, I mean I've been so taken up with our own that I haven't given any mind to Berry Woman's little one."

As she continued, thinking to persuade him, he shook his head from time to time, denying her wishes. No, they would not have any of Fitch's offspring, or his house, or anything that was his. No. No. No.

"I will have nothing to do with Fitch's get. Ever. Do not speak of it again."

She was quiet then, but he knew he had not heard the last of her desire to take in Fitch's son. She had loved Berry Woman, like her own sister, but Dan could not forget that the child's father would have murdered him. By burning.

40 ~~~

Montana Post: 2/25/1865, p. 3:

Local and Other items.

> The weather has been very cold with the
> exception of about a week, ever since Nov.
> 1st. The clerk of the weather has been
> travelling round point Zero too much for the
> comfort of outsiders. He ought to serve out a
> little more heat, which has become a cash
> article with wood at $10.00 per cord.

Dan, Timothy, and Ryder sat together on the forward-facing bench in the Overland Stage Company coach. They had hot stones to rest their feet on, and buffalo robes covered them from their chins to the floor. They gripped the robes from underneath, in the hope that their body heat would keep their gloved hands warm, too. Fitch sat between Dan and Timothy, making four men crammed into the space meant for three moderately sized people. Between Fitch's jailhouse smell and his passive, listless bearing, Dan regretted having asked Judge Hosmer to let him and the boys take the guard duty.

Simply, there was no one else for the job.

Deputy Sheriff X Beidler was needed to provide some semblance of law enforcement for Madison County, and in case of need, he could depend on their friends, the "power behind the throne," as the *Montana Post* had called them.

The Vigilantes.

So it had all been arranged. The friends would watch over Martha and the family while he, accompanied by Timothy and Ryder, made the long midwinter journey to Detroit, the closest Federal prison.

Dan asked himself if anyone, coming across an account of the legal complexities still remaining from the changes in Territorial boundaries, would make sense out of this situation. Specifically, Territorial courts were at the same time Federal courts. A conviction accompanied with a prison sentence meant serving that sentence in a Federal prison.

Which had placed him and the boys on this coach with Tobias Fitch crammed between the two young men.

Along with them, Fitch swayed, bumped, and jerked under Dan's hostile, but watchful, eyes. He did not seem to notice other people's attitudes toward him. He maintained the steady contemplation of his boots as people got on the coach or got off at the various settlements in Alder Gulch

Between them Nevada City and Junction the air rang to the sound of axes as men felled trees to sell wood for fires. Smoke thickened the air along the creek to a grayish haze. It reminded Dan of the river fogs that settled over Manhattan Island. Here, though, nothing relieved the weight of the smoke seeping into the coach. It stung the eyes and clogged the nose. There was not enough breeze to carry the smoke away. It lay on everything like a burden, a heavy blanket too thick to take into the lungs. He fastened a handkerchief around his face in hopes of filtering out the smoke, but it didn't seem to do any good.

They emerged from Alder Gulch in the area by Ram's Horn Creek, Robert Dempsey invited them to get out of the coach, stretch their legs, and go inside where a fire burned, and stew was heating on the stove. And decent whiskey would be offered.

Thinking that "decent" was a matter of opinion, Dan and Timothy helped Fitch out of the coach. Once on the ground, Ryder joined them to help him shuffle, trailing his ankle chain, into the outhouse and back after everyone had done his business. Dan gave Ryder his poke to buy a meal for them all. If he hadn't watched their prisoner all the time, Dan might have thought the stew, made of various kinds of mystery meat, was inedible. One bite he identified as possibly old horse, another was fairly fresh elk, and a third, that dominated the others, he thought might be grizzly bear.

The stage driver sat at a separate table and talked low with the owner of the station. From the looks they cast in Fitch's direction, Dan thought they discussed him. A time or two they laughed together, saying the Rebs were beat and it was only a matter of time before Lee surrendered.

Fitch moved about in a world of his own, seeming not to hear what anyone said. If he heard their cracks about Rebel losses, he made no sign.

"Do you suppose he understands anything?" Ryder wiped his bowl clear with a piece of bread and popped it into his mouth.

Timothy made a face at something he saw in the bottom of his bowl. "If'n he does, he's sure not giving any hints."

Back on the coach, Dan steeled himself for another, even longer, piece of this miserable ride. This leg would take them along the Beaverhead River, up to Point of Rocks, then across the river, skirting Beaverhead Rock, thrust up by some galactic force from the rangeland around it. Then over another bridge and up into the foothills of the mountains to Rattlesnake, their overnight stop. In the morning they would proceed to Bannack. From there, they'd cross cross the mountains and head south toward the Great Salt Lake. About sixty miles north of Salt Lake City, where the Montana Trail intersected with the Overland Trail, the town of Corinne, Utah, would – Dan hoped – give them a night's respite. Then they would change to Ben Holladay's Overland Stage Line. He planned to ride it as far east as they could to where it met the road north to Detroit. Where that road met the Overland/Oregon trail, he didn't know.

He had never had reason to know, and he wished he could remain ignorant.

He would depend on the agents of the stage line. It was their job to know. They were paid to have that information.

All in all, Dan figured, the trip there and back would take them at least two months. Maybe as long as ten weeks.

Ryder brought Dan out of his calculations. "Do you expect this man to survive long in that horrible place?"

"What do you mean?"

"Look at him. He's obviously suffering at the thought of what he tried to do."

Dan refused to look at Fitch. "His suffering is not my concern. If I had my way, we'd hang him to a good stout tree and leave him for the vultures."

"You can't mean that!"

The coach bounced over a sizable rock and threw them against each other. After they had regained their seating and settled themselves again, Ryder repeated, "Mr. Stark, you see him. He has said he'd rather die, that it doesn't matter if he lives or dies because he's in – that place already."

"How do you know he'd not being clever? That he's not pretending remorse in order to trick gullible fools?"

"I see the difference in him. I see — "

Timothy roared, "He nearly burnt his own baby alive! Just because he thought he was burning my baby brother. Because he wanted the gold in our mine. How can you have any sympathy for him? Don't you care about the little ones?"

The coach tilted upward and came down hard on its front wheels.

"Everybody all right in there?" shouted the driver.

Ryder called back, "Yes, we're doing fine."

Dan could not smile at the word, fine. His back ached from jouncing on the hard, unyielding seat cushions, People's posteriors had beaten them to board softness long before.

Ryder rubbed his gloved hands together, a futile attempt to warm them. "Of course I have sympathy for the helpless little ones. I rejoice that Mr. Stark acted so quickly and saved that baby. But the angry man who would have, er, done what he tried to do, he is not the same man we're taking to prison."

"If we'd knowed he would go to them lengths, shoot, I'd've given him the damn mine." Tim gave his stepfather a swift, sidelong peek. "At least ..."

Dan leaned down to adjust the burlap wrapping over his feet on the rapidly cooling rock. "There's more gold to be found, Timothy. The Nugget does not contain the Mother Lode. There's no such thing. Lodes are being discovered all the time, in Alder Gulch, Last Chance, Summit, and other places. The *Post* doesn't weary of listing them. The problem is not that there's a shortage of gold in Montana Territory, but that Fitch thinks there is a Mother Lode, and it's contained in the Nugget, and it is rightfully his. He's deluded. And until he loses that delusion and faces reality, we cannot trust him. Not one iota."

"But why lock him up in that prison? With all those human wolves?" Ryder's voice rose almost to desperation.

The coach rounded a curve, into a short open stretch. Wind-driven snow pounded the coach, rattled its door.

Timothy, sitting on the downhill side of the coach, blew on the window next to him and rubbed a clear circle in the glass. "I can't see nothing out there."

Intent on closing down Ryder's concern about the right thing to do for Fitch, Dan snapped, "What would you have me do? The federal prison is the best solution for my family. It locks him away from my children, and as far as human wolves are concerned, let him ask for God's protection."

The coach tilted upward in front, as the horses climbed up into the foothills.

"You can't mean that — " Ryder protested.

A front wheel of the coach lurched into a hole – as Dan thought – but it did not climb out of the hole. Instead, the coach rolled over, tumbling the men, the rocks, and all the bags they carried inside over and over as if they were pieces of meat stirred in a pot.

The coach doors sprung open.

Dan rolled several yards down, until he slammed, stomach first, into the trunk of a pine tree. He put his hand on its rough, layered bark, curled his fingers around the upward-pointing sections and pulled himself upright. Gasped for breath. Thought he might never breathe again. Yelled, heard a strangled sound.

415

Inhaled, coughed, inhaled again. Breathed. Shook his head to clear it, looked around to get his bearings, and see where everyone was.

A snowstorm had come down on the mountain, drifted over the road. Snow blew around the coach, hiding the young men from him. Hid the coach. Leaving the tree's small shelter, he clambered upward, toward horses' whinnying, men's calling. He hoped he climbed toward the coach, that the driver had escaped injury, that the horses could go on.

The coach lay partly on its side, luggage and freight strewn farther than Dan could see, but Ryder and Timothy were both unhurt. They had already set to extricating the driver from under the front boot.

Dan floundered through the snow to the horses.

"Stay with Fitch," Dan ordered Ryder. The young man had rolled in the snow and looked as much like a snowman as the real thing.

"Oh! I forgot about Fitch." Ryder looked around, seeming baffled as to where the man had gone to.

Keeping his hand on the coach, Dan hurried around it to see where the prisoner might be. The driver rose, stood upright if shaky, untangled the long reins from his gloved hands. Winced as he pointed his chin higher up the slope, where a man, ghost-like in the blowing snow, walked away from them.

Fitch.

Dan yelled his name, but he gave no sign of having heard and continued his steady pace onward. Thick snow blew between him and Dan, and he was gone from sight. Then the wind reversed itself, blew a lighter gust, and Fitch stood out from the white all around him. A heavier gust veiled him from Dan, and he was gone.

"Let's get after him!" Ryder yelled.

Timothy shook his head. "No." He was busy helping the driver straighten out the six-horse team. Careful of a frightened wheel horse's struggles, he unhooked a trace from the animal's collar, kicked it out of his way, and tugged on the bridle. The horse put his forelegs out, boosted himself with his hind legs, and stood trembling, head down. The boy stroked its neck and made soothing sounds. As it calmed, he hooked up the trace to the collar.

"Come on! He'll freeze to death!" Ryder bent himself in Fitch's direction, waved an arm to urge them to join him.

"No!" Dan bellowed. "Saving ourselves beats saving him."

The animals in the middle of the six-horse hitch were smaller than either wheel horse and had already risen to their feet. They stood, heads down, trembling, tails clamped to their cruppers.

Moving through the knee-deep snow, Tim went to the second wheel horse, which had already gathered its feet under it. Unhooking the trace, he gave the bridle a tug, "Up, there, boy." The horse rose and shook itself, scattering snow over its partner and Timothy. "Hey, you!" The boy swatted the animal's shoulder. "You mind yourself, you hear?"

"Let's find Fitch," Ryer insisted. "We can't let him be lost in this storm."

"Fitch ain't worth all this." Timothy swung his hand around to include the downed coach, the spilled freight, the horses now standing. The driver took the wheel horse from him to hook up again.

Dan carried a sprung toolbox closer to the coach. He set it down. "Get it through your head, we will not search for Fitch in this storm. I will not risk our lives to find a man who does not deserve to be found. I would have left Fitch to God in the prison. We will leave him to God now."

Ryder insisted, "In this storm he could die before he goes twenty feet. We should look for him."

"If'n we don't get this coach going soonest, we'll all find out what the Almighty does for idiots who wander off in snowstorms." The driver picked up his long-lashed whip and gave it an exploratory snap of his wrist.

The whip cracked loud as a gunshot.

"Hah! It works just fine. We better get moving."

Everyone set to helping right the coach. The driver examined the undercarriage and pronounced it safe to chance traveling. As the driver hitched up the team, the three passengers loaded the freight. Within minutes they were on their way, but slowly, for one of the horses limped. The driver hollered, "Whoa." He jumped down, ran his hand down the animal's leg. "He'll be all right, gents. He pulled something, but he's not spavined, and he didn't bow a tendon."

"We'll catch the next stage back to Virginia from Rattlesnake," Dan told the young men when they were under way.

"If we don't freeze ourselves tonight. Mam will be glad you're back so soon." Tim tucked his hands in his armpits to warm them.

Ryder pulled the skirts of his new greatcoat over his knees. "I wonder if we'll ever see Fitch again."

"No telling." For himself, Dan had an idea what he'd do if Fitch ever came near his family, but he thought better of saying it aloud.

41 ~~~

Montana Post: 2/25/1865, p. 3:

Sheriff's Sale (Reprint from 2/11/1865)

> On Saturday the 11th Day of February, 1865, at 11 o'clock, A.M., all the interest of the said William J. Robinson, in the following described property, viz: One house and lot situated on Jackson street above Idaho, and immediately back of the Planters House.
>
> Neil Howie, Sheriff
>
> J. X. Beidler, Deputy Sheriff.

Local and Other items.

> The weather is very cold.

Timothy had said Martha would be happy to have him back so soon.

For his part, Dan would be more than happy to see her, and all the family, especially his little boys, now that they were beginning to recognize him with smiles and waving limbs. He shivered harder at the thought of the danger Fitch had put them in. The horror of Fitch's attempt on the baby's life sent him shaking so hard that Ryder thought he was dangerously cold. He suggested they all sit on one bench to be warmer, if such a thing could be possible in this leaky sieve of a coach. Resettled between the younger men, Dan felt no warmer, but he was comforted anyway, somehow.

"Your mother will be happy to see you, too, Tim." He tucked his gloved hands between his legs. "She wasn't at all pleased about you taking such a chance to help with guard duty."

"She's a worrier, Mam is." The boy leaned forward to talk around Dan. "Say, Ryder, is your Mam a worrier about you?"

As they waited for Ryder's answer, the coach rumbled along at a horse's limping pace, bumping them from side to side, or forward and back, without any rhythm to catch and ease the worst jolts.

If it hadn't been for the cold, Dan would rather have walked to Rattlesnake, the Spencer guarding Fitch all the way.

When the young man answered Tim's question about his mother, his words came out in bunches as the horses negotiated the road. Dan pieced the story together from phrases. Ryder's mother 'was the Godliest woman,' 'never idle,' 'sewed all evening after supper,' 'always looking for how she could help others.'" He paused long enough that Dan thought he had no more to say.

And then Ryder cleared his throat. "She taught me to read."

Another long silence from the young man. The coach creaked and groaned, and over all, the wind shrieked, worked its frigid breath through the gaps in the walls and around the doors of the coach, through sprung joints and splintered walls.

"My father didn't see any use in education, so when I decided on divinity school, he was angry. But she told me it was the happiest day of her life."

"What does she think of you coming out here?" Tim's question came fast.

"She died of pneumonia ... two weeks ... before the battle of Gettysburg."

"Oh. Sorry."

Dan added his condolences. Along with the two younger men, he fell into a glum silence, with nothing to occupy his mind but unsuccessful maneuvers to avoid the ride's battering.

At Rattlesnake, the driver stopped the horses and hollered at his passengers, "End of the road. Take your plunder with you, gents."

They stumbled into a squalid room carpeted in men's bodies rolled in their blankets. The luckiest ones slept closest to a tall, pot-bellied stove in the middle of the room. The later arrivals lay in the order of their luck, with himself and the boys at the outer limits of the stove's heat radius. There were no women. Amid curses and complaints, the newcomers forced enough room for each of them to lie down in their blankets, fully dressed, and like everyone else, in their coats

Dan could not sleep. On the trip out to gold country two years before, he had thought he discovered new continents of discomfort, but now he searched in vain

Carol Buchanan

for a position that did not hurt in his contact with the hard floor.

Now and then a blast of cold air from the doorway announced that a man went out to relieve himself, and another told when he returned. Each time, the frigid wind found Dan, and he called down the wrath of whatever gods might linger from old myths to bar the door against the blizzard. He lay on his side, his head on the upstretched, crumpled cape of his greatcoat, his knees drawn up in an effort to hold some warmth in the middle of his body. Sometime in the endless night, he fell into a semiconscious state that was not sleep, yet neither was it waking. His last conscious thought was how the wind around the corners of the station sounded like a wolf's howl, but at some point it became a baby wailing.

In the morning, he awoke like everyone, grumbling and cursing. The station agent yelled at everyone, "Get up now! You can't sleep all day! Coach leaves in half an hour for Virginia City."

Dan paid the fares for himself, Timothy, and Ryder. Pains in his back, one hip, both shoulders, and his right elbow made him dread the return trip as he would another session in some medieval torture mechanism.

Nor did the journey surprise him. Instead, his body remembered each dip and slam the vehicle provided. Christians in a Roman arena suffered no less, he almost said aloud. One glance at the faces of other passengers warned him to be silent; even a pleasant 'Good morning' could bring on his murder. The boys, mashed

424

into a space meant for half the number of passengers, wore the same look of dull misery as everyone else.

~~~

A day and a half late, the driver drew rein in front of the Overland Stage office in Virginia City. Nat Stein, the Overland agent, left his office in a thickly padded jacket and knitted cap that covered his ears. Smelling of coal oil and warmth, he helped each man dismount from the coach. Even the youngest, Timothy and Ryder, moved like ancient souls in their sixth or seventh decade.

Here, too, the wind screamed, and snow swirled about the few unfortunate people necessity had forced out on the street. Stein's assistant came out to unhook the traces from the lead horses' collars. A stable boy ran from the livery across the street, coiled their long reins, and led them off to their stable, across Wallace Street. One of the wheel horses whinnied after them, but the coach was nearly unloaded of all its freight and baggage by the time the boy ran back to the agency for the middle team.

"That wind!" one of the passengers shouted over its whine. "It blew all the way from Rattlesnake."

"Wasn't blowing here until you-all swung into town," returned Stein's assistant.

"Yeah," Stein called down from his perch on top of the coach. He passed boxes of freight to a second assistant who piled them on a cart. "It started blowing when you crossed Daylight Creek. I had a lookout posted on Kiskadden's roof, and he saw you."

425

Dan said nothing, though the backs of his hands tingled as if the hairs lifted. Once again, the wind sounded like a baby wailing. On a sudden impulse, he handed his valise to Timothy. "You and Ryder go on home. Tell Martha I'll be along directly. There's some business I have to attend to."

As he turned his back on them, he heard Timothy shout, "Hey! Dan'l! What business?"

Without answering, he strode down Wallace, turned downstream on Main, and crossed Daylight creek on the section of thick ice the horses and coach had not broken.

In Lower Town, he felt the wind blowing stronger, and its banshee howl was louder.

The wet nurse's cabin was dark and cold. Dan left the door open, but no light came through the doorway. The place felt only marginally less cold than outside, and the stench and the screaming of the wind – no, it wasn't the wind —

A baby yowled.

On the slattern's sodden bed, Fitch's baby son screamed, but even as Dan approached, its cries became fainter. He cast about for anything dry to wrap the child in, but the slattern seemed to have emptied the place.

Then his foot touched something under the bed.

He stooped down to look, and his skin crawled.

The slattern's corpse stared at him, unseeing, through wide-open, sightless eyes.

"What is it, Dan'l?" Timothy had not obeyed his instruction to go home.

"What's happened?" Ryder, Timothy's accomplice in disobedience.

Immediately, he knew a sense of relief. He did not have to be alone in this, whatever it was. Crime, yes. The slattern had been murdered, and her body hidden under the bed, while the murderer ransacked the hovel, and abandoned the child.

Not, however, before he wrapped the infant against the cold.

And left him.

First, the baby. "Find something dry to wrap the baby in. We have to take him home."

Lighted from behind, Timothy's face could not be seen, but his smile sang in his voice: "Mam will be happy. She's been wanting —"

"Yes, yes. Hurry. We don't know how long he's been crying, but he can't last much longer."

Ryder had already found a wrapping for the child — his own sheepskin vest.

Dan put his back to the younger man. "Unbutton my cape and wrap him in that. I want nothing from this – this place – in my house, except for Nameless."

"'Nameless?'" Ryder stripped the wet, cold wrapping from the baby. He flung it away, making an extra turn of his vest around the child, to protect him as well as he could against the ferocious cold and wind.

"We have to have something to call him by. After Mrs. Stark has taken over his care, we can think of a proper name for him."

With Dan carrying the whimpering baby, as well protected against the elements as possible, they set off for home. The younger men carried all the luggage between them, though they protested mightily. Both of them wanted to carry the baby.

In Virginia City, Dan set a fast pace up the Jackson Street hill. As he walked, his mind was busy with thoughts of the future. How would this pitiful infant survive, even given good care? Even if he did survive, how would he grow up? Would he grow to a normal size, or would he be stunted in his growth? X Beidler was the shortest fellow Dan knew, but he was also one of the toughest. When he had given Nameless into Martha's care, he would see X Beidler. X was good at finding out things. He'd headed up the Vigilance Committee's Ferreting Committee, because he could ferret out nearly any secret, especially secrets of murder.

If anyone could locate Fitch – or his corpse – or the slattern's killer – X could.

Besides, Dan had to tell Judge Hosmer how he had lost Fitch.

Preoccupied, he would have gone by the path to his house, if Timothy had not called to him.

Someone inside the house heard the boy's voice and flung open the door as Dan put his foot on the bottom porch step.

"Dan'l," screamed Dorothy. "Mam, Dan'l's home, and Timmy, and Vaughn, and – and they have a baby!"

"It's Fitch's little boy." Dan had no time to say more, for Martha pivoted from the stove, with a wide, delighted smile and outstretched arms, completely forgetting that she held a spoon dripping stock across the table.

"Mam!" Dorothy snatched the spoon from her mother and thrust it into the big pot of something that smelled delicious simmering on the cooktop.

And then all was confusion, as Martha, nearly weeping at the strange child's pitiful condition, took him from her husband. "You came home so soon! And you brought Fitch's baby. Oh, the poor little mite."

"My dear, I'll be back soon. The boys can tell you the gist of our travels, but right now, I have to find X Beidler, and also explain to Judge Hosmer how I lost Fitch."

His swift pace, less careful than when he carried a baby, brought him sooner than he liked to the Court House. Even so, as he walked, he promised himself, God, and the absent Fitch, "One day, Fitch, if you're still alive, I'll find you. You can't hide from me forever. And when I do, you'll pay for your crimes."